Oath of Allegiance

Allegiance, Book 2

To Val.
[illegible] & love.

ISBN: 9798607142353

Cover design by Adriana Hanganu

Also available from Jana Petken:

Multiple Award-Winning *The Guardian of Secrets*
Screenplay *The Guardian of Secrets*

The Mercy Carver Series:
Award-Winning *Dark Shadows*
Blood Moon

The Flock Trilogy
Multiple Award-winning, *The Errant Flock*
The Scattered Flock
Flock: The Gathering of The Damned

Allegiance Series
Swearing Allegiance
Oath of Allegiance

The German Half-Bloods Trilogy *The German Half-Bloods*
The Vogels: On All Fronts
Before The Brightest Dawn

Available in Audiobook Format
The German Half-Bloods trilogy

The Guardian of Secrets
Mercy Carver series
The Flock Trilogy
Swearing Allegiance
Oath of Allegiance (coming soon)

Swearing Allegiance, Silver medal,

Readers' Favourite Awards

Editorial Review, Five Stars, Readers' Favourite

In Swearing Allegiance, the first entry in The Carmody Saga by Jana Petken, the Carmody family is forced to face the devastating consequences of the First World War. Dublin has fallen apart and the British can't keep the Germans at bay. Once an affluent family, the Carmodys now experience hardship and poverty. Readers are about to discover an interesting and entertaining family drama, set against the backdrop of war, a family story that explores secrets, politics, love, and what is left to keep a family together when everything else crumbles. It's a story of love, patriotism, war, and loyalty.

Jana Petken is a gifted writer and this gift can be seen through the expertly developed characters, the gripping plot, and the complex conflict. Danny, Patrick, and Jenny are very compelling characters, each sculpted with a complex nature and a haunting problem to face. These characters are thrust into a family drama that makes relevant references to history. The plot is well-paced, and the conflict is developed at different levels, making the story even more gripping.

From the very first page of the story, I felt irresistibly pulled in by the author's powerful and vivid descriptions, a generous encounter with one of the key characters in the story. The conflict — or at least part of it — is introduced immediately. This is a beautifully written story that explores elements of the

First World War and how different people coped with its effects. Swearing Allegiance is a family story that will resonate in the hearts of many readers, a story that will remind readers of the drama taking place in many families; it is entertaining, it is gritty, it is hard to put down.

Acknowledgements

My sincere thanks to the people who have contributed their expertise to this book:
My editor, Patricia Rose;
My proofreader and historical fact-checker, Caro Powney;
My graphic designer, Adriana Hagangu;
My Grandfather, David, an Irishman if ever there was one and the inspiration for this series,
and to those who have supported me and continue to encourage me in my writing career

Note from the author

This book is written in UK English and all spellings, punctuations, and grammar adhere to UK English, World English, and the Oxford English Dictionary

It's been a while...

Hi everyone. It's been three years since I published Swearing Allegiance, so I thought I'd introduce you to the characters again, just in case you've forgotten them. Here's a glimpse of some new characters as well.

The Carmody family

Patrick Carmody – a Lieutenant, British Royal Navy, in school for his doctorate
Danny Carmody – A British soldier and Irish Republican
Jenny Carmody – their sister, injured by a Zeppelin attack, now working in a hospital
Anna Carmody – Danny's Welsh wife
Minnie Webber – the Carmody children's grandmother

The Jackson family

Lord Jackson – a member of the House of Lords, a British Loyalist
Matilda Jackson – Lord Jackson's wife and Kevin and Charlie's mother
Kevin Jackson – A British army doctor, Jenny's love
Charlie Jackson – Kevin's brother, a member of the Royal Irish Constabulary.

Others

Michael 'Mick' Collins – IRA leader, alternative government minister
Jimmy Carson – Danny's friend, also in the IRA

Finn McClure – Danny's army chum, also in the IRA
Éamon de Valera – Overall leader of the Republican movement
Quinn – a close friend of Patrick's, in the IRA but does business and sells woollen goods regardless of political position.

Chapter One

November 1917

Dublin, Ireland,

Jenny and Patrick Carmody almost jigged their way along the streets from Dublin's Royal College of Surgeons to the Bank of Ireland situated on Sackville Street. Jenny, impatient to get this business out of the way, was delighted when, five minutes after their arrival, a bank clerk ushered them into the manager's office. It was a cold, damp room with a small high-up window that hardly let in a ray of light, and there Mr Firth, Robert Carmody's long-standing bank manager and friend, welcomed them home.

Firth took off his spectacles, came from behind his desk, and gave Patrick a brisk handshake. "Well, well, if it isn't young Patrick Carmody. My God, you're looking more like your father every day, God bless his soul. You must be glad to be home again. Is this you back in Dublin for good?"

"I am, Mr Firth, I am glad. Unfortunately, it's not for good, not this time," Patrick answered.

"And how are you, Miss Carmody?" Firth finally asked Jenny.

"Well enough, thank you," Jenny responded, stretching her arm out and getting a rather limp handshake in return.

"Please, sit," requested Mr Firth, returning to his black leather chair. "I was happy to hear you were coming in. How's your young brother, Danny? I heard he did a stint in Frongoch. And how is your mother coping without your father?"

"We buried her two days ago. She died last week of a stroke." Jenny sat in one of the two visitors' chairs.

Mr Firth's shocked eyes locked onto Jenny's; she wondered what else he wanted her to say about it. She remembered seeing the man at her father's wake, and later at the graveside where he'd looked genuinely upset; he'd shed tears. Probably crocodile ones, the hypocrite. He'd been quick enough to throw the Carmodys out of their home weeks after the funeral, hadn't lifted his finger to help. "Her death was very sudden," she said, squirming under his gaze.

"I'm sorry to hear that. Why, it's a terrible thing, and her being a young woman still. It's true what they say, it is indeed. Only the good die young, and there was none better than your sweet mother."

"Thank you."

In the uncomfortable silence that followed, Jenny looked at the clock on the wall. It was a strange-looking thing made of wood and brass and shaped like the bow of a ship. Its frame stuck out six inches and some of the numbers on the clock face were obscured by it; for instance, Jenny could see it was two-something in the afternoon.

She looked at Patrick, who was balancing his father's Gladstone bag on his knee and fumbling as he tried to open the lock. He'd warned her not to interrupt whilst he or Mr Firth were speaking. Some businessmen didn't approve of women being present during financial discussions, he'd pointed out. Sure, she'd seen that earlier with the Board at the College of Surgeons when Patrick had insisted that she sit in on the meeting. The old white-haired, bearded and long moustached men had barely looked at her. They'd not asked her a single question, nor had they consulted directly with her during any part of their discussions. Afterwards, Patrick also pointed out that she was fortunate to have a brother who wanted to see the advancement of women in the world.

"As you know, Mr Firth, I took the family to London after we lost the house." In his excitement, Patrick's tone was unusually high-pitched with a strange, girlish quiver to it. "Since then, my lawyer has been dealing with my late father's outstanding business with the Royal College of Surgeons, and to cut the long story short, the Board have settled with the Carmody family over the ownership of my father's medical research papers."

Jenny felt for her brother, holding the cheque that was to change their lives for the better in his trembling fingers. Like him, she wouldn't get over the shock of seeing the huge amount of money they'd been given until he sat her on a pub stool and gave her a glass of whiskey to throw down the back of her throat, preferably in one giant gulp. Her fondness for the stuff was growing. She blamed Minnie, for every time they received bad news or a shock, her granny insisted upon having a nip of the stuff.

Patrick pushed the cheque across the table to Mr Firth, who eyed it greedily.

"Ten thousand pounds. Well, that is good news for the family. I'm sure this will come in very useful. Would you like the money to go into a savings account?"

"No, certainly not," Patrick retorted. "We don't want to invest this money or lock it down in your bank. We want to spend it. As you can imagine, Mr Firth, life has been difficult for us since our da passed."

"You're going to spend it? All of it?"

"We are thinking about purchasing a modest house in Dublin."

"I see."

"I'd like my sister to be co-signatory on this account. Money should be available to her without me having to be present to sign for withdrawals."

Mr Firth stared at Jenny's flowery black hat tilted downwards at the front left-hand side. His disapproving eyes, looking bigger through thick lenses in silver-rimmed spectacles, settled on her flushed face and the scars that had defined her time in London. "Miss Carmody, this is an awful lot of money for a young woman to manage, especially as I know you've been through a terrible ordeal. We heard about you being injured in the Zeppelin attacks, and about what John Grant did to you – terrible – unforgiveable. And you see, the brain is a complex thing in a woman, it being more prone to lapses and hysteria, you understand. Wouldn't you rather let your brother take sole care of the family's financial matters?"

"My brain is perfectly intact, Mr Firth. It's probably as keen as your own…"

"What Jenny means is she's quite capable of looking after our money while I'm away fighting," Patrick interrupted, his tone lower than before and tetchy. "I want her to have full access to the account, and if you can't arrange for that facility here, well, we'll take our money back to London and deposit it in the Bank of England."

Mr Firth rose, hands out in a mollifying fashion. "Then I will get the papers for you both to sign."

At three o'clock, Jenny and Patrick left the manager's office. Jenny carried twenty-five pounds in her purse to tide the family over for two or three months. As always, she carried money in a shoulder strap bag that was concealed inside her coat. Ever since two thieves had assaulted her in London, she took precautions never to carry a bag that could be snatched from her hand. She had Patrick with her today, but when she went out alone, she also carried a sock with stones in it, so she could wallop any would be assailant.

Her mind was dashing between new curtains for the living room and a second bed in Minnie's room, so she could share with her granny when Patrick came home. It wasn't right that he had to sleep on the couch. Then, her thoughts turned to the tatty grey gown she wore every day for work at the hospital. It was a horrible thing. She despised it. She glanced at Patrick, deep in his own thoughts, and asked, "Do you think I could buy myself a modest new gown, Patrick?"

"You can and you will, Jenny, and so will Anna. We'll see to it tomorrow."

They strode briskly along the main Dublin thoroughfare, but halted when they reached the General Post Office, which had been virtually destroyed a year and a half earlier. The rubble had been cleared away and the only remaining parts of the iconic building still standing were the granite façade and pillars.

Jenny had grown up admiring the beautiful edifice: its romantic pillars and grand entrance, its high ceilings inside, the smell of polished wood panels and walnut wood tillers' counters, and wonderfully tiled floor. She choked up, not with shock or horror, but with hurt and a tinge of anger. "Oh, Patrick, what a terrible time that was, and to think our Danny took part in the destruction we're seeing. I don't remember it looking this bad. Sure, it was piled high with rubble the last time we were here, but now it looks sad and forlorn, like a monument to those who died. How awful to see half of Dublin brought down like this. It's almost as bad as London!"

"Except this mess was not of the Germans' making, darlin', it was the Irish Republicans and British Army. Eighteen months, Jenny, and they still haven't rebuilt it. It could take years to get Dublin back to the way it was. Ah, but sure, I don't suppose the British government will shower us with generosity, not when we were the ones who helped to tear the city down," Patrick said, studying the magnificent pillars that had been spared.

Jenny sniffed into her handkerchief; delicately, as her mother had taught her. She was disturbed by another thought. "Everything looks strange to me. I feel out of place. I don't think I want to come back to Dublin to live, Patrick, not while the war on the continent is still on and everyone is suffering."

She spotted two children sitting on the kerb next to the emblematic building's remains. Their faces were a mottled reddish blue with cold. Their eyes were red-rimmed, mucus ran from their scabby noses, and not even their tatty woollen coats hid their wee skinny bodies. Beside the children, a woman sat with a sack full of something or other resting on her lap. "Look at them over there. I could weep for them."

"There's a homeless crisis," Patrick said, also staring at the boy and girl. "Some of the oldest tenements are coming down and the city council are not rebuilding or replacing them. They're waiting for the British government to start its rebuilding programme."

"You mean they're going to rebuild all the fancy buildings that were destroyed in the Easter Uprising?"

"Yes, so they say."

"Well, that's all well and good, but what about building homes? Real homes for folk living on the streets like that family over there? Maybe Danny has a point about this independence malarkey being a good thing for Ireland."

Patrick gripped her hand and pulled her away from the Post Office. Jenny went meekly, knowing she shouldn't have talked sedition in front of a building that had been destroyed by British traitors, but then she had second thoughts and stopped walking. "Patrick, will you give me two shillings?" she asked, with her hand already out.

Patrick nodded. "Very well, but don't linger."

The suspicious eyes of the woman sitting on the kerb looked up at Jenny, eventually focusing on her fancy hat. "I suppose you're going to tell us to move along?"

"No, I am not." Jenny opened her palm. "Take this," she said, handing two shillings to the stunned woman before hurrying back to Patrick.

As they walked on, she looked back and saw two British soldiers ordering the youngsters and the woman to get up from the pavement and move on, as though they were vermin dirtying their British streets. "Sorry, Patrick, but I meant what I said. I've decided I don't like the British Army telling the Irish what to do on their own streets. Somebody has to do something."

"Things are as they are, Jenny," Patrick responded, whilst looking at his wristwatch. "If we can get to the port in a taxi, we might be able to get the next ferry to Holyhead and make it home sometime after midnight. I'll say this for the war, it's provided plenty of trains for the London routes."

"And they're all sending men to their deaths on the continent. Charming."

As they neared a tramcar stop, Jenny cheered up for Patrick's sake. "Imagine Minnie and Anna's faces, Patrick, when we tell them our money is in the bank. I know it won't help much when it comes to buying food and what not, but it will make our lives a little better."

"True. You can't buy food if there's none to be had, but you might be able to buy those new sheets and blankets you've been on about for days."

Jenny halted abruptly and placed her hand on Patrick's arm. "I was thinking that maybe we could get Minnie to move with us to a bigger house. Buying a house in Dublin was for Mam's sake, but with her gone we might as well stay put in London, at least until the war ends. What do you think?"

"Do you really not want to come home?"

"I don't. I have a job, Anna has a job, Danny will come home, eventually, and you'll be coming back from Southampton every other weekend or so." Jenny was animated, hoping her excitement would spill onto her brother. "Patrick, think about it. Danny's married now, and we can't expect him and Anna to live with us in that cramped house in Greenwich. Wouldn't it be nice to have more bedrooms?"

"It would, Jenny, but now's not the time to invest money in a house that might get blown up next week. We have no rent to pay and no mortgage on Minnie's house. Let's be thankful for what we have, eh?"

They walked on, Patrick pointedly ignoring Jenny's little pout.

******

Patrick vomited over the side of the boat belonging to the City of Dublin Steam Packet Company. Unfortunately, the direction of the strong wind threw half his dinner back at him, and it stuck to his face and overcoat. He wiped his mouth with his handkerchief, then asked Jenny for hers. "The dreaded curse of the sea strikes again," he groaned.

"Wouldn't you rather come inside with me, darlin'?" Jenny was wrapped up in her thick winter's coat. Her hand shot up to her head as a sharp gust of wind hit her. "Let's go in," she said, pressing her palm down on her hat, despite having two hatpins digging into her hair.

"No. I'm not going indoors. We men have got to keep a lookout for German submarines. You go in, get your feet up if you can. We have a long train ride from Holyhead to come after this."

As soon as he was alone, Patrick belched. He'd felt sick since the moment he'd set foot on the boat. He could blame his *mal de mer* on the choppy crossing, but the truth was he was as nervous now as he had been on the HMMS *Britannic* straight after the explosion that had caused her to sink. He hated bloody ships!

He was not alone with his fear. Men lined the railings looking for German threats. It was as dim as hell; the ship on dark-running, the sea black, and the fog gathering as night drew in. He and the other men next to him couldn't see much further than their outstretched arms, and compounding the situation, foghorns remained silent nowadays for fear of alerting enemy U-boats. The men were blinded by the harsh weather, but they'd maintain vigilance regardless of impediments until they got into the Welsh port on the Isle of Anglesey.

"Do you want a nip of brandy to settle your stomach? Works for me every time."

Patrick turned. The voice belonged to a tall man with a young, handsome face, ruddy with cold. His flat cap covered his head, and unruly black curls encroached on his ears. He wore a grim expression, matching that of every other man on the boat. He was also wearing the obligatory canvas, cork-lined lifejacket that was given to every passenger upon boarding.

Patrick nodded. "Thank you. It probably won't help me, but I don't mind if I do." After a decent slug, he felt the burning alcohol slide down his throat and into his swirling belly. "I needed that. I'm not a good sailor at the best of times, which is ironic seeing as I'm in the Royal Navy." He smiled as he wiped off the mouthpiece and gave the flask back to the man.

"Well, if it's any consolation, I'm shitting myself here," the man said with a natural, friendly smile. "Never thought I'd be brave enough to get on this boat again, what with the German submarines stalking the Irish Sea and Cardigan Bay. I was in a close enough call this year when the boat that came after mine was torpedoed and sunk. We've lost a few ships to those invisible devils – the name's Quinn O'Malley, by the way."

"Patrick Carmody." Patrick shook the man's hand and asked, "Do you know how many boats have gone down?"

"I don't know the total – propaganda suppress the news – but the Germans stepped up their submarine operations in February this year. Locals say thirteen ships were sunk in Welsh waters off Bardsey Island and the Pembrokeshire coast during that month alone. At the time, the local newspapers reported the sinking of the *Voltaire* and the *Olivia,* and they included the crew's accounts of their ordeal in the story. Some of the survivors said the Germans boarded and looted the boat's provisions before they sunk it. Apparently, they wanted British newspapers as well, to find out the latest news on the war."

Patrick was horrified at the German audacity so close to home.

"Ah, don't worry, things have calmed down in the last few months," Quinn assured him.

Unconvinced, Patrick looked again at the men standing closest to him. They searched the sea with dogged determination to battle the rolling mist and sheets of rain beginning to fall. Not wearing a hood or cap, Patrick made do with pulling up his greatcoat collar whilst saying, "I'm glad to see we're not becoming complacent. You said you had a near miss? Do you make many crossings?" Patrick asked Quinn.

"I come over to England once a month. I manufacture women's finest woollen shawls amongst other woollen apparel, and I provide a few stores in London and Liverpool."

Patrick was intrigued. "Is there call for luxury goods, what with the war going on?"

"I have high-end customers in England and France. Sure, profits are way down, and selling in France has come to a standstill, but the war doesn't dictate the weather."

Quinn proffered the flask back to Patrick, who accepted it, then raised it in the air before taking another nip. It seemed to be settling his stomach after all, or maybe the company was making him feel better.

"Here's my card with my address in Dublin. If you're ever back there, come see me. I'll give you a tour of my modest factory." He chuckled. "We're spending most of our time making good woollen items for the British Army – it's not what we're used to but it keeps us going and brings in a wage for Dubliners who were having trouble finding work – we're up to our chins in socks."

Patrick and the man locked eyes and held each other's gazes as Patrick took the card. "Thank you, Quinn. I'll certainly look you up next time I'm in Ireland," Patrick said, heading inside to check on Jenny.

"See that you do," Quinn O'Malley called as Patrick opened the door.

******

In Anglesey, North Wales, Jenny and Patrick took a train from Holyhead to London's Euston Station. It had been a long journey and the pair drowsed fitfully from sheer exhaustion. Afterwards, they'd walked halfway to Greenwich in the dark before hitching a lift on the back of a horse and milk pram carrying milk in churns for the morning round. They had done what they'd thought impossible over two very long days. It had been hard, but they'd put their best feet forward despite their grief for Susan and fear of travelling across the Irish Sea.

Patrick opened the front door and entered the narrow hallway. Jenny came in behind him, shivering as she removed her coat and hat and hung them on the coat stand. "I can't walk another step in these boots." She bent down to unlace them and shivered again as the heat in the hall began to thaw her. "God bless Anna for keeping the fire going for us."

Jenny, on one knee, fiddling with a knotted lace, suggested to Patrick, "I'll check on Minnie upstairs while you put the kettle on. I think we could do with a nice cup of tea before bed, don't you?"

When her brother didn't respond, she looked up, then fell onto her backside in astonishment. "My God, Kevin. It's you?"

The man she loved but believed she'd never see again stood in front of her in his army trousers and braces, his collarless shirt with its sleeves rolled up to his elbows covered in soot from the fire grate. Patrick gaped, and behind him Anna beamed with joy.

Kevin stretched out his arm and opened his palm. Jenny, enthralled by the sight of him, lifted her hand and placed it into his blackened hand.

"Up you come," Kevin grinned, pulling her to her feet.

Jenny began smoothing her skirt but then held her breath when Kevin crushed her to him. She felt like a pliant puppet, being pulled this way and that within his embrace, and when he kissed her, she thought she might faint with the joy of it.

Kevin's lips left hers, then he drew away. Jenny, feeling bereft, coiled her arms around his neck, gasping at the strength of her love. "Kevin…!"

"Ah, I have never seen such a welcoming or more beautiful sight than you, Jenny Carmody. I will never leave you again without saying what's in my heart. My beautiful, stubborn, Miss Carmody, you have no idea how many times I imagined holding you like this."

Kevin's soft, lyrical voice warmed her, and Jenny, mesmerised by his face and his touch, allowed his fingers to push her hair away from her face. Not even when he looked closely by the hall gaslight at the scars around her eye and hairline, did she flinch, for he was her Kevin and she felt his love, not his pity. She held her breath as he drew his finger along her sparse eyebrow and the rough-skinned eyelid, drooping at the outer edge. Then he moved it down the side of her head and touched the place where her ear used to be. She exhaled tentatively, but then sucked in her breath and held it again, as he lowered his head and kissed the unsightly spot.

"I love you, my Jenny…"

"Can I get a hello?" Patrick interrupted, breaking the spell that held Jenny and Kevin enthralled.

Chapter Two

The next morning, Jenny sat in her mother's favourite armchair, her hands hugging a cup of tea. She hadn't rested at all, for she had not wanted to give a single moment of the previous night to sleep, not even after her tiring trip to and from Dublin.

For so long, she had dreamt of Kevin's homecoming and of putting things right with him. She'd pictured a hundred different scenarios unfolding at their reunion. In almost all of them, she'd opened the front door to him. There he'd be, standing before her, unwilling to take her into his arms until he had given her a good telling-off about the fake letters, and John Grant breaking off their engagement then coming back to renew it, and the most serious of all, her failure to come clean about her feelings before he'd gone to war.

In those daydreams, she'd either defended herself by pushing the blame for everything onto Mam and Minnie, or she'd gone the other way and was contrite and begging forgiveness for the misunderstandings, of which there had been many. When her mam died, she discarded the blame scenario, for it wouldn't be proper to place the guilt on her poor dead mother.

Even now, her skin blazed from his touch, and her persistent smile revealed her love. Nothing of what she had pictured in her mind for months had come to pass. She had not opened the door to Kevin, as she'd imagined. He had not been angry or distant and hadn't asked about John Grant or why she had not revealed her feelings. Instead, he had strode out of Minnie's parlour with a face covered in soot from the fire, and with his uniform shirt sleeves rolled up to the elbows, and he had spoken of his love for her. It had been wonderful…

"Jenny, Minnie's talking to you. For God's sake, get your dizzy head away from Kevin Jackson and back here for a minute, will you?" Patrick chided with an amused grin.

"Sorry. I drifted off when you and Uncle George started talking about the Russian Bolsheviks. Sweet Jesus, can we not have one morning when we don't talk about the war? And why are we blethering on about what's happening in Russia? I thought we were discussing our Danny?"

"Don't blaspheme the Lord's name, Jenny," Minnie scolded, more herself now that the laudanum had worn off. "Russia is important. God knows what's going to happen to that poor Tsar Nicholas and his family," she brooded, looking into the fire and becoming despondent again.

"They've got enough on their plate without thinking about our war, right enough," Uncle George submitted. "Their revolution has turned into a civil war. You've got that Red Army fighting for Bolshevik socialism led by Vladimir Lenin, and the other lot calling themselves the White Army, supporting political monarchism. You wait and see; they'll end up destroying their own country without Germany having to lift a finger against them."

Jenny rolled her eyes. All morning, Kevin and Danny had been the main topics of conversation but when Uncle George arrived and gave Minnie *The Times* to read, they had begun a heated discussion about the Russians and their change in circumstances. And still it was going on … and on.

For the first time that week, Jenny was not running around making cups of tea and trying to put edible cakes together using very few of the correct recipe ingredients for the mourning folk who had come to pay their respects to Minnie and the family. Susan's death, devastating and still unbearably raw to the Carmodys, had shocked the whole street, and every man, woman, child, and their dog had come calling. Thank God the funeral was over, and they could now grieve in peace. She wondered how she was going to mourn properly when she was also full up with happiness.

Jenny regarded Minnie, who was looking better than she had the night before. She was still unusually quiet and prone to tears if someone said a wrong word, but after a good sleep, she had a little colour back in her cheeks. During the discussion about Danny, a spark of life had crawled back to her eyes.

Minnie, covered with a blanket in the armchair closest to the fire, gripped *The Times* in her hands as though afraid her family would take it off her. Sporadically, she looked up at the mantelpiece where a telegram sat and smiled. It had arrived minutes after dawn, and it held the wonderful news that Danny was even now on his way home, just as Kevin had predicted.

"This rain is spiteful. As if I'm not suffering enough, these damp, dark days have come to pull me down even further," Minnie moaned during a momentary lull in the conversation.

Jenny said, "We're almost into December, Minnie, we can't expect anything else at this time of year. At least it's not snowing."

"And this bad weather might keep the Zeppelins away," Uncle George suggested.

Minnie said to a pensive Anna, "You must be glad you don't have to work today."

"My God, Minnie, as if I could even think about delivering laundry with all that's happened. Where do you think Danny will be now, Patrick?" Anna asked for the third time.

"He's probably halfway across the English Channel," Patrick answered.

"Are you sure he'll go to the Charing Cross Hospital? What if they send him to a hospital outside London? How will we get there?"

Jenny had never met a worrywart quite like Anna. She was surprised the girl found the courage to get out of bed in the morning. "Anna, for the last time, the telegram says Charing Cross, so we must assume that's where they'll take him."

"Thank the Lord, that boy's coming home. I can see us losing this war, after what that bloody extremist party have done in Russia. Wait and see, they'll turn on us now," Uncle George grunted and returned the conversation to the Bolsheviks.

"Uncle, those ignorant madmen won't hold on to power for long," Patrick insisted for the second time.

"I'm not so sure, love," Minnie disagreed. "*The Times* is never wrong, and the journalist who wrote the article seems to know more about this carry-on than our Prime Minister and his government."

"Bloody government doesn't tell us anything nowadays," Uncle George grunted as he puffed on his pipe. "They're a bunch of lying, squabbling, toffee-nosed gits. Anyone would think they're running their own private club in Westminster instead of serving the rest of the country."

"Maybe the news is too terrible and they're afraid to tell us the truth?" Anna suggested.

"It's bad, all right, if we are to believe *The Times*," Patrick agreed. "If the Bolsheviks really have proposed an immediate peace with Germany, as the newspaper states, we'll be looking at the liberation of almost two million German and Austrian prisoners being held by Russia. And they will put those two million back into uniform before they even get the chance to say 'hello, how are you' to their families. What else did it say about that, Minnie?"

Minnie already had the newspaper open and was scrolling down its second and third pages. "It says here that the Bolshevik government of Soviet Russia and the Central Powers of Germany, Austria-Hungary, Bulgaria, and the Ottoman Empire, have signed a treaty at Brest-Litovsk and that it has ended Russia's participation in the war. Apparently, the negotiations have been going on for two months, and in the end the treaty was forced on the Bolshevik government by the threat of further advances by German and Austrian forces." She scrolled down again, then added, "This is the bit we should all worry about. It says that in concurring with the treaty, Soviet Russia has now defaulted on all Imperial Russia's commitments to the Triple Entente alliance, and this may do incalculable damage to the Allied cause."

"There, what did I tell you?" Patrick grunted.

Jenny said, "I don't understand why the proper Russian government and the sane people who supported the tsar don't put a stop to the madness."

"It's not as simple as that, Jenny dear," Uncle George told her.

"Well, it should be. Can you imagine those peasants in charge? How can they know the first thing about running a country?"

"They knew enough to go across German lines to negotiate a truce on behalf of the Russian nation," Patrick countered.

"I don't give a damn what the Russian hierarchy looks like at the moment," Uncle George continued, his pipe puffing becoming more ferocious. "I don't care if their leaders are pig farmers. Like I said, what should concern us is the likelihood of a new two million-man army of prisoners being freed to fight us in the West."

The rare sound of a motorcar pulling up in the street halted the conversation. Anna looked out of the window. "Kevin's getting out of a motorcar!"

Jenny rose from her chair, ran into the hallway and flung open the front door. After kissing him soundly in the street, and what the neighbours thought, be damned, she asked, "Who loaned you the motorcar?"

Kevin grinned. "No one. I bought it at an auction."

"You bought it? That must have been terribly expensive."

"It wasn't, actually, I got it for a song. It belonged to an army major who was killed in France a few months ago. His wife had no use for it, and it was just sitting in her garage doing nothing. And it was full of fuel. I don't suppose I'll be able to get much more once the tank is empty, apart from the official rationing for medical essential work, but we'll be able to get a good few miles in for personal needs, maybe even for social occasions before it runs out. Minnie's not fit enough to take buses and walk for miles, and I don't want you catching a cold either," said Kevin.

"What's that you're saying? It's yours, Kevin?" Minnie shouted from her chair into the hallway.

Back in the parlour, Jenny said, "It is, Minnie. Isn't it wonderful?"

"It's at your disposal, Minnie, and I'm more than pleased to see you've got over your woozy spell. How about I give you a ride through Greenwich? It'll put some colour back on those cheeks of yours," Kevin added with a wink and a mock bow.

Jenny, who was desperate for more time alone with Kevin, couldn't help wondering how he had afforded such a luxury. She didn't know anyone who owned a motorcar here in London, only one or two senior doctor friends of her da's back in Dublin. "Anna and I will put the kettle on," she said. "We'll all have a nice cup of tea, then I think we should go to the hospital. I'd rather wait for Danny there than sit here on tenterhooks."

"Maybe we should forget about the tea," Anna suggested.

Patrick said, "Hold your horses, Anna. Even if his ship has docked, it'll be hours yet before he gets to London, and hours, maybe days after that before he's allowed to have visitors."

Jenny beamed at Kevin. "Will you stay with us, Kevin?"

"I will, darlin'. I'm all yours."

Chapter Three

Kevin sat in a chair at the living room table, stretched out his long legs, and sighed with contentment. "I went to Charing Cross Hospital this morning to deliver my orders to the hospital's Chief Medical Officer. They're short-staffed, but Commander Graham's a good man, and he's honouring my leave."

"How long have you got, Son?" Minnie asked.

Kevin had told Minnie his news the previous night while she was hazy with laudanum. He surmised she wouldn't remember a word of their conversation. "Fifteen days, Minnie."

Last night had been about Jenny and himself, but he'd also had a few moments alone with Patrick when Jenny and Anna had been tucking Minnie into her bed. Patrick had spoken about his mother's sudden death, the shock of it, and the subsequent funeral. He'd not gone into specifics about the funeral cost, nor had he mentioned the payout from the Royal College of Surgeons in Dublin, but Kevin had dug beneath Patrick's painful accounting and had concluded that the family were in a much better financial position than the last time he'd been home. It had been a homecoming he'd never forget.

"Kevin, I'm sorry about last night. You must forgive me, I wasn't myself," Minnie said.

Kevin shifted his gaze from Jenny, as she and Anna left the living room to make tea. "There's nothing to forgive, Minnie, but promise me you'll lay off the laudanum now. You know it can be addictive, and we don't want it getting its hooks into you, do we?"

Tears slipped from Minnie's eyes. Patrick and Uncle George gazed sympathetically at her, but she focused on Kevin, as though he were the only other person in the room. "Son, I have to say … well, what my Susan and I did to you with those letters wasn't right. I wish I could take back all the lies we told … I do."

"It's all right…"

"No, it is not. My Susan isn't here to apologise to you, but if she were, she'd say the same thing. I know she was sorry for what she did to Jenny and you, even though it was because we were trying to protect our girl."

Kevin got up, went to Minnie, bent down and kissed her forehead. "Let's put all that nonsense behind us. Jenny and I have sorted out our differences and we couldn't be happier. Ah, Minnie, I wish I could take away your grief and make you feel better. I'd do anything to see that fighting spirit back in your eyes."

"Me, too." Minnie began to cry in earnest. "It's not right, taking my Susan like that. It's not fair, so it's not."

Uncle George went to comfort her, at which point Patrick rose from his chair at the table and motioned Kevin to join him in the hallway.

Kevin closed the living room door behind himself, then put on his coat and followed Patrick onto the small porch. "What's up?" he asked Patrick.

"I've got something to tell you. I didn't mention it last night because I was delighted to see you alive and well and didn't want to spoil your homecoming. The thing is, Kevin, I have to go back to sea next week."

Kevin's face fell. "Did they not give you compassionate leave?"

"I got a two-day extension to my existing leave, but that's all."

"Well, that's better than nothing, I suppose. Most men at the front aren't being granted *any* leave on compassionate grounds. It's a damn shame, but it's just not practical. This war's not going well for us."

"No one's being spared?"

"I've seen a few soldiers slip through the net, but the decision to ship a man home is discretionary and the decision hardly ever goes the soldier's way. You made the right choice when you opted for the Royal Navy. I know I'd rather look at the sea than the muck of the trenches and the burnt, stinking landscape covered in rotting flesh, bones, and body parts. I don't think I could have taken any more of it. It enough to drive the sanest of men mad."

Patrick nodded. "I don't think I can take another stint at sea, either. We all have our crosses to bear. Sure, but even crossing the Irish Sea yesterday was full of stress and perils." Then he averted his eyes.

Kevin, sensing Patrick's resentment, said, "Sorry, mate. I'm an eejit for saying that to you. Commander Graham at Charing Cross gave me some advice this morning. He said I've not to bottle up my feelings or my bad memories. People might not want to hear about the horrors in the trenches, he said, but he suggested I talk about my time on the Western front with someone who might understand." He sighed, "I forgot you went through hell on the *Britannic.*"

Patrick came around. "Your Commander Graham was right. You should talk to someone trustworthy, otherwise your memories will fester inside you and one day the poison will spill out of you and hurt someone you care deeply about. If you're marrying my sister, I suppose you should talk to me."

Kevin leant against the inside wall of the porch to shield himself from the freezing wind. "You know, I could tell a thousand people about the trenches, but unless they've spent time in them, they couldn't picture the horrors men endure there, hour by hour, day in, day out."

"I think we can all imagine them being the most hellish places on earth," Patrick responded with a pat on Kevin's shoulder.

"And likewise, quid pro quo, know I'm here for you too, Patrick. How *are* you doing after your ordeal at sea?"

Patrick shrugged, then answered with a wry smile, "I'm having nightmares about going on a combat ship, but apart from that, I'm fine."

"I can't even imagine what you must have gone through when it was sinking. I should have replied to your letters, to tell you how glad I was that you got off it safely. I'm sorry for being a stubborn, stupid bugger."

"I don't blame you for being angry at the Carmodys, Kevin. Bloody women and their emotional games, eh?"

Kevin chuckled. "That's the fairer sex for you, I suppose. You know what hit me the hardest when I came home on my last leave for a few days?"

"When was that?"

"A while ago now. I wanted to surprise Jenny, but I was the one who got the surprise. I stood on the pavement outside and saw your sister kissing John Grant in the living room. That bastard saw me gawping at him through the window before he leant forward to lock his lips on hers. I was raging and walked away instead of knocking on the door and asking her what the hell was going on."

"Well, I can tell you, hand on my heart, that their meeting ended badly. She threw John out. Told him never to come back."

"Good, I'll punch him all the way back to Dublin if I see him sniffing around here again." Kevin paused, then asked, "Tell me more about your posting?"

"I'm joining a seaplane carrier, HMS *Ark Royal*. She's the first one the Royal Navy has built, apparently. She's in the Dardanelles operating as a depot ship for our seaplanes in the Royal Naval Air Service for that area. I've got to get out to her, which means she won't be returning to England any time soon. I don't know when I'll get home again, Kevin."

"Jesus, Patrick, why haven't you told the family? They have a right to know. Jenny thinks you'll be home every other weekend."

Patrick ran his fingers through his hair, then bowed his head. "Ach, I don't know. We've had too much bad news lately. Her worst nightmare is me going back to sea, so I thought I'd write to them once I'm settled on board."

"It's not a damn cruise liner you're going on!"

"I know!" Patrick snapped back.

Patrick's nerves had already started to tingle. The thoughts of being at sea again terrified him; thoughts of seeing waves batter the ship in rough weather, of seasickness, vomiting, and spending nights awake because he was too afraid to sleep in case the ship was hit and he drowned below deck. He'd been on a ship that had sunk, and the images of that experience had crammed his mind ever since. Christ, he had thanked God when he'd got off the ferry from Dublin the previous night, and that crossing was in the narrow Irish Sea!

To brush aside his fears, Patrick focused on a happy event, saying, "Kevin, marry my sister. Don't wait for Danny and me to get home. Life's too short and unpredictable to delay the happiness you both deserve."

"Patrick, I'd marry her tomorrow, but it doesn't seem right to have a wedding this soon after your mam's passing."

"Ah, but that's my point. My mother wasted so much of her life pining for my da, she forgot how to enjoy her independence. While the world and everyone in it went on without her, she got herself stuck in a bloody waiting room watching the clock and wishing the time away. She wasn't a happy woman, Kevin, not even when my father was alive, and she had every luxury you can think of at her feet. I envy you and Jenny. You have something I crave, the love I dream of having but can't seem to find."

A spark of excitement coloured Kevin's cheeks, but he hesitated. "I don't know…"

"What don't you know? Sure, you could get one of those special licences and marry in a registry office in the city or in Greenwich Town Hall. We can always have a wedding party after the war ends."

"I'll think about it. Do you think she'd give up on having a grand wedding in the white dress and a church full of flowers, and the reading of the Banns and all that palaver she's always wanted? I mean, can I take away her dream?"

Patrick laughed. "If you had asked me that question a year ago, I'd have said you weren't the full shillin', and no way will my Jenny give up her grand plans for her big day, but now? No, I don't think it'll bother her at all. She loves you more than the frills that would go with a wedding. Look, it makes sense. You two get married, you live together, and she doesn't end up choking the life out of Minnie. It's a win-win situation."

"No." Kevin shook his head. "I won't ask her to leave Minnie. You should have seen the state of your granny last night. She needs help now that your mother's gone, and you can't ask Anna to look after her, what with her job and Danny coming home."

Patrick took out his Woodbine cigarettes and shuffled the box until one popped up. He proffered it to Kevin, saying, "It's true what you say. Uncle George has been a great help to Minnie this past week, but he's got that bad leg from the Boer war and can't get about like he used to…" Patrick's voice trailed off as he lit Kevin's cigarette with the trench lighter he'd acquired; a spare one from a grateful Tommy in exchange for cigarettes during a hospital ship repatriation run. Then he straightened, cracked the front door open, and peered into the empty hallway. "Keep this under your hat, Kevin," he said, keeping the door on the latch. "Jenny and I didn't tell Minnie we were going to Dublin to get my da's money."

Kevin asked, "Why the secrecy?"

"Minnie would have panicked had she known we were going across the Irish Sea, what with the thought of free-floating mines and U-boats, an' all. Mind you, I don't think she stayed awake enough to even notice we were gone for two whole days. Anna told her we'd gone out to do business in London each time she asked for us. My granny's not the spunky woman she was." He pointed to his head. "She's still got it up there, but she's worn down. I think age and grief have caught up with her. The thing is, we're okay for money, and we will be in the future if we're careful. Jenny suggested yesterday that we rent a bigger house for us all. Would you consider living with Minnie after you and my Jenny wed?"

"I'd have to think about that."

Patrick studied Kevin, who was no doubt getting tangled up in the idea of living with the in-laws or getting his own house, which he could well afford to do. "Tell me, does my Jenny know who your family are?" he asked.

"No, I haven't told her."

Patrick chuckled, "Well, at least you know she's not after your wealth or title. Imagine her face when she finds out you could buy and sell John Grant ten times over."

"Don't say a word to her. I'm not telling her until I'm ready to take her home with me." Then he aired his thoughts. "I'm not against the idea of Jenny continuing to live with Minnie, Patrick. Last night, she talked about her job at Shooter's Hill hospital. She enjoys it, and I'd hate to move her across the river to be nearer to my hospital."

"You'll be working all the hours God sends, right enough," Patrick mused. "Are you sure you know what you're taking on with a wife?"

"I'll take your sister on with pleasure, but first, I need to get to Cork to see my parents and brother for a few days. If you're not here when I get back, do you want me to tell the family where you've gone?"

"Would you do that for me?"

Kevin nodded. "It'll be better coming from me than from you in a letter. I'll tell Danny as well."

Patrick sighed with regret. Danny was his main concern, and he wouldn't be around to support his young brother. "You know me, Kevin. I'm not a man to pray, but I hope to God my Danny doesn't fully recover until the day after this war ends."

"You wouldn't say that if you'd seen him…"

Patrick and Kevin broke off their conversation when Jenny and Anna made a racket coming from the kitchen. Both men went in, took off their coats and followed the women into the living room.

Anna, who was pouring the tea, said, "Right you two, a quick cup of tea, then we're off to see Danny. And before either of you say it, I don't care about the hospital's set rules allowing half hour visiting times. Kevin, you'll be a big man there soon, so you can ask them if they'll allow us a special visit, just this once."

Patrick whispered to Kevin, "Welcome to the family. Get used to being bossed around."

Chapter Four

The journey from the casualty clearing station based at Remy Farm at Lijssenthoek had taken its toll on Danny's state of mind. Apart from his other injuries, he was suffering from the dreaded Trench Fever. Although not confirmed, many army doctors believed the sickness was brought on by the lice that invaded a soldier's body whilst in the trenches. The parasites nested and laid their eggs in the seams of clothing, shirt tails, and body hair, and left men with raised temperatures and shivers so profound their teeth rattled like a woodpecker knocking holes in a tree. Danny was burning up, and his condition was compounded further by the searing pain in his neck, face, hands, and for some reason, his legs and shins.

His blistered body stung from the inside out where the gas had seeped through his skin and flesh and settled in his bones. He was scared, suspecting that the angel nurses at Remy Farm weren't angels at all and had lied about his circumstances or had left out the dreadful things that could happen as a result of the gas attack injuries.

Halfway across the English Channel, Danny got himself into a nervous state. He needed to talk to someone. With a soft voice, he called out to a wounded man who'd been kind enough to narrate their journey from Lijssenthoek, hoping he was still lying next to him and wasn't fast asleep. "Walt, are you still there? Are you awake?"

"I am now," the grumpy Scottish voice responded.

"I was thinking, Walt, I shouldn't have spoken to that woman with the Geordie accent at the farm. Remember her?"

"I do. She was looker, right enough."

"Her voice was soothing, I'll give her that, but I think she understated the extent of my wounds."

"How come?" Walt asked.

"Well, she kept saying, 'I've seen worse than you, pet. Give it a year and you won't even have scars.' I've been thinking about her. She probably told every man she saw they'd be all right while knowing they were going to die."

"Aye, you might be right. I've seen it happen. Just before a poor bugger called Reg got his leg amputated and then died, her sweet smiling face looked down at him and told him he'd make a good recovery in England. I mean it's her job to comfort dying men and the likes but to be honest, I think Reg would have been happier to hear a priest say a few words to him."

"I suppose," Danny mused. "A doctor told me before we left that the effects of the mustard gas can be delayed for twelve hours, and then it quite often begins to rot the body from both within and without. I'm scared, Walt. He said men died of the stuff up to four or five weeks after being hit – tell me the truth – how do I look?"

"The same as you did an hour ago. And I wouldn't worry about what that clown of a doctor said. He wouldn't have said that to you if he thought you were going to die."

Danny sighed, loving that response. "You might be right. He back-peddled afterwards; said I'd been saved just in time from a lethal dose; still, I'm not convinced I'm going to live through this carry-on."

"Shut up, Danny, or you won't live through this voyage!" a familiar voice from the trenches called out.

“Is that you, Charlie?” Danny called back, trying to smile at his old friend, despite splitting a couple of the gas blisters on his lips.

“It is, and if you don’t stop talking about dying, I’ll come over there on my one leg and finish you off myself!”

Danny didn’t feel as though he were dying. He was breathing well enough and wasn’t bleeding out of his nose and ears or any other orifice. The pain and burning he experienced felt superficial, yet it was quite possible that he was being eaten alive by an invisible poison capable of decaying his heart and liver and every other organ inside him. Never would he ask another medical question in his life, for however long that might be.

As if the thought of dying wasn’t enough, his mood darkened further with the lack of answers to questions about his eyes. It wasn’t unreasonable to ask if he was going to be blind for the rest of his life, yet not one person had been able to give him an answer to put his mind at rest. They’d taken the bandages off a couple of times when he’d been in the clearing station ward and had bathed his eyes, but he was still blind. He wasn’t even seeing outlines or misty figures like the ones he’d seen in the trench straight after the gas attack. In fact, the last face he’d seen had been Kevin Jackson’s, of all people.

He listened to the noises surrounding him and all he could think about was living in this ethereal darkness, hearing voices and being jumpy at the sound of every approaching footstep, or the rattling of tin cups or plates being dropped or set down near to him. But the worst part of it all was his reflexively shocked response to a rifle or pistol firing. Thankfully, he’d slept during most of the train journey, but God only knew how he’d managed that. Men were crying for their mothers and moaning in agony as the train chugged, jerked and shivered to a stop on frozen tracks near the front line. It seemed like hundreds of men had been confined in that carriage. He could feel their spittle on his face when they coughed and smell piss and shite-filled clothing as though the crutch of a pair of their trousers had been wafted underneath his nostrils.

During that stage of the journey, a medical orderly had pricked him with a needle; more morphine, he presumed. He remembered being in agony and begging for help when they carried him from the train, but later, while listening to the roar of a ship's engine growling as it docked alongside, he'd drifted off to sleep. There was a lot to be said for that morphine stuff. It was no wonder Jenny hadn't wanted Patrick to take it off her when she was getting over her burns.

"Danny, we're well over the halfway point," Walt's voice came back. "I've just heard someone say they sighted land. Blighty, here we come. I can hardly believe we're on our way home. Christ, I never thought I'd make it off that battlefield alive, never mind a wagon ride, a train ride and a voyage."

Danny turned his head in the direction of the voice. "I knew you'd make it, Walt. It'll take more than a German field cannon shell to take you down."

"They took my arm, though, the rotten bastards."

Danny tried to smile, but where his blisters had oozed and dried, his lips felt as though they were glued together. Walt had been in a neighbouring bed in the hospital at Lijssenthoek. He'd lost his arm six weeks earlier, yet one would think he was the happiest man alive. He talked a lot, but he'd been a godsend, insomuch as letting all the poor blind buggers know what was going on in the ward.

Danny dozed off, lulled to sleep by Walt's voice. He woke with a start: excited voices, people laughing and crying, boots thumping the deck's floor, stores being moved, and the strange noise of the ship's engines revving loudly just before they were cut. He panicked at the sounds invading his oversensitive ears. "What's happening? What do you see, Walt?"

"Ach, there you are, back in the land of the living. We're here, Danny. We're in Southampton. They've started to disembark the walking wounded. The stretchers will be next."

"I wish they'd take this bloody blindfold off me. I can't stand this darkness!" A hand touched Danny's arm and he jumped with fright. "Jesus Christ, Walt, don't do that!"

At that moment he felt his stretcher being lifted, and an unknown voice stating, "You're next, Corporal." Having presumed that Walt had pawed him with his one hand, he muttered, "Sorry, I'm blind."

"I'll be on the stretcher right behind you," Walt said, giving Danny some comfort.

A new thought struck Danny as he was bounced along on the stretcher, and he aired them aloud. "I hope my wife and my mam know I'm coming home. The first thing I'm going to do is ask to be allowed to recover in my granny's house. With my Anna beside me, and my mam clucking around me like a hen, I'll be well in no time."

"My da's not going to be happy with me coming home with one arm. I'm supposed to be helping him run the farm when this is over. I suppose I'm not much good to anyone now, am I?" Walt called out with a miserable voice.

Danny concentrated on the noises going on around them. His heightened hearing was picking out voices and the sound of vehicles. His face was hit by a cold gust of air, and raindrops hitting parts of his face not covered by bandage. “Aww, that feels good. British rain, British voices, and no guns. I can’t hear a single gun. I couldn’t wish for more. Can you tell me where we’re going after this?” he then asked the invisible stretcher bearers.

“The train station, then on to London,” a voice answered.

“I don’t care where we’re going,” Walt piped up, still on the stretcher behind Danny’s. “I’m finished with the war and good riddance to it.”

Much later, Danny was given a bed in a ward at Charing Cross Hospital. As soon as he’d been tucked in, the doctor arrived and introduced himself. “Hello, Corporal Carmody. I’m Doctor Spratt. I’m going to remove and replace your eye bandages. Let’s see how far you’ve come, shall we?”

Danny was anxious and excited as Doctor Spratt began unwinding the cotton strips wrapped around his head and eyes. He was also praying. Would he see or was it too soon to have his sight back? Would the doctor be pleased with the progress that had been made or had there been no progress at all since the mustard gas had blinded him?

“I’m not expecting miracles, but I would like to know if it’s looking a bit better,” Danny muttered through his cracked, blistered lips.

“Well, Corporal, I didn’t see what you looked like when you were first wounded, but I’ve seen enough men to know if you’re going in the right direction. Even so, don’t get your hopes up just yet. It’s still early days.”

Silence followed the removal of the eye pads. Danny, holding his breath, saw not a glimmer of light, but he did feel cooling air hit his eyeballs, and the fingers of the doctor’s sterile surgical rubber gloves pressing the area around his hairline.

"You might feel a pulling of your sore eyelids and something hard pressing on your skin around the eyes. Sorry, I must have a closer look at your corneas through my magnifying glass."

After an excruciating wait for the doctor to speak again, Danny asked, "Well, Doctor, what's the verdict?"

"I don't have one yet. Your eyelids are red-raw, puffy, stuck together, and covered in great mustard-coloured blisters, as I would expect them to be. The good news is that your cornea and sclera don't look too badly burnt. How is your breathing now?"

"Better. When it happened, my throat closed, and I had to fight to catch a breath. I thought I was going to choke to death. What are my chances, Doctor? I've heard stories about men dying from this after they thought they were getting better. You wouldn't lie to me now, would you? I need to know so I can prepare my wife for the worst."

Is that a chuckle I hear coming from the doctor? Danny wondered, as further silence followed his question.

"Don't get carried away, Corporal Carmody," the voice eventually came back. "The gas kills about one percent of soldiers who have been exposed, and I don't believe you will fall into that category. Mustard gas is far more effective as an incapacitating agent. If you're lucky it will take you out of action for the duration of this conflict. If you're unlucky, you'll be fit enough one day to resume your service to our wounded country."

"Oh, shite – no offence, Doctor Spratt, but in the spirit of honesty, I'm hoping the war will be over before I'm well enough to go back to it."

Chapter Five

It had taken two full days before Anna, Jenny, and even Patrick, as a qualified doctor, were given permission to see Danny. The stringent rules at Charing Cross Hospital dictated that only one family member at a time could visit at the patient's bedside, and that patients could not receive a visit for more than thirty minutes in any one day. Kevin, with his new posting there made public, used his influence to convince the ward sister to allow Anna and Jenny to go into the ward together whilst he and Patrick waited their turn downstairs in the general waiting area. The pair determined they would see Danny, despite the rule stating that there should be no exchange of visitors during visiting time.

In case Patrick were denied entry, on this his last day at home, the family gave Jenny the horrible task of informing Danny about their mother's death. The news came as a shock to her younger brother, as expected, and it had also caused the ailing spirits of a man who was already suffering the agonies of war to plummet further.

Outwardly, he appeared to take the news well. He hadn't cried behind his bandages or demanded answers as to why his previously fit and healthy mother had suddenly passed away. He had nodded, and said, "I see. God bless her soul." Jenny had decided not to go into the nitty-gritty details of the massive stroke their mam had suffered. Danny had enough to contend with, and the specifics of their mother's passing could wait until he felt better and more able to cope. She reminded herself to tell Patrick before he blabbed.

The listless, silent figure lying in the bed was as a stranger, making Jenny think, *this is not my passionate, wild brother who left England for war.* Strips of linen bandages covered the top half of his face, but the shape of his bared, blistered lips and stubborn jawline were also unrecognisable. She was glad he couldn't see the silent tears rolling down her cheeks, or Anna's horrified face as she stared at the man she loved.

Jenny stood at the bottom of the bed to allow Anna to have a more intimate conversation with her husband. Patrick had remarked that morning to the family that he'd seen men in similar conditions to Danny on the *Britannic* hospital ship and at London's King's Cross Hospital. According to him, it could take weeks or months for a man to fully regain sight after a gas attack, which could be a good thing, Jenny had thought then. The longer he was blind, the longer he would stay in England. Later, when Kevin had added that some poor buggers never got their sight back, she'd crossed herself and had asked for forgiveness and a speedy recovery.

Jenny knew her brother better than Anna, and he was not only dispirited but also in a foul mood. He was trying to hide his feelings, but each laboured word he'd spoken had been clipped and hard-edged and that had nothing to do with his sore, swollen mouth.

Anna held Danny's hand, and kept bending down to kiss it, like he was her lord and master. She was being brave but as soon as they left Danny, she'd likely break down and cry until her tears ran dry. That was Anna; always a tear at the ready.

"Danny, my darling, I know this is terrible for you. You're injured, your mam's dead, and I can't imagine your suffering and pain, but something else is bothering you. What is it?" Anna asked.

Her sister-in-law's intuition impressed Jenny. Perhaps Anna *did* know Danny as well as she did. Love usually revealed the deepest, most hidden traits of a person.

Danny didn't want to or couldn't speak, but Jenny didn't need to see his eyes to know he was now struggling, even silently crying beneath his bandages. "Tell us, Danny?" she pleaded, moving closer to the side of the bed by his head.

"They've told me I've got to stay at least another three weeks in this hospital," Danny finally uttered through his split half-open lips. "Then they'll move me to a military convalescent home or depot."

Anna's face crumpled. As predicted, she was quick to come to tears; as if they were waiting in the corners of her eyes to spring out on command. *Poor Anna,* Jenny thought. *Within twenty-five minutes, the British Army has stomped on her dream of looking after Danny at home.*

"Where will they send you?" Anna sniffed.

"That's it, I don't know. I pleaded with the doctors to let me recuperate in Greenwich, at Minnie's house, but the doctor who's dealing with me said I'll go at the appropriate time and wherever the army sends me based on my condition upon leaving the hospital."

Jenny had also tried to keep Danny close. She'd suggested to his ageing doctor that he should transfer her brother to Shooter's Hill Hospital where she and Anna worked. It was much closer to Greenwich, she'd contended, and Anna would raise his spirits. Keeping a soldier happy was an important medicine, she'd pointed out, and she should know; it was her job. But the doctor had flatly denied her request.

"… I'll try to visit every day they allow visiting, but it won't be easy." Anna was now saying, as she gently caressed the back of Danny's hand. "Kevin has bought a motorcar, and he'll drive me here whenever I get time off to see you. There's no such thing as regular bus times in London nowadays. Most of them have been shipped over to France to ferry troops, and some have even been used as pigeon lofts for the carrier pigeons to send messages, so I was told..."

"Finding fuel is also next to impossible. Kevin can only use the motorcar if it has petrol in it," Jenny reminded Anna.

"He said he'd let me drive it," Anna said, ignoring Jenny's pessimism.

Danny, who was still unusually subdued, asked, "Jenny, you and Kevin are getting along, I take it?"

"We're engaged, Danny. I wish you could see my ring. It's much nicer than the one John Grant gave me. Remember the day you and I went to London to sell it?"

"How can I ever forget; if it were not for that bloody ring, I wouldn't have gone to war. You'll not be selling this one, I suppose?" Danny at last cracked a smile, but then moaned with pain as his blistered lip split yet again.

"No, I will not. Oh, Danny, I love Kevin. You were right, I should have told him a year ago."

"You should have seen them both, my *cariad,"* Anna said, the Welsh endearment for her husband coming musically to her lips. "It was like watching a fairy tale unfold when they ran into each other's arms and kissed before saying as much as a "Hello, how are you?" I don't think Jenny got more than five minutes sleep last night."

"When the gas got me, I couldn't help myself, I thought I was a goner," muttered Danny, tiring now. "I know I said a lot of terrible things in the past about Kevin, but I ... I wouldn't be here were it not for his quick thinking … his actions. He saved my life, Jenny. Would you thank him for me?"

"You can thank him yourself, Danny. He's waiting outside, hoping to see you. He's going to work here soon, so you'll have plenty of time to get to know each other…" Her words trailed off, but she then decided to be honest with her brother. "He's going to be your brother-in-law, Danny. I would like you and he to be friends. Will you promise me you'll put the past behind you and try to like him for my sake?"

"I will, Jenny. I won't deny he's a good man."

"Jenny has more good news for you too, cariad. Go on, Jenny, tell him."

Jenny leant down until her lips were almost touching Danny's ear. "We're rich, Danny. We've got ten thousand pounds in the bank in Dublin. The Royal College of Surgeons settled with us for the value of da's research papers."

Danny gasped. "You went to Dublin?"

"Yes. Minnie doesn't know yet, so don't say anything to her. Patrick will tell you more about it when he comes in."

Jenny backed away to let Anna say her goodbyes. The latter kissed Danny's hand, then said, "We're going now. "We promised to let Patrick and Kevin in to see you for five minutes. Patrick's leaving tomorrow for Southampton, and Kevin's going to Ireland for a few days. I'll be back tomorrow when I finish work, all right, dearest?"

Danny squeezed Anna's hand and then turned his head as if searching for her face. "Before you go, Anna darlin', I don't want you driving a motorcar. It's not right."

Anna retorted, "Have you been lying there chewing that over in your mind, Danny Carmody? Of course, it's right that I should drive."

Jenny concurred. "Sure, if she can drive a laundry truck, she can handle a four-seater Ford T motorcar."

"No. I don't want my wife driving anything that moves on wheels with a mechanical engine," Danny insisted.

"Don't be daft, Danny, the streets of London are full of women driving buses now. We're able to do everything a man can do and do it just as well. You saw that for yourself before you left for the front."

"I doubt you can do what we're doing in the trenches," Danny mumbled.

Jenny gritted her teeth, but Anna seemed to want to make her point. "We'll be getting the vote soon, Danny. The House of Commons has already passed the Representation of the People Act bill, and by a huge majority at that, and that will give women over the age of thirty their say in who runs this country."

"Only if they own a property," Jenny reminded Anna.

Anna leant down and kissed Danny's bandaged forehead, saying, "We don't need to talk about politics, my love. You concentrate on getting better. And don't think about what that doctor said about you not being allowed to come home. He's a civilian, and Kevin probably outranks him. When he starts work here, he'll be in charge, and if he says you can come home, that'll be that."

Jenny vowed to keep her mouth shut for the rest of the visit, lest she be accused of upsetting her brother and sister-in-law with the fact that Kevin was answerable to a higher ranking officer who would ultimately decide what would happen to her brother according to their rules and regulations.

Danny then surprised Jenny with his response to Anna's statement, "I understand why they want to keep me in the hospital, darlin', but I don't understand why they think I'll recuperate faster in an army depot or a convalescent home than in my own home with my loving wife looking after me."

"You're in the army," Jenny reminded him, breaking her vow of silence within seconds of making it. "Men in the convalescent barracks stay as fit as they can be. They're retrained before being sent back to the war, and they maintain their discipline. I know you, remember? If you were to stay at Minnie's, you'd lie in bed all day letting your wife spoon feed you."

Danny turned towards Jenny's indignant voice. "Is that right, little-miss-know-it-all? And how would you know what goes on in the army?"

"The army have programmes going on at the convalescent bases. A few weeks ago, I was talking to a wounded soldier at Shooter's Hill. It was the second time he'd come back because of war wounds. He said when he arrived at a recuperation depot the first time around, a medical board interviewed and examined him. They assigned him to one of the four cavalry squadrons at the Depot. He had to wear a coloured slide on his epaulette and that depicted his squadron and how fit he was. He had bayonet practice and was marching up and down two weeks after getting there. You won't get any discipline at Minnie's."

The ward's handbell rang, signalling that visitors had five minutes left. Jenny stared at the double doors and saw Patrick's impatient face behind the glass. "I love you, Danny. See you soon. I'd better let Patrick in before he breaks that bloody door down."

Chapter Six

March 1918

London, England

Danny left the underground station, walked up the stairs to Bond Street, and crossed the road to Durrants Hotel. Before going through its fancy entrance adorned with white pillars and glass windows, he ripped the convalescent hospital's Red Squadron slide from his epaulette, crumpled it in his hand, and shoved it into the pocket of his new uniform trousers.

His heavy army sack held the possessions he would need to go back to war, apart from his rifle. He had packed earlier that morning and everything he carried was precious, either to use or to barter with: straight razor, shaving brush, shaving strop, Pears shaving stick, toothbrush, dentifrice toothpowder, comb, needle, thread, buttons, a half pint tin cup, pocket knife, spoon, and a few knitted comforts. His heavy, cumbersome greatcoat sat at the top of the sack in case it rained and he had to get to it quickly. He had folded it flat numerous times and inside the doublings he'd laid two spare shirts and a spare pair of puttees for his ankles. The Army gave each man one uniform, and if a soldier ran out, tore or lost his kit, he went without, begged, or took from the dead.

He set the sack on the pavement, then buttoned his jacket's top button and pulled his cap further down his forehead. Within minutes, he would hold Anna in his arms, free of the stares of the other patients during his and Anna's short farewell kiss at Orpington's convalescent hospital. They had allowed her to visit him once during his three-month stay – *whoop-de-bloody-doo!* Yes. He was free of all constraints until the following morning when hell would once again open its jaws and sweep him inside.

He would kiss Anna hard when he saw her, but he wouldn't make it last too long or draw attention to himself. This was Jenny and Kevin's big day, not his, Kevin had warned him in a telegram. He'd received it the previous night, telling him the news and details of the lunch venue today; he had thought it a coincidence that it had come only an hour after he'd received his marching orders from the hospital. Danny deduced that Kevin must have known about the hospital's intentions before they'd relayed them to their patient. That'd be Kevin, right enough. He had his fingers in a lot of pies, that one.

Inside, Danny asked the hotel's receptionist for directions to the restaurant, and after being told where it was, the man suggested to Danny that he leave his army pack in storage. A good idea, Danny thought, admiring the posh furniture, pictures and wall coverings. He wondered who had chosen this posh venue. He was still taking in the news that he wasn't poor anymore, and that his sister and brother were sitting pretty with their da's money. He also knew about Kevin's wealth, but Patrick had sworn him to secrecy. He wondered, *has Jenny discovered her husband's family history yet?*

Danny spotted Anna from the restaurant entrance doors. She had her back to him, but he'd recognise her blue-black curly hair and the line of her shoulders anywhere. Jenny spotted him, squealed, and rose from her chair. *This is it,* Danny thought, waving to her. The moment he'd been waiting for. The months of torture were over.

The round table for six, decorated with seasonal freesia and daffodil flowers, was situated in an alcove. Danny crossed the main dining room to Anna and kissed her soundly before saying "hello" to his family. Eventually, after a kiss that had lasted longer than deemed appropriate in a public place, he reluctantly drew away from her to congratulate the newlywed couple.

Jenny, dressed in a delicately hand-embroidered and lace gown the colour of the champagne they were drinking, looked radiant. Danny had noticed her hair before her gown. She wore her curly mop down. It now touched her shoulders, covered most of her unsightly scars and was decorated with a feather-type clip, also a champagne colour. Danny kissed her cheek and held her outwards at arm's length. Her damaged eye looked a little better. Yes, its eyelid was still crooked; drooping at the corner nearest her hairline, but it was less so than it had been a year earlier. He could cry with joy for her. She looked like her old self; the Jenny he loved but had also disliked for most of his puberty years.

He left his sister and leant down to kiss Minnie, who was looking grand in a dark blue dress with a frilly collar. Her thinning white hair was swept up in a bun that sat high on her head. It was held in place with a gold comb and her trademark silver pins to keep the wispy sides tamed. He grinned at his grandmother's made-up face. He was guessing his Anna had painted Minnie's lips with rouge. He hadn't seen her looking this elegant for years.

After Minnie, Danny shook hands with Uncle George, then finally, he paid attention to Kevin. "Well, you got her in the end," he gave his new brother-in-law a genuine smile.

Kevin, in his full-dress officer's uniform, beamed and said, "I did indeed. I'm glad you made it, Danny. Now we can start the party."

Danny sat next to Anna. He was shaking and held her hand for support. She wore a radiant smile. Her eyes were sparkling and devouring his face, which caused him to avert his. He was going to tell her about his posting, he was. He'd planned the way he would say it on the train, but how he'd manage a cheery face and spirited voice without a tremble was beyond him. Sure, rehearsing his speech in private was not the same as telling her to her sweet face; he forced his mind to other topics. "I'm sorry I couldn't get to the ceremony. I take it the deed is done?"

Jenny laughed, "You make it sound as though we've committed a crime. Yes, Danny, the deed is done. I am now Mrs Jenny Jackson – Jenny Jackson – it has a nice ring to it, don't you think?"

"No offence, but you'll always be Jenny Carmody to me," Danny said.

The waiter poured Danny champagne in a tall lead crystal glass flute. The others at the table raised their glasses to meet his as he toasted the couple. "Congratulations. I wish you both a long life of happiness together." Danny drank the glass dry, and after he'd asked for a refill, added, "I never thought I'd live to see this day, after all the carry-on it took for the two of you to get here."

Kevin had already ordered a set menu for the family but had not given the waiter the nod to serve it. Danny supposed his new brother-in-law wanted to savour his wedding breakfast, not rush it like the uniformed naval officers at the next table who were chomping their food down as if it were their last supper. Patrick came to mind. Anna and Jenny had not mentioned him in their letters. "Does our Patrick know you got married today?" he asked, while giving the waiter the eye to refill his glass yet again.

"No. He's at sea. We don't know where," Jenny answered.

"He's all right, Danny, but he'll get a clip around the ear from me when I see him," Minnie chimed in. "The little tyke didn't tell us he had another ship. He left that gem of a job to poor Kevin."

After the waiters served bowls of spring vegetable soup in which early new potatoes, carrots, split peas, onions, and fresh spring greens were dished up in a chicken-based stock, Minnie asked Danny how he had enjoyed his time at the convalescent hospital in Orpington, near Bromley, Kent.

As Danny stirred the vegetables, probably grown in someone's back garden or allotment, he considered how to answer Minnie's question. Bromley was only eight miles from Greenwich, and thirteen miles from London, but he'd felt a hundred miles away from his beloved Anna. "They treated us well enough, Minnie," he finally answered. "The hospital was full of Canadians and men from other parts of the Empire. I was the only Irishman in the place."

"I thought that might be the case," Kevin put in. "When I pushed for you to go there it was because it was much closer to Greenwich than the other convalescent places. I was hoping Anna could visit you once a week."

"I would have, were it not for work. I've been working hard, Danny. Every hospital in London is overflowing with patients, and our days off are cancelled until further notice. I really did try to get to you."

"And what did you do with yourself every day?" Minnie asked Danny.

"The first few weeks were hard, Minnie. There's not much a man can do while he's blind. Once I got my sight back, I was able to move about safely and even learnt how to play croquet. They had cricket matches for those who were fit enough to play, but I never did like that game. And the doctors wouldn't let me play football either. They didn't think me getting hit with a ball in my face would do my recovering eyesight much good. I took on your habit of reading donated newspapers as soon as my sight improved enough; when I was lucky enough to get hold of one, that is. And in the last couple of weeks, I started to go on organised runs and do the compulsory army keep-fit callisthenics."

"Isn't it wonderful to see our Danny fit and well, and to have this happy occasion to celebrate?" Minnie giggled, and had another tipple of champagne.

"I'm sorry your parents couldn't get over from Ireland," Uncle George said to Kevin. "I've no doubt they'll give you and your new wife a warm welcome when you manage to take Jenny home with you."

"I suppose they'll be happy Jenny didn't insist on a Catholic ceremony," Danny piped up after finishing another glass of champagne, then he belched. "A Protestant and a Catholic. Who'd have thought it, eh?"

Kevin threw Danny a disapproving look, noting the glasses around Danny's serving plate were accumulating faster than the wait staff could take them away. Jenny said, "Today was about a legal marriage on license, Danny. We'll decide when and where to either have a proper church blessing in Kevin's church, or have what's called a *convalidation* in our church…"

"A conval… what?"

"It's where we receive the marriage sacrament. And before you ask, Kevin is quite happy to convert to our religion, so that we can continue our marriage with a priest's blessing."

Kevin squeezed Jenny's hand, then lifted it to his mouth and kissed it.

Danny, with another full glass, was happy for his sister, but the Carmodys were staunch Catholics, not British loyalist Proddie-dogs like Kevin's family. Jenny was deluded if she thought Kevin's parents would welcome her with open arms or allow their son to become a Fenian; that ugly name they gave to the members of the Irish Republican Brotherhood. All in all, it was a tricky situation. "Your parents live in Cork, do they not, Kevin?" Danny said, knowing the answer but feeling the devil coming out of him. Or was it the effects of the champagne? *Who cares?* He was going to have more of it. He'd be drowning in the stuff before the day was finished.

"They do. Unfortunately, my father couldn't leave the farm. It's a busy time in the fields for him, and its lambing season."

Danny chuckled and thought, *Farm? Wait till Jenny sees the farmhouse!*

As the second course of fish arrived, the conversation moved on to Jenny's plans to continue working, despite now being a married woman. She'd cut down her hours at Shooter's Hill Hospital, she told the others at the table. Maybe she would only work three or four days a week instead of six. Kevin wanted to rent an apartment for them close to his place of work. He had offered her the same job she was doing now at Charing Cross Hospital to cut down on travelling time, but she had refused. She was fond of the people who worked at

Shooter's Hill. They were like family, especially Doctor Thackery and his wife, whom she saw often.

Danny listened, feeling like an outsider. He'd been gone from home for over a year and was still having trouble reintegrating. What was the point of trying to feel as though he were home when he was going away again the next day?

"What a treat this fish is. Still, the government's doing the right thing with their rationing laws. It's only fair," Minnie added.

"It is fair, Mum," Uncle George agreed as he tucked into the plump fish meat.

"I think we can all agree on that," Kevin also concurred.

"You know, my George was telling me last week that because of rationing, the poorer folk in England are getting better fed than they were before the war. Isn't that right, George?"

"Yes, and the rich are finally learning what it means to go hungry," George grunted a snide response.

"That lot will never go 'ungry," Minnie corrected her son.

"Well, they'll at least have less choice, and less to waste."

"That's down to impartial distribution, Minnie," Anna joined in the conversation. "People are only allowed to have certain amounts of sugar, meat, milk, and butter, regardless of how much money they keep in the bank or under their mattresses."

"Well, this ample lunch must have cost a pretty penny, so money can still talk a good talk," Uncle George suggested.

"I've always been one not to waste anything," Minnie told the family, who knew fine well how tight she was. "Before the war, well-off young people were throwing away their old clothes or giving them to the destitute, but now that Britain's resources are being directed to the war effort, even high and mighty women are repairing socks and stockings and underwear, and patching up their husbands' torn shirts and trousers, and the like."

"And cobblers are doing well, what with men with money hammering new soles and heels onto their boots and shoes," Uncle George said. Then he asked Minnie, "You know Bert, Mum? His premises are near London Bridge."

"Oh, I know Bert all right. He asked me to marry 'im when I was seventeen, cheeky bugger."

Kevin said, "I take it he wasn't your cup of tea, Minnie?"

"Oh, 'e was nice enough, Son, but I was already engaged to Susan's father."

"My granny was very popular with the boys in her youth," Jenny giggled.

"Anyway, Bert is making more money doing shoe and boot repairs than he ever did," George finished his somewhat flat anecdote.

Minnie chuckled. Danny thought it a strange sound coming from his old granny. Seemed the champagne had got to her brain as well. He leant into Anna, kissed her, and then raised a newly filled glass of red wine to go with the meat course.

The waiters took away the fish plates and moments later pork chops arrived with a smidgen of mashed potato on each plate. "Three courses, eh? Rationing be damned at this table, then," said Uncle George, licking his lips.

Chapter Seven

Danny's mood darkened as the plates with pork chop bones were carried away. Even with the levity created by Minnie's demands on the waiter that he should bring the meaty bones back – wrapped in waxed paper – for her ever-ready black-leaded range's savoury stew-jar, Danny felt depression tugging at him.

He tried to shove his black thoughts to the back of his mind. He reminded himself that this was the happiest day of Jenny's life, the conversation was jolly, as it should be, and the food was the best he'd had in years. Kevin had probably paid a fortune for the lunch, but the drink was going straight to Danny's head and bringing out every morbid thought living there – *aw bejesus, he felt like shite being beaten up in a bucket!*

He'd been in high spirits on the journey from Kent, although he suspected this day was going to be hard for him. On the train, he had focused his energy and thoughts on Anna, and Jenny whose big day he was celebrating. His sister had refused to marry Kevin until at least one of her brothers could be present.

He should be ecstatic. His family were having a gay old time; a wonderful day. Trouble was, even with the good things that had happened in the last few months: getting his eyesight back in both eyes, no longer being in pain, being fortunate that his liver and kidneys had recovered well and that the nasty infection in his urine had gone, he couldn't shrug off the terror and bad dreams choking the life out of him.

"…and it was a lovely surprise to learn we'd be staying here tonight. When I was unpacking upstairs earlier, in the honeymoon suite, no less, I looked out of the window and saw Regent's Park right in front of me. Kevin knows how much I enjoy long walks, Uncle George, so he's taking me to the Zoo tomorrow," Jenny was now saying.

"I read in *The Times* that Zoo officials have offered reduced or free admission to those who are suffering most from the war," Minnie informed the family. "I think it's a marvellous way to boost morale for those poor Belgian refugees, and our soldiers and their families as well. Wounded soldiers are being treated to refreshments, and according to the newspaper, there are long queues for free rides on the llamas and elephants. They're so popular, the staff rerouted them to reduce the danger from those damned air-raids rather than stop them altogether."

"How wonderful. Can we go once you've settled in Danny? Maybe next week?" Anna's large round eyes widened further with excitement.

Jenny said, "I think I was about ten years old the last time I visited London Zoo. Remember that day, Danny?"

"Danny, are you feeling all right?" Kevin looked concerned.

"I'm as fit as a fiddle." Danny took another large slurp of his wine. It wasn't doing its job; it was heightening his emotions instead of dulling them, as had been his intention. His mouth set in a tight line. His eyes, glazed with alcohol, were hard and angry, and so deep and dark were his thoughts he didn't realise the family were staring at him until Jenny slammed her glass on the table.

"What's wrong with you, Danny?" she demanded. "Kevin arranged my wedding for today because you were coming home, and you're sitting there like a bloody mute with a face on you like a cow's filthy backside. Can you not cheer up for five minutes?"

Danny raised his eyes to his sister and then poked his finger at Kevin. "Ask your husband why he picked today for your wedding and not tomorrow or Friday? Go on, ask him." Danny then glared at Kevin, and without waiting for his answer, snapped, "You knew about my posting before I did, didn't you, Kevin?"

"Danny, that's enough. Whatever has got into you?" Minnie chided her grandson.

Danny's tongue was on fire; flames felt like they were bursting forth. He finished the wine in his third topped-up glass, fully committed to blaming Kevin for his foul mood. "What's got into me, you ask, Minnie? Well, how about I found out this morning that I'm going back to France tomorrow. 'Corporal Carmody, you are fit for duty and will leave tomorrow for the front,' I was told when I went for my discharge papers – tomorrow!"

A sob tore from Anna's throat. Her hand shot up to her chest where she pressed it hard against her heart. "No … oh God, no, Danny. You told me you had weeks of leave owed to you. You said you might not even go back to the war, seeing as you've been out of it for so long. You said that!"

Jenny took Anna's hand, and as her own tears dripped onto her cheeks, her voice cracked, "Oh, Danny … I'm sorry … I didn't know."

Kevin, his eyes full of sympathy, muttered, "Bad news."

"Its bad news, all right," Danny was raging. "They're sending me back to the trenches tomorrow morning, and I won't survive them a second time. I can feel it in my bones."

"Don't say that!" Anna cried.

"Oh, my poor brother," Jenny mumbled.

"That's right, Jenny, and your poor brother blames your husband for not warning you what was going on with me. Look at the state of my Anna!"

Anna wept into her napkin. Minnie was furious but had not made it clear if she was angry at the army for sending Danny back to war or with his appalling behaviour at the table. Uncle George gave Danny a baleful look of disapproval, but said nothing, and Kevin lowered his guilt-ridden eyes.

"I'm sorry, Danny," Kevin broke the awkward silence that had also come over the other diners in the restaurant. "One of the doctors in Orpington told me a week ago he'd cleared you for duty. They don't like to inform recovering soldiers about their orders for active duty until the morning they're discharged because it brings them down. It wasn't my place to tell you or anyone else."

Danny gestured to the nearby waiter to fill his glass.

"You've had enough wine, Son," Minnie said.

"Are you kiddin' me, Granny? This is my first and last day of freedom. Will you deny a condemned man a glass of something?"

Kevin pleaded, "Can we talk about this after you've had a bit of wedding cake in your stomach. For Jenny's sake?"

"Sure, why don't we do that? Let's forget about me and where I'm going in the morning. Tell you what, Jenny, when you and your husband are feeding the monkeys at the zoo tomorrow, spare a wee thought for your brother. The bloody apes will be having a better time of it than me."

"That's *enough* now, Danny. You're making a scene," Anna said, surprising everyone with her harsh tone. "And you're spoiling Jenny's wedding day."

The waiters retreated from the depressed atmosphere at the table, but not until after one of them pleaded with Kevin to keep his guest in order. Danny returned the maître d's filthy looks, but when Anna began to cry, he was jolted back to civility. He gasped, then shook his head, trying to clear the cobwebs and dark places of smoke and blood, of death and smells of rotting flesh in a captured trench.

He covered his crown with hands that shook, and dragged his fingers through his scalp, his nails digging into his skin. "I can't go back – Mother of God, I can't do it again!"

Kevin stood. He looked down at Jenny's shocked face and Minnie's teary eyes. "I'll be back in a minute," he told them.

Danny looked up. Kevin's hand was on his arm; not gripping it but placed there for comfort and encouragement. "Kevin, can you help me get out of this mess?"

"I can help you today, Danny. Come outside with me for a wee minute and we'll talk about it."

Danny lurched to his feet. His fingers holding onto the tablecloth and pulling it towards him as he fought to balance himself.

"Oh Christ, I'm sorry," he muttered, as glasses fell over and Kevin's expensive wine spilt.

Outside in the street, Kevin forced Danny to squat down and put his head between his knees: "That's the way, Danny boy, breathe that crisp spring air into your lungs."

Danny, raised his head and slurred, "Sure, it's the last fresh air I'll have … for the rest of my miserable life … right enough."

Kevin struggled to hide Danny's condition from passers-by. He was wearing the king's uniform with gravy stains and red wine mingling together on his chest, and holding him still was no easy task. Danny was a broader, stronger man than he'd been in Dublin at seventeen. "Will you talk to me about it?" Kevin urged.

Danny, breathing deeply through his nose, looked at Kevin as the latter propped him against the hotel's façade. He was dizzy as hell and seeing double. Kevin was one person, then he was two, then one, as his secondary figure jumped out of him and then back in.

"I knew it, Kevin. I knew it as soon as they got me lifting weights and running around that bloody field in my shorts. They had medical officers watching us, studying how much we could lift, how far we could run without collapsing, how high we could climb ropes and vault feckin' wooden horses. There they were, scribbling furiously in their little notebooks, calculating when they thought a soldier would be fit enough for them to go back to war to get slaughtered. They almost did a bloody jig in front of me this morning!"

Danny's breath came in short, sharp bursts, but finally grew quieter; as the fog started to clear, his senses returned, and he calmed down. "This one officer told me I would be re-joining my battalion. "What bloody battalion?" I asked. "They're probably all dead!" He didn't like that. They reckon if you can see, walk, talk, comply with orders, hold a rifle and shoot it, you're fit enough to get back to the front to be gassed again or killed. Those words, *fit for duty,* have broken my bleedin' heart."

Chapter Eight

The next morning, Jenny and Kevin met a contrite, hungover Danny at Victoria Station. As always, the train station was packed with soldiers, their backpacks making their figures bulky, crying mothers, and proud fathers stoically holding themselves together. After a brief discussion with a ticket officer, Anna learned the arriving train was delayed an hour, and she suggested they go to the tearoom across the street instead of standing on the platform to be jostled and bruised.

In the café, Jenny lifted her cup, full of weak, barely coloured tea with only a tiny drop of milk and a smidgen of sugar per person. The British tradition of copious tea drinking was limited to one cup per person in most places now. She stole a glance at her husband. She still felt wrapped in his love, flushed and glowing after their honeymoon night in the hotel suite, and she was grateful he was not going back to the front as well.

Loving Kevin was emotionally overwhelming, frighteningly intense, and glorious at its core. And now that they'd shared the most intimate and physical part of their marriage, she desired him even more. She shuddered with pleasure and felt heat rise from her neck to her face. Despite experiencing some discomfort at the beginning of their lovemaking, it had been the most wonderful experience.

Danny spoke, jolting Jenny from her beautiful recollections. Feeling guilty about having joy in her life, she gave her brother the forgiveness he was hoping for. "How are you feeling, Danny, darlin'?"

Danny, concealing part of his face with his cup, answered, "I'm sober. Sorry, Jenny – Kevin – I hope you'll both forgive me for ruining your big day."

Jenny reached out and gently pulled Danny's cup down. "If you're apologising, at least look at us properly."

Anna gave Danny's arm a nudge. "Well, cariad, what have you got to say for yourself?"

"I'm truly sorry. Will you both forgive me?"

"Yes," Jenny responded, squeezing his hand.

"You didn't ruin it," Kevin told Danny. "No one could have spoilt our happiness yesterday, not even you, ya' fumblin' Dublin."

Jenny giggled. Anna frowned and asked, "What's that you're calling him?"

"It's a slur for drunk Irishmen who are usually found under the influence outside one of Dublin's pubs," Kevin grinned.

Danny smiled. "In my defence, yesterday was the first time I'd had a drop of alcohol in over a year. I can't remember the last time I had a Guinness, never mind all that fancy drink you put on the table. Where did you get the champagne, Kevin? Last I heard, the pubs in London were running short of alcohol."

"Kevin paid a lot of money to make our day special, Danny. His dad was kind enough to send the champagne over on the ferry, and the restaurant allowed its waiters to serve it. A friend of Kevin's brought it personally."

"Oh, and where's he?"

"He volunteered for the army. He's going over to the Continent today," Kevin answered.

"I suppose we should have taken your glass away from you when your eyes started crossing," Jenny said with a wry smile.

Danny grew serious, as he took an envelope out of his pocket and gave it to Jenny, saying, "Will you give this to our Patrick the minute he gets home? Don't send it to him, even if you know where he is and that he can receive mail through the Royal Engineers Postal Section. You hear me, Jenny? Hand it to him. This is important. If anything happens to me..."

Jenny opened her mouth, surprising herself when a sob rushed out. Anna, never short of tears, chorused Jenny's weeping and clung onto Danny's jacket sleeve.

Danny pulled himself up, sitting bravely despite his fear. Kevin leant slightly across the table to his new brother-in-law. "Danny, I know you don't think it's fair that you're going back, and I understand. You gave it all you had the first time around and nearly died."

"It's not right. I knew I might have to go again, but they only gave me one day – one bloody day at home, Kevin," Danny complained. "Yesterday, everyone was happy, dressed up, drinking and eating good food, and laughing at Uncle George's silly jokes, and there was I, feeling as if I was passing through your lives on my way to the fires of hell. I was angry and jealous, and I'm man enough to admit it."

Whilst Kevin consoled Danny, Jenny stopped crying and chided an almost-hysterical Anna. "Pull yourself together, Anna. This place is full of wives and mothers who are losing their menfolk to the war, and you're not helping any of them or us."

"It's all right for you, Jenny Carmody. Your husband isn't being sent to fight again," Anna stopped crying to fling in Jenny's face.

Jenny hit back hard, "My husband has done his share at the front and is still saving lives, the way he saved our Danny's."

Not convinced, Anna blew into her handkerchief, gave Jenny a filthy look, and then clung to Danny's arm as he continued to complain to Kevin about the injustice.

"...and they should give me the same dispensation Anna's brother Dai had for a while. I'm the man of the house..."

"Every available man in Britain is being pushed out to France and going straight to the front this week," Jenny joined the conversation. "And to be fair, you're not looking after me anymore. Kevin is now my husband and provider, and Minnie has Uncle George."

"That's right," Kevin nodded. "You don't have a case for dispensation. Every man of fighting age is going, Danny. Yeomanry Territorials are also being shipped out, and the divisions on the East Coast are being replaced by volunteers and sent to France. The government's even trying to bring in conscription in Ireland."

"Good luck with that," Danny smirked. "They'll be facing mass assemblies of civil disobedience if I know anything about our fellow Irishmen. We all know the Irish don't like following British rules and laws. We'll not be having it in Dublin, not after they executed our leaders – the bastards."

Jenny tried to calm the situation again. "Shh ... careful what you say. There are no Irish Republicans in here."

"Danny, this new offensive against the Germans could finally end the war," Kevin said.

"And if the Americans hurry up and send their troops, the end could come sooner than we think," Jenny added, injecting a note of optimism.

Kevin put on his cap and rose from the table. "C'mon, Danny, let's get you on that train."

Jenny noted the warmth between the two men. She was proud of the way Kevin handled her brother; it wasn't easy to change Danny's mind about someone, especially when he was in one of his moods.

Jenny, Anna, and Kevin waved as the steam engine pulled the train away from the platform and chuffed down the tracks. Jenny tucked her arm into Anna's, then gave Kevin a nod. Their honeymoon was over. Anna was inconsolable, and family always came first.

Chapter Nine

7 August 1918

Amiens, the Somme Area,
France.

The Somme area was a morass of mud and debris extending as far as the eye could see. Once, it had been a green and pleasant land with rolling chalk ridges liberally dotted with villages, farms, and woods. Danny imagined it being an unspoilt, mainly rural scene, splendidly colourful in summer and white with frost and snow in the winter. He pictured how it might have looked before the war as he marched in lines of three past stumpy trees torn to shreds, and brown mucky fields that had long since lost any semblance of production or beauty. It was the most desolate battleground he had ever seen, with not a sign of life; a pitted, muddy landscape of stinking, rotting corporeal death.

He recalled his arrival from England at the end of March. Back then, the fields had not been dull, with spent shells lying everywhere, but washed with a morning dew that had made the sprinklings of spring blue and yellow wildflowers weep.

Having completed a four-day stint in the forward zone where he'd followed the routine of two hours on duty and four hours off, Danny was now taking his five-day rest period in the town of Amiens, which was outside the German's firing range and situated two miles from the British trenches.

Since his return to the war at the end of March, Danny had served with the British III Corps, commanded by Lieutenant

General Richard Butler, who was under the overall command of the British Fourth Army under General Sir Henry Rawlinson. During his first weeks back, Danny had asked dozens of men for his old mates; Jack, and Brian McCallum, the Scotsman who was in love with the poet, Robert Burns. After having no luck, he deduced that those men and others he had known before being wounded were either dead or based in another maze of traverse lines snaking across the land from the Somme to Western Flanders and Belgium. He had more chance of seeing God shaking his fist in the sky than bumping into Jack and Brian.

The man marching on Danny's left said, "Thank God that's over, eh, Danny? We've done well, gained some ground, I think."

"Freckles, if you think gaining two miles and losing thousands of men in the process is *doing well,* you should revaluate your usage of those words," Danny responded with a grunt.

"Aww, come on We've taken over the front astride the Somme."

"Only after we halted our retreat and fought our arses off."

"Well, fighting our arses off gave us a victory over the Hun who outnumbered us. You should be as proud as I am," countered Freckles.

"You're English. You lot are brought up on excess pride."

Chalky White, the man marching on Danny's right, piped up, "I heard the captain telling another officer that the Germans had superior numbers afforded by as many as fifty divisions. Apparently, the Russians have withdrawn from the war, and in a show of good faith, they released all their German prisoners. They signed some treaty with the Hun in a place called …

damn it, I've lost it. It had something to do with titties. I got a lovely tingling feeling in my John Thomas when the captain said the name … wait, got it. Breast something or other. Anyway, I reckon if we can gain ground against those odds, we can beat the Germans all the way back to Berlin."

Danny snapped, "Brest-Litovsk – the place was, Brest-Litovsk – now shut up, both of you, and let me concentrate on where I'm putting my feet."

Danny marched on, preferring his own thoughts to those of the men he'd just silenced. After defeating the Germans at the town of Amiens, he had followed the same tedious routine: repairing damaged trench walls and parapets, standing watch for gas attacks and sniper fire across the blackened stretch of *no man's land,* and eating tinned bully beef or, for a change, streaky bacon fried inside his food tin, using slivers of personally dried wood kindling so the fire wouldn't smoke too much.

Still on the move, Danny lifted his water container to his mouth and drank deeply from it. Tea and drinking water still tasted like gasoline. The men's drinking flasks came from the red *cleaned* petrol canisters, which were not clean at all and often caused widespread dysentery. But despite the horrible taste and threat to health, he, like everyone else, needed to quench his thirst during this hot French summer.

Routine and life at the front were fraught with danger and discomfort. Men died every day, not always because of battles being fought, but often through bad luck or questionable judgement. Danny couldn't count the number of mates who had been killed because they'd inadvertently stepped on a live landmine or had raised their heads an inch too high above the parapet whilst taking a sneaky look towards enemy positions.

Snipers on both sides made it their business to spot and shoot heads, helmets or any other cheeky body part peeking above the trenches. Between the enemies was no man's land, stalked by the sniping bogeymen who would kill anything that moved. Danny had spent many an hour picking off Germans who had come into his rifle's sights – his kills had earnt him the nickname, *Brain Smasher*.

He hated everything about the trenches: lying on his belly, his heart pounding against the ground as the Hun lobbed their bombs over the top of the British positions was terrifying but strangely normal. The thought of him failing to spot mustard gas rolling silently above the tortured ground in a pale-yellow cloud, however, was an indescribable terror that consumed his thoughts day and night. Being gassed again was worse than any other horror he could imagine, apart from death; not even the dreaded stinking, painful trench foot, caused by wearing permanently wet socks and shabby footwear, matched his fear of the gas.

Danny had suffered the beginnings of trench foot, that terrible condition where one's toes eventually turned black, skin peeled from flesh and then greenish flesh peeled from bones. And the smell – oh, but the stink of dry gangrene, or worse, the deadly, wet, gas gangrene in men's limbs. That stench was far worse than that of a thousand dead and rotting rats piled high, inches from one's nostrils. Fortunately, the nurses had treated his feet whilst he'd been in hospital for blindness, before the rotting poison could take hold.

A line of British soldiers, also marching three by three but heading in the opposite direction, shouted greetings to Danny's beleaguered column as they passed by. "What's it been like up there?" one man heading to the front line, shouted.

"Bloody awful. Enjoy!" Freckles shouted back.

"Shut up," Danny elbowed Freckles in his ribs.

"Oy, you, watch it. What would you have said?" Freckles nudged Danny back.

"Well, for a start, I'd have wished him good luck instead of telling him to enjoy himself. Sure, it'll be us going back again soon enough." Danny liked Freckles. He was a chatty man who enjoyed telling tall tales about his life as a professional gambler in Blackpool. He had a knack of making one forget the horrors they were living through even if it were for a couple of minutes at a time. Freckles' naturally pale complexion hadn't fared well in the summer sun, hence his nickname. His skin was peeling, the tip of his prominent nose covered in sunspots and a mole of significant size sitting above his top lip, just under his left nostril. It was unfortunately placed, for it looked as if he had a permanent crusty snot sitting there.

"What are you going to do with your five francs, Danny?" Freckles asked as they neared the destroyed town's outskirts. Payday came after each stint at the front. In English money, the French francs came to ten pence, which was close enough to a shilling. Danny liked to save a couple of francs, but he was finding it more and more difficult not to spend it all on frivolities. He wasn't certain if the money he put aside would even reach home, despite the facilities set up to allow men to *save,* and, apart from that, the family were no longer skint, what with his da's money coming through before last Christmas. They didn't need *his* pittance. "I don't know yet. I'm feeling adventurous. I'd like to get drunk. What about you?"

"I'm going to the brothel as soon as I get paid. A man needs what a man needs, and if I don't get there before our lot, I'll be last in line and get that old fat cow I had the last time. She nearly bloody suffocated me, with her buttocks sitting on my face."

The men marching behind Danny and Freckles laughed. Danny tried to picture the scene and immediately regretted the attempt; it wasn't pretty.

As always, when they arrived in town, they lined up first for their food. A loaf of bread was divided up and fed sixteen men. With it came the bully beef stew that was hot instead of being lukewarm and congealed as it was at the front. It tasted glorious by comparison.

When the exhausted men had got their food tins filled, they found a place to sit. Thousands of men were already assembled on the roadside or in the mucky field across the road from the brothel and piles of rubble from destroyed buildings. It didn't matter how devastated a village was, it always had a whorehouse full of scantily clad women up and running.

Danny and Freckles, along with the bulk of the men they'd marched into town with, sat in front of the men in the field who were in a variety of relaxed positions: some prostrate, others leaning against the backs of other men for support or curled up in balls covered with their coats for privacy and to give the illusion of night time, while others sat cross-legged staring at everything and nothing with blank, dull eyes.

"This is the best we'll get," Danny said, plopping down on the ground.

"Sheer bloody bliss," Freckled agreed as he wriggled his backside into the soil to get a softer spot.

The men tore into their dinner. Danny dipped his crusty bread into the stew and picked up every crumb that had fallen onto his uniform while he chewed. He raised his eyes from his bowl and looked across the road to one of the brothel's occupied rooms. A recent explosion had blown the window in and damaged part of the façade, leaving a sizeable hole that gave onlookers in the street an excellent view of the bed and the people having sex on it.

Men surrounding Danny began to whoop and cheer, as they watched the theatrics beginning between a woman and an overly excited, howling British soldier on the torn mattress. Then their faces fell as the woman dislodged the man in the throes of his glorious climactic moment, came naked to the hole in the wall, and drew a thick curtain across the gap, thus ending their entertainment.

Disappointed, Danny ate in silence. He conjured up images of Anna, and what had happened after she'd forgiven him for his behaviour at Jenny's wedding breakfast. They'd made love as quietly as was possible in Minnie's house, which unfortunately, had made it less passionate than it might have been otherwise. His granny still had a good pair of ears, and Anna's bed, which used to be his, squeaked with the slightest pressure on its broken springs.

He realised now he'd had sex four times in his life; three when he was on his honeymoon and that one time before embarkation in March. A horrible thought crossed his mind, and he was ashamed to be even thinking it. Still staring at the closed curtains, he asked Freckles, "Is it worth it?"

"What?"

"Spending your money on a woman?"

Freckles wiped gravy from his mouth with the back of his hand. "Bar girls wearing lace undies and displaying their titties? Of course, it's bloody worth it. I look at it this way … I'm not spending it on a woman, as much as I'm spending it on my own needs and pleasure. It does me the world of good, Danny, and what the wife doesn't know, doesn't hurt her, right? You should try it. If you want, I'll point out the best woman I've had in there, so far. You might have to wait in line for her, but she's got plenty of stamina."

Danny thought about it with what was, in his opinion, a fair and balanced mind. Cheating on Anna was not a nice thing to do. He loved her. He was Catholic, and the church frowned upon infidelity. But shooting off his load now and relieving his painful blue balls, as another soldier had once termed his relief, might be a good thing in the long run. A bit of practice in the art of lovemaking wouldn't go amiss, and it might relax him, like a good game of football. He was uptight all the time and could do with a distraction from the war for a few minutes or for however long he could make it last. And what if he died, having only done it four times? Odds were, he would get killed and wouldn't make it back to his wife. He hadn't met a man there who thought he'd make it out alive – the shadow of death loomed over all of them. It watched, it waited, it struck...

"Stay where you are, men!" Captain Strutton's booming voice smashed Danny's wondrous, and sometimes morbid, thoughts. "Pay attention. I need a few things from you before you begin your leisure time."

"Well, here it comes," Danny whispered to Freckles. "Clean your boots and buttons, get the mud off your uniform, shave and wash, line up for pay, wash shirts, and get ready for inspection first thing tomorrow. He never fails to give his pep talk and orders, does he? It's as if he can't let go of his rank for five minutes."

"Nope. And here we are, weary men desperate for five bloody minutes' peace. It's not right. I'm telling you, Danny, he'd better not pull out the list of names he's chosen to go on work details. I'm sick of getting called up for them before I've even had a decent rest."

"Sure, you're right there," Danny spat. "Damn cheek calling this a rest period. The top brass should be honest and say they bring us back here to do their heavy lifting." What man wanted to come off the line, physically and mentally exhausted, only to be given the even more physical jobs of carrying supplies, planks of wood, steel to make the light railway tracks, and rolls of barbed wire and shells, and in the boiling hot August sun, too? Danny thought.

"I'd better not be on his list this time. I did my share of humping stores the last time we were in town," Freckles repeated as the list came out of the captain's pocket.

"...that will be all," Captain Strutton finished reading out the names, which didn't include Danny or Freckles this time. "Corporal Carmody, report to me when you've washed up," Strutton spoke directly to Danny.

After his wash and shave that came an hour after he'd queued up for a water bucket, Danny went in search of Captain Strutton at the bivouac site, where senior officers had tents. Soldiers cringed whenever the brass singled them out. It was never a good ending for the men in question.

Strutton was sitting outside his tent on a groundsheet, smoking a pipe and stirring his steaming tea in his tin mug. He looked up at Danny, who saluted then removed his cap and stood at ease.

"Ah, corporal." Strutton went into his pocket and pulled out a piece of paper. "You've been promoted to sergeant. Go to stores, get another stripe, and sew it onto your jacket before tomorrow morning."

Danny held the order in his hand. The division's commanding officer had signed the order and it took immediate effect. "Thank you, sir."

"Before you go, Carmody, you ought to know that our orders have changed. Our division will be moving out at dawn."

"Are you joking?" Danny blurted out. "My apologies, sir, but with respect, we've just got here for our rest."

"And now we're going back. Do you know how much we've achieved in the last week, sergeant?"

Not used to the rank, Danny uttered stupidly, "Who, me?"

"Yes, you, damn it."

"Sorry, sir … erm … no, I don't, to be honest. I'm a nobody, a grunt. I do as I'm told when I'm told, and I don't ask questions best left to officers. I do know we lost hundreds of men."

When Danny's insolence went unchecked, the captain answered the question he'd just posed. "Four days ago, we pushed the Germans ten miles east of what was our forward position at that time. By the end of the following day, we captured thirty thousand German prisoners and over three hundred artillery pieces. Two days ago, the French Third Army launched attacks in the southern sector of our advance. They recaptured the commune of Montdidier, and because of that victory, the Paris-Amiens railway line is once again in Allied control. Tomorrow, with the help of God, we will push the Hun back again, and we will keep pushing them towards Germany until they no longer have the will to move forward against us. Do you agree, Carmody, that the sooner we defeat the Germans, the sooner we'll go home?"

"Yes, sir."

"Very good, then. There will be a briefing at 2000 hours with NCOs and officers in Lieutenant General Butler's headquarters. I expect you to be there, so check your trench watch is accurate. You may go."

Thanks for nothing, Danny thought, depressed by his new rank. NCOs were the first to fall. They died like hot flies and in even greater numbers than the officers. No one wanted to be a sergeant, for it meant going first over the top.

He was a goner.

Chapter Ten

October 1918

The Greek Port of Piraeus

Patrick Carmody and Christian St. Davis had started their climb earlier that morning. Near the top of the rugged hill of Kastella, they sat side by side on a large rock and drank water from their flasks. Summer was over but the weather had remained mild and dry. It was a cloudless day with hardly a breeze to cool them on what had been an ambitious outing.

As they caught their breath, the men admired the panoramic views over Athens and the Saronic Gulf. Piraeus was stunning, Patrick thought, his eyes following the horizon. Situated in the southwest part of the central plain of the Attica Basin, Mount Aigaleo bound the rocky peninsula to the northwest and the Saronic Gulf bound it to the south and west. Patrick been told it had originally been an island in ancient times. He imagined that sea levels had risen over the centuries, and that this was how the island's three natural harbours had been born. What beauty the crews from those ancient ships must have viewed when they'd sailed into them.

Piraeus was also connected to the rest of Athens' more urban regions to the east and northeast, as it had been since antiquity. He loved the place; its history, the archaeological sites and defences of the ancient 5th century BC Themistoclean Walls and Eetioneia, the large circular tower at the entrance to the harbour. He was like a kid being handed a bag of sweeties after being denied for months. He'd be happy in a desert today;

anywhere other than a vessel that floated on water, and the stinking hospital where he was treating a deadly illness he didn't fully understand.

He stretched his tired legs while contemplating his new posting. He was still officially a member of the *Ark Royal's* crew, but two weeks earlier he'd been seconded to the Allied hospital in the port. Since being ashore, he'd weighed up the pros and cons of the move, and he'd wondered a few times if his job on land might be even more dangerous than being on a ship where one worried about potential German torpedo strikes.

Months onboard had taken its toll on his body. This morning, he felt as though he were using muscles in his legs for the first time. Stores and wounded men waiting to be transferred crammed the ship's sickbay. The decks were jam-packed with sailors, Royal Marines, and seaplanes, while below, ambulance vehicles, other mechanical trucks, and an array of supplies occupied the hangars where many of the sailors slept on hammocks and makeshift palliasses filled with whatever they could find to make them softer than the floor...

"What's going on in that head of yours?" Christian, an engineering officer, interrupted Patrick's thoughts.

"I'm thinking how good it is to be on dry land. For months, I saw the officers and ratings I worked with being rotated with stints on land and sea, but I didn't get off that ship for more than an hour at a time. This is bliss, Christian. Right here, right now, I'm in heaven."

Christian gave Patrick a playful nudge, "Go on, admit it, you'll miss the *Ark Royal*. I once did a whole year onboard back in '15, during the Gallipoli campaign and heavy fighting at the Macedonian Front. Now *that* was hell. She's one of a kind, Patrick."

"As you keep telling me."

Christian shrugged. "Because it's true. She has no equal. When the Royal Navy purchased her in '14, they had laid her keel but the ship was only in frames. The Blyth Shipbuilding Company in Northumberland were building her as a large freighter, probably intended for the coal-for-grain trade in the Black Sea. Then the navy came along and modified her design almost completely, to accommodate our modern warfare use of seaplanes. Trouble was, the extensive changes to the ship came at a cost for the navy."

"What cost?" Patrick asked, getting his pack of cigarettes out.

"She was too slow. She couldn't keep pace with the Grand Fleet. You see, they converted her to a seaplane tender, with the superstructure, funnel, and propulsion machinery moved aft and a working deck occupying the forward half of the ship. The deck was not intended as a flying-off deck, but for starting and running up of seaplane engines and for recovering damaged aircraft from the sea. Look at the size of the aircraft hold – one hundred feet long and forty-five feet wide and fifteen feet high – it's revolutionary in scale, even down to the amount of fuel she's carrying. Imagine how long it takes to load four thousand imperial gallons of Shell aviation petrol for her aircraft in standard commercial two-imperial-gallon tins. She's probably carrying more petrol than London has for all its needs."

Patrick offered a cigarette to Christian. He accepted it but stuck it behind his ear for later. "I suppose as an engineer you would be genuinely interested in her construction, but I'm afraid she's just a ship to me," Patrick said after lighting his own Woodbine.

"Well, she's not just a ship to me. They drummed the *Ark Royal* into me. I'm from a village in Northumbria. My father and I helped build her, right up until December '14, when they commissioned her. That's why I got this posting and not one on a convoy frigate in the Atlantic or North Sea. Thank God for small mercies."

"What do you think of the Royal Navy Air Service and Royal Flying Corps merging to form the Royal Air Force? Do you think that name will last any longer than the others?"

"I do. Amalgamating the two Air Corps was a good idea. Before we know it, our planes will become faster, fly longer distances, and carry more efficient and powerful bombs and machine guns. We're moving with the times, I suppose."

Patrick stared at the beauty of the sea, shimmering as the sun hit it. He'd seen action against the enemy and some seaplanes going down, spiralling in flames before they hit the water, but he'd also had boring days onboard, where nothing extraordinary happened and the ship was only a supply depot. During the most inactive periods, claustrophobia and an anxiety he couldn't quell gripped him.

"I take it you're not a naval career man, Patrick?" Christian asked, disturbing Patrick's thoughts again.

"No, I'm afraid a life at sea is not for me."

"Never mind, before you know it, you'll be back in London and out of uniform for good," Christian said with conviction.

"You sound sure about that." Patrick cocked his head and looked over at him. "Have you heard something I haven't?"

"No, I don't think so, but I'm convinced the war is almost over. I hear things from the pilots. They're seeing less enemy resistance in the sky. We've driven our offensive from Greece into occupied Serbia. We've broken through the German, Austro-Hungarian, and Bulgarian lines along the Macedonian front. Bulgaria has already signed the Armistice of Salonica with the Allies in Thessaloniki, and we've taken back all of Serbia. Hungary is the only holdout, and I don't think we'll even need to invade. You'll see, they'll offer their surrender soon."

Danny came into Patrick's mind. "What about the Western Front?"

"Our lads are pushing the Germans back there, too."

"I heard there were massive casualties in September."

"When aren't there casualties?" Christian sighed, then asked, "How come you don't know as much about what's going on as I do?"

"This is the first time I've been able to leave the hospital in over a week," Patrick smiled wryly. "At least the place has a nice garden."

"They're working you hard, eh?"

Patrick studied Christian's face. They'd become good friends onboard the *Ark Royal,* but he was hesitant to tell him about the crisis doctors were facing and had faced for over a year. "Can you keep something to yourself?"

"Of course."

Ach, to hell with it. The disaster is public knowledge now, for the most part, Patrick thought, and the Medical Board were saying the worst was over. "Do you know about the flu that's been going around?"

"I heard about men being transferred to the base hospitals because of chest infections. It's a bad one, apparently."

"It's a killer. Thousands have died already, and it might kill hundreds of thousands or even millions before it's finished. It seems to have spread almost worldwide."

Christian flinched as though Patrick had struck him. "Are you kidding? As bad as that?"

"Yes. I'm afraid it is. The military censors minimized the severity from their first reports of the illness and its high mortality rates in Allied countries to maintain morale amongst the troops. Even the most senior doctors on the *Ark Royal* and at the hospital in Piraeus didn't know the extent of its reach, or about the vast number of fatalities it's caused. I suppose the generals didn't want to spread panic amongst the rank and file, what with our men having to face death every day on the battlefields."

Christian's face drained of colour as he waited for Patrick to take another drink of water.

"I shouldn't be telling you this, Christian, but sod it, you're not the sort to spread gossip, and it's becoming public knowledge now anyway," Patrick eventually said. "The British censors, and I suppose the French and Germans ones also, couldn't stop journalists reporting on the flu's statistics in Spain because it's a neutral country. And unfortunately, or fortunately depending on how you view it, these stories have created a false impression of Spain being the hardest hit, or the origin of the disease. I think the governments around the world have encouraged that idea to deflect from the serious crises in their own nations. The British Medical Board have even given the sickness a nickname … they're calling it *Spanish Flu.* But no one knows where the sickness originated."

"Why are we not talking about this onboard?" Christian uttered, posing the question to himself aloud.

"Be thankful you're *not* hearing a lot about it. Can you imagine if men knew they were susceptible to a new killer, more insidious than gas or bombs or bullets that strikes them down in the theatre of war? Sure, we all understand the vile nature of weapons and what they can do to a body, but this thing has been rampaging through overcrowded camps and hospitals, and indiscriminately killing thousands of victims of chemical attacks and other injuries. It's also affecting previously healthy people and members of staff. Our hospitals and camps are ideal sites for spreading a respiratory virus."

"How contagious is it, for God's sake? Will this affect our families at home? Christ, it doesn't bear thinking about."

Patrick had been keeping his own council about this epidemic for months. He didn't want to say more about it to his friend, who was not a doctor, therefore not privy to information or treatment protocols. *Damn me and my big mouth,* he thought, seeing Christian's worried face. "It's contagious. The consensus is, it's being spread through poultry and piggeries that are kept near the front lines to feed the troops. It also infects people through spittle and coughing, and those gathering in large numbers."

"You mean breathing or being close to another person with it, will do it?"

The sun was becoming brighter as the last of the white clouds burnt away. Patrick fetched his flat cap from his pocket. He pulled it down his forehead and continued, "Some people are immune. I read a report from a private describing such. In June, he and members of his regiment slept in a cowshed. They all, apart from the private, caught an intense fever and were treated in a nearby military hospital for the Spanish flu."

"Christ, I hope my children are all right."

Patrick's stress levels were heightening, and again, he cursed himself for bringing up the subject. "Christian, don't overanalyse this. Our families at home are probably fine. The flu is hitting military personnel hard because of living in close quarters and having continuous massive troop movements. You've got to understand that when an infected person sneezes or coughs, hundreds or even thousands of virus particles can spread to those close by. I believe this war has hastened the epidemic. It's probably increasing its transmission and perhaps even making it more lethal to men who are already weakened by malnourishment, the stresses of combat, and chemical attacks increasing their susceptibility. The good news is that it seems to be dying out, with less new cases being reported in Europe."

Patrick got to his feet and swept dust from his trousers. Then changing the conversation, he said, "I'm starving. Shall we eat something in the port?"

Christian eyes were full of scepticism for Patrick's jolly mood. "Thanks for telling me, Patrick. You be careful in that hospital of yours."

"I will, but will you give me your word that you'll keep this information to yourself?"

"Of course."

Patrick nodded, then began walking down the shallow slope to the Port, praying there would not be a resurgence of the Spanish Flu that he'd heard had already killed thousands in England alone.

Chapter Eleven

10 October 1918

Near the town of Cambrai,
Hauts-de-France region, France

Danny rested in the funk hole he'd nabbed in the captured German trench before one of the men following him could take it. One had to be quick to get the most comfortable positions in any trench, Allied or German, when foul weather was on the way.

He was jubilant; it was a strange emotion to have after a battle where horrors had taken place and men had died, but the Allies had prosecuted their assaults exceptionally well. He was seeing progress amongst friendly forces. After every battle, Danny performed an autopsy on the day's fighting; it was almost medicinal for him.

He suffered flashbacks that came with waves of pain from all of his senses: sight, the god-awful images he would never be able to forget, blood and bandages and more blood, the corpses and carcasses still twitching as they died; sound, the screams of the dead and dying, explosions, detached limbs slapping the ground inches from his face; touch, the sensations of the very earth rocking beneath him when rounds got too close, the unforgettable experience of accidentally sticking his hand in the mud, surprised to find it so warm, only to glance over and see the viscera of a fallen comrade coating his fingers; smell, the odours of blood and excrement overwhelming everything except the scent of cordite … and so Danny had begun analysing the battles in military and strategic fashion, thus keeping his mind busy and, hopefully, fending off his more morbid recollections.

Today's win was thanks to the Canadian Corps. The previous day, they had overwhelmed much stronger Hun defences and weakened three German lines, spanning some seven thousand yards – about six and a half thousand metres to their French and Belgian allies. Ten minutes earlier, he'd heard his company officer tell another that the Germans' feeble defence was due to the Allied general offensive across the Western Front and the bombardment by over three hundred tanks.

The strange and noisy iron demigods had been successful this time, unlike the debacle of 1916 when many of the tanks had stuttered with mechanical problems and the remainder failed to reduce the German strongpoints in front of them. Danny had heard men talk of the fiasco in which their officers left the infantry behind the tanks to attack well-armed, well-prepared German defenders in virtually untouched enemy trenches. And as always in badly planned attacks, or those that simply went wrong, there had been a great loss of British and allied lives.

Today, before the infantry attack, he had studied one such beast traversing no man's land. At one moment, its nose disappeared, then with a slide and an upward glide it climbed and clanked to the other side of the deep shell crater which lay in its path. Its antics had enthralled him. Big and ugly as it was, clumsy as its movements appeared to be, the thing seemed imbued with life and possessed of uncanny intelligence and understanding.

Would they have won today without these beasts of war? He couldn't say, but they had sown panic and confusion amongst the Hun and allowed the British 3rd Army to enter the deserted town of Cambrai significantly faster and with fewer lives lost than expected.

The pelting rain came at dusk. It marked the end of the warm spell and the fighting, at least for now. Ally and enemy alike were knackered and would be glad of the wet weather, Danny knew, for with the discomforts wrought by sodden trenches, the rain also brought a respite from the big guns and gas attacks.

He cradled his sore left arm. Shrapnel caught him the week earlier and one of the no-nonsense Red Cross nurses had removed the metal and wood splinters, sutured the wound, and then given him his orders to return to the front after a cup of hot chocolate. It had been worth getting wounded for that sweet delight, the pretty, smiling face of the nurse's aide, and a wee lie-down on a real cot.

Danny's mates, Freckles and Geordie, hunkered below him on the trench floor. When they had captured the German defensive position, the ground had been dry and hard. The three men had looted all manner of accoutrements left behind by the fleeing Hun and then divided the spoils between themselves. A German greatcoat that had been hanging on a wooden upright beam now served Danny as a blanket. He'd swallowed the still-warm, albeit disgusting-tasting tea from an abandoned tin cup, and on his wrist were the two Swiss trench watches he'd taken from dead Hun officers: one a Girard and the other a Cartier, which he would barter with when he needed something more useful to him. Or he might take one home for Patrick. He was also sitting on a woollen blanket in good condition, apart from having been invaded by lice that would probably mate with the lice in his uniform seams, delivering to him thousands of fresh and hungry Anglo-German louse babies. How nice.

The hard trench floor was starting to disappear under water. He hung his head over the edge of the funk hole and saw a big, fat rat scurrying through men's legs and skirting the walls. The little buggers ate the dead and found scraps to eat in the dugouts. They were probably enjoying the war.

"The water won't soak through the hard ground for a while yet, but you two will float soon. Get yourselves up from there," Danny called to his two mates.

"C'mon Danny. We have to sit somewhere," Geordie complained.

"Suit yourselves." Danny retreated further into the hole. He wasn't in the mood to chat or go for food, nor give advice and comfort to the other new recruits who'd just experienced their first outing. Bejesus, some of them looked no more than fourteen. They probably weren't.

His mind turned to optimistic thoughts, the likes of which he'd not had in years. The Allies were finally winning the war, no doubt about it. The Germans had left their big comeback too late, and unless they conjured men from thin air, they would keep on running away. He supposed they'd realised their only remaining chance of victory had been to defeat the Allies before the United States could fully deploy its overwhelming human and material resources. But how could they have anticipated the might of an army now in possession of fully functioning tanks that could traverse almost all landscapes whilst firing devastating rounds that tore up structures and soldiers with equanimity?

The British had come a long way but had lost hundreds of thousands of men in their advances. Danny recalled the day in August when the Allies began their counteroffensive with the support of over one million newly commissioned American troops, backed up by improved equipment, artillery and techniques, and operational methods. He'd believed then as he did now that they were on the road to victory. How long that road might be didn't matter to him, for he was okay with fighting battle after battle if the Allies were going towards Germany and not backwards to the British Channel.

"Bloody 'ell I'm getting soaking wet down 'ere, right enough," Geordie groaned and shot to his feet.

"Told you –" Danny sucked in his next words as a sniper's bullet went through the thin layer of sandbags and ripped into Geordie's head.

"For feck's sake, how many times have I got to tell you eejits to keep your bloody heads down?" Danny groaned, getting out of the funk hole and crouching beside Freckles, who was on his knees, wiping Geordie's blood and brain matter off his face.

"The stupid git should have known better." Freckles' voice broke, as he stared at the friend who'd been chatting away only minutes earlier. "Aw, Christ, he was waiting for his first child to be born."

"Well, he'll have to look down upon it from above now. Help me carry him back to the medical station before he becomes a dam for this water." Danny grunted at men to get out of the way, as he and Freckles struggled to get the body to the forward medical aid post. His rest was over. Another mate was dead.

"Sergeant Carmody!" The call, although soft in volume, was urgent in tone, and it found Danny when he returned to his earlier position, now occupied by a snoring infantryman.

"The new captain wants to see you."

"Another new captain? Hope he goes for longer than the last one. Has this one got a name?" Danny asked.

"Don't know. Don't bother taking much notice of what they're called nowadays, Sarge," the private answered.

******

Danny crouched to enter the officers' recently captured dugout. The soldier guiding him pointed out the gaunt-faced captain, saying, "Good luck with this one." Then he left.

Danny saluted the dour-looking man before removing his helmet, then peeked at a map lying on a wooden trestle table. "You wanted to see me, sir?"

The captain looked up from the map and appearing irritated by the interruption, said, "I don't know, that depends on who you are."

"I'm Sergeant Carmody, sir."

"Then yes, it's you I want." He folded the map, put it into his jacket pocket, then took all the time in the world to lift his tin cup and sip whatever was in it.

Danny felt his skin crawl, as it often did when speaking to jumped-up officers, fresh off the boat. He could always tell when men had not tasted blood on the battlefield. They lacked the humility and grim sobriety that came with campaign experience. Men of this ilk reminded him of the British officers who had marched the Irish Republican Volunteers through Dublin's streets after the Easter Uprising – toffee-nosed bastards brought up by nannies and milk fed till they were old enough for their public schooling at Eton and the like.

"I have a job for you." The captain didn't bother to give his name, but Danny caught the 'P. Lewis' on the tag of his uniform shirt. "The Prussian and Bavarian forces are digging in some five hundred yards behind what used to be their secondary line. According to our scouts, the Germans' new forward post is manned by only a handful of German soldiers who got stuck there during their retreat. I want you to take ten men and raid that defensive position with the goal of retrieving provisions and one or two live prisoners to question about the Hun's plans. You will do this as quietly as possible, understand? It must be done as if you were never there – no rifle fire, no pistols. Understand?"

Danny was raging. He didn't need to hear *understand?* twice. He gritted his teeth and forced himself not to answer with his usual unmannerly dexterity. "I understand, all right, sir, but I don't approve," he told the shocked captain. "This is not a job for an NCO. Two officers should lead a raid like this … one giving directions and the other making the rush in. And sure, the only plan the Hun will have is to scurry back to Germany as fast as their bowed legs can carry them. I'd have thought that obvious. Begging your pardon for my cheek, sir."

"Are you a coward, Sergeant?"

Stunned, Danny laughed. "I am not. I've been fighting this war for two years and I have never shirked my duty. If you don't mind me asking, how long have you been on the front lines, sir?" Danny clamped his insolent mouth shut. *Shite, too late to worry about the cock-up now.*

The soft-skinned captain glared at the entrance to the dugout, dismissing Danny. "Report to me when you get back,

Sergeant Carmody. And whilst you're there, look for your balls in no man's land."

"Let's hope it's not a bullet I find, eh, sir," Danny retorted as he left.

Back in the trench, Danny asked for ten volunteers. He got four names in return; Freckles, who liked to stick close to his sergeant, being one of them. Danny picked the other six men himself. He recognised all of them but didn't know them well. It was a hard thing to see a trench full of strangers at the end of each battle, because those he had known and fought with were lying dead somewhere else. He no longer made friends easily, for it was an added hardship when he lost them, as losing Geordie had just so proved.

At midnight, Danny led his raiding party across no man's land towards the German trench, which before that day had been part of the German secondary line. Luck favoured them as the heavy rain and thunderclaps without lightning masked their presence. Bomb craters and uneven ground also aided them in their advance, as did the cover of black, heavy clouds and smoke bombs.

The men, armed with rifles, garrottes, freshly sharpened bayonets, pistols, and knives, slithered on their stomachs for the final approach. They were a good distance from their own lines but an even greater distance from the bulk of the German forces, which bolstered their spirits.

Success depended on Danny and his men surprising the unknown number of abandoned soldiers and killing them quickly and silently. 'Don't fire your pistols,' the officer had ordered – *pogue mo thoin* – kiss my arse, Danny thought now, as he neared the ditch. If he needed to discharge his weapon to save his own life or that of any of his men, he'd blast away till morning and to hell with the officer's instructions!

He halted the men to observe the trench at close quarters and to listen for noises coming from it. Silence – which meant there were very few Germans in it, as the captain had suggested, or they were asleep. Either way, Danny and his men were ready to make their move.

Danny found his first German as soon as his feet touched the trench floor. The man was dead. The rest of the British soldiers bellied over the edge of the parapet at different points, knives between their teeth and rifles with bayonets prepped for hand-to-hand assault.

Bent over, Danny cautiously made his way along the length of the trench. He stood on his second dead German – and a third – then he found more dead bodies lying in contorted positions. He knelt in the thickening mud and lifted the arm of one of the corpses. It was not stiff but pliant. Rigor mortis had not yet set in.

"They're all dead, Sarge," one of Danny's men hissed behind him.

"I can see that. Find provisions … nothing that rattles, mind."

Danny neared the dugout. A ground sheet covered its entrance. Unable to see what was behind it, he stretched out his rifle's bayonet, poked it through the material, and tugged hard until the curtain fell. Then, like a jack-in-the-box, a soldier sprang up and took a run at him. Danny stepped back in shock, tripped over the body on the ground, fell backwards with his legs lying across the corpse, his arms flailing, and the rest of him flat out in the muck.

He'd dropped his rifle and had already raised his hands to protect his face when he heard the American accent.

"What're you doin' here, Tommy?" the soldier asked. Behind him came five more men, loaded up with the treasured provisions that Danny's raiding party should have nabbed.

"I might ask you the same thing," Danny said, hauling himself out of the mud.

"Guess our officers are going to have to work on their correspondence and cooperation skills," the American joked. "I goddamn near killed you."

"I doubt that."

Danny's men joined him and the now-six Americans. The British were raging.

"Is this a bloody joke? Are we going back empty-handed?" Freckles asked Danny.

"Looks like it," Danny replied, looking at the American closest to him in the dimmed lamplight from the dugout. "What time were you given the order to come here?"

The American, a lanky man with a cheesy grin, answered, "Don't know, buddy, I didn't have a watch." He pulled his sleeve up and grinned again, "Guess I have three now, thanks to these obliging fellas."

Feck it. Danny turned back to his men, unable to see their faces, but sensing their anger; then he returned his baleful gaze to the Americans and noted that two of them were chewing on crusts of bread. "I don't suppose you'll give us something to eat … a few tins, maybe?"

"Sorry, Tommy, finders-keepers," the American corporal answered.

"Bloody great. You've been in this war for five minutes and you think you own it." Danny squinted at the men behind the Yank in charge. "Well, did you at least take any prisoners?"

"Nope. No one told us to take one alive."

"Feckin' good game this is," Danny muttered, planting his body in a crouched position. He saw no point in asking for intelligence material or anything else. He would kill the little shite who'd ordered him here. "Right then. I can't say it's been a pleasure, but I wish you well," he told the American. "We're leaving now. I take it we won't bump into each other on the way back?"

"Nope. We're stayin' put. We're taking this trench as a forward outpost."

"Of course, you are."

After getting back without incident, Danny went straight to the captain's dugout. A soldier lying across its entrance was dozing. Danny kicked the man's foot and grunted, "I need to speak to the captain … don't know his name."

"Sorry, Sarge, he and a few more officers are kipping in there. I'll get shot if I disturb 'em."

Danny looked at one of his wristwatches. It was almost three in the morning. He'd lost sleep, had taken his men into danger, and all for nothing.

Fuming, he stepped over the soldier, clipping back at him with his heel before entering the bunker. A few candles lit the first space he saw. The dugout was full of wooden boxes with German writing on them. He took a shifty look around and realised he was alone with his curiosity. Come what may, he was going to give the men who had risked their lives with him something to show for their trouble.

The boxes were already open, and he was able to lift the lid off the first one without making a sound. He muffled his gasp and took a step backwards as if bitten by the contents. French brandy stared back at him, and he saw that someone had already helped themselves to a couple of bottles out of the straw-packed box.

He looked behind himself again, opened his greatcoat, and slipped two bottles inside his own home-made extra pockets, designed for spoils of war. There was plenty of room; he'd lost over a stone in weight.

Outside, he apologised to the soldier, "Sorry, mate, I shouldn't have done that. I didn't wake the captain after all."

"What's your name, Sarge?"

"Smith – Sergeant Smith from four division."

His soldiers' morale was rotting away, just like their socks and drawers. Danny and the men in his company were suffering from exhaustion and cold, as the pitiless rain pelted down on their crude shelters. It froze them to the very marrow.

There never seemed to be any respite from the tension. It had escalated the previous night when one of the company commanders arrived with the rum jar. Danny, his temper frayed to the snapping point, had been physically restrained from hitting his superior when the first man to taste the drink declared it was not rum but bloody whale oil! Now, Danny grinned in mockery of the cheesy American as he crouched and made his way along cradling the bottles. Yes, up the officers' arses, right enough.

The rain was still pelting down on the men sticking close to the trench walls and none of them would get any kip. The walls were crumbling to mud and lumps of melting soil and planks of wood plopped into the now ankle-deep water on the trench floor. Discrete nips of brandy wouldn't go amiss tonight.

He and his men deserved it.

Chapter Twelve

End of October 1918

Greenwich, London, England

Earlier that morning, Jenny had left Kevin's apartment on Charing Cross Road. She'd taken two buses to Greenwich and had arrived soaking wet at Minnie's house, despite running all the way from the bus request stop at the end of the street. It was a wet and windy midmorning; dark, with a heavy, slate-grey sky and not a patch of blue or white to lift one out of the doldrums.

But Jenny wasn't in the doldrums; she was overjoyed.

Before leaving for the hospital a little after daybreak, Kevin had pleaded with Jenny not to go to Minnie's alone. 'You'll catch a cold in this, darlin,' he'd said whilst she was putting her coat on. What he'd really wanted to say was: 'There's a terrible sickness going around; don't catch it. The bridge might be weakened structurally; don't go across it alone. Don't go near Greenwich docks; a bomb might hit you on the head.' Kevin was overprotective at times, but he wasn't an old nag like some of her friends' husbands. His concern was born of love, and she loved him for it.

The male gender frequently annoyed her; at least, those who remained in England. Men still thought their wives were fragile creatures unable to fend for themselves; this, despite women in all sectors of industry doing hard jobs, such as working in the horrible bomb-making factory she had visited two years earlier. Husbands could no longer use air attacks over London as an excuse to order their wives to hurry home or to stay indoors, for Londoners weren't afraid of the Zeppelins anymore. The beasts hadn't dropped their bombs on England since early August, when four Zeppelins bombed targets in the Midlands and the North of the country – there had been nothing since then. The Germans were gasping their final, violent breaths, and any day now the war would end with the desperate Hun begging for peace.

Jenny wiped her muddy boots on the iron boot scraper, then opened Minnie's door with her latchkey. Inside, she removed her mucky ankle boots and slipped on her comfortable old house-shoes, which Minnie still stored in the locker by the door. "Hello, it's only me!" she shouted into the living room.

"We're in here," Anna called.

Jenny removed her coat and shook off the excess rainwater from the heavy woollen garment. Being married but continuing to live with Minnie had not been one of her brightest ideas, she reflected, pleased to be visiting her old home rather than residing there. Whenever she came to Greenwich nowadays, she was glad when the visit was over and she could return to the north side of London Bridge. Being separated from Kevin had been hell. He worked long hours at the hospital and had had no spare time to visit her in Greenwich, and she'd become fed up of travelling backwards and forwards to his comfortable apartment so they could spend the odd night together. Strange though, that it had been Minnie who had urged Jenny to give up her job at Shooter's Hill and move out of the Greenwich house. "I don't need you, love. 'Ere's you mopin' around 'ere and your new 'usband moping around there, when you could live together like a normal married couple and mope together."

Jenny smiled, as she often did nowadays. She'd found new reasons to love Kevin since moving into his rented two-bedroom apartment near the Charing Cross Hospital. She was his queen; at least, that was how he made her feel. It was as if her affections for him were boundless; growing daily and developing in their intensity.

In the living room, Minnie and Anna scanned the newspaper, not even lifting their heads when Jenny walked in. Annoyed, she glanced at her granny, then at Anna, whose eyes were puffy from crying. "Morning, Minnie – Anna," Jenny said before kissing her granny's forehead. "What's got you teared up, Anna? Is there more bad news in *The Times* today?"

Minnie sat in her chair with the creased, well-read *Times* newspaper resting on her lap. Beaming, she finally paid attention to Jenny, saying, "Oh, love, I'm glad you're 'ere. The paper's got lots in it this morning. I swear I'm about ready to burst. I nearly leapt out of my chair when I read about…"

"Don't say it!" Anna, who'd been sitting on the wooden arm of Minnie's chair got up, gave Jenny a bear hug, then went back to perch on the wooden arm. "It's about my Danny. It's wonderful news, Jenny. I've been crying with happiness. I want to run down the street and tell everyone, and I think I might just do it."

"Anna, why don't you make us a nice brew with the last of that tea in the caddy? This is a celebration," Minnie said.

"I will, but you mustn't say a word about it until I come back, Minnie. Promise me?"

"I won't. I'll let you read the newspaper piece aloud to Jenny after tea's made. Danny's your 'usband and it's only right that you should be the one to tell 'er."

"I've got something to tell both of you, too," Jenny said.

"Well, let it wait until after we've told you our news. Off you go, Anna."

Jenny grunted her displeasure. She'd spent hours getting here, but as usual, Danny came first. Always Danny; like the bloody sun shone out of his backside.

"Oh, Jenny, we're up to high-do here. I want to know your news, honest I do, but let's get the news about Danny out of the way first. There's a good girl."

Jenny's tolerance snapped "For God's sake, Minnie…"

"Ooh, who's put a bee in your bonnet this morning, Little Miss Impatient?" Minnie stared at Jenny. "What are you doing here anyway? Look at the state of you. Your dress is soaked through."

"I had to take two buses and there was a long wait for the second one."

"Couldn't you have come with Kevin in that fancy motorcar of his?"

"He can't get any more petrol for the Ford till the first of the month, and that's if there's any to be had." Jenny took a calming breath. She was desperate to tell them her wonderful news, but she wouldn't, for not until her granny had given her commentary on world events would *her* announcement get the attention it deserved.

"'Ere, listen to this, dear," Minnie said, going back to the first inside page of *The Times*. "I'll ignore that awful Spanish Flu that's going around. The further from us it stays, the better." Minnie pushed her glasses up until they were sitting on the bridge of her nose. After months of listening to her complain about her eyesight, Kevin had insisted Minnie get her eyes tested. Now, wearing her new steel-framed spectacles, she was reading not only newspapers but as many books – even novels – as she could beg, borrow or … well, borrowing was as far as she got down that path, as far as Jenny knew.

"Right, 'ere it is. I won't go into too many details, so keep up, all right, love?"

"Yes, Minnie."

"Last week, British forces routed most of the German army from Selle River in France, capturing the French commune of Le Cateau by the end of the day." Minnie turned the page and continued, *"The Germans evacuated the Belgian coast right up to the Dutch frontier. Zeebrugge is also in Allied control."* Minnie kept flicking her eyes and finger back and forth, then spoke again when she found what she was searching for. "Ah, yes, it says 'ere, *"Great joy reigns in Paris over the liberation of Lille. The population have shown demonstrations of respect and love in front of the statue of Lille in the Place de la Concorde, in Paris."* She looked up to add, "Apparently, our Ambassador to France deeply touched the French people by laying a wreath at the foot of the statue. They say 'ere it was a gesture of admiration and solidarity from the people of Britain."

"What else is happening in the war?" Jenny asked, her enthusiasm now matching her granny's.

"There's a disturbing account in here about Russia. Nothing to do with us, mind you, but terrible nonetheless." Minnie turned several pages, as if she knew where she was going from memory. Periodically, she licked her ink-stained thumb as she flicked the paper's top outer corners. "Got it. According to this article, those Bolsheviks are killing off the leisure classes." She looked up. "I suppose that means the wealthy, although I'm always at my leisure in 'ere and I'm as poor as a church mouse! Apparently, the Bolsheviks are shooting the country's most powerful and aristocratic people in the streets, and then after they've looted the poor souls' belongings, they leave the bodies to rot."

"I think this Russia situation is more dangerous than we first thought, Minnie. It wouldn't surprise me if Britain were to send men or arms to help the monarchists fight off Lenin's supporters."

Minnie nodded her agreement but was already moving on to another page. Jenny looked on with eyes full of affection. Without the kindness of their wealthier neighbour, who made sure Minnie got her newspaper every day once he had finished reading it, her old granny would sit in her chair staring at the fire and four walls, waiting for visitors to give her news. Few in these parts could afford *The Times,* which the upper classes read religiously. Their neighbour's kindness had an additional boon for Minnie: *she* was the source of news for almost all of her friends. They popped in to ask what the latest war tidings were and ended up visiting with Minnie and providing her with information or debate points of their own. Other than grieving Susan still, Minnie was more content than she had been in ages.

"What are you looking at now?" Jenny asked.

Minnie flicked the pages again, then said, "Ah, yes, this caught my eye. It's a bit of a strange one. Listen. *"Sir Cecil Herbert Edward Chubb, First Baronet and the last private owner of Stonehenge prehistoric monument, Wiltshire, has donated the land on which the site stands, to the British government."* Who'd 'ave thought someone owned that in the first place? Remember the day your father took us on an outing to see Stonehenge?"

"Barely. I think I was about five? I remember I was sick in the carriage on the way home." She grimaced.

A moment later, Jenny sighed with relief as Anna entered carrying a tray with cups, saucers, a milk jug, and a sugar bowl that held less than two spoonfuls of sugar in it. She set it on the table next to Jenny, then went out again to fetch the teapot.

When she returned, Jenny poured the tea while Anna giggled like a lovesick girl as she watched Minnie turn the pages.

"Oh, will the two of you get on with it?" Jenny grumbled, now at her wits' end with both women.

Finally, Anna began to read. *"The British Military Medal has been awarded to Sergeant Daniel Carmody for most conspicuous bravery, leadership and personal example during an attack and in subsequent operations. Sergeant Carmody, while in command of a platoon, single-handedly took a machine-gun post, rushing the Germans manning it with his rifle and bayonet. Upon seeing him advance, the enemy scattered to lob hand grenades at him. Regardless of all danger, and almost without halting his rush on the post, this NCO shot and killed at least six of the enemy.*

"Later, upon seeing another platoon requiring aid, Sergeant Carmody led his men to them, took command of the situation, and captured the objective. During the German counterattack on the following day, he led a section forward and restored a portion of the line. Per his commanding officer, Captain Peter Lewis, 'his bravery, skill and initiative were outstanding. His conduct throughout exemplified magnificent courage and was an inspiring example to all.'"

Jenny, for all her impatience and resentment over her own news taking second place to her brother's, began to weep.

Never had she felt as proud of or as happy for Danny. What would her da have said were he alive to see his son being singled out for bravery in the British Army? “Oh, Anna, my brother has done us proud! I don’t know what else to say except I’m thrilled.”

“It’s a wonderful day for the family, right enough,” Minnie said. “Your mother would have been over the moon to hear about this…” Then Minnie began to cry, wretched sobs that came from deep within her. “Oh, my Susan, my poor girl!”

Anna comforted Minnie whilst Jenny glanced at the clock. No buses were running in the afternoons anymore. She’d have to leave now if she were to make it back to the only bus request stop that serviced Central London.

“Well, what’s your news, Jenny?” Minnie finally sniffed.

“I’m pregnant,” Jenny said, standing, “and if I don’t want to miss the bus home, I’d better be off.”

Chapter Thirteen

November 1918

Belgium, the Western Front

The assembly of men in the trench waited for the order; those going over the wall first with bayonets outstretched on their rifles and those behind carrying bags of bombs. Teenagers who had come up to the front for the first time stuck to Danny like mud on his boots. He supposed it was because he'd outlasted most of the other NCOs who'd been shot to pieces in the last six days. This advance eastwards through Belgium from the Condé Canal on a thirty-mile front towards Maubeuge-Mons had been brutal on the Allied troops. That he still breathed was a surprise.

Danny searched the terrified faces of his men. That afternoon, a young recruit had asked, 'Sergeant Carmody, how do you manage to look calm all the time? How can you do this week after week, month after month?'

Without a thought, Danny responded truthfully to the seventeen-year-old. "I endure it because I am afraid of being afraid and of displaying my fear to men like you. I see it this way … if I die, it will be knowing that the world will never see another war like this one. This *has* to be the war to end all wars."

Now, a young private faced the mud wall, muttering, "Mam, oh, Mam."

Danny clipped the lad's ear and said, "Shut up. You won't find your mam's teat here."

"Up yours," the offended soldier spat back, and began muttering again.

"Don't mind him, Sergeant, he's not the full shillin'," a fellow Dubliner whispered to Danny.

The Irishman's arrival at the front two weeks prior had cheered Danny, for he had brought news from home. Finn McClure was his name, but the men called him Sharky. Finn didn't mind what he was called, so long as it wasn't *Fenian.*

The tall Irishman was also a friend of Jimmy Carson's. Jimmy was one of the men who'd been arrested with Danny and Donal Doyle when the three had been trying to hide rifles at the old tannery factory in 1916. Back in Dublin and firmly committed to Ireland's independence movement, he was helping the cause in the run-up to the December elections, Finn had informed Danny, adding that all good Irishmen prayed for a Republican Sinn Féin victory at the polls.

Danny looked at the boy he'd slapped, regretting his harshness. "What's your name?" he asked the young soldier.

"Steven Thomson, Sergeant," the boy muttered, his face reddened.

Well, Private Thomson, did anyone ever tell you about the time I was that nervous I squeaky-bummed my way across the front? No kidding, I farted all the way through no man's land and right into the German trenches." Command had passed down the order for silence so the men around Danny chuckled deep in their throats, behind closed mouths.

The kid smiled, only just, and Danny knew his words had reassured him and the other men in the vicinity. Danny began to tremble and faced the wall to hide his own fear from the men. The silence was the worst part of waiting for an offensive to begin. It gave those new to war the false perception that they were alone on the battlefield; however, Danny knew if he were to call out, thousands of enemy soldiers would answer.

After only two days' respite from the front, command gave Danny and his men their full marching orders. *Here we are again, brave wee soldiers marching to our useless deaths,* he'd thought. These had been the longest and shortest hours of his life. He'd not slept the previous day or night under the continuous bombardment of a thousand shells coming over the top of their hastily dug trench and another thousand coming back.

His nerves were wrecked and, even worse, he was constipated. Human waste had been inside him for far too long. He'd hoped for a result the previous day, but an accident had occurred at the latrine and it had stuffed him up. The men had dug their shite trench, and as customary, placed a concrete block at each end and one halfway along it for support. They'd then laid a flat narrow board along the entire length of the ditch for men to sit on.

Danny had used this type of make-do toilet many times, but yesterday, as he and four other men sat on the bench to 'do their duty' with their bums enjoying the crisp air, the plank of wood snapped, and they fell backwards into the trench's muck and shite. Danny had taken more than a mouthful of excrement as he'd lain in thigh-deep rainwater, piss, and mud, alongside the maggot-infested dead rats. In a war full of horrible experiences, he had to rate this one near the top. He didn't think he'd ever shit in peace again.

No one was saying it aloud, but he believed this could be it: the final week of the war. The Allies had exerted ceaseless pressure on the Germans, and the hammer blows against them over the previous few months were bearing fruit. After the battle for the Sambre River a few days earlier, German resistance had significantly weakened. And when the French First Army came from the direction of Valenciennes to join the British, Danny couldn't shake the tantalising possibility that the Hun were at long last on the brink of collapse. The Allies had broken through all the Germans' prepared lines, apart from the one they would face today. After they saw it off, which they would, only extemporised defences would stand between the Allies and victory. That wasn't a wish; it was something he believed.

The French soldiers Danny had met the previous day were also upbeat, as were the Canadians his unit had bivouacked with some days earlier. They all believed they were winning, and not because their officers said so; the behaviour of the German soldiers spoke volumes. They were changed men, dogs with their tails down…

A loud bang jerked Danny from his thoughts. A man whispered something to him.

"Quiet," Danny hissed back. An hour earlier, the men had handed over all their belongings to the company officer. Danny placed letters he valued above all else into the hands of a plush-arsed bugger who would remain behind the lines in his comparatively safe bunker whilst non-commissioned officers and lower ranks went 'over the top'. He wondered if he would live to see the hours after sunrise.

Having come this far, Danny was now desperate to survive until the Allies won and the powers-that-be declared peace. He'd been thinking more deeply than he'd ever thought before: about Ireland and freedom for its people, about his Anna and his hasty promise to her that he would settle in England and not look for a fight against the British, about his family and what their lives would look like in peacetime, about what he would make of his future as a father and husband. Would he be a success or a failure at the most important job a man could have? He had got to the stage where he was not afraid to die but was terrified of losing an arm or leg. He would be a hero if he died but a burden if he lived with limbs missing. He hated that thought.

The British bombardment began. The ground shook and the German retaliation came with unexpected ferocity. When dawn broke, Danny ordered a ration of rum to be passed around to the men; as much as they could drink. Afterwards, the men checked their bayonets, and waited again under heavy weapons fire coming over the top of their trench towards the nearest town where Allied guns were based. Soon, the noises of death and destruction blasting above them in opposite directions rose to an eardrum-clouting crescendo.

Danny positioned himself behind his men with a revolver in his hand. He hated this part of the job, but all NCOs were ordered to give soldiers this final 'pep talk,' as the officers called it. He regarded the shivering men, never letting his eyes settle on an individual's face, as he snapped, "If anyone goes up that ladder then turns around and runs back here, I'll shoot him myself. There is only one way to go, and that's forward!" Then he nodded to the lieutenant standing next to him, thinking, *no doubt, he'll shoot me as well if I don't go up the damn ladder.*

Minutes later, Danny went back to the ladder in question to lead by example. He took a deep breath and exhaled as he shouted down the line, "Over the top! Let's give them hell!"

The world became a loud chaotic mess where rational thought and fear no longer existed. Danny led his men through no man's land a hundred yards at a time. No one ran or ducked or retreated; instead, they held their lines as they trudged through the knee-high cloying mud, slipping, stumbling, sometimes falling face first into it, laden as they were with infantry equipment. Though he couldn't hear the sound today, the mud made a loud, wet sucking noise as one pulled his legs out of it, back in and out again. *Squelch – squelch – squelch.*

At first, the lack of machine-gun fire bolstered Danny's courage, but he soon realised the Germans were controlling their fire until the bulk of British troops came into range. And, as he'd predicted, the door to hell swung open. The Hun found their range, and a barrage of fire broke loose and swept across his line.

Men dropped to the ground on Danny's left, to his right, in front of and behind him. A soldier shot in the leg continued to move along, his bayonet between his teeth and his rifle serving as a make-shift crutch. Wounded survivors screamed, sometimes looking around themselves for their missing limbs. A man cradled his intestines in his arms like dirty washing and he made eye contact with Danny, looking dazed. Danny pushed on, seeing next a soldier who had lost his left arm and left leg. His eye was hanging by a thread on his cheek, and he was calling out, "Nani!" Danny shot him to put him out of his misery and moved on.

The British broke lines as German machine-gun fire intensified. Danny leapt into a shell-hole dropper and found a dead sergeant wearing field glasses. He nabbed them, along with the man's bullet pouch. Most of the soldiers who had gone over the parapet first were dead. He now heard no orders, no commands at all, but duty screamed that he should get out of the hole and continue his advance.

After he'd climbed out and proceeded ten yards, Danny's rifle flew out of his hand. He looked down at the hole in his palm, then bent down to retrieve the mud-soaked weapon lying next to a dead man. The gunshot had not been that painful, he realized. The impact felt like that of his old teacher's cane whacking his hand when he'd been naughty. He surged on, ignoring the blood and stinging. He now gripped his rifle in his left, weaker hand, taking a moment to appreciate the smoke-filled air, almost like London smog, and the bullets still whizzing past his ears. Allied soldiers' bodies were piling up, forcing him to step over and on them, but still he advanced on the spitting German machine guns and lines of enemy riflemen.

He finally came to the barbed wire hills, erected to protect the German enclave from most of the gunfire. The wire was uncut despite the intense fire, and dead soldiers stuck to it like flies on a spider's web. Not even a rabbit could get through the jagged tangled mess.

Danny set to work, despite not having British cover fire. Determined not to falter and using dead comrades as shields, he blocked out the growing possibility of being gunned down or bombed as he cut the sharp, whipping concertina wire. Over the months, the thought of being hit had impacted Danny, causing him to get thin in the face, haggard and jumpy. Everyone knew that one day a beer-swilling Kraut would load a shell into a Krupp gun, and an invisible hand would write in invisible ink the name of a British soldier. Men often asked, "What will it do to me? Will it be a clean blot out, blinding insanity, or searing, white-hot pain?"

And what if it were his turn to get bombed or shot; what could he do? He wasn't alone. Fifty – a hundred men – were trying to cut through the wire enough to be able to crawl beneath it to the German lines, even though rounds were exploding close by and the men were being showered with cinders and clots of earth. He had one hand to work with; the other was useless and hung at his side or, when he remembered elevation was good, across his chest. His fingers wouldn't work. He couldn't grip anything or even squeeze his hand closed. Jesus, he could see right through his bloody palm!

Before long, bodies at the wire piled high. The mounds grew until it became possible to climb over them and clear the top of the razor-wire fence. *Not soldiers. Not people. Just a means to an end,* Danny thought, using the shoulder of a dead man to brace himself as he crested the rise.

A few Germans rushed Danny and the hundreds of British infantrymen with him as they neared the crude enemy ditch. A Hun with a canister on his back ran forward, spraying fire with a hose. Danny dropped to the ground, petrified of this new monster of war which had burnt to death at least twenty men on his right. He rose to his knees, got the man in his sights, and awkwardly put one in his chest. Then as more Germans came at him, he squeezed the trigger until the weapon's chamber ran dry.

Danny dropped his rifle and jumped into the enemy's shallow trench with his knife in his left hand. In the calf-deep mud, men were fighting hand-to-hand. Any gunfire posed the threat of killing a countryman, and there wasn't the space to point a rifle with a bayonet sticking out two feet further than the barrel. Most men were using their knives or fists. Many fell to the ground and were trampled to death or were pushed face first into the mud and drowned. Danny slashed his way into the fray, his desire to live overshadowing his fear.

When he tripped over a body and fell, a German officer on the ground next to him struggled to rise. In the fight that ensued, both men battled each other and the squelching brown liquid pulling at their feet, affecting their balance. Danny, through sheer force of will, got on top of his opponent. The back of the man's head went under, but both his hands shot up and gripped Danny's knife-wielding wrist.

As he pushed down against the German's superior strength, Danny's hold on the knife weakened. The Hun officer's face resurfaced, the whites of his eyes a stark contrast to his brown muddied nose and cheeks. He gasped for air then his mouth opened fully to let out a roar of exertion as he pushed the knife back towards Danny's throat. The men locked eyes and shared the mutual understanding that only one of them would survive the next few seconds.

With a sudden jerking movement, the German's fist struck Danny's face full on. Caught off guard, Danny's head whipped to the side. He lost his grip on his knife, then heard his own primaeval scream of rage as his body rolled off the man and squelched into the mud, face up.

With supreme effort, Danny tried to shift the German's legs to straddle him at the waist. Instead, his head sank, his mouth filled with bloodied brown water, and a dead rat's tail teased his lips. Danny squeezed his eyes shut. He was drowning, unable to squirm his way out of the predicament. He was dying, and it was a horrifying, ugly, painful end.

Strong fingers gripped Danny's collar and pulled him out of the filthy mire. He got to his knees, dizzy, blinded by dirt, and choking on the mud at the back of his throat and nose. He pinched his nostrils one at a time whilst blowing slime out of the open one, then he wiped his eyes and looked up to see Finn's face red with blood.

Unable to speak, Danny nodded his thanks. The German officer who'd almost killed him lay face down atop other dead men. Finn had stabbed him in the back, and his knife stuck out of the corpse, still jerking with its dying gasps. Danny pulled the blade out and wiped it before handing it to Finn, nodding his thanks again at the Irishman who'd saved his life.

On the ground next to the dead German, an unconscious Hun officer lay with part of his lung hanging out of a terrible chest wound. Engrossed, Danny watched the organ expand then contract and expand again with his breathing, like a balloon being blown up, deflated, then up and down again until it remained still, looking like a raw piece of meat.

So many bodies were now amassed, they formed a dam; a human bridge grotesquely rising from the mud along the length of the trench. Finn disappeared, leaving Danny to fight for breath and composure. *Thank you, thank you, God, and Finn and all the angels and saints and devils that abound,* Danny's inner voice cried.

He looked behind himself, still coughing and spluttering up filth. The Allies had grouped ten Bavarians with their hands in the air. They were being pulled up to ground level by the French, while British soldiers from Danny's company trained their rifles on the prisoners. The defeated Krauts were skinnier than the average Allied soldier by at least a stone. They looked relieved; many were smiling and saying, *"Danke, danke,"* thanking their captors with sincerity. It was a strange old war.

Freckles and Finn were relieving the Germans of their valuables: lighters, trench watches and time fobs. Danny, still suffering the effects of half-drowning in mud, lowered his eyes to the barricade of dead men in front of him. He noticed now that the trench was also packed with German corpses in the stage of death where their faces and hands were inky black or held a grey-greenish tinge, and the whites of their eyes and lips drawn back from their teeth gave them a gruesome, skeletal appearance. He sighed and tilted his head to the heavens. It was over. The fighting had stopped for the moment, and the noise of gunfire was rolling away like thunder peeling in the distance.

Chapter Fourteen

After a brief respite in the eerie silence, an officer ordered Danny and his men to begin the clean-up operation. Danny squished in the deep mud towards the concertina wire he'd helped cut hours earlier. Dead men were no trouble, he thought, watching soldiers cut the corpses down and load them onto the horse-drawn wagons. Neither were the walking wounded, who took themselves to the medical stations. The badly wounded men needed the most attention. It took time and effort to arrange the transportation for those being relocated from the waterlogged charnel house of the battlefield to the nearest clearing post for evaluation.

Every step a man took in no man's land could still be his last.

It was not common for German or British snipers to shoot men rescuing the wounded. Sometimes men lay for hours unattended, and the enemy, while picking up their own dead and injured, left the Allied soldier to his fate. This battle, however, had been a huge defeat for the enemy, and Danny knew the Prussians would take their revenge in any way they could.

Danny delegated the tough job of combing no man's land to look for casualties to subordinates he didn't know well. He wanted Freckles and Finn with him. To lose either of them now was unthinkable.

Earlier, he'd got his hand sutured, front and back. The doctor had strapped it up with a bandage, but Danny still couldn't make a fist or grip anything. The days of him being a stretcher-bearer, a labourer carrying crates, a guard on the forward lines, an infantryman going over the top were over, regardless of how long the war continued. It was hard to take in, but as day turned to night, he realised that he might be incapacitated enough to be sent home. Ah, but sure, with his luck they'd tell him to shoot with his other hand. The sound of that order tasted bitter on his tongue, and he squashed all sense of hope with the same finality his boots reserved for pinned rats.

Danny, Freckles, and Finn saw to the influx of German prisoners. For hours, they had herded Bavarians and Prussians into order. It had been an enterprising day; Danny stole five watches and three fobs, and Finn got a fancy silver flask with a pretty engraving on it. Freckles, though, seemed uninterested in his loot, which surprised the other two.

On the march into town with prisoners later that night, Danny struck up a conversation with a German officer. The man was having trouble walking and shuffled along like an old woman. Danny looked at the German's boots. "Take them off," he ordered, expecting to find feet so swollen with 'trench foot' he could no longer bear to have them restrained by leather.

The two men sat on a blackened tree stump, and after the Hun removed the first boot, Danny regarded his mucky, sodden socks. Then he looked inside the boot and found a thick wad of wet, ink-running envelopes bound with string. "No wonder you can't bloody walk with that lot in there. I suppose you've got the same in your other one?" he said, handing the envelopes back to the man.

The German spoke decent English, and to break the monotony of the prisoner march, Danny elected to sit awhile on a felled tree trunk. Together, the two men smoked a cigarette, and the German, Claus, showed Danny the photographs inside the letters. Before long, they began talking about who they had left behind and about the war in general. They agreed the conflict had been useless. The German, like many of his fellows who had echoed the sentiment, believed Germany had already lost the war and that they should have surrendered weeks earlier. They, like the British, were fed up with the whole thing and couldn't care less who won. Claus just wanted it over so he could go home to his wife and four children.

Danny liked the man who couldn't wipe the smile of relief off his face. Under other circumstances, they might have been friends.

******

The British forces rested in a town they called, 'the town.' No one cared to ask the town's name or if they did, to pronounce it correctly. It was like every other place they'd been in; the buildings in ruins, the ground like thick, brown soup.

Danny searched Freckles' face with concern. The man was a jittering mess. His body jerked with strange spasms that had not been present earlier that day. His hand was waving ten to the dozen, and he was dazed and unresponsive to questions. It was as if his mind had suddenly split from his body and he had become two separate entities. Danny had seen many men in this condition; they looked and acted insane. A soldier with it rarely recovered before the following day's battle, but they were repeatedly pushed over the top and into incoming fire; or worse, unable to function, they were marched out and shot for cowardice.

"C'mon, let's get you to the doctor," Danny said, pulling Freckles to his feet. "There'll be no fighting for you tomorrow. I'll make sure your soldiering days are over."

On the way to the makeshift hospital, Danny, Finn, and Freckles passed hundreds of exhausted men curled up on the rubble towering above the filthy thoroughfare. Further on, soldiers piled mountains of horse dung whilst others shovelled it onto the back of horse-driven carts. The animals were tethered in lines, and veterinarians were patching up those that had got injured but could still be saved. As they walked on, Danny heard a gunshot and presumed another horse was being put out of its misery.

After the doctor had examined Freckles, he handed the shaking man back to Danny. "He's suffering from shell shock, Sergeant. He is unfit for duty, but I have nowhere to put him here. You must look after him. Find him a quiet place to rest … as little noise as possible."

"Are you joking, sir? There are thousands of soldiers here. I'd have to walk him five miles out of town to find a quiet spot. What does 'shell shock' even mean, anyway?" Danny asked the last question partly to distract from his insubordination and partly from genuine curiosity. He had heard the term but didn't know its proper medical meaning.

"It means he could have a concussion. A shell doesn't have to mutilate, bury, or lift a man off the ground to cause injury. I have seen men drop dead in this state with no external injuries."

"Jesus. I see," Danny said, but he didn't understand at all.

"Shell shock is a debatable matter, Sergeant, but I feel confident in my diagnosis."

"Then beggin' your pardon, sir, but shouldn't he be here with you?"

The Captain searched Freckle's sightless eyes and watched his body's severe, irregular spasms for several moments. In a rare turnabout, he answered, "You've got the cheek of the Irish, Carmody, but all right, leave him here." Then he gestured to Danny's hand. "Let me see what's under those filthy bandages."

When he'd finished examining Danny's hand, the doctor passed him over to a nurse who cleaned the wound with iodine. Her liberal use of the antiseptic caused Danny to bite his lip hard enough to draw blood. When she was wrapping clean bandages around it, she said, "You might have damaged some nerves. You won't be holding a gun in that hand any time soon, or perhaps ever."

"Don't get it dirty again, Sergeant," the captain called over as Danny left.

Danny wondered what magical, sterile world the captain lived in.

******

Two days later, Mr Gossip, a corporal from Danny's brigade who always seemed to know what was going on before anyone else did, informed Danny and the men with him that the Germans were negotiating an armistice. Some hours later, a poster appeared on a partly destroyed facade. It stated: *All hostilities on the Western Front have ceased at 1100 hours on the 11th of November. Shine boots and buttons.*

Upon reading the news, men threw their helmets into the air. Some of them linked hands and danced and skipped around like kids playing *Ring a Ring o' Roses.* Later, however, a peculiar lethargy came over the thousands of soldiers. The silence disturbed Danny. It was as if most of the men were too exhausted and deflated to enjoy the moment or couldn't take it in. He remained seated on a large bolder near the poster, observing the sea of men stretching to the end of the town's boundaries and beyond. Those closest to him looked relieved at the news but they were not as high-spirited as one would expect. The earlier cheering, whooping, singing, and jigging had stopped. They were all too tired to bother with the carry-on.

It was an anticlimax for Danny; a flat moment almost incomprehensible in its lack of feeling. The military had just sacked him from his job and he was without direction now. Soon, men started to slump away, some putting Danny's thoughts to words. "What are we supposed to do now?" After four years, three months, and sixteen days of war, no one had answers. Men, accustomed to crouching in the trenches, still hesitated to stand lest a sniper shot them, and when darkness fell, they lay down as they had on any other night in any other town.

Finn sat with Danny. Both men smoked their cigarettes in silence, trying to wrap their brains around the fact that they'd be leaving Belgium and going home soon. Only when Finn remarked, "We were bound to win, Danny. It was a given the moment we brought those tanks onto the battlefield and got more aircraft in the air," did Danny's lethargy surface as anger.

"Have you already forgotten the damage the German machine guns did to us? I got the casualty figures from the last few months, Finn. Since August, the Allies have lost over *seven hundred thousand* men. You must excuse me if I don't feel up to celebrating the end of a war that should never have happened."

"Sure, I haven't forgotten the men who died," Finn retorted, looking more hurt than angry. "I lost plenty of pals, too, but we can't bring them back, can we?"

"No, we cannot."

"Then I'll ask you not to rob me of my enthusiasm. I'm looking forward to going home to Ireland." Finn peered furtively about him, then whispered, "Mark my words, before long we'll be in another war, and it'll be a much more satisfying conflict for Irishmen than this one."

Danny kept his own council until Finn nodded to the crowds of men and said, "See all these knackered buggers here? We'll be kicking the likes of them out of Ireland for good soon."

"Do what you want," Danny shrugged. "I'm going home to my Anna, and just so I'm clear, the only fight I want now is the one for success in my life for myself, my wife, and however many wee babies she'll produce in our home. I met my wife when I was in Frongoch Prison Camp, and she won't forgive me if I'm arrested for sedition a second time. No, I'll fight no more, Finn. I've seen enough death for a lifetime." He looked at his bandaged hand and added, "Besides, who would want to go to war with a one-handed soldier?"

Danny let out a long, tired sigh and lay down. He covered his face with his helmet to block out Finn, who was being an annoying git with his talk of Irish independence, and finally he closed his eyes and let the thoughts come as they would.

For the last one hundred days, Danny's brain had been on constant high alert, perched between horror, dread, and panic. His thoughts routinely centred upon terror of dying some horrible way, depression from the sight of death in every direction, the fetid smell of unwashed bodies, and the even worse stink of rotting corpses turning black in the sun. The fear of being buried alive under a mountain of soil when a shell exploded near the trench would never leave him, nor would the memory of the stomach sickness that had caused shite to run down his legs while Freckles harangued him to keep running when he would've been happier for the Hun to shoot him for the mercy of it. He had killed countless men, seen the ubiquitous deaths of comrades, and witnessed the capture of thousands of Germans in recent battles. What had started at Amiens as an Allied counterattack had culminated in all-out victory for the Allies and a humiliating capitulation for the German nation. Yet, he felt nothing like a victor.

He turned on his side, curled up, and behind his helmet, began to cry. He was going home to loving arms, and hopefully, a lifetime of peace. It was raining, leaves were falling, muck was thickening like a stew, yet there was nothing sad about this day, for the guns had finally fallen silent.

Chapter Fifteen

Early December 1918

Wimbledon, London

Danny returned to England during the second week of December. After taking the train from Haselmere to Wimbledon, he reported to the Army's demobilisation station where he was amongst the fourth batch of thousands of troops waiting to be demobilised.

He blew into his cold palm; medics had strapped the other with layers of bandages, making it resemble a thick mitten. He'd been standing in this long queue for over an hour, awaiting his turn to enter his designated marquee. His boots' soles had worn thin. One of them had a hole in the centre of the leather, and rainwater had seeped through it, soaking his sock, foot to ankle, beneath. The rain was pelting down, making his cap soggy and his green army overcoat heavy on his skinny frame.

"It's bloody freezing," Danny remarked to Finn whilst shuffling from one foot to another to keep them from going numb.

"My nose is frozen solid, and my snot's turned to icicles. Not the warm welcome we expected, eh, Danny?" Finn McClure, Danny's Irish friend, had come back in one of the first batches because he was the son of a farmer and was, therefore, needed. Danny, classified as wounded in action and requiring ongoing treatment, had also been put in the fourth group of men to gain passage and return home under the army's demobilisation system.

The two men were discussing how long they thought it would take to bring millions of soldiers home. Danny was angry at having had to wait in Belgium for a month after Armistice Day, and angrier still on behalf the men still waiting, but Finn disagreed with Danny. For the first time in his life, Finn McClure stuck up for the British Army.

"How can you of all people agree with the army keeping men on the Continent?" Danny grumbled to Finn. "Can you imagine yourself being stuck in France or Belgium for another few months, just because the army says you have to wait your turn? The war's over, and they should let every man who fought in it get back to their families now."

Finn, wringing out his wet cap, repeated his earlier contention. "Danny, you know me. I'm not one for backing the British and their rules, and you know I hate the king, but this time I think you're wrong. Millions of men were serving on the Western Front, not to mention those in other countries. It's not possible to demobilise that many soldiers all at once in an orderly fashion. It'd be chaos were it a free-for-all."

A man standing behind Danny piped up, "He's right, Danny. They couldn't have done it any other way. The system of grading might not be fair, but at least it got *us* home for Christmas."

"And what about the thousands of poor sods stuck on the Continent and God knows where else? They might be there for months or even a year!" Danny retorted.

Johnnie, a Scotsman who'd sat next to Danny on the train, grumbled, "I'm with Danny. If you ask me, the military's top brass will get themselves into trouble for holding men like prisoners. Did you know they're sending thousands of troops to Germany as an occupying army? Those poor bastards *could* be there for years!"

"It's a disgrace." Danny shook his head in disgust. "You'll see, there'll be resentment and mutiny … riots, even."

An hour later, Danny went into the marquee and marched up to a desk.

"Name and rank?" the young corporal behind the desk asked.

"Sergeant Daniel Carmody."

"Pay-book, Sergeant?"

Danny handed over his pay-book. In it was his record of service, including the reports of his injuries sustained in battle, his mild form of trench foot that medics had treated in Charing Cross Hospital, and a record of his Military Cross award. After going through the book, the corporal looked up and said, "You'll have to have a medical. Standard regulations for everyone being demobbed."

Danny's mind fast-forwarded to the hours he'd have to wait to see someone in the medical corps. The medical tents were crammed with men who'd stupidly agreed to see a physician or nurse, but he was desperate to get home and was having none of it. "I don't want a medical. I'm fine."

"That might be so, Sergeant, but you can't leave your unit until you're medically examined and given Army Form Z22. Without that, you can't claim for any form of disability arising from your military service. Ever. Are you rich?"

"No," Danny grumbled, understanding now why other soldiers had agreed.

"Then medical it is," the corporal said.

After shuffling papers, the clerk continued with yet more surprises. "With this Army Form Z44, you can get your plain clothes. And this is a Certificate of Employment showing what you did in the army…"

"I killed Germans. I'd have thought that was bloody obvious," Danny whinged, dismayed to see the paperwork mounting up.

The corporal carried on without comment. "This is form Z18. It's a Dispersal Certificate, recording your personal and military information and the current state of your equipment." He looked up. "If you lose any of your gear after this point, we will deduct the value from your outstanding pay."

"Right, is that it?" Danny asked, calculating the hours before he was a free man.

"No." The corporal handed over another form along with railway warrants to London via wherever.

"What does Z12 Protection Certificate mean?"

"Keep that safe when you leave. It entitles you to receive medical attention during your final leave – looks like you'll be needing it," the clerk replied, nodding to Danny's hand.

The corporal began writing in a ledger, ignoring Danny for a good five minutes until he finally raised his head and spoke. "Right, Sergeant, that's you sorted. This is what you're due."

Danny looked at the book with tiny writing and numbers he could hardly read. "What does all that say?" he snapped with impatience.

"It's your demobilisation account. It reads: *Balance due to soldier on the date of arrival at the dispersal station. Two pounds and eighteen pence. Twenty-eight days' furlough at eight and tuppence: Eleven pounds, eight shillings and eightpence. Twenty-eight days' ration allowance at two and a penny: Two pounds and fourpence. Allowance for plain clothes: Two pounds, twelve and sixpence.* That's nineteen pounds, eighteen and fourpence, payable by demobilisation postal draft – here it is."

Danny admitted to himself that it was a good sum of money, but no less than he and every other bugger in the queue deserved.

When Danny came out after doing everything required of him, he found Finn, who was eventually going to Euston to catch a train to Holyhead and then the ferry to Ireland. He'd hung around to catch the train to Haslemere with Danny so they could say a proper goodbye. Like most of the men, he looked happy enough, but he also had an air of uncertainty about him.

"Well, that's it, Danny, all done. We're free men," Finn said.

Danny nodded. "Free and with a bit of money and a four-week ration book in our pockets. Sure, it'll come in useful." He looked at Finn's hand, noticing the Dubliner's fingers tremble as he lit his cigarette. Finn was nervous. Danny understood; he was feeling anxious himself. It had been a long time since any of the demobbed soldiers had fended for themselves. The Army, despite all its ugly parts, had given the men a home and purpose; a sense of unity, mutual support, and solidarity. He'd heard a regular soldier remark that some men missed the camaraderie to the point they were institutionalised, which eventually made them vulnerable in the outside world.

"Before we get the train, take this," Finn said, handing Danny a piece of paper with his address on it. "Look me up as soon as you get back to Dublin."

"I will, Finn, but I don't know when that'll be. I need to look for a job first and then get a house sorted out for me and my wife. God knows, I love my granny, but I don't want to live with her nor have sex with my Anna every night in dead silence with Minnie in the next room."

"Every night? Jesus, but you're a lucky bastard," Finn laughed.

Danny playfully punched his friend's arm, "To be honest, I think my Anna and me will go to see her mam and dad in Wales before I'm allowed to even think about a visit to Ireland. It's only fair, seeing as she's not seen them in more than a year."

As they began their walk to the train station, Finn chuckled to himself and then said, "See, that's the reason I'm married to a shy, submissive type. She never says boo, never questions me like some naggers. I'm what you might call 'a free spirit.' No woman will tie me to her apron, by God, they won't."

"That's probably why she doesn't give you sex every night," Danny joked. "Ah, but sure, marriage is a wonderful thing. Having a wife to share the good things in life with is the best a man can ever hope for."

"Well, that might be true for both of us, but I know you, Carmody. You'll not be able to resist the pull of Ireland once the Republicans get started on their path to Independence."

"I told you, my fighting days are over."

When the two men said their final goodbyes, Finn again reminded Danny to look him up in Dublin. Danny shook his pal's hand, and with moisture in his eyes, said, "Wherever you go and whatever you do, may the luck of the Irish be there with you."

"You, too, Sergeant."

After walking for half an hour, Danny had pushed thoughts of Ireland to the back of his mind. At London Bridge, he looked back and saw a line of army ambulances making their way along the embankment. He didn't know where they'd come from but he presumed they were carrying wounded soldiers and heading to some hospital or other. The sight of them reminded him of his last days in Belgium. Word came through that Axis soldiers had wounded or killed dozens of Allied soldiers only minutes before the guns fell silent – maybe seconds before the end of the war. Christ, it didn't bear thinking about, but he couldn't stop his mind from going there.

He couldn't get Freckles out of his head, either. Danny had watched his friend's condition worsen during the long weeks they had spent in Belgium waiting to find out which demob group they were in. The war had finally broken him, and the man had gone mad. He was fatigued all the time, unable to sleep at night but dropping off for minute-long naps during the day, blubbering like a baby, convinced he was going to be sent back to the front. It was as if he were still living in the war and didn't even know the bloody thing was over! His tremors and sweats were shocking. He was confused and suffered terrible nightmares, and as if those symptoms were not bad enough, his sight began to fail. Plus, he couldn't seem to hear a bleedin' thing anyone said to him.

Danny had fought tooth and nail to get Freckles transferred to the Army Medical Corps for further evaluation. He'd not taken no for an answer, risking reprimand. 'The army and the war did this to him, so you fix his mind before he kills himself,' he'd demanded of a captain. He supposed he'd never know if his intervention helped Freckles, but eventually, they had taken him away to the hospital.

Danny neared his granny's house and felt moths in his stomach fluttering their wings with excitement. He had never been this eager to see his wife. He was glad he hadn't had sex with the prostitute in Amiens, for now, although he was out of practice, he was as pure as a baby monk.

On his way, he'd stopped to buy a bunch of flowers from a street market seller. He should have known there were none to be had. Hot houses were not priorities during the war, the man at the flower stall had told him. Still, he'd not done badly. He'd got dried honesty and teasels with rose hips wrapped with ribbon, and a bit of sparkly mistletoe. Anna and Minnie would be pleased enough with his bouquet.

He reached the front door and straightened his new tie while looking at the tired façade of Minnie's house. The long Zeppelin scar ran from the rain gutter beneath the roof's eaves all the way to the ground. The council had patched it up with cement, but it was ugly; a constant reminder of the night Jenny was hurt. His first task was to get Anna a home of her own. What a grand day that would be for them both.

He knocked on the door, having lost his latchkey a year earlier. Anna answered, glorious in a turquoise gown, her hair swept up, and her eyes sparkling with love. He'd never seen her looking so beautiful. "My darlin' girl," he uttered.

He stepped into the hall and crushed her to him, croaking, "Oh, my love … my love."

Anna tilted her chin upwards for a kiss. He obliged her, and whilst they enjoyed each other's lips, Minnie, Jenny, and Kevin appeared in the hallway to welcome Danny home.

Chapter Sixteen

20 December 1918

Greenwich, London

Sunrise crept into Danny and Anna's bedroom through a crack in the curtains. It wasn't a pinkish glow or a timid stream of yellow that would strengthen as the clock ticked on but rather a dull, grey hue that bathed the walls and made the room feel colder.

The angry pitter-patter of rain hit the windowpane in an unsteady pattern. The bare branches of the garden's hazel shrubs whooshed and cracked together as the wailing wind blew through and against them, with the odd one snapping under pressure. The lamenting howling sneaked in between the window and its frame where it didn't close properly, and at intervals, peals of thunder echoed in the distance, reminding Danny of the folklore: 'thunder in December, there's a cruel, bitter winter to come.' He shivered at this portender of doom, the hairs on the back of his neck rising.

Danny didn't mind the harsh sounds of the weather, for they made him appreciate the cosy bedcovers and the proper sprung bed he was in. After being home for almost a week, he still felt the joy of civilian life and the freedom he awoke with each morning.

But he was not keen on the reverberating rumbles and loud booms that followed in the angry sky. They made him jumpy. They sounded like heavy guns firing in the distance, and they brought images of a desolate wasteland of fire and brimstone instead of the peaceful one in which his beautiful wife was lying next to him and he was safe from bombs. The peals of nature's fury made his muscles tense, and in those confused moments between sleep and wakefulness, he expected shells to explode and the ceiling to crash down on him. He jolted himself out of his fearful, melancholic thoughts, then swung his legs over the side of the bed. Today was a new day in a peaceful world and he was determined not to let the weather interfere with his plans to shop for Anna's Christmas present.

"You're awake, Danny," Anna said. Her eyes were closed, and her skin had a strange sheen to it. "I'm going to stay here a while longer. It's too cold to get up."

"You do that, darlin'. It's a wicked day outside. I think I'll bring you up a nice cup of tea and get back into bed with you. We can go into London this afternoon instead of this morning. How about that?"

Danny, having dressed in his pyjamas and dressing gown, went to the window. He pulled open the billowing curtains and pressed the back of his hand against the bottom of the window frame where cold air and noise seeped in. "I must do something about this frame. The wood's rotting, and it won't come down as far as it should."

Anna opened her eyes to gaze lovingly at Danny as he fetched another pair of pyjama trousers from the wardrobe. He stuffed them into the narrow space between the bottom of the window and the frame to block the air from outside, then used a towel to mop the wet floor beneath it. "That'll do it for now, Anna. At least, it's stopped that wind and rain from coming in." He looked at his wife. "I promise you, sweetheart, we'll get our own house, you and me. As soon as Christmas is over, I'll start looking. We'll not spend 1919 here."

Anna coughed. It was not a morning cough to clear one's throat but an intense, coarse sound that rose from deep in her chest.

Danny returned to the bed. Since opening the curtains, the room had become brighter, albeit only with a greyish light. He studied Anna's face; the droplets of sweat on her forehead, the bluish tinge to her skin and lips. "You're not well," he stated.

"I have a headache and a cough, but I'll be all right after that cup of tea you promised," she said, her voice hoarse. "Go on. Don't fuss."

Danny found Minnie in the kitchen. "Anna's ill. She's got a headache, a cough, and a fever. I think I should go for the doctor."

"What does she look like?" Minnie asked, going pale and slumping in her chair.

"She's coughing, and she said she was tired. Her lips are blue. I told her to stay in bed a while longer."

Minnie stared out the window, a frown deepening her already furrowed forehead.

"Minnie, you don't think it can be that Spanish flu you told me about?" Danny whispered.

"Go for the doctor, Son."

Danny was calm as he put his coat and flat cap on, but when he left the house, his hands began to shake, and as he broke into a run toward Doctor Branston's home, he panted, "Not Spanish flu … not Spanish flu."

He'd learnt more about the disease from Minnie and Anna three days after he'd got home than he had from all the doctors in France. He had gone to Dr Branston, whom Minnie spoke highly of, to get his injured hand seen to. The bullet hole had closed, the doctor removed the sutures, and it was healing nicely. He had abnormal tingling sensations in three of his fingers, from the middle finger to his pinkie. It would never be a pretty hand. The lateral edge was deformed and looked like crumpled tissue paper.

'It's lame, I'm afraid,' the doctor had said, as if he were talking about a horse. 'I suggest you wear a leather glove on that hand to protect it. It's early days, but maybe you can get a specialist to look at it further down the road. He might be able to do something to get the feeling back … nerves occasionally knit over time, but they can't be mended.'

Danny went home that day and brought the subject of the flu up to the women after seeing people wearing face masks at the doctor's office. Doctor Branston was as old and as worn as Moses at the end of his forty-year journey from Egypt to Israel. He was fit for nothing but the knacker's yard, although his mind remained sharp. He'd not been encouraging about Danny getting the feeling back in his fingers, nor had he been forthcoming with an explanation of why two of the patients in his waiting room wore facemasks and bags of camphor around their necks.

Now, Minnie opened the front door to the doctor and Danny, and said, "She's not looking well at all. I've just been up to see 'er, and she's got a high temperature and the ague."

"Have you and Anna been taking the recommended precautions?" Doctor Branston asked as he hobbled past her, nearly crushing her slipper-clad foot with his walking cane.

"Yes, we have. We've carried potatoes in our pockets, and we've been eating the raw onions you suggested, but Anna 'asn't been able to keep away from other people, not with 'er job at the hospital. I thought this flu 'ad run its course."

"We thought it had, Minnie, and believed it for certain when the council reopened the schools and theatres a few weeks ago. Don't go thinking the worst. It might not be the big flu..."

"Do the pair of you think you could continue this discussion after you've seen my wife?" Danny interrupted. "All this talk won't help Anna."

Doctor Branston nodded and staggered on bad hips towards the stairs. Danny wondered how long it would take the old codger to get up them.

"I'll see your wife myself," Doctor Branston said, stopping Danny from following him into the bedroom.

Danny nodded, but Minnie made sure he obeyed by pulling him back. "I'll make tea, Son," she said, still gripping Danny's arm.

"I don't think your magic tea will sort anything this time, Minnie."

Danny went into the living room. He wished Patrick were home; he would know what to do. They had received a telegram from him two days earlier, saying he'd not get discharged from the navy until at least the start of the New Year. He was not on a ship but on some island with a funny name. It had been over a year since they'd seen each other.

"'Ere, drink this, and don't fret," Minnie said, appearing with a cup of steaming tea on a saucer.

Danny thanked her. He set the saucer on the dining table and said, "I'm scared, Granny. Anna mentioned how bad this flu was in the summer. She said tens of thousands died, and not just the very young and old."

Minnie was silent.

"Minnie, please, be honest with me. She said she could spot the symptoms a mile away. She told me folk were fatigued and had fevers and headaches and could die within hours of their first symptoms. She saw plenty of cases at the hospital … patients turning blue –" Danny's voice broke and he let out a loud sob. "Oh, bejesus, no. She's got it."

"Let's not jump to conclusions, love. She's got a fever, but this might be the normal flu. We've 'ad such bad weather…"

"Don't do that, Minnie," Danny's wet eyes flashed anger. "Don't you, of all people, lie to me! She's upstairs with all those symptoms. She looks like she's at death's door, for Christ's sake." He was terrified. Anna had looked exactly like the people she'd described.

Danny wept in earnest for a full five minutes then stood up, wiped his eyes, and made for the stairs before Minnie could stop him.

"Don't go up there, Danny Carmody," Minnie sobbed, as he took the stairs two at a time.

In the bedroom, Doctor Branston wiped Anna's mouth with his own handkerchief. Danny approached the bed but abruptly halted when he saw the blood on the cloth. His round, frightened eyes widened further as he searched his wife's face. She stared up at the ceiling, sightless with fever, oblivious to who was in the room.

"Come into the hall with me a moment, will you?" said Doctor Branston, pulling Danny away from the bed by his jacket sleeve. He opened the bedroom door and stood there until Danny was in the hallway. "You've been away, Mr Carmody, so you don't know all the ins and outs of this illness."

"Nor do I want to, Doctor," Danny retorted.

"But you must."

"Are you confirming she has this Spanish flu?"

"I'm afraid I am. I've seen enough of it to know when it's staring me in the face. Your wife is a young woman, Daniel," he stated the obvious, using Danny's formal Christian name. "She's in the most susceptible age group. This is a strange disease with sudden, savage changes. We have much to learn from it, but we know already that it is more deadly in young people between the ages of twenty and thirty-five. I'll be honest with you. She is very ill."

Danny was speechless, his worst fears crawling up his spine. The stoop-shouldered doctor hung his head as though already defeated, his stethoscope hanging limp around his neck, and when he raised his tired eyes to Danny, he confirmed the worst in a whisper, "I'm sorry, Daniel. She is unlikely to make it through the day. She's already developed the gravest of symptoms and this bu –" He ensured Minnie wasn't in earshot and then continued. "This bugger works fast."

Danny's mind was dulled to the pain of losing his love, his ears deaf to the doctor's prognosis. "What treatment do you suggest?" he asked.

Doctor Branston sighed as he walked along the landing to the stairs. At the top of the staircase, he stopped and said, "We don't have medicines that will help, apart from aspirin to keep the fever down. If you can get her to swallow two or three crushed on a spoon, they might help, but mind she doesn't choke. You can also keep her cool with cold, damp cloths. Make her comfortable. I'm afraid I can't suggest anything else that would do her any good; she's too far along. Stay with her, Daniel."

Minutes later, Minnie stood at the front door with Doctor Branston, nodding as he explained the situation.

"I thought it was over," she murmured.

"We all did, but it seems it returned with our soldiers from abroad. It's a virulent form of influenza, Minnie. I've received a report on the army camp at Catterick. They've had thousands of deaths in the past few weeks."

"I suppose with all those soldiers congregating in camps, an infection could make the rounds easily enough."

"And at great speed. The morgue has been forced to stack bodies like cordwood in the corridors. They don't have enough coffins for all the corpses, nor are there enough people to dig individual graves. So far, this is happening in only one camp we know of. God knows how many others it will affect. Hospitals all over England are reporting the same rise in death rates due to the massive influx of repatriated soldiers. We must brace ourselves for this third wave and pray it won't be as deadly as the second."

"Those poor boys surviving the trenches only to come home and die of the flu. It's not right." Minnie broke down in tears. "I don't know how my Danny will ever get over this, if she goes. *I* should be the one dying, not that young woman. She's only twenty-one, for God's sake!"

Minnie blew into her handkerchief, then stoically straightened. "Doctor, I wonder if you could do something for me. It's important that Jenny and Kevin come here. You have one of those telephones in your surgery and my grandson-in-law has one in his apartment … for work, you see. Could you telephone him for me? Tell them to come over as soon as possible. Danny will need his sister before the day is out."

Minnie handed Branston a piece of paper. "I've written his telephone number."

"Of course. I'll make the call as soon as I get back to my house." With that said, Doctor Branston left. Minnie went to the stairs and looked up their length, then slowly climbed them, a broken woman.

******

That evening, relentless rain battered the window. Darkness had fallen and the bedroom was flooded with orange light from the lamps on the bedside tables and several candles on the dresser. Anna's head lay propped against the pillows. She was awake and looked peaceful, apart from the gasps that interrupted her breathing.

Danny sat on the edge of the bed and held her hand. At the foot of the bed stood Minnie and Kevin. They had not allowed Jenny into the bedroom, despite her pleading. She had to think of herself and the baby, Kevin had told her in an unusually harsh tone. He had suggested to Minnie that they allow Danny and Anna privacy in their last moments together, but Danny had insisted his wife be surrounded by family; her not having her own in London.

Anna smiled at Danny, oblivious to or ignoring Minnie and Kevin's presence. "My love, it was only a matter of time before I got it, I suppose," she uttered in her beautiful, lilting Welsh accent. "I'm so grateful I got to see you … first. You mustn't be sad, Danny. I don't want you to … I need you to be brave … *fy cariad* … promise me?"

"Hush now, darlin', the doctor said you'll be fine. Sure, after a few days' rest, you'll be eating Christmas pudding," Danny answered in a cheery voice.

Between bubbling, rasping breaths, she smiled and whispered, "Liar."

Danny cursed his tears. Throughout the war he'd learnt how to control his emotions, but he'd never been as scared or broken as he was now. It was unconscionable that his Anna should leave him. "I love you with every vein in my body. You'll not be leaving me alone. I won't have it, my sweet girl."

"Don't fight the British Army," Anna said, her eyes boring into her husband's with sudden ferocity. "Even if there's a revolution in Ireland … don't you go. You must move forward, not backwards to rifles and war … promise me, Danny."

"But my darlin', Ireland is at peace…"

"Liar," she used that word again. "Oh, my Danny, you're so headstrong. I love you for your passion. Never go back to prison … I couldn't bear it."

When Anna's eyes closed, Danny squeezed her hand. His own tear-filled eyes searched her face, then his breathing quickened as a last wisp of air left his wife's body, and her hand grew slack in his. He gave her a brisk shake and whispered, "Anna, wake up – Anna, breathe!"

A gentle hand rested on his shoulder. He looked up to see Kevin, tears running down his face as well. He was such a big man, Kevin, but here he was, bubblin' like a baby.

"Let me see to her, Danny," Kevin choked.

Danny struggled to stand, and when he was on his feet, he staggered backwards to give Kevin his place. The latter felt for a pulse, and afterwards used his stethoscope to listen for a heartbeat. Immersed in grief, Danny jumped as Minnie tucked her arm into his, her ashen face riveted on Kevin's downturned profile.

"Is she still breathing?" Danny asked, fighting to negate the silence. "She'll pull through this, right?"

Kevin left Anna and went to Danny whose look of horror made him hesitate. "Danny…"

"Tell me she's all right?" Danny begged in a high, quivering voice.

"Anna's gone. I'm sorry."

Danny pushed Kevin aside and went back to Anna. This time he fell to his knees at the bedside and lifted her hand to his lips and kissed it. "Oh, my Anna – oh my darlin' girl – my love. Wake up. C'mon, open your eyes for me."

"Danny, dear, she won't. Anna's passed away," Minnie told him.

******

The next morning, Minnie and Jenny waited in the kitchen for Danny to come downstairs. Before he'd left for Central London the previous night, Kevin had explained to a distraught Jenny that a family death was no excuse to take a day off work. If that were the case, there would be a constant shortage of staff in the hospital. He promised, however, to send Anna's parents a telegram. It was not the way Danny wanted to notify them of their only daughter's death, but neither the Walters nor their neighbours had a telephone.

"Danny won't be able cope with this, so I suppose we had better make the arrangements for Anna's funeral," Jenny said.

Minnie, who had stayed up all night in case Danny wanted to talk, asked Jenny, "Do you feel up to this, love? You mustn't distress yourself. It's not good for the baby."

"I'm already distressed. Anna was my sister-in-law, but she was also my best friend. I didn't even get to say goodbye to her. I let her down."

"Nonsense. You didn't let anyone down."

Jenny burst into tears. "Oh, Minnie, I don't know what I'll do without her to cheer me up and make me smile at her giddy ways. I thought we'd got away with it. Even Kevin believed we'd beaten the Spanish flu. I can't believe it. I feel as if I've lost a part of myself, and one of the better parts. That beautiful girl up there meant so very much to me … to us all. How will we ever recover?"

Chapter Seventeen

End of January 1919

Greenwich, London

Three months after the military leaders signed the armistice, Patrick was out of his Royal Navy uniform, back into civilian clothes, and walking along Minnie's street in Greenwich. He'd been anxious on his voyage home from the Greek Islands. The war had ended; hostilities had ceased, but every morning the ship's crew had conducted survival drills. Added to those were alarm bells set off by officers on watch because of reported sightings of a static or drifting mine in their shipping lane. The ship had made it home without incident, but the drills and alarms were a constant reminder of an event he'd rather forget.

Patrick would hate sea travel for the rest of his life.

During the last months of the war, he had managed to curb his nightly sweats and dreadful memories of HMHS *Britannic's* sinking. Being on a shore base had helped, but so had talking to sailors who had survived torpedo attacks and minefields in the North Sea, Heligoland Bight, and Straits of Dover. The men who came to him had endured the traumas of escaping ships that were blown out of the water or had suffered a slow, humiliating sinking. Each man had his own unique perspective of the experience, as did Patrick, who could personally relate to most of the stories. He wasn't certain how or when *he* had recovered from his own nightly terrors, but he guessed it stemmed from being a comforter and not a victim with the distressed sailors he cared for. The first step to healing himself was … to heal others. Who would have thought that?

After tears of joy at seeing Patrick, Minnie calmed down enough to make tea. "It's still a luxury, Son," she told him, "but if we can't 'ave it to celebrate the little things in life, when can we, eh? Take our Jenny … now there's a girl who needs to keep 'er spirits up if ever I saw one. I swear she's got thinner since Anna's death, and 'er being pregnant."

Patrick carried in the tray with cups and saucers from the kitchen and set it down on the dining table. Minnie followed with the teapot and a plateful of dubious-looking homemade biscuits and placed it next to the cups.

"I'm 'appy you're home, dear. We've 'ad a terrible time of it 'ere," Minnie said "Go on now, you sit by the fire. I'll bring your tea over."

Patrick did he as was told, sighing as he wriggled his backside on the well-padded cushion. "Ah, this is lovely," he muttered to himself.

"I expected you hours ago," Minnie said, handing Patrick the hot tea. "Your telegram from Southampton yesterday said you'd get 'ere this morning. Were you caught up in the unrest in London?"

Patrick nodded, taking a sip of tea and feeling its heat run down his throat. "My journey through London took much longer than I expected. You probably know the electric train drivers have downed tools today? They've paralysed the London Tubes, and the congestion below ground has transferred to the omnibuses. I've never seen so many men tramping the pavements from east to west, trying to get to their work or wherever they were going. The queues for buses and trams stretched for miles. I gave up on the idea of waiting my turn. My feet are killing me, Minnie. I walked here."

"Well, you get those feet up now. It's been rotten 'ere. We've got all those soldiers returning from the War expecting to find a land fit for heroes, and instead they're getting poverty as bad or worse as when it all kicked off. I don't know what's goin' to 'appen, I really don't."

"How long have these strikes being going on?" Patrick asked.

"It's 'ard to know when they started, but a forty-hour strike broke out in Glasgow and Belfast last week. *The Times* said thousands of munitions workers are facing unemployment up there while engineers in work are suffering a fifty-four-hour week. We've 'ad the British police forces striking on and off since the end of last year. It's got so bad, the government 'ave convened a committee under Lord Desborough to look at all aspects of police forces in England, Wales, and Scotland. I was shocked when I learnt 'ow little they got paid. Did you know the wages of agricultural workers and unskilled labourers 'ave outstripped those of the police? It's a bleedin' disgrace, if you ask me."

"No, I didn't know that," Patrick said dutifully. He was more interested in learning how Danny, Jenny, and Kevin were, but until his granny gave her daily report on the state of the world and everyone in it, he would nod and feign interest. She'd eventually get around to her other grandchildren.

"There's no uniform pay structure for the police," Minnie said, biting, unsuccessfully, on a hard biscuit. She grimaced and threw it on the table. "These biscuits 'ere must've been made with cement."

Patrick smiled. "Go on, you were saying, Minnie?"

"Well, according to the Desborough Committee, the average constable serving in a provincial force with five years' service, and who's married with two children, earns about two pounds fifteen shillings, and that includes all their allowances, like rent and child allowance. Then you 'ave a street sweeper in Newcastle-on-Tyne, who's on the same rate of pay as a constable in the provincial force! Is it any wonder the policemen don't want to pound the streets, what with the crime rate 'avin' risen and those poor soldiers coming 'ome from war without a job or a wage to look forward to? I sometimes think we were more united and civilised when the conflict was going on."

"I can't say I know what it's been like here, but I did see a lot of angry men in the streets today, never mind the poor sods on crutches or with limbs missing. The train station was full of beggars."

"Breaks my 'eart, so it does," Minnie grumbled, then she picked up her biscuit again and dunked it in her tea. "On top of everything else, we've got racial riots against black people taking place in ports from Glasgow to London," she continued. "I understand there's not enough jobs to go around and that people are ragin', but British seamen shouldn't take their frustrations out on Africans and other foreign workers."

"I hadn't heard about that," Patrick said, eyeing the plate of biscuits, wondering if he should chance one. He was starving.

"The troubles started when a group of white indigenous British seamen accused the blacks of stealing their jobs and taking 'ousing that should belong to them. We're turning into a country of barbarians, so we are. Mark my words, we'll be going in the same direction as Russia if we're not careful."

"It'll sort itself out, Minnie. These things always do," Patrick said, slipping the words in when Minnie lifted her cup of tea.

"I suppose you're right. Well, that's enough of my news. What about your plans?"

"I got some good news. I'm going to begin my formal training as a general surgeon. The Royal College of Surgeons in Dublin has offered me a place. Did you know they're going to name a new wing of the hospital after my dad? They told me in my acceptance letter. I can't wait to tell Danny and Jenny about it."

Minnie's lip began to tremble. She looked as though she'd just been informed of a death

"Are you all right, Minnie," Patrick asked her.

"Oh, don't take any notice of me, Son. I'm getting dour in my old age. I'll miss you if you go to Ireland. It seems you'll all be leaving me soon – and what with poor Anna gone…"

They hadn't spoken about Anna's death yet, but Patrick wasn't ready to talk about it. "We'll not leave you alone, Granny. You know that. I'm excited about going back to Ireland to live. I'm thinking of buying myself a cottage … something modest in County Dublin."

"That's nice, dear."

"I don't know what Jenny or Danny are planning to do with their share of the inheritance, but I've decided to split the money evenly between the three of us."

"You're not buying a house together, then?"

No. it doesn't make sense now that Jenny has Kevin, and Danny … well who knows what Danny will want to do now."

"Oh, Patrick…" Minnie's words trailed off, then she lifted moistened eyes to him and said, "You might as well know,

now you're back. Danny's not doing well at all … not at all. He spends most of his time in the pub, and 'e 'as no interest in getting a job. I'm at my wit's end with 'im."

"Jenny told me in her last letter that he was misbehaving again. To be honest, I thought he'd be grieving, not drinking himself into a stupor. He wasn't a drinker before the war started." Patrick noted Minnie's eyes, soaked with tears, and accepted that the conversation was going to get even more depressing. "I still can't believe Anna's gone. I was devastated when I heard," he croaked.

Minnie blinked her tears away but allowed herself a sorrowful sigh. "It was quick, so that was a godsend. She had a cough in the morning and was gone by that night. The funeral was 'ard. Anna's mother and father managed to get down in time – her brother, Dai, is still away in the army – gone to Germany with the occupation forces apparently."

"Mr and Mrs Walters must have been in a terrible state."

Minnie sniffed into her handkerchief. "They were as you'd expect. They were nice enough to Danny, but they couldn't get two words out of 'im. He sat in 'is bedroom most of the funeral day, and the day after. He wouldn't even come down for the tea I laid on, and 'e didn't say goodbye to Anna's parents when they left for the train to Liverpool. Kevin took them to Euston station."

Patrick was heartbroken for Danny, and for Anna who'd been taken far too soon. She'd been a light when things were at their gloomiest, a ray of warmth not only for Danny, who'd not spent much time with her, but for Minnie who'd seen her as an attentive grandchild. "Jenny told me in her letter that our Danny goes to the pub around the corner most days. Is that still the case?"

"Yes, unfortunately. 'E'll pickle his liver in no time if 'e's not careful. Spends most of 'is time in the Sportsman's Arms, getting into fights. It's as if 'e wants to get beaten up to dull his pain..." Minnie's voice ebbed away. She blew into her handkerchief, then finished with, "I 'ardly see 'im. 'E's a changed man, Patrick."

Patrick stared pensively at the fire before picking up the poker and rearranging the red-hot coals on the grate. He'd expected this bad news about his brother's behaviour. Danny had always had an excess of passion and pride, and Anna's death had probably pushed him over the edge and sunk him. "I'm glad to see your coal bucket is full," he said absently.

"Uncle George managed to get a sack from a friend of 'is."

"Where's Danny now?"

"I told you, 'e's never out of the Sportsman's Arms."

"Right, I'm off to get him. I'll bring him home and we'll have a good talk."

As Patrick rose, Minnie said, "Whatever you do, don't mention Anna. 'E won't have us lifting 'er name."

"All right. You know best," Patrick said, dreading going back in the cold to look for his errant brother.

******

Danny went to The Sportsman's Arms Pub, which was situated two streets away from Minnie's house, for the sole purpose of insulting the British and venting his anger on anyone who cared to give him the time of day. He'd been barred twice for fighting, but the landlord always let him back in because he spent a lot of money. On days when he felt generous, he even bought a round of drinks for strangers at the bar before riling them up with his anti-British rhetoric. He'd been advised in the strongest terms many times by fellow drinkers to make an Irish pub his local, but Danny wanted to fight, to feel physical pain, to dull the agony of losing his beloved Anna. What was the point of going somewhere he'd be popular?

Today, the place was packed with men who had stayed away from their jobs in solidarity with the electric train drivers. They were joined by ex-soldiers who had not managed to get work since their return from the war, and who spent their days whining about the injustices set against them. It was ironic, he thought, looking at the faces at the crowded bar: unemployment was rife, a shortage of jobs plagued the nation, yet big and small unions were refusing to work during days or weeks of strikes while their families went hungry. The country, according to Minnie, was being thrown into an age of darkness, straight after it had come out of the wearisome gloom of war. That about summed it up, but he didn't give a shite anymore about British suffering, nor his own.

At the bar counter, Danny's melancholy exploded during a rendition of the wartime song; *Keep the Home Fires Burning,* being played on the piano. As the men sang in their drink-slurred cockney accents, his thoughts crossed the sea to Ireland and the momentous decisions being made regarding its freedom from the oppressive, imperialistic British yoke. *The day is coming, ye load of Sassenach gobshites,* Danny thought, as the song ended and men cheered.

Hating their smug faces, Danny shouted, "Freedom for Ireland. Down with their English oppressors, and up with the Irish Republican Army! We'll…"

"Shut up, ya Paddy git!" someone yelled. Then another drinker slammed his fist into Danny's cheek.

Danny's head whipped sideways. A back tooth came loose. Dazed, he felt it dislodge from his gum along with a stream of blood and saliva that spewed through his half-open lips. The next punch hit him full on the nose, the force of it causing blood to burst forth from both nostrils and bringing with it the familiar coppery smell and taste he knew from the battlefields of France and Belgium.

"That's it, look at ye all … takes a whole pub to gang up on a single Irishman. C'mon … is that all you got, ye feckin' bunch of shitehawks!"

Danny ducked the next blow that swept over his head, but as he straightened, a fist crashed into his face full on. Others joined in. He had no idea how many men were coming at him, but they were not enough to stop him from yelling again, "Freedom for Ireland…!" Then, the breath was punched out of him as an upper cut ploughed into his stomach.

As he doubled over, unable to breathe or think, Anna came to mind. All the daft promises he'd made to her on her death bed about not joining the IRA were out the window. He was going. "Ireland…," he gasped defiantly, as he straightened to receive a crushing fist that split his bottom lip and sent him reeling to the floor.

"… I said get off him. Get off him, the lot of you!"

The gruff voice was familiar to Danny's ringing ears. Still lying flat on his back, he lifted his head, enduring multiple explosions of pain and peered up at the ring of faces looking down at him. "Patrick … bejesus … it is you," he slurred as he took a deep breath and made to rise.

"I'm taking him. It's over," Patrick said to the man whose fist had done most of the damage to Danny's face.

Patrick helped Danny to his feet, but then the latter's legs buckled as he was being pulled towards the door. His eyes smarted with painful tears, making his vision blurry, and his pride had also taken a beating. "Freedom … Ireland," he muttered like a petulant child before spitting blood out his mouth.

The man Danny had goaded into the fight after spewing hatred about the British government, finally stepped aside, but not before grunting, "My brother was killed in the Easter Uprising, ya bloody, pot-lickin', Fenian bastard. The IRA is nothing but a sewer for thugs."

Danny chuckled, making Patrick pull at him even harder.

The landlord, who'd come out from behind the bar counter, shouted after Danny and Patrick as they reached the door, "Don't bring him back here, you hear me? I'm sick of his antics. He's banned for good!"

"Up yours … up the lot of you," Danny slurred back. "I fought for the king, which is more than can be said of some of you Proddy war-shy bastards, who didn't even go to the front."

Patrick pulled Danny behind him as he opened the door, but Danny refused to leave until he had his final say, and as he was disappearing out the door, he blasted over his shoulder, "I'll never fight for the British Army again. From now on I'll be supporting the Sinn Féin MPs taking their seats in the Irish Parliament in Dublin … you lot can say goodbye to your occupation of my country … that's right, our day is coming. Up with the Irish Republican Army!"

A bull of a man followed the two brothers out of the pub, his face creased with rage as he raised his fists and snapped, "If you don't shut 'im up, I'll close his mouth, good and proper.

We ain't 'aving no treasonous talk in Greenwich, you 'ear me? You keep that bastard off our streets!"

In the street, under a light drizzle and an early evening fog, Patrick held Danny at arm's length and studied his battered face. Danny lowered his head and spat blood from his mouth, then he peered at Patrick through his tears. "You're back then?" he whimpered.

"I am, and this is not the homecoming from war I expected, ye daft bugger," Patrick responded, giving Danny a great bear hug.

Chapter Eighteen

"I don't know what more I can tell you. It's as if he's begging to get himself killed," Patrick told Jenny and Kevin in Minnie's kitchen. "He's been like this since I got here over a week ago. Maybe you can talk sense into him, Jenny?"

"I doubt he'll listen to me," Jenny responded, slumping into a kitchen chair. She and Kevin had arrived in Greenwich late that morning. Kevin had got a two-gallon can of petrol from an ironmonger on the Charing Cross Road, which had thrilled Jenny. At six months pregnant, she now dreaded having to wait for buses and then walk the length of the long street to get to Minnie's house.

Patrick filled the kettle, then lit the new gas stove he'd bought Minnie to help ease her workload. It was significantly easier than having to deal with the old, open-fire cooking range, and she was enjoying new culinary skills because of it.

Jenny, who noted marked differences in Patrick's appearance since the last time he'd been home, worried about the added anxiety he'd have if he had to look after Minnie *and* Danny. He was gaunt in the face and his clothes were hanging off him. She glanced slyly at Kevin whose eyes were also on Patrick, and asked her husband, "Darlin', what do you think we should do about our Danny?"

"I know what we have to do," Patrick answered instead of Kevin. "I propose we split da's money between the three of us and give Danny his part along with the option to stay here or go home to Ireland. I was thinking we might all go to Dublin on Wednesday. Kevin, you're on a week's leave from tomorrow. What do you say?"

Kevin was not keen on the idea. Jenny watched his mind work; the sigh of disappointment, the anxious shadow flitting across his face. He was tired and needed a break. She imagined the last thing he'd want to do with his leave was keep her brother in check and make the long journey to Dublin. "We don't have to go," she suggested, stroking Kevin's arm.

"No. Patrick's right. You should get your inheritance sorted out. It'd be better for all of you if Danny chooses his own path. He's a grown man, and you two can't be thinking and worrying about him when you have enough on your own plates to deal with." Then Kevin spoke directly to Patrick, surprising Jenny with his bluntness. "I'll not have my Jenny upset, so make it clear to Danny that if he lives here, he must stop the drinking. This situation is not good for Minnie's health."

"And if he wants to return to Ireland?"

"Tell him if he wants to live in Dublin or wherever, you won't run to his aid if he gets into trouble with the law."

Jenny had found out when she arrived that Minnie was staying with Uncle George for a couple of days. It was fortuitous for all of them, for she had a feeling that today was the day the Carmodys would have it out with each other and set terms for their futures, not as a family, but as individuals. "What time will Minnie be home?" she asked Patrick.

"I don't know. Uncle George will probably bring her back after lunch."

"Well, I agree with Kevin. Danny will put our granny in an early grave with his carry-on."

"Is that right?" Danny stood at the kitchen door, throwing filthy looks at his brother and sister, and no look at all at Kevin. He wore his suit, white shirt, and green tie. His hair was wet, combed back from his face and sitting flat on his head without a parting. He looked better than he had the last time Jenny had seen him, with his then-dishevelled appearance, purple cheek, and black eye. On that day, she had chided him over his drunkenness and bad behaviour towards Anna's parents the day after the funeral. They hadn't spoken since.

"You're all so certain you know what's best for me, yet none of you have had the decency to ask me what it is I want to do with my life," Danny accused.

"You've not been in a sober state long enough to tell me what it is you want to do with your life," Patrick snapped. "God knows, Danny, we sympathise with you over Anna's death. Losing that dear girl was a terrible blow to all of us, but you need to pull yourself together now and make something of yourself. She wouldn't want to see you like this."

"Typical," Danny spat. "You've been home five minutes and already you've started playing the big brother and telling me what to do. You do know I managed to survive the Somme and the whole bloody Western Front without you? I think I can make a straightforward decision by myself."

"And I don't think you're clear-headed enough to tie your own boot laces!" Patrick blazed back.

Jenny shifted in her chair and unconsciously placed her hand on her swollen stomach. "We only want what's best for you. We worry that you'll go to Ireland and get involved with that new IRA group or Sinn Féin." Hardening her tone, she added, "You're like a bottle with a bad cork. We never know when you'll pop off and get up to something no good. Anna worried about that side of you too, you know?"

"Did she now?"

"Yes, she thought you could be reckless, and if I know anything it's that she'll be turning in her grave, watching you make a fool of yourself."

"Anna's dead." Danny's lips quivered as he spoke. "She's not turning anywhere. She's gone."

"Yes, she's gone, but you're not," Patrick pointed out. "You're still here, and whether you want to or not, you *need* face the future without her." Patrick paused, then he suggested to everyone, "I thought we might go to Dublin on Wednesday. We have money coming to us, and as soon as we get our shares divvied up, the better for all of us."

"We'll make a holiday of it," Kevin finally agreed. "It's time Jenny met my family. We could all go to Cork – Minnie as well – do you think she'd like that?"

"I'm way ahead of you lot." Danny pulled an envelope from his jacket pocket and waved it maliciously at the others. "I picked this up from the post office yesterday. It's from Jimmy Carson. He's invited me to stay with him while I get sorted out." He returned the letter to his pocket without reading its contents to the others. "So, you see, I'll be on the boat on the night sailing…."

Jenny said, "Change the ticket, so we can go as a family."

"No. I can't stomach another day in this house. I can't sleep in that bed without my Anna. I can't stand seeing her stuff lying around the place, and her perfume still lingering in that room upstairs. I'm going today. My future is not with this family, it's with my own kind who are fighting for independence. That's the truth of it, and if you can't accept it, tough, that's your problem."

Jenny, disappointed, said in a feeble voice, "You promised Anna you wouldn't."

"As you keep reminding me," Danny spat.

"And what sort of Irishman would break a promise to his dying wife because it's not bloody convenient for him? Does your word mean nothing to you?"

"It means everything to me, ye cheeky mare!"

"Have some respect when you speak to my wife!" Kevin snapped. "Personally, I don't care what you do. You can go to hell as far as I'm concerned."

"I might just do that."

"Stop, both of you," Patrick jumped into the fray. "Danny, are you sure you want to go back to all that carry-on in Ireland?"

Danny now turned on his brother. "Carry-on, you call it? Do you not read the papers? Sinn Féin have swept the polls throughout much of Ireland. They've got an overwhelming parliamentary majority. Michael Collins, as a senior Sinn Féin representative, is now an elected MP for Cork South, and may sit in the House of Commons in London if he has a mind to. The *Dáil Éireann* – Assembly of Ireland – have officially met in the Mansion House in Dublin where they announced a unilateral declaration of Irish independence…"

"And on the very day when the Dáil sat for the first time, the IRA shot and killed two policemen in Tipperary," Patrick retorted. "You can dress up a rebel in respectable clothes and give him a seat in government, but he's still a killer, Danny. Do you really want to hang your future on the same line as the assassins roaming the country, collecting weapons and killing representatives of the crown?"

"We're not assassins. We are a legal organisation with the Irish vote behind us. According to Jimmy Carson, there were tens of thousands of people on the streets of Dublin celebrating our win. We're on our path to freedom, and if on that path we have to kill some traitors, so be it."

Danny glared at the others, but then he appeared more bemused than angry at their attitudes. "What's up with the lot of you? We're all Irish here," he said. "Do you not want to break the British yoke around our necks?"

"Not with violence. We had enough bloodshed in the war. I'm surprised you want to stomach more of it," Kevin grumbled.

"Oh, shut up, Kevin. You're a bloody loyalist through and through. I'm not listening to anything you have to say –"

Patrick butted in, saying, "That's enough of the cheek. It's because of Kevin's bravery that you're not in a grave on the Somme."

"And you'll never let me forget it, will you, Patrick?"

Hurt crossed Kevin's face. He'd been nothing but good to Danny, Jenny thought, but her husband wasn't a saint, and he looked set to lose his good humour. "Why don't you go into the living room and put your feet up," she suggested.

"I'm part of this family, Jenny. I'm staying," Kevin answered with an unusually stern tone.

Patrick was biting his tongue, but Jenny knew that look of his; where he was struggling to control his temper, but if it came out, he'd go through Danny like a dose of salts and put him on the ground with his fists. She wanted to throttle her younger brother for the havoc he was causing. His behaviour stemmed from grief, but she couldn't stand him when he was in one of his self-pitying and rebellious moods.

In the tense silence that followed, Danny sniggered as he glared at the others one by one. "Look at the three of you standing there, ganging up on me and wondering what else you can say to make me look small. You'll not be so high and mighty when I'm proved right about our independence, will you? Oh no, you'll be thanking the likes of me who had the balls to fight – what, nothing else to say, Patrick? What about you, Jenny? Are you not going to stick up for your Protestant husband?"

"Don't you dare bring religion into this!" Jenny finally found her voice but was then surprised when Danny laughed in her face.

"You're delusional, you always have been when it comes to romance. You thought John Grant was a fine upstanding fellow until you found out he was a Republican rebel. Are you still stupid enough to think your husband's uppity parents will accept a Fenian into their family?"

"That's enough. We're not here to talk about my parents," Kevin warned Danny.

"It's enough when I say I'm done speaking. It's about time you told my sister the truth, Kevin Jackson."

"Danny, I'm warning you, let it go," Patrick said, gripping Danny's jacket sleeve.

"Get off me," Danny hissed, as he jerked Patrick's arm off him. Then he ogled Jenny with victorious eyes. "Well, do you want to know or not?"

Jenny got off the chair to stand and face him with an outward bravado she didn't feel. This moment reminded her of the dinner the family had the day after her father was killed. Danny had come out with the stunning revelation about her then fiancé, John Grant. She wanted to cover her ears now, so she didn't have to listen to what he had to say about her husband. If it were something horrid, she'd die! She stared at Kevin who bowed his head. He had delayed her meeting with his family on two occasions. He'd told her who they were, but only after she'd accused him of being ashamed of her. Some of what Danny was saying had a ring of truth to it. Why else would Kevin not let her see letters from his mother or tell her what the Jacksons truly thought about his marriage?

"Kevin has told me all about his mother and father," she finally responded to Danny. "I know his father is a Lord and his mother is the Earl of Cork's cousin. I also know they're wealthy and own more land in the County of Cork than the Earl does. There's nothing you can say that will be news to me."

Danny nodded pensively, then said, "How about if I told you that Lord Clifford Jackson is a member of the British Parliament in the House of Lords, and that he voted against all the bills that would give the Irish more autonomy. Did your husband tell you that his father also expelled his Catholic tenants after the Easter uprising?"

"That's enough, Danny!" Patrick shouted, as he too got to his feet.

"It's the truth!"

Jenny, both embarrassed and angry with Kevin for not telling her that significant detail, felt her enthusiasm for the upcoming first meeting with Kevin's family wane. She had decided on her wedding day not to make their differing religious or political views an issue between them. She put the question of a Protestant church blessing for their marriage or a full-blown Catholic mass with communion on hold until she met his family in person. That event had seemed a long way off at the time of their civil ceremony in central London. "What has this got to do with Kevin? He's not his father any more than you were yours."

Danny seemed pleased with himself for bringing his sister close to tears. Now, he tittered to himself as his eyes narrowed with contempt. "You two think you have it all, don't you? Here you stand, Jenny, with a baby coming and the perfect husband by your side. Sure, you've got the good life of a doctor's wife to look forward to, and plenty of money in the bank to buy your pretty party dresses. You're so bloody fortunate you need to be careful you don't trip over your own giddy steps. Oh yes, you've got it all, and I'm betting you haven't given a single thought to your poor sister-in-law's death or about my broken heart and broken dreams."

"There it is. I wondered how long it'd take you." Jenny began to cry in earnest. "I loved Anna…"

"Oh, did you now? Well, that's news to me. She used to tell me in her letters how you looked down your nose at her … thought you were better off ... treated her like she was *shant* from an old tenement."

Kevin opened his mouth to speak, but Jenny threw him a vicious look that might kill a lesser man. "No Kevin, you'll not be saying what's on my mind. He's lying. I can tell by that shifty look in his eyes. The truth is, Anna was too bloody good for my brother."

"That she was. I'll not deny it," Danny agreed, putting his hands up in surrender. "But what I said about you is the truth. You're a snob, Jenny. You're looking down your nose at me right now and you don't even know you're doing it."

"You're a cruel bastard, Danny," Patrick, who had allowed his siblings to vent their anger, finally lost his temper. "If you're going, get upstairs now and pack your bags. We don't want you here – go on, get out!

Kevin added, "He'd better go. If he doesn't, I'll not be responsible for my actions.

Danny sniggered, undaunted by Kevin's veiled threat. "What are you going to do to me, Kevin … call for your brother in the RIC to evict me?"

"What are you talking about? Who's in the RIC?" Jenny demanded to know.

Danny spat at Kevin, "You didn't tell my sister that your brother, Charlie, is an officer in the Royal Irish Constabulary, did you? He's a loyalist, Jenny, just like his father. He and his fellow officers torture and kill Irish Catholics for a living. The feckin' traitor serves the crown…"

Jenny and Patrick gasped when Kevin's open palm slammed into Danny's cheek. Danny staggered backwards but quickly regained his composure. Red in the face, he disregarded Kevin and Patrick, and instead informed Jenny, "Just so you know, anyone who stands in the way of Irish independence will be severely dealt with, including Charlie Jackson. It's time for you to choose a side, Jenny. And know you'll be no sister of mine if you convert to your husband's Protestant religion. I swear to God Almighty, if you do that, I'll have nothing to do with you or your child. You'll be dead to me. You hear me, Jenny? Dead to me."

Danny, with tears that spoke more of grief than anger, brushed past Kevin and Jenny on his way out. Then he took to the stairs, two at a time, muttering something they couldn't hear.

Jenny choked on a sob as she rushed into Kevin's arms. Disgusted and shocked by her brother's seditious talk, she uttered, "Please don't follow him, either of you. I've had enough."

As Jenny snuggled into her husband's chest, Patrick swept by them on his way out of the kitchen. He was probably going to the porch to smoke a cigarette and calm down. "We're better off out of it," she mumbled into Kevin's thumping chest. "Let him get his suitcase and leave this house. We can meet him on Thursday at the bank in Dublin to sort out the money, and afterwards I'll be happy if I never see him again." She gazed up at Kevin; her eyes enraged, threatening as she added, "My unborn child will *not* hear Danny's hatred and bigotry. I will keep him or her away from him, and even Patrick will respect my wishes on this." Then she continued with another threat, this one for her husband. "Our child will *not* be a pawn in a religious feud between your family and mine. It will be Catholic, and that is the end of it."

"Let's not worry about that now, darlin'," Kevin responded with a tender smile.

Chapter Nineteen

End of January 1919

Dublin, Ireland

"I slept better last night than I have in years, Jimmy. I mean it," Danny said, cupping a hot enamel mug of tea.

"God bless you if you think lying on my floor on an old ground sheet with an overcoat to wrap you was comfortable. I hate to think where you've lain your head these past two years," Jimmy Carson grunted, as he looked at the damp, mildewed walls and splintered wooden window frames.

Danny casually viewed the room, careful to keep the disgust from showing on his face. Jimmy's tenement block was like all the others the man had lived in for most of his adult life, but this was the smallest. Since he was a bachelor, they'd allocated him one room, big enough to house an open fire with a hook to hang a kettle or cauldron on and for cooking the stews he loved so much. That, a small table for storage and eating meals, a chair, a stool, and a narrow bed not quite long enough for Jimmy's tall frame was all the room consisted of. He shared a communal kitchen-*cum*-laundry house and outside closet accommodation with too many people to count.

Jimmy had joked the previous night that they had to swim to the privy in wintertime. 'You know how it is, Danny. After heavy rain, the backyard turns to mud then becomes a pond, and in late winter the bloody lot freezes over and no one has the guts to sit on the loo and shit there. Apart from that, our outside toilet is a 'tippler', and when it tipples, it comes with a roar of rushing water that scares the living daylights out of any poor bugger who happens to be sitting on it. To be honest with you, I use a piss-pot most of the time and throw the contents out the window when no one's looking.'

Danny had been holding his 'morning constitution.' He wasn't above using the outside toilet – he'd shat in worse places, but he wasn't keen on the sanitary methods here, and would rather wait for a better venue. 'Our bog doesn't flush,' Jimmy had informed Danny when the latter had asked to use it. 'It's an old cinders bog, I'm afraid. We pile ash on top of what we pass as solids, and the night soil man collects the waste for manure on local farms. Sure, we've got a bit of a problem with worms and lice, but not much we can do about those.'

The place was a dump, Danny thought, but no man liked to hear he lived in one, even if he thought as much himself.

"Ah, but it was heaven knowing that the floor I slept on was under a ceiling that was under an Irish sky. That's what counts, Jimmy. It's grand to be home at last," Danny assured his friend.

Still frowning and looking around the room, Jimmy said, "Away with ye. This is even worse than the place I rented before I went to work in the countryside. Do you recall that one?"

"I do, Jimmy. How could I forget the last time we were in it together? Jesus, the trouble we got ourselves into that day."

Jimmy chuckled. "I curse that old tannery every time I pass it by. It wasn't one of your better ideas, Danny."

"Have you seen Donal Doyle since then?"

"Not since they arrested him with Éamon de Valera and the rest of them. Far as I know, he's still in Brixton Prison over in London."

By mid-afternoon on that rainy Wednesday in Dublin, Danny sat on a squeaky, rickety wooden chair at Jimmy Carson's table, slightly hungover from the night before when he and Jimmy had polished off a bottle of Irish whiskey in the wee hours of the morning. Jimmy had bought it especially for Danny's homecoming.

The two men had talked all night, but Danny had skirted any mention of the war. He didn't think he'd ever be able to speak of it. No one, not even in their wildest imaginings, could picture correctly the horror of it if they hadn't seen it for themselves. And he didn't want to describe it to anyone, not even to Jimmy, who knew all his secrets and lies, including the depth of his sorrow for Anna. He'd been the only person from Ireland to write to him throughout the conflict, the only Irish Volunteer from the Easter Uprising to remember him.

He now asked Jimmy, "What time should we leave for the meeting?"

"In about an hour."

"Ah, Jimmy, I can't tell you how much I'm looking forward to seeing all my pals from Frongoch. Now, you're certain Michael will be there?"

"He said he would be, and when Michael Collins gives his word, you can believe it's true."

Jimmy fell silent. Danny, gulping down the hot tea, felt it warm his insides. He looked at the grate with the blackened remains of last night's fire. The room had seemed cosy during the night, for Jimmy had kept the flames going with some coal he'd nicked and a bit of kindling. Strange, how different the atmosphere in a room could be in the cold light of morning with a dead fire and the cloth for curtains opened to reveal the bare brick wall of a neighbouring tenement, so close he could almost stretch out his hand and touch it.

He looked at Jimmy, who'd taken the day off work. He was still the same shaggy-bearded, long-haired, ruddy-faced man who'd left captivity in Frongoch, Wales, promising to continue the fight, but he had a tiredness about him now that made him look worn out. "When I get my inheritance on Thursday, Jimmy, I'm going to buy a house. I can afford a detached property with three or four bedrooms, I reckon. I'd like to offer you a room there. You can have the run of the place, and I'll make sure the rent is the same as you're paying for this dump. What do you think?"

Jimmy's eyes widened with excitement. "Do you mean it, Danny?"

"I do."

"Then I accept. You'll make sure it's in the city centre, will you not?"

Danny frowned. "I don't know about that; I'll get a bigger property in the suburbs. Come to think of it, living away from the city centre isn't a bad idea. Could be a good bolt hole for when the Metropolitan Police or British Army are sniffing about – might even be able to use it as a safe house – you know, for when the real fighting begins."

Jimmy got up. He looked uncomfortable, turning his back on Danny as he went to the old chipped wash basin and enamel water jug on the table to swill his face. When he'd done that, he dried it on his shirt tails.

"What's up? You don't think it's a good idea?" Danny called out.

Jimmy turned, tucking the damp tails of his shirt in his unbuttoned trousers as he moved. "Aw, Danny, I should have told you this last night. You see, when I told Michael Collins and the others you were coming back to join us, they were surprised … you know … about your dubious past. They thought..."

"My dubious past?" Danny said, as Jimmy sat on the stool.

"Yes. We've uncovered a few British spies, you see. They've been dealt with, but the IRA are concerned about infiltrators, and what with you winning a medal in France and wearing a British uniform and serving the crown in the war as a sergeant no less, they worry…

"Who worries, exactly?" Danny's heart was thumping furiously, which aptly described his mood. "Well, Jimmy? Who's worried about me?"

"That'd be John Grant, for a start, and his da, of course. That pair of backstabbers never do or say anything on their own. It's always a double whammy with the Grants."

Danny instinctively clenched his fists at the mention of John Grant's name. "You know, I've always felt he and I still have accounts to settle."

"What like?"

"I don't know, but if I make a fist every time his name is mentioned it's because I still want to punch his head in. Tell me what the bastard said about me?"

"He and his da' have been spreading rumours. They're saying you changed when you got to London … that you started to feel a certain loyalty to the British after your sister was bombed. John told Michael Collins you even got a job in London making ammunition that would be used against the Irish, eventually."

"Are you feckin' kidding me?" Danny leapt to his feet, raging that his good name and loyalty to Ireland were being questioned, and that lies were spreading all the way up to the top of the IRA chain of command. "Do *you* think I might be an agent of the crown, Jimmy?"

"No, I don't, ye daft bugger, but you know the Grants. I told you a long time ago not to get on John's bad side. He and his da are throwing money at the organisation and they hold a lot of sway. You've always known that."

Danny, still hurt, on the warpath, and ready to tear John Grant limb from limb, croaked, "The very thought of me betraying the Irish cause makes me feel sick to my stomach … for him … for that bastard to even suggest…" Danny shut up, and his lips set in a tight line as his mind played a tune of murder. "Right, that's it, we're going. I'm not waiting a minute longer. I want to see Michael Collins and the rest of them, now, right now. The sooner I get this cleared up, the sooner I can prove my loyalty."

******

He wasn't happy about it, but Jimmy eventually agreed to take Danny to the house the IRA had bought and was using to conduct their new ministerial duties. Most of the Dáil Ministry existed only on paper or as one or two people working in a room of a private house. Given the circumstances of the brutal murders of a pair of Royal Irish Constabulary officers, Republican ministers were liable to be arrested or killed at a moment's notice by the Royal Irish Constabulary or the Dublin Metropolitan Police, known as the DMP.

Jimmy had told Danny that the killings perpetrated on the day the Dáil had convened its first official meeting at Mansion House in Dublin, had been carried out by IRA volunteers from the 3rd Tipperary Brigade, but he'd not gone as far as to mention their names. Evidently, Jimmy didn't trust him enough to give away their identities.

As Jimmy recalled, the four men had attacked the RIC officers who were escorting a consignment of gelignite headed to the quarry in Soloheadbeg, County Tipperary. Jimmy was adamant that the two policemen were not targets for assassination, but rather in the wrong place at the wrong time when they were shot dead during the engagement. It was, Jimmy had added, the first shots fired in what was going to be a war of attrition until victory was claimed by the Irish independence movement and the British were routed from their Emerald Isle.

Two men were standing in front of a parked motorcar at the entrance to the street where Michael Collins lived. The vehicle's bonnet was up, and the men were trying to look busy fixing whatever was apparently broken, while glancing furtively around. There was nothing that needed fixing, Danny surmised. They were IRA lookouts.

Jimmy nodded to the two men, then he and Danny walked along the street, passing a row of terraced houses before coming to three detached properties. Further on, at the corner of the street, another two men leant nonchalantly against the wall next to the grocer's shop window.

"He's got four in the street, and I noticed two more behind the curtains of one of the terraced houses," Danny said; the *he,* referring to Michael Collins. "I'm used to keeping my eyes peeled, and I can tell ye, Jimmy, they're as inconspicuous as elephants walking down Sackville Street."

Once they'd gained entry to the fancy detached house, Jimmy introduced Danny to the man posted in the entrance hallway. Then he ordered Danny to wait there until he was called.

Danny was nervous. He knew Michael Collins as well as any man in the organisation could. His bunk had been directly opposite his own in Frongoch Prison Camp. They'd spoken at length many times. Danny had told him about his love for Anna, who'd worked in the shop at the time. He'd explained how his da had died in a Dublin street. He'd assured Michael that he was prepared to continue the fight for Ireland even if it meant his execution, yet he felt now as if he were a stranger being vetted, as if his contribution to the Easter Uprising had counted for nothing.

Minutes later, Jimmy returned and said, "You're in luck, Michael will see you now. Make your best case, Danny."

Chapter Twenty

Danny hesitated at the doorway to Michael Collins' office. The spacious former living room was full of men; at least ten of them standing before Michael who sat behind a bulky oak desk stacked with documents and loose sheets of paper. The men parted to give Danny an aisle in which to approach the great man; Danny's hero – his mentor.

"Well, well, Danny Carmody has come home from the war," Michael Collins said, looking Danny over.

Danny turned to his left in response to someone's loud snigger. John Grant and his father stood side by side throwing him dirty looks. Danny, hiding his anger, turned his gaze on Michael. "I've come home to Ireland for good, Michael. I'm ready to join one of your brigades and get stuck into doing whatever it is you ask of me. You'll not forget my willingness to fight on Easter Monday, will you?"

John Grant sniggered again, but this time Michael raised his hand to silence him. "If you can't show respect to a fellow Irishman in this room, John, I'll ask you to leave. Danny has offered his services, and I mean to hear him out." Michael flicked his all-seeing eyes back to Danny and said, "It was good of you to enlist. How *was* the British Army?"

"I'll not lie, it was hell. And just so we're straight, I didn't enlist. I was shunted into uniform by the police after I beat the shite out of a thief molesting my sister. It was the army or back to prison for me." He looked at the men in the room and noted their surprised expressions.

"Then you didn't volunteer?" Michael asked, flicking his eyes to John Grant.

"Certainly not." Danny spun around to John. "Is that not the way *you* told the story?" he asked feigning surprise.

The room fell silent until Michael spoke again, "I heard you won the military medal for bravery."

"That's right, and I threw it from the train into a field on the way back to London. They can shove it up their arses. The only medal I want is one that says Republic of Ireland on it." That was a lie. The medal was in Greenwich, at Minnie's house. She'd already got it in a glass case on her mantelpiece.

"What was your job in the army?"

Again, Danny perused the men surrounding him. This felt more like a trial than a welcome home party. It was nerve wracking and insulting. "I was an infantryman and a sniper – are you going to have me, Michael, or is this a bloody court case?" he asked, revealing his ire.

Michael nodded slowly, as though he were still thinking about what answer to give even as he gave it with the affirmative bob of his head. "All of you take a break. I'd like a word in private with Danny," he told the men present.

When the group of men left, leaving Michael and Danny alone, the former asked Danny to sit. "We'll take you back, Danny, but a lot has changed since the last time we rose. We're not going to fight this war with guns blazing like we did in the '16 uprising. This time we're waging a war of intelligence against the British until we wear them down."

"When you say, wear them down, does that mean peaceably or with a certain amount of violent persuasion attached? I ask because Jimmy said the deaths of the two RIC men at Tipperary were accidental. It leaves me wondering if we can win a war against the British without intentional use of force. They'll kill us quick enough."

Danny saw Michael's hesitancy, and it stung him. "Look, Michael. John Grant and I have history together over the way he treated my sister. The last time I saw him in London, I punched him to the ground in the middle of a busy street and then abandoned him while he was cryin' broke and beggin' for fare to get back to his daddy. You know I'm loyal to you and Ireland. If you didn't, I'd already be at the back of this building with a bullet in my skull. Now, I'm here offering to join you, just as I promised you I would when we were in Wales, but Michael, I need to know what I'm getting myself into, and you need to trust me or throw me out on my ear. I won't dance this jig with you."

Michael regarded Danny a moment longer, then committed himself. His words both thrilled Danny and scared him, for they were candid, which made them dangerous. Michael was conveying information that could never be un-heard.

"The RIC officers' deaths in Tipperary were no accidents. The only way to start a war, Danny, is to kill someone, and that includes anyone belonging to the foremost and most important branch of the enemy forces. We want to start a war, so the day we held our first Dáil, I sent men to steal weapons and to kill as many policemen as they could. My only regret since that ambush is that there were only two policemen involved, instead of the six we had expected."

Danny still wasn't sure if he would leave Michael's house with his head and reputation intact. He swallowed, wishing he had a bucket of water next to him to douse his burning skin. They had put men in the ground for less startling evidence of violence than he'd just received from the head of the IRA. "I see. I like the way you think, Michael … show the bastards who we are," was all he could manage.

"It's all about stealth this time," Michael began again, equally candid. "Getting in and out, quietly, efficiently, and without loss of Irish lives where possible, is key to our operations. We have spies but so do the British, and they're using them to their advantage. Before the Dáil's first meeting at Mansion House, moles in my network tipped me of plans to arrest our members in overnight raids. Éamon de Valera, and others in his circle, ignored the warnings. They thought if such a thing happened, it would be a propaganda coup. They thought in terms of politics and how the optics of such actions would play out. Well, our intelligence proved accurate and de Valera, along with Sinn Féin MPs who followed his advice, were arrested. They're still in prison in Brixton, and I'm sitting here waiting for the British to throw more trickery at us so I can throw it back at them."

Danny was pensive, and as he listened to Michael's smooth-talking tongue in action, he thought, *He's giving me straight talk from the heart. This is a good sign.*

"Jimmy Carson tells me your sister has married a member of the Jackson family from Cork?" Michael now said.

"That's right, it's Kevin Jackson."

"You know his father is Lord Jackson, a leading Protestant who has strong political ties with the British government. He advocates for heavy-handed responses to any Irish rebellion, whether peaceful or through violence. He hates us Fenians."

Danny took care not to blurt out a defence or explanation of how Jenny and Kevin ended up together; instead, his response must be honest and to the point. "I know all that, but Kevin is a decent man. He's good to my sister and granny, and he's not involved in politics. He's a Doctor of Medicine and is still serving in the British Army. He's bringing my sister over on the boat tonight. We've got family business in Dublin to attend to tomorrow, and afterwards we're going to Lord Jackson's estate in Cork. Kevin's family haven't met my Jenny yet, and they've invited us all to stay for a couple of days."

Danny leant forward and clasped his hands atop the desk. You've been honest with me, Michael, so I'm doing you the same courtesy…"

"I appreciate that, Danny."

"The way I see it, who my sister marries is none of the IRA's business, and even if it were, I guarantee you, Kevin Jackson cares most for two things … healing people and my sister. Fighting Republicans doesn't even get a look in." Danny stopped talking, but then added for good measure, "I'm here today because of him. He saved my life at the Somme and got me home to my Anna."

Michael lit a cigarette. Danny also got his packet of Woodbines out, lifted the flap, and gave it a nervous shake until he got hold of a cigarette. He stuck it between his lips and then lit it with his German trench lighter.

"Can I see that?" Michael asked, gesturing to the lighter.

Danny handed it over, and as a fine gesture, said, "Keep it. A gift from me to you from the trenches."

Michael was quiet as he flicked the lighter's lid up and down, up and down. Danny was uncomfortable during the ensuing silence, apart from the sound of the metal lid making a grating clicking noise. He wondered if Michael were thinking about Kevin or had turned his thoughts closer to home? His silence didn't bode well. Had Jimmy Carson related the whole conversation from the previous night to Michael and the group of men who'd been in the office when he and Jimmy had arrived? His tongue was quick enough to ramble away in the space of time it took him to get back to the hallway. That was Jimmy to a tee; more loyal to the Republic than he was to one of his best friends.

"I was sorry to hear about your Anna," Michael eventually said. "She was a good girl. I remember going to the shop after they released you. She told me she missed you, kept asking me if I'd received any letters from you. Ah, sure love for you shone in that girl's eyes, Danny."

"It was her da's fault she didn't get my letters. He never passed them on to her." Danny's eyes welled up; hearing that Anna had missed him when he'd left Frongoch was both sad and wonderful. "Ah, Michael, she was the best thing that ever happened to me." He sniffed, but continued, "It was fast … so bleedin' fast … coughing in the morning and dead that same night." Danny sucked in the smoke from his cigarette, then blew it out hard along with a sobbing breath.

Michael cleared his throat, and looking uncomfortable, pointed to Danny's gloved right hand. "I take it that's a war wound?" he asked.

"Yes. I'll show you where the bullet hit." *Michael wants to change the subject. Good,* Danny thought. He wasn't keen on talking about Anna. His feelings were still too raw to mention her name without blubbering.

As he gingerly pulled the glove off by the fingers, Danny said, "It still hurts come the end of the day. The skin is red, and it burns then itches like hell sometimes."

The skin surrounding his scarred palm, pinkie, and the finger next to it looked like frayed tissue paper, and the centre of his open palm displayed the damage done by the German bullet. Michael stared at it in silence as Danny turned his hand over to display the closed wound on the back of it. "See, went right through my palm."

"Jesus Christ – excuse the pun, but it looks like you've got the stigmata," Michael joked.

"It's ugly, right enough, but at least I've still got five fingers and a bit of feeling back in them. The whole thing was numb for weeks."

"Can you hold a gun and shoot with it?"

"I can, and my aim's as good as ever."

"Right then, put your glove back on for now, but when you I call on you, you'll do the job wearing a pair of leather gloves. The enemy looks for recognisable traits to help them identify us. T'would be a surprise if your mugshot's not already on the Peelers' walls at Dublin Castle."

Danny hadn't thought about the glove being an impediment in that regard, but what Michael said made sense. "You're right. I'll see to that today."

Michael stood, calling an end to the meeting, but as the two men shook hands, Danny was in the dark about what his job might entail. Although the conversation had gone well to his mind, it had not been enlightening. "Who do I report to?" he asked.

"Richard Mulcahy."

"Is that the Mulcahy who was in Frongoch with us?"

"The very one. He's a good man; they released him same day as me and he re-joined the Republican movement before he stepped out of the gate. He's now the Commandant of the Dublin Brigade of the Irish Volunteers *and* our assistant Minister for Defence. Jimmy Carson will take you to him."

Danny let out a sigh of relief. He was in the game. "Right you are, and thank you, Michael. It's good to be back."

"One thing more before you go, Danny."

"Sure, then."

"The threat a person poses to us determines who we target for death. I'll pass the word not to touch your brother-in-law, the doctor, but his father and brother are fair game, understand?"

"Yes."

"Good, because this is a war where an enemy is an enemy – period. It's not personal. We will target whoever poses a threat to this organisation or person serving in it, and that includes people we might be fond of."

"I understand, Michael." Danny said, and he did.

"Send Jimmy in, there's a good lad."

After Danny left the room, he sat in a chair in the hallway to wait for Jimmy who'd gone back into the office to have a further word with Michael. He had a lot to think about, but his eyes kept drifting to Michael's men – including John Grant and his father – lounging in chairs and couches in a spacious room opposite him. A woman was serving them tea, and a rousing debate was going on. The door being open allowed Danny to shoot daggers at John Grant. Danny's expression said, *I'll have my revenge, ye lying sack of shite,* while John's replied, *Try it, Carmody.*

When Jimmy went back into Michael's office, the latter gestured to Jimmy to close the door, then said, "I want you to stick close to Danny for the next few weeks. Let me know where he goes today, who he talks to, and what he tells you in private. If he has any British sympathies, I want to know about them."

"Aw, c'mon, Michael, you can't think Danny's a spy?"

"I'll think what I bloody like!" Michael retorted.

"Well, I don't. He's as keen now as he ever was. And to be fair, tens of thousands of Irishmen fought and lost their lives for the British in the Continent. I wouldn't hold that against him, and neither should you. It's John Grant we should be minding. He likes stirring things up for the Carmody family, and if he does it to them, he'll do it others. I think he wants your job, or near as damn it."

Michael's tone softened, "Your loyalty to young Carmody does you proud, Jimmy, but don't let it cloud your judgement. Jenny Carmody has just married a Jackson, and I'll be monitoring her and her husband as well. I don't think Danny sees the bigger picture yet, but he will. Give me an hour before you take him to Mulcahy. I want to speak to Richard before Danny sees him."

Jimmy nodded. "You've got it, Michael. I know what to do."

Chapter Twenty-One

End of January 1919

Lord Jackson's driver drove the Rolls Royce Silver Ghost along the beautiful winding country lanes of County Cork at a sedate pace, as though savouring every bend in the road and every tree, shrub and field he passed. Jenny sat in the back seat of the posh motorcar, holding Patrick's hand whilst thinking about her other brother sitting in the front with the driver. Danny's decision not to return to London hadn't shocked her, but she was surprised he didn't want to return to Greenwich to pick up his and Anna's belongings. 'You sort through Anna's stuff, Jenny. You'll know what to do with her clothes and the like,' he had said when he left the rotten job to her.

"I'm glad we got yesterday's business out the way. Have you decided where you'll buy your house?" Jenny asked Patrick.

"Not yet, but I fancy myself in a cottage. When I eventually start working, I'll be staying in digs near to the college, so when I'm off it'd be nice to get to the country for some fresh air."

"You're old before your time, Patrick," Danny called over his shoulder. "You should live in the centre of Dublin, so you can find yourself a good woman."

Patrick patted the back of Jenny's hand, and ignoring Danny's comments, said, "You're looking peaky, darlin'. It was a tiring day for you yesterday, so don't overdo it today."

"I won't, Patrick. It was the arguing with Danny in the restaurant yesterday that took it out of me," Jenny said, loudly enough for Danny to hear.

"Didn't our father say sarcasm is no alternative to wit, Jenny?" Danny reminded her without turning in his seat.

She and Danny had called a truce the previous day, but he had tired her out, nonetheless. First, she and her brothers had gone to the bank, then a lunch that had been tense with disagreements over Danny's house-hunting preferences and future ambitions being at the core of matters. The siblings hadn't spoken about their row in London, but it was clear to both Patrick and her that their young, impetuous brother was getting involved in the murky world of politics and rebellion, and nothing they could say would change his mind.

She looked at the back of Danny's head. He was wearing a peaked cap, an overcoat he'd purchased five minutes after leaving the bank, and a silk scarf around his neck. She let out a nervous sigh. If his good behaviour on this visit matched his respectable clothes, they'd be all right.

"How are you feeling?" Patrick asked Jenny again.

"I'm nervous and excited. I miss Kevin…"

Danny laughed, "Aw, for God's sake, Jenny, it's only been twenty-four hours."

"That might be so, but I'm pregnant and feeling fragile. Maybe if you'd stop your sniping, I could relax enough to enjoy this holiday."

"Well, excuse me if I'm not as excited as you two about things. I'm barely getting through the days."

Jenny was annoyed with herself. Danny was suffering, and she was not being sympathetic; instead, she was trying desperately to put Anna to the back of her mind, as he was apparently doing. Anna would've slapped him over the head by now for his petty behaviour. "I know this is hard for you, Danny. Take no notice of me. I'm nervous about meeting Kevin's parents. What if they don't like me?"

"What's not to like?" Danny retorted. "Your father was one of Britain's finest surgeons, and you're as good as any woman the Jacksons might have chosen for Kevin. They're lucky to have you." Danny gave the driver a sly, sideways glance, then added. "Sure, I hear they're nice people."

Surprised and delighted by Danny's rare compliment, Jenny said, "Thank you for saying that." Then she asked Patrick, "Do you think Lady Jackson and Minnie are getting along?"

"I think Minnie's probably been lapping up the luxury of her surroundings," Patrick smiled. "They'll be fine. Lady Jackson is nice enough once you get to know her."

It had been Kevin's idea to take Minnie with him to the estate a day early. It was a good idea, Jenny thought. Their granny had nothing to do with the proceedings at the bank, and she'd have found it tiring to walk around Dublin. The only parts of Minnie's body that still worked well were her brain, her tongue, and her eyes.

Jenny gasped as the chimney stacks and roof of the Jackson's stately home rose above the treetops in the distance. "Will you look at it, Patrick? It's as big as Buckingham Palace."

"That's a slight exaggeration," Patrick chuckled.

Jenny, still overawed, said, "Why did you not tell me it was as grand as this?"

Danny turned in the front seat, and sneered, "That was Kevin's job, not Patrick's. And what's grand about it? This is the twentieth century. Why would one family want to live in a cold draft-filled place that size if not for their Protestant Anglo-Irish egos? Give me a small, cosy house any day of the week."

The motorcar came to a shuddering stop outside the front entrance. A row of servants to the right of the open double doors stood to attention in their crisp black and white uniforms. They kept their eyes front, as if they'd been told not to look directly at the guests. To the left of the doors stood Kevin, and beside him an older man and woman who stared at the car with the same benign expressions as the statues on the porch.

Two footmen came forward to open each of the vehicle's passenger doors. Jenny's stomach was growing rounder by the day, and she had difficulty getting in and out of Kevin's motorcar – not this one, though. The Rolls Royce had a wide door and, although high off the ground, there was a step to help her descend. She thanked the footman for holding the door open and then met Kevin in an embrace. "One day, and I was going mad without you, darlin'," she whispered before their brief kiss on the lips.

"I felt the same." Kevin smiled tenderly as he drew away. Then he greeted Danny and Patrick. "Well, this is it," he said, taking Jenny's hand in his own before escorting her to his parents.

"Mother, Father, this is my beloved wife, Jenny."

Although dwarfed by her husband and son's statures, Matilda Jackson towered above Jenny. Her long thin face was aristocratic, yet attractive. It held a mixture of curiosity, but then changed to one of repugnance as she scrutinised her daughter-in-law's scarred eye and crinkled skin where her ear used to be. *Typical,* Jenny thought, *that the wind should pick up and blow my hair back from my damaged eye and ear at this crucial time.*

"I'm pleased to meet you, Jenny. You look tired after your long journey," Lady Jackson said, her cool tone not matching her warm words.

"She doesn't look tired at all, Mother. She looks splendid, as always," Kevin quipped.

Next, Kevin introduced her to his father, who looked remarkably like his son apart from an abundance of wrinkles around his eyes and a mouth bare of moustache and beard.

"I'm pleased to finally meet you, Miss Carmody," Clifford Jackson said after a long perusal.

"It's Mrs Jackson," Danny informed him, and then came to stand beside his sister.

Jenny noticed Kevin and Patrick's worried glances at Danny, but in this case, she agreed with her younger brother. "It's nice to meet you, too, Lord Jackson. And Danny's right, I'm now Mrs Jackson. It says so on my marriage certificate, my bank account, and identity papers," she said with her sweetest smile.

"Yes, well, I suppose I must get used to calling you that. Perhaps when you and Kevin marry properly in the eyes of the church and before God, I'll feel more comfortable using your married name," said Lord Jackson. He had a 'public school accent,' not a hint of Irish brogue.

The Jacksons' open hostility when Kevin formally introduced Danny to their hosts struck Jenny. They did not conceal their distaste under a layer of etiquette or behind welcoming words; it was laid bare in their narrowed eyes that gazed down at her brother from an invisible perch of condemnation.

"You're the soldier, the NCO?" Lord Jackson asked, though he already knew the answer.

"Not anymore," Danny responded with an uncustomary politeness in his voice. "I served the king, as was my duty, but that's all behind me now."

The Jacksons quickly moved on to Patrick, surprising Jenny with their affectionate embraces with him. "A naval officer, what," Lord Jackson said proudly. "It's good to see you, my boy."

"And you too, sir – Lady Jackson, you look as lovely as ever."

"Oh, please, Patrick," Kevin's mother preened at Patrick's compliment. "Your grandmother is inside. Why don't we all go in? Tea is being served in the drawing room."

"Tea is being served in the drawing room," Danny mimicked in a toff's voice behind Jenny.

"Shut up, Danny" Jenny hissed over her shoulder, as she stepped back onto his toe.

******

That evening, Lady Jackson sent a lady's maid to help dress Jenny. When the girl had finished, Jenny stared at herself in the dressing-table mirror. Her hair was perfect; wavy, not curly, shaped strategically so it fell across part of her eyes and covered her damaged ear. Angela, the lady's maid, had even applied rouge to Jenny's face and lips and had highlighted her eyes with a black kohl pencil.

Jenny thought, *this is a far cry from my lifestyle in London*, but it was also daunting. Years ago, her mother had employed a personal maid, but the woman was engaged as a companion rather than for any service she could provide. It had been a waste of money, for being served hand and foot had not brought Susan Carmody happiness. Only Robert, her darling, flamboyant, and often absent husband could light his wife's doe eyes and blush her cheeks.

Strange, Jenny thought, peering at her reflection. She was not feeling a rush of satisfaction. In her youth, her ambition was to have a house full of servants, a wardrobe filled with the latest Parisian fashions, and a doting husband at her beck and call; however, with all those luxuries now at her fingertips, she felt intimidated by her new family's opulent surroundings and by the Jacksons themselves. She wished for Kevin's small, cramped London apartment, and her part-time job at the hospital reading to the sick.

At the loud knock, she looked eagerly toward the door. "Come in," she called, presuming it was Kevin. He had his own set of rooms and would have to visit her bed, apparently. They'd both had a good laugh at the thought of them not sleeping together, but Matilda Jackson had been adamant that this was 'how it is done.'

Kevin entered. The maid, Angela, set the hairbrush down on the dressing table, and asked, "Will that be all, Madam?"

Jenny looked at her neck-length wavy hair, the ornamental silver hair comb twinkling halfway between her ear and her crown, and the intricate embroidery at the neckline of her new silver and red evening gown. She was the picture of a perfect fashionable society lady. "Thank you, Angela. You've done a grand job."

When Angela left, Jenny turned in her chair and smiled at Kevin. He looked like a stranger – entitled, handsome as any man she'd seen in upper-class magazines featuring people who moved in royal circles, but a stranger, nonetheless. "The last man I saw dressed as you are now was my father. We attended the Royal College of Surgeons' Christmas ball in Dublin the year before he died." She got up, crossed the room and went into his arms. "You look marvellous in white tie."

"And you are beautiful every day, my darling," Kevin said, then kissed her hard on the lips, properly smudging the rouge Angela had just applied.

She giggled as she reapplied her lipstick, and then she pulled on her silver elbow-length evening gloves, saying, "What a carry-on for dinner at home. I felt as if that maid was getting me ready for a royal function at the palace." She drew away, and then spun. "Will I do for your parents?"

"You would bedazzle a king in anything you wore."

"Hmm, I don't think your mother would agree. Her eyes went straight to my scars and my pregnant bump."

"Don't take any notice of Mother. She's warm and fuzzy on the inside, you'll see. She thinks you're delightful."

"Liar," Jenny said, picking up her cashmere evening shawl from the bed. "Sure, she was all over our Patrick, but don't stand there and tell me Danny or I delighted her. I've felt warmer blocks of ice on my face."

Kevin led Jenny to the four-poster bed and sat her down. He sat next to her and stroked her perfect hair, careful not to ruffle the coifed style. "Give them time, Jenny. The current political crisis has them on edge, and to be honest, Minnie didn't help the Carmodys' cause last night."

"Oh no, what did she say?"

"She told my parents how proud she was of Danny for getting his valour and gallantry medal, but then her tongue got the better of her, and she explained how he and Anna had met at Frongoch Prison Camp."

Jenny scoffed, "I shouldn't worry about that. Your father probably had us investigated the minute you married me. I don't think Minnie could say anything that would surprise him."

"When did you become this cynical creature?"

Jenny had decided before she even got there that she would fight Danny's corner, should the Jacksons disapprove of him without reason other than he was politically at odds with them. Her brother was all that he was and more, but he'd suffered terribly with war wounds and grief, and she'd not let the Jacksons disrespect him for that, not even if it put her out of her husband's good graces.

"I'm worried about Danny," Jenny mused aloud. "Maybe we shouldn't have brought him. He's oversensitive and gets moody at a drop of a hat, as well you know. He's all set on joining this new IRA, and I don't think he'll back down if your father or brother bring politics to the table. We may have made a terrible mistake including him in this weekend party."

"You mustn't worry. My parents would have made an excuse had they not wanted Danny in their house," Kevin said, not sounding convinced. "My family, including the earl, will have to get used to having Catholics in their midst. I am the heir to this estate, and my father could buy and sell the Earl of Cork's assets ten times over. The Jacksons are bankrolling my second cousin, and I'll be expected to carry on propping up the earl's coffers when I'm lord of this manor, as well as looking after my mother and brother," Kevin chuckled, continuing, "If they know what's good for them, they'll be especially nice to you, lest they witness my wrath and be locked in the tower."

Jenny laughed at Kevin's comical interpretation of a feudal lord. "Well, if you put it that way, my Danny has nothing to worry about, has he?"

Kevin stood, put his hand into his jacket pocket, and fished out a long, black velvet box. He opened it and showed her the contents, "I planned to give this to you before we left London, but then I thought you might like to wear it tonight with your new gown. My family is lucky to have you, Jenny Jackson, and they're blind if they can't see that."

That Kevin was wealthy was not a shock. Since their marriage, it had become plain that he could afford whatever she wanted for the small, modern apartment they'd made their home. But the truth about his family had come out of him like a slow-dripping tap. Patrick and Danny had left it to Kevin to tell her he was as wealthy as Croesus and would be even richer when he inherited his father's estate. While Jenny was happy not to be as poor as a stray dog in Battersea, she was not happy that he'd kept his family's secrets from her.

She beheld the diamond and ruby bracelet, breathless at its beauty. "I love it," she murmured.

Kevin took it out of its box and put it on Jenny's wrist. When he'd clicked the clasp into place, he said, "There, the finishing touch for a beautiful lady. You need not be anyone but your glorious self, my darling. You'll dazzle my family, as you dazzle me."

Chapter Twenty-Two

Danny eyed the group of people sitting in the high-backed chairs around the Regency period, oval mahogany dining table. Lord Jackson sat at the head of it, nearest the door. Lady Jackson was at the other end. The new arrival, Kevin's brother, Charlie, sat on his father's left, opposite Minnie who looked queenly in her pearls and best royal-blue gown. She'd decided not to stay in deep-mourning black any longer for Anna, as had Jenny, but the decision had been at Danny's urging, not the ladies'. He was glad to see they'd listened to him. His Anna wouldn't want them shrouded in black garb. The love of his life had been a happy woman with a colourful personality. *She'd have loved this opulence,* he thought. *What he wouldn't give to have her sitting next to him now.*

Next to Minnie sat Patrick, looking grand and comfortable in his white-tie dinner suit, as if he'd been born to wear it. As a naval officer, he'd have dressed for formal occasions, Danny remembered.

Danny sat opposite Jenny, sitting prim and proper next to Kevin. She was nervous. She always fidgeted with her napkin when she was anxious. Danny felt a swell of love for her. He'd been unkind to the family since Anna's death, and Jenny hadn't deserved to be at the end of his sharp tongue. Jenny Carmody was as good a person as Lady Muck Jackson, who'd not given her new daughter-in-law a warm welcome, or any genuine welcome, come to think of it.

Finally, as the first insubstantial course of consommé soup came, Danny focused on Charlie. He was also wearing white tie, and not, thank God, his Royal Irish Constabulary uniform.

He'd been pleasant enough when they'd first met in the library before dinner. He was respectful to Minnie and Jenny, and he seemed to be fond of Kevin. He'd even given Patrick a hug. *Nothing for me, though. All I got was a terse 'Hello.'* Never mind, Danny thought. He didn't need to spend an evening with the loyalist police officer to know the two of them would not get along. He was nothing like Kevin to look at or in character. Charlie Jackson was a cold fish with a naturally baleful glare.

Danny fidgeted with his bowtie. Jenny had tried to make him spend good money on a suit, but he'd taken the fancy outfit on loan from a shop in Dublin. The owner of the tailor's shop had told them he had a surplus of men's dinner attire because of the massive number of Irish deaths in the war. The official number stood at thirty-five thousand, but that number might not be accurate, the man had added. 'Who knows how many bodies are under the fields of the Somme,' he'd said, as if the know-it-all sixty-year-old had fought in France and knew the terrain.

"... and have you decided if you'll leave the army or make a career of it?" Charlie Jackson was asking Kevin.

Danny had missed part of the conversation. He focused. This was an important night, and he didn't want to mess it up. All eyes were on Kevin, who seemed to struggle to answer his brother's question. He looked at Jenny and smiled, then he appeared more confident. "I'm resigning my commission in May, in time for my son or daughter to be born. Jenny and I have decided to come back to Ireland to live."

"How marvellous! It will be lovely to have you home, darling," Lady Jackson said, making no mention of Jenny or the baby.

"We decided to come back because of the cleaner air. We don't want our child to grow up in the London smog," Jenny added.

"I'm disappointed, Son," said Lord Jackson, looking down his nose with narrowed eyes. "The British Army need experienced officers to put down those rabble-rousers in Dublin. If we don't get a grip on the situation with the IRA and their affiliates in the Sinn Féin, we could be looking at another conflict on home soil."

"Father, maybe we shouldn't be talking politics at the table," Charlie suggested.

Lord Jackson glared at his youngest son. "This is my table, Charlie, and I'll talk about what I damn well please when it pleases me."

"I still can't get over the Irish refusing to be conscripted into the army during the war, and at a time when the country needed them most. They'll go down in history as cowards," Lady Jackson said, opening another vein of contention.

Politics and religion at the dinner table never went down well at the best of times, Danny thought, keeping his mouth shut. He was surprised that Lord Jackson would bring up such a combative subject, knowing that his guests, apart from Minnie, were Catholic, and that one of them had fought for the Irish Volunteers in '16. Maybe he deliberately wanted to stoke a fire to highlight his son's 'unfortunate' marriage to a Fenian? If so, he'd get as good as he gave.

"The move by the British government to impose conscription on Ireland last year was, at best, naïve, Mother," Kevin spoke up. "They should have foreseen the vigorous opposition they'd get."

Patrick concurred, "I agree with Kevin. The trade unions and Irish nationalist parties were never going to agree to military conscription, and neither were the Roman Catholic bishops and priests. In my opinion, Lady Jackson, the proposal and backlash only achieved to galvanise support for political parties which advocate Irish separatism."

"Hear, hear, Patrick. Well said," Danny said with a mischievous glint in his eye.

All conversation at the table ceased. Minnie rolled her eyes at Danny, warning him to shut up. In return, Danny gave her a wicked smile, and added, "Ah, never mind, us Carmody boys did our bit for king and country, so you're in good company, Lady Jackson." Then he stared at Charlie. "Tell me, did you get muddied in the trenches?"

"No. I was busy keeping the peace here."

"Can't argue with that, can I?" Danny responded with sarcasm while silently cursing the man who was now, according to the IRA hierarchy, classed as an enemy combatant.

As the two footmen removed the soup plates, Danny studied the part of the room that he could see from his position at the table. He was not in the least bit daunted by the Jackson ancestry looking down from the formal paintings on the walls, nor did he enjoy the pictures of hunting scenes of horses and dogs and riders in red. He thought the candelabra and chandeliers vulgar, and the flowers, three different types of wine glasses, and myriad silver cutlery on the table unnecessary. The Jacksons had gone all out to impress, but the Carmody family were not country bumpkins. They had seen and done all of this before, albeit a long time ago.

"Tell me, Danny, what did you make of two RIC officers being murdered at Soloheadbeg quarry in Co Tipperary, on the same day as the IRA's first Dáil meeting at Mansion House?" Charlie asked, interrupting Danny's ponderings. "Did you support…?

"I think we've had enough politics for one evening," Kevin interjected.

"I think we're just getting started – well, Danny?" Charlie responded with a sickly smile.

Danny had vowed to behave. There was something poetic about it being a Jackson who was stirring the pot, and not a Carmody. Either way, he didn't intend to answer the question, at least not with an honest opinion. "I don't have anything to say on the matter, Charlie," he said with a friendly tone of voice. "To be honest, I've had bigger problems to contend with than the state of Irish politics." Then he cocked his head to one side and added, "The deaths of fellow Irishmen are tragic no matter who fires the shots, are they not?"

Charlie glared at Danny; his raised eyebrow displaying his scepticism. Patrick cleared his throat with a cough, recording his displeasure in his usual tepid way, and Lord Jackson became strangely quiet, as if he were willing to allow the discussion to play out.

Kevin, however, tried to shut the subject down, failing miserably to ease the tension at the table when he stood and said, "I'd like to make a toast to my new wife. Not only has she married me once, but she has agreed to say *yes,* a second time, with a blessing in St John's church…"

"What church is that, dear?" Minnie asked.

"St John's, Minnie."

Danny said, "What she meant was, *what* church?"

"It's the Protestant church in Cork city," Charlie answered.

"Well, at least your heir will be brought up on the right side of the fence," Lord Jackson said, nodding his approval at last.

Losing his perfectly polished manners, Charlie aired his own thoughts, "You're damn right, Father. I'd have hated the thought of a Fenian baby eventually getting his hands on what's ours."

"Please, Charlie, that's enough of that talk!" Lady Jackson looked horrified.

Danny took deep breaths, trying to keep his temper in check, and the anger spitting from his eyes from becoming verbal. Minnie also looked furious; not with a rage borne from religion or politics, Danny surmised, but because of the Jacksons' continuous insults against her grandchildren.

"It's all right, Minnie," Danny assured her.

"No, it is not, Son. It's the use of such words – Fenian, in this case – that foments the unrest and 'atred on this island," Minnie snapped. "It's beyond me 'ow you men can talk of violence and bigotry when we've just seen millions of men die on the Continent. Maybe if you were to replace that incompetent and inefficient administration in Dublin Castle, you might see some progress leading to a peaceful resolution for Ireland! If you ask me, that Lord Lieutenant of ours, is leading this country down a slippery path to anarchy, and I don't care which religion 'e follows."

That's it, Minnie, you tell them, Danny thought, proud of his granny. He looked at Lord Jackson, whose face was a mixture of indignation and respect. That observation was proved correct when he said, "Minnie, you seem to know a little of what you're talking about, but I must urge you not to read too much into gossip."

"Don't patronise me, Lord Jackson. I do *not* read gossip; I read *The Times.*"

"There's not much my grandmother doesn't know about current affairs," Patrick said, stifling his laughter.

Danny wanted to kiss Minnie. He was also glad Patrick had finally joined the conversation. The perpetual peacemaker was sticking up for his family at last.

"She's knowledgeable about all sorts of things," said Jenny. Then she looked at Patrick and Danny. "While we're on the subject of Minnie, you two, Kevin and I have talked it over with her, and she's agreed to live with us in Dublin."

Patrick was thrilled, as was Danny, who said, "That's grand, Jenny. Thank you, Kevin. It means the world to us that she'll be close by."

"And what about your house in London, Minnie? Didn't you say you owned it?" Lady Jackson asked.

Minnie, enjoying the attention, answered proudly, "That's right. I own it outright, without a penny of debt on it. It's in my son's name, of course, but that's a minor detail."

Jenny said, "She's going to sell it. Aren't you, Minnie?"

"I might as well. My George 'as no children, and 'e 'as a nice house of 'is own. He won't want mine."

Danny wanted to laugh in the Jacksons' faces. The snotty gits were probably thinking, *a common woman owns her own house! She reads* The Times!

Lady Jackson seemed to be working up to her next question but before she could ask it, her husband said, "I don't suppose you'll get much for it, being in Greenwich, but it will see you right for a few years, I imagine."

"I only have a few years left, Lord Jackson, and 'opefully, it'll be enough time to spoil my grandchildren and great grandson or daughter." Then Minnie threw him a haughty dismissal, as she added, "Not many people know this, but Greenwich is one of London's most sought-after boroughs. The way I see it, if Greenwich Mean Time, GMT, is being used worldwide as a reference time independent of location, the place it comes from must be important. Oh, yes, Lord Jackson, we might 'ave been 'it by Zeppelins, but the council is going to invest a lot of money to rebuild Greenwich. And rebuilding means more jobs, and more jobs mean a better economy. I'm convinced I'll have a queue of forward-thinking men at my door, begging me to sell to them."

Lord Jackson muttered into his wine glass, but Lady Jackson inadvertently, or purposely, aired her morose thoughts to Jenny. "What was it like being bombed by the Zeppelin?"

Minnie and Patrick gasped with dismay while Kevin fumed, "Mother, must you ask my wife about her terrible ordeal?"

"It's all right, Kevin," Jenny said, giving him a grateful smile. Then with great poise, she answered her mother-in-law. "There's not much to say about it, Lady Jackson. My memory is not as it was before the bombing. Sometimes I forget what I did five minutes earlier but can recall events from five years ago. I do remember that night, though. It was dark … not just because it was night, but for the low blanket of clouds that blocked the moon and stars." She swallowed and continued, "I saw the Zeppelin above us, just ahead, concealed at first, then gleaming amidst the partial concealment of the clouds. I thought it looked like a bright golden finger pointing to some place beyond it…" Jenny's words trailed off as she took on a faraway expression. "There was a flash near the ground – a tremendous shaking force and noise – and then darkness. And nothing else until I woke up in the hospital in agony. Those are my recollections."

A hush fell over the table, allowing Jenny to compose herself. Danny was furious that Jenny had felt the need to talk about that horrific night to please her new mother-in-law. He well remembered the horror of it, his sister's poor burnt face, her agonising screams. *Shame on that Jackson woman!* "My sister's a stunner, don't you think, Lady Jackson?" Danny asked rhetorically. "If you ask me, the fact that she came through the ordeal and achieved what she has is simply remarkable. Of course, I don't expect you to understand what it was like for her and the others who were killed or wounded that night. You didn't experience the war, did you? I suppose it was just something you read about in the newspapers over breakfast."

"Danny," Patrick warned.

"What, Patrick? I'm just pointing out that they weren't bombed here. They didn't hear the rumble of guns or see enemy aircraft flying so low you could almost touch them. They never saw thousands upon thousands of men dying or lying dead on the battlefields. There is no one in the Jackson family apart from Kevin who has any idea what it was like to fight and survive that war." He spread his arms wide, exaggerating his point. "I mean, it's like you Jacksons were in a completely different world to the one we've just lived through. 'What was it like to be bombed by a Zeppelin?' What sort of bloody question is that to ask a survivor?"

The Jacksons gasped with indignation at the language and insinuations, and Minnie tittered. Danny thought, *this is beyond a shadow of a doubt the most obnoxious family of Proddywhoddys I've had the unfortunate luck to meet in my life.* He hoped to God his Jenny wouldn't have to live with the pretentious *Orange* bastards, and that he could talk her out of becoming a Protestant or letting her child be brought up as one. It would kill him – kill him!

After a long and tedious four course dinner that included salmon from the Jackson's' river and beef from one the Jackson's' herds, and having to listen to polite, superficial nonsense without any further reference to the struggle for Irish independence, Danny made his excuses to forgo the brandies and cigars with the men in the library. He'd heard and seen enough; the Jacksons had caused the disharmony tonight, not the Carmodys. Oh, he'd get a battering from Jenny, Kevin, and Patrick tomorrow, but not from Minnie. No, his Minnie had been with him all the way at that dinner table.

Chapter Twenty-Three

Patrick heard Danny moving about his bedroom, which was next door to his own. He looked at the loud ticking clock on his bedside table; its hands showed three a.m. *The longest night ever.* Gazing up at the ceiling, he traced black dancing shadows being generated by the flickering candlelight, then shot up in bed when he heard Danny open his bedroom door. *Aww, Danny, what the hell are you up to now?*

When footsteps shuffled past his room, Patrick got up, pulled on his dressing gown, and followed. Danny could only have gone in one direction, for their bedrooms were at the end of this corridor in the guest wing. He was going downstairs because he needed to eat or drink something or he was up to no good, and unfortunately with Danny, the latter was the most probable.

As quietly as he could, Patrick made his way towards the main staircase so as not to wake Minnie, who was sleeping in a room further down the hall. Before leaving London, Minnie had warned Jenny and Kevin not to bring Danny to Cork. She worried that his passion for Irish independence might clash with the Jacksons' contrary political views. 'You know Danny. His devil-may-care tongue will get him shot one of these days.' Not a tasteful thing to say, Patrick had told her then, considering Danny had fought for his country and had a bullet-riddled hand to prove it.

Downstairs, Patrick glimpsed Danny's black figure carrying a lit candle. He disappeared through an open doorway leading into Lord Jackson's office and closed the door behind him, leaving Patrick to decide whether to follow or retreat. He chose the second option and went back to the main entrance hall; the place Danny would have to pass to get back upstairs to his room. *Damn you, Danny,* he thought, sitting on the staircase's bottom step.

Whilst staying with the Jacksons during a university term break, Patrick had regularly gone to that office with Kevin. Lord Jackson had enjoyed lecturing his son on the correct comportment of university scholars, and he'd included Patrick in his pep talks. The man was a bore; always had been. He believed he knew everything about everything and everyone, which was a statistical impossibility at the least. Kevin could never successfully contradict his father, whose outdated notions of university life no longer existed. He knew best, and that was that. No wonder Kevin had enjoyed being with the down-to-earth Carmody family and its patriarch, Robert, who'd showed Kevin a more light-hearted view of life.

Almost fifteen minutes later, Danny emerged into the hallway and shut the door behind himself.

"What were you up to in there?" Patrick whispered, when Danny reached the staircase.

Danny gasped and took a step backwards. "Christ, Patrick, but you scared the bejesus out of me. I nearly dropped my candle. Can I not even go for a wee walk without you trailing behind me?"

Patrick noticed something bulging at Danny's waist and within the folds of his dressing gown. It was hard and ill-concealed, even in the dim candlelight. Furious, but without damning evidence, he pinched Danny's ear, squeezed his fingers into its lobe, and marched his brother into the drawing room.

There, Patrick lit Danny's candle again, since it had gone out on the way. He set it on a table, then held out his hand, palm up. "Give it to me," he said.

"Give you what?" Danny answered innocently.

"Whatever it is you're hiding in there. Give it to me, Danny, or I swear I will put your arse on the ground and take it off you."

Danny took another step backwards. Patrick repeated his demand, "Give me whatever it is you've got on you before Lord Jackson or Charlie find out about you stealing their property. Your sister's six months pregnant. Are you daft enough to hurt her and Kevin with your shenanigans?"

"You don't know what you're talking about, Patrick. I've stolen nothing. Why do you always assume I'm up to no good? I think you've been reading too many British newspapers, spouting slanderous untruths about Irish Republicans."

"Oh, for feck's sake, listen to yourself. I don't need to read a bloody newspaper to know you've been up to no good. You went into Lord Jackson's office, which begs the question of *why?* You can't be stupid enough to think he'd leave anything of value lying around with us in his house, so what did you take?" Patrick took a menacing step closer, but then his tone softened. "I know it was hard for you tonight, but despite Charlie Jackson trying to goad you into a corner, you kept your temper in check. Please, don't do anything to prove him right about you."

Danny sighed with impatience. "If you would just trust me, Patrick … just once, I'd be a happy man." He looked hurt as he slipped his hand into the folds of his dressing gown. "Here, it's a book. That's all, a damn book," Danny said, holding it out to Patrick.

Patrick took the hardback book over to the table and lowered it to the candle. *A Concise History of Ireland, Volume One;* the title read.

"When Kevin's father gave us the tour this afternoon, I noticed this book. He said I could read it while we were here," Danny said.

Patrick was not convinced. He had not gone on the tour – he already knew the house – but he didn't believe for an instant that Lord Jackson had taken Danny and Jenny into his office. He opened the book and flicked the pages from beginning to end, in case he found something; anything that might get his brother into trouble. "I…"

As the door opened, Patrick instinctively reacted to protect his brother by slipping the book inside his dressing gown. Then he followed Danny's lead and sat on the couch facing his brother's.

Charlie Jackson, also dressed in his night attire, walked in and glanced over at Danny and Patrick, lounging casually in the drawing room, chatting. "What's this? You two can't sleep, either?" Charlie asked.

"No. It must be all that rich food. We're not used to it," Patrick said.

Danny added, "After years in the trenches, rich sauces play havoc with my digestive system. You know how it is … oh, wait, you don't, do you?"

Patrick glared at Danny, then turned to Charlie. "I think I'll get back upstairs. I'm going to walk with Kevin tomorrow – I mean today, and I remember his route used to take us about four hours."

"Stay for a brandy. It might help both of you to sleep," Charlie suggested.

"No, thanks all the same," Patrick responded with a yawn.

Danny yawned too. "I'll walk you up, Patrick. I've got an early start in the morning."

"You're not staying the weekend?" Charlie asked.

"No, I'm buying a house in Dublin, and I have papers to sign."

As Charlie poured himself a brandy from a decanter, he said, "Tell me, Danny, what plans have you now that you're out of the army?"

"I have none at present, apart from buying a home. I'm still wounded, according to my demobilisation papers. Got to get this hand of mine sorted before I even start looking for work."

"God knows, Danny deserves to have some free time before joining the workforce." And with that said, Patrick rose from the couch.

"It won't be easy getting a job. I hope you're not planning to work for that group of illicit political ministers the Fenians have set up?" Charlie turned, swirling the brandy in the glass, his eyes half closed as he lazily studied Danny's candlelit figure. "It wouldn't look good for my brother or your sister if you got involved with rebels." He slugged his brandy down, even as Danny stood to leave.

Patrick's temper snapped. "We're guests in your house, Charlie. We haven't come here to discuss the political crisis or religious differences between us. We're here to support our sister, who's now your sister-in-law." He looked Charlie over, his anger at the arrogant bastard growing. "Remember, I know you. You were a bully as a schoolboy, always preying on the most vulnerable, always needing people to follow you about to make yourself look big and powerful. I didn't like you then, and I like you even less since you've put on a Royal Constabulary uniform."

Charlie tittered and placed his hand on his heart, "Ah, but I'm hurt, Patrick. And here's me thinking we were friends."

"I'm surprised you joined the RIC, Charlie," Danny added, full of himself now that he had Patrick's support. "You're outnumbered by Catholic brethren in your ranks.

"True, we have more Fenians in the lower ranks, but sixty percent of our officers are Protestant, and remember … we wield the whips."

Patrick warned Danny to keep quiet with a thunderous look, then turned his own ire on Charlie. "Let me give you some free advice. If you don't want to lose your brother, I suggest you make a genuine effort to welcome his wife into your family. She's the bravest, sweetest woman I've ever known, and Kevin loves her more than you can possibly know." Admittedly, calling Jenny 'sweet' was a bit of an exaggeration. She could make Charlie Jackson weep blood with a tongue lashing, Patrick thought.

"I have nothing against your sister. Granted, we would have preferred Kevin to marry a Protestant. You can't blame us for that, can you?"

Patrick, his arms crossed, protecting the book within his dressing gown, looked strangely encumbered as he crossed the room to the door. "I'll bid you goodnight, Charlie," he said, leaving the room.

"Righty ho. Same here," said Danny, smiling to himself as he followed his brother out.

Chapter Twenty-Four

Dublin, Ireland

Jimmy Carson stood at the entrance to Dublin Station and welcomed Danny home with a wave and a loud shout, "Over here, Danny!"

Danny waved back, but he was not amused by Jimmy's gruff voice screaming his name aloud in the busy station where police routinely patrolled.

"All right, Jimmy, let all of Dublin know I'm back, why don't ye?"

"I didn't think I'd see ye until Monday. What's the crack, then?" Jimmy asked, giving Danny a vigorous handshake.

"I came back earlier than planned, that's all." Despite his disastrous visit to Jenny's in-laws, Danny chatted cheerfully to Jimmy about the trip as they walked along Montgomery Street, where Dublin's ladies of the night serviced the city's lonely men. As he spoke, he realised a guilty conscience did not encumber him; instead, he was proud of himself, victorious even. He'd completed his first mission for Michael Collins, and it had been no mean feat.

"So that was that," Danny said, ending his in-depth view of the Jackson family only when he and Jimmy entered Michael Collins' street sometime later.

Jimmy, who'd seemed fascinated by Danny's impressions of the Lord and Lady from Cork, chuckled, "When all is said and done, it seems your Jenny has married into a right bunch of twats."

"They're a bunch of snooty bastards who thought my Jenny wasn't good enough for their precious son, that's what they are. I'll tell you, Jimmy, I'll not be going back there in a hurry."

Two different men from the two he'd spotted the last time he was in this street were standing by Michael's car outside his house. "What's been happening here?" Danny asked Jimmy.

"Nothing much. Ye've only been gone a couple o' days."

"Has anyone been talking about me?"

"If you mean John Grant, then no, but I haven't seen him again since you left."

"Well, he'd better keep his mouth shut about me. I'm thinking of paying him a wee visit. We have some outstanding scores to settle."

"Don't!" Jimmy halted mid-step to place his hand on Danny's shoulder. "Be under no illusion, Danny, the IRA will take John and his da's side over yours, anytime. I mean it, this is it for you. You're in today or out on your ear, so you need to keep your mouth shut about one of our biggest donors."

"John Grant won't intimidate me, Jimmy. I don't give a feck if they shower their money on the IRA or Dáil government or the bloody Vatican! No one spreads slander about me and gets away with it."

Jimmy shook his head. "And here's me thinking the British Army might have taught you about restraint."

Again, Jimmy asked Danny to wait in the hallway while he reported to Michael's secretary, but this time he was back within seconds, saying, "Michael and Dick Mulcahy are waiting for us."

"Danny, come, take a seat," Michael Collins offered, gesturing to Danny to join him.

Danny approached the couch where Michael and Richard Mulcahy sat. He was anxious. It stemmed from his previous meeting and Jimmy's recent comments resonating through his brain that this was it. 'You're in today or out on your ear.' He flicked his eyes from Michael to Dick, wondering, *which is it? Am I in or out?*

When in France, Danny had often mulled over what the IRA might be up to, but at times he was too busy staying alive to care if the movement remained strong or if the entire thing had disbanded and shrunk to a small, insignificant social club where men talked of their unreachable goals and dreams of what might have been in 1916.

It had been easy to forget the Irish struggles when he was desperately trying to keep himself alive on the battlefields, as it was easy now to forget his vow made to Anna as far back as in his letters to her from the Front Line in France. *'I promise you, my darlin', I'll not get involved in Ireland's troubles when I come home,'* he'd written. With Anna, he'd been tethered to a bright, peaceful future. But she was no longer here, and he was not the same man with expectations of a loving wife and children. He'd never fall in love again, never be tethered, never be whole.

Jimmy sat on the chair opposite the couch. Danny followed, taking the other chair but shifting awkwardly in the well-padded seat before settling.

"I think I have something for you," Danny said, breaking the uncomfortable silence in which Mick and Dick perused him from head to feet with hawkish eyes. "I don't know if it will be any good to you, but it was the only thing I could get hold of. The man had locked every office drawer."

"As he would, I suppose," Dick said in a clipped business-like tone.

Danny went into his jacket pocket and pulled out three sheets of paper. "I copied these notes from his appointment book."

Dick Mulcahy looked impressed. "No one saw you?" he asked.

Dangerous question, Danny thought. "No, I went down in the middle of the night and made sure nobody was around before I went into Lord Jackson's office." *His first lie to the Republican Brotherhood.*

"Let's have a look," Mick said, stretching his hand out.

Danny gave Michael the papers, then waited in silence until the two great men had read what was scribbled on the first one. It was a strange feeling, knowing that he might have given a pivotal piece of information that could lead to a successful mission, whatever that might entail. He'd not been confident he'd find anything of interest in the office, but he'd have stolen a paperweight and brought it back to prove to the IRA he was loyal.

"We could hit him here on the fourteenth of April." Michael pointed to a specific line on the page and drew his finger along it. "He's travelling from Cork to Dublin Castle. Some of those Cork roads are quiet, narrow lanes bordered by trees and hedges. If we pick the right spot, we could ambush his car and kill him and whoever's in his entourage and get out of there long before the next motorcar or horse and cart came along."

Danny's eyes widened in surprise upon hearing *kill.* Dick nodded. "He's written down his appointment time with the Lord Lieutenant at the castle, so all we have to do is calculate his journey time and route, pick the spot, as you said, and – bang – done. Leave this with me, Mick. I'll study these more closely with my IRB boys." Then Dick asked Danny, "Where did you get this from, exactly?"

"Jackson's diary. It was sitting underneath a pile of papers on his desk. I took a notepad with me as you suggested, and jotted dates and places down. He'd written a lot more in the book, but I couldn't take the chance of being caught, so I went as fast as I could and got out of there."

"I'm surprised you got this. Careless of him," Dick said.

"It was," Danny agreed. "An oversight, probably. Like I said, everything else, apart from a few receipts to do with his estate, must have been locked away."

"Can I say something?" Jimmy asked.

"Yes, Jimmy," Mick said.

"I asked Danny earlier if he thought Lord Jackson might have planted the diary there. I mean, would he be that daft to leave it in the open, knowing he had a known Republican rebel in his house?"

Michael returned his gaze to Danny. "Well, Danny?"

"I don't think so. I believe it was an oversight on his part. He'd been drinking a lot at dinner … probably forgot to lock the office door. Maybe he never does. Maybe he thought he was secure in his own house."

"Well, whatever the reason, good work," Dick said. Then he lit a cigarette and exhaled whilst staring at Danny with eyes that seemed to see into a man's very soul. "How do you feel about us assassinating your sister's father-in-law?"

Danny involuntarily gulped. He wasn't shocked that they wanted to kill Jackson, or by the uncomfortable question, but he'd rather not answer it. His eyes shifted from Mick to Dick, and back again, trying to gauge whether this was a loyalty test. Two pairs of questioning eyes becoming impatient met his open gaze. He said, "I'll be honest, I don't know how I feel. I'm still not sure what your strategy is. I thought this was going to be a more passive sort of war than the '16 uprising. 'A no guns blazing affair,' you said, Mick…" His words trailed off as Jimmy's earlier warning came to mind again. 'This is it. You're either in or you're out on your ear.' "I suppose taking down a member of the House of Lords will send a strong message to the British government. He's made his malicious feelings known about the IRA, and from what you've told me, he's hitting our sympathisers hard in County Cork."

"That's why we want him gone," Dick said.

Michael was silent and staring, as if he were not yet convinced of Danny's commitment. Danny felt his back being pushed into a corner. He had only two ways out of this; the first would be his acceptance of the men's plan for Lord Jackson, and the second would be his own death for disagreeing with the assassination of an extended family member. He now understood the importance of Jimmy's warning and plunged himself, body and soul, into the Irish Republican Army, now being universally called the New IRA. "The way I see it, soldiers, police, and politicians of the invader should be treated exactly as invading soldiers would be treated by the native army of any country. Does that make sense?"

"Spoken like a real trooper," Dick applauded. Then, as if engrossed in some aspect of Danny's appearance, he said, "Here's a thing. You're a sniper, and by all accounts a good one. We'd like you to use your talents in the IRB. How would that suit you, Danny?"

Danny blinked in surprise. The Irish Republican Brotherhood, known in Irish as: *Bráithreachas Phoblacht na hÉireann,* was a secret, oath-bound fraternal organisation dedicated to the establishment of an independent democratic republic. Mick and Dick Mulcahy had been members for years; even before the 1916 Easter Uprising. The organisation worked under tight secrecy, and its operations were known only to those right at the top of the command chain. Danny gave Jimmy a sideways glance. He thought it strange to be talking about this when Jimmy was in the room.

"Ah, don't you worry about Jimmy. He's already in. He has been for over a year," Mick added, reading Danny's mind.

He's a bit of a dark horse, our Jimmy. Never said a thing to me about this at his house. He straightened in his chair and said, "I'd be honoured. I used to listen to your lectures in Frongoch, Mr Mulcahy, and back then I saw myself as being in the Brotherhood. I won't let you down."

Michael was pensive. His eyes continued to bore into Danny as he began to expand on the tactics and aims of the New IRA organisation. "I touched on this before, Danny, but before you take an oath to commit yourself to us, you should know how we plan to win this war."

"Of course, Mick. I'm all ears," said Danny relaxing in his chair.

"The Däil and Sinn Féin are going down the political route, but we're going to mimic the successful tactics of the Boers during the Boer War in South Africa … fast, violent raids without uniforms. You might hear that some republican leaders, notably Éamon de Valera, favour classic conventional warfare to legitimise our new republic in the eyes of the world, but I and the broader IRA leadership oppose de Valera's tactics…"

"I agree. If you ask me, going in armed to the teeth with rifles blazing is what caused the military debacle of '16."

Jimmy chipped in, "That's right, Danny – sorry, Mick, don't mind me."

Mick continued, amusement crossing his eyes, as Danny and Jimmy's enthusiasm broke through. "Now, you know me. I'll never say a bad word against our other esteemed leader, Arthur Griffith, but he prefers to tip the scales the other way by using a campaign of civil disobedience rather than any type of armed struggle. He thinks violence will make us unpopular with the Irish people…"

Dick continued, "But we're betting that heavy-handed British responses to our violence against the army and RIC will popularise our cause among much of the population."

"I think you're right," Danny concurred, feeling terribly important to be part of this discussion.

Michael leant forward in his seat and clasped his hands between his long legs. "From now on, you will lie to your sister and brother, to your granny and friends, and to any woman you might want to bed in the future. You'll be leading a double life … one where you will kill our enemies and the other where you'll work in a low-paying job at the docks, keeping your nose clean, and your political opinions to yourself."

Dick added, "You'll be asked to pack up and go somewhere at a moment's notice. You'll be told where and why, but apart from what your battalion commander tells you, you will not ask questions, including the names of others involved until they themselves tell you who they are. The only way the IRB works is if we keep our cells separate and our missions secret. You cannot even tell your priest about your involvement. No confessing to murder, understand?"

"Sure, but I do … it's just that …. well, won't I need to let the family know I'm working as a labourer? They won't be happy about me choosing that sort of career after my father put me through a fancy grammar school. We're all coming back here to live, including my granny. And we're a very close-knit family."

Mick answered, "The way I see it, it's none of their business what work you do. You come up with whatever excuse works and stick to it. The most important thing about this dockyard job is that you're going to work for a man who works for us. He'll give you time off as and when you need it, no questions asked."

Mick turned to Jimmy, "Jimmy, go to the archives and bring the proclamation. Danny might as well read the Oath of Allegiance while Dick and I are here to witness it."

Chapter Twenty-Five

Excitement ran through Danny while he waited outside Michael's office for Jimmy's return. He sat in a chair beside a desk where a man was hitting the keys on his loud typewriting machine. Under the somewhat hypnotic sound of tapping, his thoughts drifted off. Good old Jimmy seemed to have authority in the organisation; he could listen in on high-powered discussions, had access to important IRA documents, and moved freely around the ground floor of what was a substantial detached house. It was almost as big as the Carmodys' old house, which the bank had repossessed in 1916 after the uprising.

Danny studied the man typing away, cigarette clinging limply to his lips, his eyes squinting as the smoke rose. This was an altogether different setup to the one he'd taken part in on that long-ago Easter Monday. It was a much more structured and far-sighted organisation. This would not to be a week or month of violence but a year … two … five. They had committed to fight for however long it took to push the British out of Ireland. The IRA's intentions were to chip away at the British establishment, wearing it down until His Majesty's government no longer thought occupation a viable proposition. He liked the plan.

When Jimmy returned, he carried documents in his hand. Danny recognised the first one instantly. It was the Declaration of Independence Proclamation of 1916. A surge of memories overwhelmed him, bringing back that terrible time of loss, imprisonment, and the execution of men he'd admired. "I've read it already," he said.

"Yes, but this one includes ratifications," Jimmy responded, handing him the document. "It still demands the removal of the English garrison, but this time we've issued an appeal to the free nations of the world. That part's down at the bottom. Read it all again before I take you back in for the oath."

Danny stared at the proclamation, looking as bold today as it had on that Easter Monday when Pádraig – Patrick Pearse – had read it aloud, and the Republican spirit shone brightly on English tyranny.

Poblacht Na H Eireann
The Provisional Government of the Irish Republic.
To the people of Ireland...

Under a swell of tears, Danny tried to read the proclamation, but his eyes kept wandering to the bottom where the seven members of the Provisional Government of the Irish Republic had signed their names and subsequently been shot or imprisoned for their devotion to a free Ireland.

"Did you read that bit?" Jimmy asked, pointing to the paragraph near the bottom.

Danny sniffed, and still charged with emotion, read the new ratification aloud with all the devotion he could muster:

"For these among other reasons, Ireland – resolutely and irrevocably determined at the dawn of the promised era of self-determination and liberty that she will suffer foreign dominion no longer – calls upon every free nation to uphold her national claim to complete independence as an Irish Republic against the arrogant pretensions of England founded in fraud and sustained only by an overwhelming military occupation ..."

A surge of patriotism flamed through Danny as he read the words. In that moment, his love for Ireland sprouted phoenix-like from the ashes of a war he had not volunteered to fight in. He stared up at Jimmy and said, "I was lost, Jimmy, but bejesus, I'm found, I'm whole again. Since I returned to Dublin, I've been thinking about my Anna and what she'd say about me breaking my promise to her, but I swear to you, I am at peace with that. I'm committed. I'll kill as many British loyalists as I must to see this through to the end. I will do my duty alongside you, Jimmy."

"Good lad, Danny," said Jimmy, giving him a hearty pat on the back. "Right then, we'd better get back in. You're being honoured. Michael and Dick rarely witness the readings of the oath." Then Jimmy surprised Danny by going nose to nose with him. "I've vouched for you despite the Grants' opposition to you joining us. Don't you let me down, you hear?"

Danny nodded solemnly, noting in passing that Jimmy didn't seem as young and easy-go-lucky as he'd always been.

Moments later, Danny stood in the centre of the room, his heart pitter-pattering like the rain outside. "I'm ready to give my life for Ireland," he told Michael and Dick. "If I betray this cause, I'll take a gun and shoot myself in the mouth, so I hope you two will never have cause to mistrust me again."

Jimmy held the oath up to Danny and said, "Read this and mean it."

Danny placed his hand on the bible, cleared his throat and began. *"In the presence of God, I, Daniel Carmody, do solemnly swear that I will do my utmost to establish the independence of Ireland, and that I will bear true allegiance to the Supreme Council of the Irish Republican Brotherhood and the Government of the Irish Republic, and implicitly obey the constitution of the Irish Republican Brotherhood and all my superior officers and that I will preserve inviolably the secrets of the organisation."*

Panting with the many *ands* in the text, and puffed-out with tears of pride, Danny's dreams of a free Irish nation reignited while his oath to Anna crumbled into memory.

"Jimmy, bring four tumblers," Mick said, as he went to his desk, opening one of the drawers and raising a bottle of Irish whiskey in the air. "Ah, Danny, I knew you were a good man the minute I met you. I told Dick you wouldn't let us down."

"You did, Mick," Dick confirmed.

Michael banged the bottle with pomp and ceremony on the low table between the chairs and couch, and continued, "We'll drink a toast to this and to your Anna. You were a lucky bugger to have had the likes of her. No man who was at Frongoch will ever forget –"

The explosion that followed shattered the window glass in Mick's office and blew him off his feet. Dick and Jimmy, who had been sitting, also hit the floor in those confusing seconds.

Danny, drenched in small shards of glass, crawled the few feet to Jimmy, who was using the upholstered chair as a shield against a possible second attack.

"What the feck was that?" Danny groaned.

Jimmy moaned in response. "Aw, Danny, I'm hit … it's bad … I'm dying."

Danny's eyes followed Jimmy's, which went to his stomach. "Aw, Jesus Christ, no, Jimmy!" Danny cried upon seeing a larger shard sticking out of his stomach.

"Pull it," Jimmy whimpered.

The door burst open. "It's over. It's over, Michael. We've secured the area," a Republican man carrying a rifle shouted.

"Who was it?" demanded Michael, now on his feet. His face, like those of the others in the room, had cuts and abrasions, and he was furious. "Did you see them, man?"

"No, but…"

Michael reached the man before he'd got the answer out – more – he had him in a stranglehold against the wall. "But what, Mikey, what?" he hissed.

"Joe was fiddling with the motorcar. I went for a piss, and … and before I got back the bloody thing had exploded. I'm sorry, Mick, but it was Joe. He ran off. Two of our lads further along the street followed him. It was Joe – he was a feckin' traitor or spy, I don't know..."

As Mikey's words trailed off, Mick let his hands drop to his sides. He staggered backwards, muttering, "Joe O'Donnell? Jesus, I've known him since he was a kid. The bastard!"

Danny, who was cradling Jimmy in his arms and already deaf to the conversation, squeezed his eyes shut while shaking his head to relieve the images and sounds from the Somme. The assault on his senses was so fierce, his mind replaced the people entering the room and the sounds of shouting that followed with more intense sensations yet. Sweat poured down his face. His ears began to ring under the familiar noise of gunfire and bomb blasts, the squeaking iron tanks dipping and rising from dirt craters like giant mammoths, planes buzzing overhead, and there, amidst the chaotic orchestra, the screams of men dying on the battlefield …

"… Danny – Danny – for God's sake man, pull yourself together!"

Danny heard his own screams of, "Stay down!" A heavy weight then pinned him to the mud – a German – a tree trunk? He screamed again, as he pushed his arms against the heaviness, then he finally cracked opened his eyes and stared up at Michael Collins' face. *How long had he been reliving the past?* He didn't know, but some mind monster had swept him off to the place that usually only cursed his dreams at night. And Michael had sat on his chest to hold him down.

As he came to, Danny remembered Jimmy. "Where is he … where's Jimmy?" he panted.

"They've taken him off to hospital. He'll be all right, Danny," Mick said, lurching to his feet. "What the hell happened to you?"

Both Dick and Mick stared at Danny, and behind them, others who'd come in did the same. The room was packed.

"I'm sorry. I don't know what happened," Danny said, scrambling to his feet, his fed reddening under the universal scrutiny.

In an unusual display of affection, Michael brushed the crystal-like glass from Danny's hair. "Listen, the lot of you. None of us went, so we can only imagine the horrors Danny experienced in France. It must have been hell … hell for any man to witness, worse to endure. No one talks about Danny to anyone outside these walls, you hear me? No one, or you'll have me to answer to."

Dick added, "You were gone, Danny. You scared the bejesus out of us."

Danny saw the faces of the men in the crowded room and realised he hadn't seen them enter, hadn't heard what they were doing about the assassination attempt or who they thought had made it, hadn't seen Jimmy being carted off. "It won't happen again," he muttered.

"Right, pack up, lads. Start in here. I want the place emptied in an hour," Michael said to his men. Then he turned back to Danny. "Go home, lad. We'll be in touch with you in a couple of weeks. You're in, but you're not ready for combat."

"But Mick…"

"No. I'll not have you putting anyone else's life in danger. Off you go. We'll find you when we need you."

Danny nodded. His humiliation was complete. He stooped to pick up his cap, lying on the floor in a pool of Jimmy's blood.

He shook the glass shards off it, and told Michael, "I don't have a home to go to."

Chapter Twenty-Six

February 1919

Dublin, Ireland.

Patrick walked along Sackville Street and then crossed the busy junction at Burgh Quay, which led to his destination in Dollier Street. He held a crumpled piece of paper with an address on it. As he walked, he smoothed it out to make sure he had remembered the correct street number. When he was satisfied it had not changed from twenty-two, he looked at the address of the shop he stood in front of – number eight. He was on the correct side of the street and getting closer.

A short walk later, he halted at number twenty-two. The entrance to the factory was not as he'd expected, but it was the right place, as the name above the glass double-entrance doors indicated: *Quinn O'Malley, Fine Woollens.*

Patrick shoved the piece of paper into his jacket pocket, then cleared his throat. *This might be one of the daftest ideas you've ever had,* he thought, opening the door and entering, *but to hell with it. You've come this far.*

The inside was set up as a shop with fancy displays made from polished light oak wood, set against darker oak-panelled walls. Even the woollen beige carpet his feet sank into was of the finest quality, as were the intricately carved hat stands and wooden electric wall light panels with the latest Bakelite switches. It seemed Mr Quinn O'Malley was an affluent man whose business had not suffered because of the war or had weathered the storm because he'd had plenty of money in reserve.

Patrick browsed the goods on display and noted clothing articles from hats, scarves, shawls and socks to ladies' cardigans and men's jerseys in Aran and luxurious cashmere. The stock was expensive and probably priced well out of reach of the average man on the street, yet five people were browsing and another three were waiting to pay for articles at the till counter. Two middle-aged men were working at the counter. Another man out in the store front came up behind Patrick and asked, "May I help you, sir?"

"Yes, please. I'm looking for Mr O'Malley," Patrick answered.

"Who shall I say is calling, sir?"

"Patrick Carmody," said Patrick, his voice pitched annoyingly high, revealing his nerves the longer he stood there.

"One moment."

A dark green, finely woven scarf caught Patrick's eye. He took it from the display hangar and wrapped it around his neck, admiring its appearance in one of the many appropriately placed mirrors in the shop. *I should buy something while I'm here…*

"Patrick?"

Patrick spun around with the ends of the scarf hanging down both sides of his jacket's lapels. His fingers trembled as he removed it and hung it up, and they still shook when he stretched out his hand to shake Quinn's. "Hello again, Quinn. You said I should look you up the last time we met, and as I was in the neighbourhood, I thought I'd do just that. Nice shop – I'll take this lovely scarf." He sounded like a bumbling fool and was glad no one apart from Quinn was paying attention to him.

Quinn gave Patrick a beguiling smile in recognition. The latter studied the man who'd captivated him on the steam-packet boat from Ireland over a year ago, only this time he saw him in daylight: his tall athletic figure was evident even beneath his suit. His handsome face, now bright with amusement, sported an unusual neat black beard that matched his blue-black curly hair. He was even more attractive than Patrick remembered, but as always, Patrick was prepared to be disappointed and erred on the side of caution when he next spoke, "I'm also interested in buying something nice for my grandmother. It's her birthday soon. What do you recommend?"

Quinn smiled again, but this time, his green Irish eyes twinkled with mischief. "Come into my office. Let me show you my catalogue. We can have a catch-up at the same time."

Patrick was almost certain Quinn suffered the same cursed affliction that had followed him throughout his own adult life. Only in these rare times, when the evidence of mutual attraction was so strong, would he openly seek a man he was drawn to. He'd felt Quinn's pull on the boat, had sensed his mutual interest, but his perception of someone had been wrong once before. He'd gone through hell trying to cover up his egregious sin against God and man, as society saw it to be. It wasn't a mistake he would repeat.

Both men sat in leather-padded office chairs, facing off in what was still unknown territory. To break the silence, Patrick remarked again, "You really do have a nice place here. I expected to see a factory line and people knitting or weaving…

or whatever. Do you make your products here?" *Christ, he sounded like a half-wit.*

"The factory space is at the back. I'll give you a tour later, if you like?" Quinn suggested, then looked at his wristwatch.

"I don't want to keep you," Patrick rushed out.

"You're not. In fact, I was just about to have lunch. Will you join me? It's nothing much – a few sandwiches … oh, and cake. One of my secretaries brought in some fresh-baked Gur cake this morning."

Patrick smiled. His mother never had Dublin Gur cake in the house. She thought it was for poor people and too base for her family. It consisted of a thick layer of filling between two thin layers of pastry. The filling was a dark brown paste, containing a mixture of cake and breadcrumbs, sultanas and raisins, and with a sweet tasting binder. It was Danny's favourite. "I never say no to cake. It's been years since I tasted a slice of Gur."

After Quinn's telephone call, a woman brought in a tray laden with cups, teapot, milk jug, a plate of sandwiches, and another with that of Dublin's famous cake. She set it down on the round conference table and said, "Shall I tell everyone you're in a meeting, Mr O'Malley?"

"Yes, please, Mary. I don't want to be disturbed unless it's important."

When the two of them were alone, Quinn poured the tea into the cups while saying, "You didn't come here to buy a scarf, Patrick, so tell me, why have you come to see me?"

Patrick looked into the sparkling eyes across the table and crossed the line of no return. "I think we've both been around long enough to know when we meet someone of like mind, Quinn. You know, one of my biggest flaws is that I procrastinate, but after going through a war and coming close to death a few times, I thought, 'Sod it, life's short and men like us need to take the occasional risk if we're to get anywhere … if we're to have any hope of finding a spoonful of happiness.'"

Quinn nodded, and Patrick went all in. "That night on the boat, I saw something in you I liked, and that you're sitting before me nodding makes me believe you liked me too. If I'm mistaken, there's no harm done. You can insult me and tell me to leave, and I'll never darken your door again."

"You're not mistaken, not at all," Quinn responded in a serious tone. "I've thought about you often, Patrick. I kicked myself for not taking your address on the boat. I was afraid you wouldn't seek me out. I'm a bit like you regarding hesitation. We can never be certain, can we, and so we fail to act and live to regret our cowardice." He grinned. "We're like bats, hiding in the shadows by day but flapping about blindly even when we are set free. I'm happy you're here. I was drawn to you the moment I saw you peering into the night over the side of the boat, looking terrified."

Patrick's muscles stiffened as Quinn left his chair and came to stand over him. "I've known one man in my life, Patrick, and he abused me terribly then threw me away like an old sock. I don't take this lightly. It terrifies me. If decent people knew what I was, I would lose my business and my family, and the law would probably take my freedom and shove me in some prison."

"I'm scared too," Patrick said, hypnotised as he craned his neck to look up at Quinn. Then he stood, as if some magnetic force were propelling him to his feet.

"I've watched my sister and brother falling in love," Patrick murmured, nose to nose with Quinn. "They're both passionate about the people they fell for. My brother, Danny, has just lost his wife to the Spanish flu. I don't know if he'll ever recover, but I do know he was blissfully happy for a time. I want to feel what he had. I have always wanted that joy, that connection to another person, but I never have and never will know it with a woman. I know I'm a homosexual, an abomination, a faggot, a terrible mistake in God's grand plan. I…"

Patrick's thoughts vanished as Quinn swooped in to kiss him. It went on and on, the kiss, and it took him to a place he'd never been before; to a bliss he'd always imagined existed but had never known for himself. He'd dallied with a man in a London bar once, but he'd never kissed or hugged or had any physical contact with another that had made him feel as though his entire body were on fire.

After they broke from the embrace that had carried him off to some heavenly place, Patrick slumped into his chair. He panted, not with exertion or anxiety, but with an elation that left him breathless.

Quinn, his eyes flashing with passion, swayed on his feet as he added, "Then we're both mistakes in God's eyes, and I refuse to believe it so. That aside, I think we needed that. What do you think?"

"I don't think we should talk about the why or wherefore," Patrick answered in a broken voice. "It is enough that we feel the same about each other. You've made me a happy man. You've just breathed life into me."

"Then why don't we start from here and figure out the rest of it as we go along?" Quinn suggested.

Still immersed in the memory of the kiss, Patrick responded by rising to kiss Quinn again. *Yes. Still as sweet.* Afterwards, he agreed. “We’re both cautious men, and I trust you, so yes, let’s start from here and see where this craziness takes us.”

Chapter Twenty-Seven

Beginning of May

Kilbolane House
The Jackson Estate,
County Cork, Ireland

Jenny attended yet another luncheon at Kevin's family home while privately plotting to make it her last, at least for a while. In honour of Kevin's final meal at home before his return to London, the Jacksons had invited their cousins; the Earl and Countess of Cork. Charlie Jackson was also present, although it was clear to Jenny that he didn't want to be there any more than she did.

She looked across the table at Minnie, who openly rolled her eyes, signifying her boredom. Jenny couldn't blame her granny, for the talk at the table was enough to put an elephant to sleep: problems with crop growing, unreliable and troublesome tenants, trespass and poaching, illegal removal of fences, the cost of potatoes, the price of rents needing to go up, and the countess' plans to renovate their manor house being the sum of the conversation. Jenny and Minnie were being ignored – slighted – insulted. They were present but might as well have been apples in the fruit bowl on the table for all the attention they'd received.

Finally getting off the subject of electricity being installed in the countess' personal suite of rooms, the earl asked Kevin, "Where are you thinking of setting up home when you leave the army?"

"I've made enquires with various medical practices and hospitals in Dublin. I am even considering Coombe Lying-in Hospital, caring for new mothers and infants. I'm testing the waters … looking at where I might fit in when I sign my army discharge papers."

"Really, dear, I don't think women's problems are for you, and I certainly don't want to hear about them at the table. No, Kevin, you must practise medicine in Cork. You've been away from us long enough, don't you think?" Lady Jackson stated, rather than asked.

Jenny glared at her new mother in law, who seemed to think it was her decision to make. Indignant at the cheek of the woman, she said, "I'd prefer to live in Dublin, Lady Jackson. Kevin will work long hours regardless of where he practices medicine, and I have two brothers who will settle in the capital. And Minnie also wants to be near her grandsons."

All conversation halted. The earl and countess' forks froze in their hands. Kevin's mother and father glared at their new daughter-in-law, who'd had enough of the Jacksons' snubs and snobbery. Charlie seemed to enjoy the awkwardness. His lips twitched in amusement, and his arrogant eyes flashed with victory at his brother. Minnie gave Jenny a tender smile, as did Kevin, who was unaware of Charlie's spiteful pleasure.

"Miss Carmody, I think you are being rather selfish. It really isn't your concern or decision to make, but Kevin's," Lord Jackson told Jenny in a harsh, unyielding tone. "What you must learn is despite Kevin choosing medicine against my wishes, he is *still* the heir to this estate, and it's important that he's here to learn the ropes. After all, when he takes over from me, you will reap the benefits of his title, which will, down the line, give him a seat in Parliament's House of Lords."

"My husband is right," Lady Jackson agreed, albeit reluctantly. "When a woman marries, it becomes her sworn duty to support and obey her husband in all things. Her own needs *must* be secondary to his, because as we all know, it is our husbands who shoulder the burden of responsibility."

"Hear, hear, my dear," Lord Jackson echoed his wife.

Jenny felt like a schoolgirl being slapped on the wrist in front of the class. They still called her 'Miss Carmody.' Was she supposed to agree, remain silent like a good girl, give up her opinions? Ask Kevin to tell them for the umpteenth time that she was a *Mrs* and not a *Miss*? She pitied Lady Jackson. The woman couldn't seem to bring herself to call her own husband by his Christian name! For three days, she had called him Lord Jackson this and that when speaking of him to Jenny or Minnie. Minnie, as astute as ever, had suggested in private that Lady Jackson did not intend for the Carmodys to address her or her husband in any familiar way at all, ever. Her reasoning made sense. 'It's clear as day, dear. It all comes down to class divide.' Minnie had made her point when the two women were walking together in the gardens. 'You mark my words, Lady what's-her-face would rather 'ave you and me curtsy to 'er, than 'ave us sit at her dining table.'

Minnie had read Kevin's mother to a tee, Jenny thought. Thank God, she, Kevin, and Minnie were leaving Cork straight after lunch. She wouldn't be coming back in a hurry, baby or no baby.

"Tell me, Kevin, dear, is it important to you that your wife be content?" Minnie now asked Kevin.

No! Jenny groaned inwardly. Minnie was still angry and not willing to drop the subject of wifely duties until she'd made her point. This, it seemed, was now a battle between two strong-minded matriarchs who wanted their voices heard. Jenny determined she was not getting involved.

"What a strange question. Of course, it's important to him, but sometimes one's contentedness must take a back seat to duty," Lady Jackson answered before Kevin could lay down his fork.

"What a load of tosh," Minnie scoffed. "I don't care what anyone says, a marriage should be between equals, and it certainly should not have to answer to the in-laws, whatever their station in life. I know what's going on 'ere. You and your 'usband are miffed because your eldest son didn't come straight 'ome to help run your family business. You can't control 'im, can you…?"

"Minnie, please don't…" said Kevin, trying to defuse the situation.

"No, I'm sorry, Son. I know you love your parents and that's 'ow it should be, but no one should tell you or Jenny where to make your 'ome or 'ow to live your lives, not these days, and not after all the 'ardships you've been through together." Undaunted by the Jacksons' gasps of indignation, Minnie continued, and this time, she directed her anger at her hosts. "I've been sitting 'ere for four days, watching you two insult my granddaughter. And I'll 'ave no more of it, you 'ear me? 'Er name is *Mrs Jackson*, Mrs Jenny Jackson. She and my other two grandchildren 'ave been through 'orrific times in the last three years. The children have lost both parents. Danny was wounded twice in the trenches, and now he's just lost 'is beautiful wife, Anna. 'E needs his sister and brother's support, and Kevin's, come to think of it. That's why they want to live in Dublin."

Jenny and Kevin cringed in their seats, but Minnie returned Lady Jackson's glare, and added, "You might think Jenny's not good enough for your son, but I can assure you, she is every bit, if not more the lady you are. For a start, she 'as manners."

"I think that's enough, Minnie," Lord Jackson rumbled.

"It's Mrs Webber to you," Minnie retorted.

Lord Jackson blinked, surprised she had called him out on his impropriety.

The earl and countess continued to watch the spectacle without getting involved, but Charlie, who had said very little during lunch, threw an even bigger spanner into the works when he blurted out, "Were I the heir of Kilbolane House *and* the earl's title, I'd be spending all my time with father and Cousin John, learning the business. Did it ever occur to you, Kevin, that you've put our family's future well-being in jeopardy? No one wanted you to become a doctor or marry a Fenian, but oh, no, the great Kevin Jackson doesn't give a damn about anything or anyone but himself. Isn't that right, Father?"

Kevin lurched to his feet, fists clenched by his side, his good manners holding on by sheer will power. Jenny also stood, but she swayed on her feet as the shock of what Charlie had said hit her. "Kevin, you are the heir to the earl's title as well as your father's estate?"

"He didn't tell you?" Charlie asked her, with a vindictive grin aimed at Kevin.

Jenny felt the room swimming, and as the footman pulled her chair out from behind her, she gripped a handful of the tablecloth to help steady herself. "If you'll excuse me, I'll go pack my things," she said to her parents-in-law, her tone as cool and patronising as theirs had been. Then she glared at Kevin. "I want to leave for Dublin. Now."

Kevin threw his brother a look of disgust, then he apologised to his aristocratic cousins. "I thought it would be a nice idea to introduce my wife to you, but as you can see, my parents and brother must have left their good graces in the library."

"How dare you!" Lord Jackson raged, as he too scrambled to his feet.

"How dare *you,* Father!"

Several minutes later, Jenny stared across the bedroom at Kevin, furious. The atmosphere downstairs had been cold, but it was positively icy between them now. "I can put up with you being the future Lord Jackson. But really, Kevin, an earl as well? When were you going to tell me about that little gem?"

Kevin took a step towards her. "I should have told you I was to inherit. My cousin can't …"

"No, wait. We'll talk about you becoming Earl of What-not later," she cut him off. "First, I need to pack. After that carry-on downstairs, there can be no question of me staying here while you're in London. They don't like me, and I will not stay where I'm not welcome."

Kevin raised his hands. "Darlin' I suggested you stay here because we haven't found a house yet. I won't drag you back with me to London this late in your pregnancy, so don't ask me to. It's madness."

Jenny's eyes narrowed in anger, but she was now calm, for nothing he could say would change her mind. "For the last time, I will not stay here while you're across the Irish Sea or gallivanting in Dublin with Patrick or anywhere else doing anything else. I don't care if I'm almost eight months pregnant or nine months and in the process of dropping a baby in your lap. I will sleep on Dublin's streets before I stay here."

"Think about what's best for the baby, Jenny…"

"Don't!"

"Don't what?"

"Don't lay guilt on me. I won't have it." She slumped on the bed and laid her hands on her tummy. The baby was kicking. "I can't believe this is happening. I was excited about meeting your family. Call me daft, but I pictured them taking me to their hearts and being happy about welcoming a grandchild that will bear their name. I'm disappointed in the Jacksons, and in you for not nipping their bad behaviour in the bud. They haven't even tried to get to know me. I'm a Fenian. Not good enough for their son … an undesirable addition to your illustrious family. That's all I'll ever be!"

"Jenny…"

"No. Jenny, nothing. Minnie knows I'm right. She loves all the pomp and ceremony of being served and having a maid to dress her up in the evenings, but even she can't wait to get out of this place."

Jenny sat on the dressing-table chair and sniffed into her handkerchief. Kevin, standing behind her looking helpless and lost for words, stuck his hands in his trouser pockets. *He knows I'm right,* Jenny thought. "Well, are Minnie and I coming with you to Dublin or shall we walk there ourselves?"

Kevin let out a defeated sigh. "Yes, I'll book a couple of rooms in The Davenport Hotel. It's near the river and close to the centre."

"We won't stay there for long," Jenny said, then sighed with relief. "I'll get Patrick to help me find us a nice house at the price and in the areas you and I discussed, but I promise, I won't say we're buying anything until you've seen it for yourself and agreed to the sale. You'll be back in no time, darlin'."

"Well, I suppose I might get the odd couple of days off to come over."

Jenny rose from the chair. Kevin looked dejected, and she hated seeing him feeling embarrassed about his spiteful family when he didn't have a spiteful hair on his head. She went to him, and softening her tone, said, "You did what you thought was best for me, but what's best is not always the most comfortable. I agree with you about me not returning to London. I want our baby born in Ireland as much as you do, and to tell you the truth, I don't fancy another boat crossing. But our son or daughter doesn't have to be born in your ancestral home in County Cork. We still have time to greet our child in our new home, don't we?"

"About me becoming the earl one day…"

"Shh … not now, Kevin. I don't want to be a countess, and by the look on your face, you're not keen on being the Earl of Cork, either, so let's leave that conversation for another day when we're both a bit more settled. Please, will you go help Minnie down with her baggage?"

"Yes, and I'll send a maid to help you pack…"

"No, you won't. I'm perfectly capable of folding my own clothes, thank you very much."

Kevin stood at the door, shifting his feet like a chastised little boy who didn't know what to say or do. She went to him and laid her cheek against his fast beating heart. "Go on, darlin'. I'll be all right," she said in his embrace.

"My parents will warm to you, I promise."

"But that time is not now, Kevin."

Kevin squeezed his words through tight lips, surprising Jenny with their intensity, “They’ve embarrassed you and me for the last time, Jenny. I hope you’ll forgive them. I don’t know if I ever will.”

Chapter Twenty-Eight

End of May 1919

Dublin, Ireland

For two hours, Kevin had sat with Danny and Patrick, stood aimlessly, drunk tea, and paced up and down the new, ten-foot long Persian rug adorning his living room floor, muttering curses with each turn at the end of the carpet. Periodically, he took his eyes off the multi-coloured woollen threads of the spectacular floor covering and raised them to the ceiling. Above the men, his beloved wife was in agony, her screams becoming louder and more desperate as the hours ticked by.

He'd had enough waiting and wondering and listening to Jenny's pain. Despite Minnie's, Patrick's, and the doctor's orders that he remain downstairs like any other father-to-be, he was going up there to deliver his own child. He turned to the window where Patrick rocked back and forth from heel to toe and Danny stared out at the pretty garden, rich with green grass, tall yellow flag iris by the pond, and an abundance of other vibrant late-spring flowers.

"I've had enough. I'm going up," Kevin announced.

Patrick let out a long, impatient sigh. "Kevin…"

"I know. We've talked about this … but Christ, Patrick, this has been going on since last night. That baby should be out by now."

Patrick left the soothing window alcove and set a reassuring hand on Kevin's shoulder. "Yes, we did talk about this, and you agreed it wasn't right that you deliver your own child.

You're a bloody mess. Look at your hands shaking. You couldn't even hold a cup of hot tea, never mind see to that business upstairs."

"I'll never forgive myself if she dies in childbirth while I'm here walking her new carpet bare."

"Nothing will happen to her," Danny piped up. "Jenny's in good hands. You've spent a fortune on a full-time midwife and the best doctor in Dublin. Besides, we'd know if she wasn't doing well. Our Minnie would've come down here by now if she thought there was a problem."

Danny's words didn't convince Kevin. To hell with what was "right and proper". He was going…

Another scream came from upstairs and then there was silence. After several moments of staring at each other, the three men craned their necks to look at the ceiling, each holding their breaths. Another long moment passed, then a baby's cries, strong and piercing, replaced the silence and the sounds of Jenny's suffering.

Without waiting for the doctor's announcement, Kevin bounded up the stairs to the front bedroom and stepped inside. The midwife and Minnie were helping Jenny sit against fluffed-up pillows.

Jenny beamed at Kevin, her eyes shining with happiness. "You have a son, darlin'," she uttered in a hoarse, exhausted voice, her eyes drifting to the swaddled bundle in the doctor's arms.

"A son, is it?" Danny said, he and Patrick crowding behind Kevin in the doorway.

Kevin rushed over to Jenny's side while Minnie went to the door and linked arms with her grandsons. Unlike Jenny, who was tired but seemed pain-free and composed, Minnie was weeping for joy. "A great-grandmother – me! 'Oo'd 'a thought I'd ever live to see this, eh, Sons?"

"I'm proud of you, my love," said Kevin, kissing Jenny's clammy forehead.

"Yes, well. Don't be asking me to do this again, at least not for a good while," Jenny responded with an exultant smile.

After checking the baby's colour, airways, spine, fingers and toes, Doctor Pearse handed the little bundle back to Jenny, saying, "He's perfect, Mrs Jackson. Congratulations on your healthy boy."

Jenny, who started shedding tears the second she felt her son's warm body on her skin, uttered, "Hello, my beautiful lad."

"Who does he look like?" Patrick asked, as Kevin sat on the edge of the bed.

"Tell us he's a Carmody," Danny called out.

The midwife who was tidying the room, quipped, "Mrs Jackson needs her rest. Why don't you three wait downstairs till she's had some private time with her husband?"

"Let them see their nephew and great-grandson before they go," Jenny said, grinning at her brothers and Minnie.

Patrick and Danny leant over Kevin's shoulder at the bedside, peering at the baby.

"You're a fine son for any man, aren't you?" Kevin croaked emotionally, as he perused the perfect little face blinking up at him.

Patrick concurred, "He is that. He's got your nose."

Kevin laughed, for it was far too early to distinguish facial features. "On you go, take Minnie downstairs and open that bottle of good Irish whiskey I've been saving."

******

Long after the doctor and Danny left for the evening, Kevin snuggled beside Jenny and the baby in bed. "I never thought I could be this happy," he whispered, watching the infant feed from Jenny's teat.

"Me, neither. I have the home of my dreams near to where I grew up, a beautiful garden for our child to enjoy, and the best husband I could ever have hoped for. It's a far cry from three years ago when everything was gloomy, and all those terrible things happened to us." She sighed. "I only wish I'd seen you for who you are long before I did. How could I not love you right from the beginning?"

"Ah, my darling, love sometimes needs to ripen. You weren't ready when your father died, nor after you were injured. The most important thing is that we found each other. And here we are – the three of us a family."

Jenny sighed contentedly, "My mother would've loved this beautiful house…"

"She'd have loved seeing us with servants."

"True. I imagine she'd not have anything to complain about," Jenny mused.

"She'd have spoilt her grandson rotten!"

Kevin looked around the spacious room filled with the finest oak wood furniture and soft golden fabrics on the windows and upholstery. When he'd come over to sign the papers and purchase the house, he'd been thrilled with his wife's choice. Jenny had done well finding this substantial home in his absence, along with the three servants to go with it, he thought. It had five bedrooms, a living room, a front parlour as a reception room, a dining room, his study, and a large kitchen with the most modern appliances Jenny could find. Jenny had got it decorated and ready to move into only one week after his return to Ireland with his final discharge papers from the army and as it turned out, with only five days to spare before the birth of their son. It was a bigger home than he'd envisaged they'd have, but he liked it. One day, he might even open his own medical practice on the ground floor. He kissed her again, knowing he'd have bought her whatever she'd wanted.

After two quiet taps on the door, the midwife, Lizzy, came in and ordered Kevin out. "This is a lovely scene, Dr Jackson, but why don't you join Minnie and Dr Carmody downstairs. I'll take the baby to the nursery when he's finished his feed. Your wife needs her rest now."

"It's not 'the baby' anymore, Lizzy," Kevin said, smiling at the young woman. "He's called Robert Joseph Jackson."

Jenny added, "Robert for my dear late father, and Joseph for Mr Jackson's grandfather."

******

Downstairs, Kevin joined Patrick and Minnie in the dining room. Patrick wasn't staying the night but had promised to keep Minnie company until Kevin returned. Minnie, who was tipsy after drinking two ample glasses of whiskey to celebrate the new arrival, was in fine fettle. "Come and sit, Kevin. You must be starving. You 'aven't eaten all day."

Kevin gave Minnie a tender kiss on her cheek and took a seat. "I think I might be too excited to eat."

"Nonsense, I won't 'ear that. You'll eat and enjoy it. Cook's made a lovely dinner. She said she'll send a light meal on a tray up for our Jenny when she's rested. She's a good woman, that Mrs O'Hara."

"You're too good to me, Minnie."

"Aww, Son, I can never pay you and Jenny back for all you're doing for me. I don't mind saying I was unhappy when I thought you were all leaving me in London. I know 'ow hard doctors work, Kevin, and although I might not be able to climb up and down stairs like I used to, I'll look after Jenny for you when you're out all day." Minnie, not usually prone to tears, sniffed, "If my Susan were 'ere, she'd be taking over by now. Oh, how my girl would have loved this baby."

Kevin patted Minnie's hand. Patrick, who hated to see his granny crying, changed the subject. "Kevin, Danny rushed off soon after our wee toast to the baby. He said he was off to meet Jimmy Carson for a drink at the pub to wet the baby's head. A fine old tradition."

"'E 'as an early start at the docks tomorrow," Minnie added.

"I was glad to hear Jimmy had got over his accident at the docks," Kevin said to Patrick.

"It seems so. Danny mentioned last week that he'd started work again."

"That boy Jimmy's been a godsend to our Danny. Getting him that job in the docks came just in time. I know, I know what you will say … it's beneath 'is station in life, but a job is a job, and it'll give 'is mind something positive to focus on."

"It'll be the making of him, Minnie," Patrick agreed about Danny's new job.

"Have you been to Danny's new house?" Kevin asked Patrick, as William, the manservant, served the first course of soup.

"I went with him when he got the keys to move in. It's a nice house, but I thought it was too big for him, and too far away from the docks. He said he'd make money renting out the three spare bedrooms…"

"See, 'e 'as a good business 'ead on 'im. You wait and see, our Danny's not stupid," Minnie said, her spoon waving in the air as she spoke.

Patrick was less convinced than Minnie regarding Danny's business acumen. Jimmy Carson and another man he called *Tom* were living with him, but Danny had told Patrick only today that he didn't have the heart to charge them money for staying there. "Not to worry, they'll pay me back further down the road. Jimmy's just getting back on his feet after his accident, and Tom's a good lad but can't find a job. A wee bit of charity goes a long way, Patrick," he'd declared.

After a long discussion about Jenny and the baby, the conversation at the table turned to Patrick's affairs, with Minnie asking him, "How are you enjoying your surgical course at the college?"

"I'm enjoying it very much, Minnie. It seems my experience in the war has stood me in good stead. My professor thinks I might skip a year and go straight to my finals."

"I should think so. You've operated on hundreds, perhaps thousands of men and under terrible conditions. You must be way ahead of the other students," Kevin noted.

Patrick didn't want to agree, but it was the truth. He'd learnt a lot in the navy and was not finding the course daunting at all, at least not the practical side. He studied Kevin, his face glowing with the happiness of fatherhood, and wished he could tell his friend and Minnie that he, too, was happier than he'd ever been. He and Quinn saw each other at least three times a week. He often spent the night at Quinn's apartment, which was close to the docks. He was in love and bursting to tell someone.

"... Patrick?"

Patrick's head shot up. "Sorry, Minnie?"

"I asked when you thought you might buy your own place."

"Soon. I've been too busy to think about it, to be honest. My lodgings near the college are handy for work – maybe at the end of the year or before, even. I've seen a cottage I like. It's thirteen miles outside of Dublin, but I'll buy a motorcar to commute. When do you start at the practice?" he asked Kevin, turning the conversation away from himself.

"I've still got two weeks discharge leave left. I'm not going anywhere until my wife's lying-in period is over and she's back on her feet."

Patrick glanced at the clock. It was eight o'clock. He was going straight to Quinn's apartment. As always, a surge of love swelled in him whenever he thought about his nights with the young man who'd brought light into his life. "I think I'll leave dessert if you don't mind, Kevin," he said. "I've got a heavy day tomorrow, and I want to have some steam left at the end of it so I can come back and see Jenny and the baby. I didn't even get to hold my nephew."

Kevin screwed his face up and said, "My parents and brother are coming for a visit tomorrow and staying for dinner. You'll be doing me a huge favour if you'd join us."

"Yes, quite right. I think you should be here for us," Minnie said assertively.

Patrick couldn't think of anything worse, but family was family. "Thanks, I'll look forward to it."

Chapter Twenty-Nine

May 1919

Ballagh, County Tipperary, Ireland

Danny studied his reflection in the three-quarter length mirror in a room above a pub in the town of Ballagh, County Tipperary. Satisfied that his navy-blue suit, white shirt, and green and blue tie looked good, he turned arms wide and asked Jimmy, "Well, will I do?"

"Bejesus, you'll break a few hearts tonight, Danny," Jimmy teased. "Shame about the leather gloves, though."

"I won't break any hearts, and there's nothing I can do about my hand, Jimmy." Danny studied the gloves, nonetheless. "Would you rather see me in those fashionable pansy suede gloves some men are wearing?"

Jimmy took over from Danny at the mirror, and as he brushed down his sleeve with Danny's clothes brush, he said, "Remember, this is a secret volunteer dance, so no getting drunk and falling over, no talking business with anyone unless you know and trust them or they're introduced by someone you know well. And no running off with a girl at the end of the night. We're not known here, and the RIC in this area are looking for any excuse to come down heavy on strangers, same as in County Mayo. The RIC arms its constables with carbines and revolvers and they'll shoot a suspect they think is IRA as soon as look at him – how's my tie?"

"It's not good. Here, let me do it."

Whilst Danny made a neat knot in Jimmy's tie, the latter asked, "Do you think I might meet a nice girl tonight?"

Danny finished what he was doing, took a step backwards, and studied his friend. Jimmy had gone to great lengths to look handsome. He'd taken off his beard, opting for the more fashionable clean-shaven look. The shave had brought out his facial features, including his acne scars, which added to his somewhat attractive, rugged appearance. He was infinitely more presentable now than when he'd sported the caveman-look. His barber, after a few remarks about not seeing him for so long, had given him a stylish haircut slicked back with the old-fashioned, coconut-scented Macassar oil at no additional charge. He'd lost weight since his injury, which had damaged his insides and caused him to undergo two cutting-edge and dangerous operations. He was lucky to have pulled through, but there was no denying he now looked fitter and younger.

"Sure, you'll never be a handsome man, Jimmy, but you'll turn a head or two tonight," Danny finally said.

As Danny laced up his shoes, he said, "Tell me, if it's a secret dance, how will women know to come to it?"

"Oh, they'll know all right. Ballagh's riddled with Republican sympathisers. They'll all be there with their pockets full of money. Mark my words, we'll raise a bucket load at this fundraiser tonight."

Danny was nervous and desperate not to let the boys down. Finally, Dick Mulcahy had allowed him back into the Brotherhood. *'Back into the fold,' he'd said, like I'm a bloody sheep,* Danny recalled.

"Won't the RIC know the dance is being held?"

"Probably, but they won't come in if they know what's good for them unless we cause a rumpus. The Peelers here are a bunch of gobshites. They report anyone with suspicious political leanings to their officers, and those bastards go straight to their district inspectors, who in turn report to Dublin Castle. Come over here, let me brush down that jacket of yours. Jesus, it's full of fluff. When was the last time you put it on?"

"Anna's funeral."

"Ah, Danny boy, sure but you'll not be in the mood for dancing, will you?"

"No, I'm not, but if the women are queuing up for me, I'll do my duty."

As Jimmy brushed the back of Danny's jacket, he remarked, "We're doing well. I know you've not been around much, but our bite is getting under British skin. If we could get our hands on more money… now that would make a difference. By God, it'd make all the difference in the world! Raising funds like we're doing tonight is important, Danny, and being in the company of the South Tipperary boys is an honour. They're hard men, know what they want, and how to get whatever it is they're after."

Danny nodded. "Like I said, I'll do my bit, Jimmy. If there's money in a man's pocket, I'll get it out of him."

******

The dance was going well. Jimmy had been right; plenty of women had come dressed to the nines, ready to part with their money, whether it be a halfpenny or as in one case, a gold sovereign. Danny wasn't a dancer; never had been. He was a good footballer because he was on the stocky side and had near perfect balance, but he'd never been nimble on the dance floor. Half through the night, however, he had danced the reels with the lads and lassies, and had held a woman in his arms, letting her take the lead in a dance called the 'One-Step.' Stupid name, he'd thought, for it had a lot more than 'one bloody step' to it, and he had tripped over his feet numerous times while praying for the end of the music.

She was a pretty girl – Mildred – a dark beauty, Danny thought, as they'd moved around the dance floor. But she might as well be a toothless, flat chested dwarf for all the enthusiasm he had for her. He was empty, bereft, and felt as if he were being unfaithful to his Anna with someone who couldn't lick the dainty leather boots she often wore. His heart was hurting, a physical, throbbing ache, like a permanent toothache. He wanted his Anna, and no matter how many pretty girls he looked at, none would compare to her in beauty and spirit. Danny had thanked the girl who'd looked disappointed when he didn't offer to take her to the drinks' table. She was still throwing him dirty looks now. *Well, what of it?* She'd already coughed up a shilling, had done her bit, and he'd done his.

To get rid of his melancholy, Danny went to the drinks' table alone and asked for a Guinness Extra Stout with a whiskey chaser. He was already feeling the effects of the alcohol he'd had earlier and was trying his best to enjoy himself and keep a smile on his face. Jimmy, he saw, was off talking to a couple of girls. Since his recovery from the motorcar bomb that had put a shard of glass in his guts, he'd been much more outgoing with the opposite sex. He had his reasons for 'going full at it,' as he'd termed it, and he'd enlightened Danny when he was recovering in the latter's new house. 'When I thought I was dying, I wasn't afraid of death, but it *disappointed* me that I'd never married or fathered a child. I'll need to get onto that straight away. There's no time to lose,' he'd declared.

Danny still wasn't sure why the Tipperary lads invited him and Jimmy to this *ceilidhe* at Éamon O Duibhir's house. Yes, Jimmy was originally from Tipperary, but he was just a baby when an English Landlord had confiscated his father's farm and thrown his family into the street like dogs. Since then he'd lived in Dublin; first with his family, then on his own after his parents succumbed to tuberculosis. Jimmy knew the lads who'd invited him along, but Danny only knew *of* them. The four major players were being hunted by the British army, and the RIC, also known as the Peelers. Danny felt as if he were part of a game but didn't know the rules or what its objective was. Yet, he was every bit a player on the board as anyone else in the room.

To hell with it, he thought, cheering up again as he went for another refreshment. He was dancing right in the middle of a martial law area where he could expect a British raiding party to break open the door any minute. Or maybe someone there could slip away and report the goings on to the nearest police barracks, situated two miles away. All sorts of things could go wrong, yet no one he could see looked in the least bit bothered. The sense of living on the edge excited Danny, reminding him of the more successful campaigns he had autopsied to keep himself sane.

"Ah, the whiskey's grand. I'll have another," Danny requested to the elderly man serving the drinks. Someone had done up the spacious basement nicely. They'd decorated it with Irish tricolour flags and banners. Long trestle tables lined one side of the hall, as it was being called for the evening, and atop them were bottles of spirits, glasses, and small barrels of

Guinness Dublin Porter, Guinness Foreign Extra Stout, and other stouts donated by the brewers, Beamish Crawford, and Murphy's. Two fiddlers, an accordion player, and a bodhrán drummer were supplying the music, and a man and woman were periodically singing songs with Irish Republican themes. It was a good atmosphere and despite his unenthusiastic promise to accompany Jimmy, the Guinness and whiskey chasers he was drinking were going down a treat. For the first time in months, he saw a sliver of light in his gloomy world.

To make sure he didn't get too drunk, Danny filled up with sandwiches, pickles, and soda scones with lashings of butter. He savoured every bite, every morsel of scone and slice of cheese. They were treats that had been denied to him for years. He still hid food in his trouser pockets in case he got hungry when he was out; always carried a biscuit or piece of cake wrapped up in greaseproof paper on his person. Since the deprivations of war, his need to save food for an emergency had become a built-in mechanism in his brain…

"Sergeant, is that you there, all clean-faced and smartened up?"

Danny spun around with his half-full glass of Guinness in his hand and gasped with pleasure. Finn, his mate from the trenches, stood before him in a dark-grey suit, white shirt and emerald green tie. His hair was in the same style as Danny's, shaved at the sides and back and longer on the crown.

Shaking Finn's hand, Danny said, "Of all the places to meet up, eh?" Then he grew serious. "I've got a bone to pick with you. You gave me a dodgy address, ye daft bugger. I went to look for you as soon as I got back, and an old man answered the door. Said you'd moved out a year earlier."

"That'd be my wife that moved. Sure, she left a forwarding address with the people who rented our old place, but I was raging when I finally caught up with her and the kids. I gave that bloody address of mine to I don't know how many Irishmen I met in France and Belgium. Just as well Dublin's a small world."

Danny grinned again. "Jesus, it's good to see you with a clean face. I hardly recognised you."

Finn laughed. "You too. Look at ye, dressed up in your burial suit. What are you doing here?"

"I'm with Jimmy Carson," Danny said, pointing to the man in question, now dancing with a woman and looking as proud as the punch that was being served.

"Ah, good for Jimmy. We'll find him a wife, yet."

Danny laughed. "Since his brush with death, he's been on a mission to marry a good Catholic woman. Now finding one doesn't seem to be a problem for him, but he doesn't seem to understand that a man has to court a girl before giving her the big proposal."

Finn chuckled, as he said, "Living as if there's no tomorrow, eh? That attack on Michael's headquarters won't be the last, Danny. Did they find the arsehole who did it?"

"I believe they did and rubbed him out as a traitor. He won't be blowing anything else up."

Finn scowled, scanned the hall, and spat, "The British will never recognise the IRA or the Dáil. We need money, Danny. It's costing a fortune to keep the leadership safe. Did you know de Valera is going to America next month? He'll ask the Americans for official recognition of the Irish Republic and to float a loan to finance the work of our government."

"I hope some of that money will go towards our military operations."

"It will. Mark my words, it'll go a long way if we can get the American people on our side. The Americans are good fundraisers, and they're proud of their connections to Ireland."

Danny, heeding Jimmy's warning not to talk business, took a furtive look around. He saw people dancing and drinking, laughing and shaking hands, and doing what one would expect at a function such as this. If British spies were present, they'd be hard pushed to see anything other than folk having a good time. "Have you heard from Freckles?" he asked switching topics.

"Not a peep. Poor bugger's probably still in hospital."

"Do you ever get nightmares, Finn?"

"Every night, or near as damn it. They're easing a bit, but every time I hear a gunshot or a motorcar backfiring or any loud, sudden noise, I nearly jump out my skin. My bleedin' heart pounds like it will explode at any second and I start sweating. It's like feeling the fire of the Somme on my face."

Danny was strangely comforted that he was not suffering the after-effects of war alone. "Me, too. It's our curse."

"Might well be, Danny, but we'll have to learn to live with it or we'll end up like Freckles. Come to think of it, is it true you had some sort of fit?"

Danny shook his head, angry at having found out there'd been gossip about himself, saying he'd cracked under pressure. "No, Finn, it was nothing of the kind. I got caught up in the explosion and my mind wandered … it wandered back to the trenches … that's all. Jesus, I'm sick of feckin' rumours about me."

Finn placed his hand on Danny's shoulder. "You need not tell me about the mind flashing back to France. Like I said, I've gone there a few times myself, and it's as real as … well, you know. I'll put a stop to any of the talk about you unless it's good talk. Just know you were a good soldier, a good sergeant. Fancy another drink? We might as well enjoy ourselves."

"Ah, why not? I don't think I'll get Jimmy out of here anytime soon, by the looks of it," Danny answered.

Chapter Thirty

Ballagh, County Tipperary

"… Danny, wake up … wake up, will ye?"

Danny opened one eye, stretched out his arm, and took the hot cup of coffee Jimmy handed to him. "Ah, good lad."

"I had to go downstairs to the pub and beg the landlord for it, so drink it all," Jimmy said, looking agitated.

Danny raised himself enough to take a sip, then set the cup on the floor. He groaned, "Jesus, I will never again drink whiskey. I feel as though my guts are on fire." Then he swung his long johns-clad legs over the side of the bed and promptly vomited on the carpet. "Aww, feck it. Sorry about that," he mumbled, raising his head and wiping his mouth boorishly with the back of his hand.

"We've got bigger problems than last night's booze coming up," Jimmy answered, as he threw a towel at Danny. "Clean that up, then get dressed. We're in trouble."

At those words, Danny felt another bout of vomit dancing around in his stomach. He remembered everything from the previous night. He hadn't been in a stupor, hadn't fallen over, hadn't started a fight, verbally or physically, and he'd been sociable with everyone he'd met. Unlike the pub in Greenwich, he'd loved everyone at the ceilidhe. "Did my tongue run away with me last night? Did I upset anyone?" he asked.

"I don't know. I was smooching with a girl most of the night. She gave me her address. I think she might be the one."

"Well, that's good, so why do you look like a mule has kicked you in the face?"

"It's Séan Hogan. He met a girl and went off with her."

"Where to?"

"I don't know exactly, but we'll find out. All I know is the stupid bugger got himself arrested by the Peelers."

Danny left the vomit-soaked towel on the carpet and sat on the edge of the bed, picturing the young, good-looking man in question. He'd met Séan Hogan for the first time at the dance, but he'd learnt about the youngster's exploits earlier through Jimmy. He was already one of the most wanted men in Ireland, one of the big four. "Christ, the police have him, and him being hunted for John Milling's murder?"

Jimmy nodded; his face was ashen with worry. "Bloody nitwit. He was warned not to leave the hall. Finn came for us twenty minutes ago. He's taking us to see some lads about mounting a rescue, so hurry and get dressed. And leave the floor the way it is."

"I can't leave this mess…"

"Danny, we're in a pub. It won't be the first time the landlord has found vomit on his floor. C'mon, get dressed."

Ten minutes later, in the premises of O'Keeffe's of Glenough, Danny and Jimmy met Finn and three other wanted IRA men in the same Tipperary battalion as Séan Hogan, the man they were now planning to rescue.

Jimmy introduced Danny, and the latter spoke briefly to the men: Dan Breen, a short, stocky man with the hard-as-nails build of a blacksmith, Seán Treacy, almost six feet tall and as solid as a tenement block shit-house, and Séumas Robinson, a wiry, skinny man who looked like a knackered horse.

Danny listened to the conversation that ensued.

"JJ would decide the same as we have, were any of us in his situation," Dan Breen said.

"...we're agreed on a rescue, then?" Seán Treacy said, more a statement than a question.

Finn, who'd informed the men about the capture of JJ – Séan Hogan's nickname – asked, "Where are you thinking of mounting the rescue?"

"First, we have to find out where the bastards took JJ," Breen answered. "But we can't go out now ... no, it's too early. We're bound to bump into a British army patrol or the Peelers."

"They could have already moved him to Thurles, Tipperary, or even Cashel," Treacy mused, then added; "Wherever he is, with every hour that goes by, he's in greater danger of being locked up in a place that's out of our reach. We're already passing the word to our informants for information; we may get a lead through them."

Danny straightened as Breen looked him over before flicking his eyes to Jimmy. "Jimmy, the landlord's got a bicycle. Give it a wee while then take a turn on it. See if you can trace our JJ."

Finn stubbed out his cigarette in the ashtray, and surprising the Tipperary men, said, "Look, I know you don't want to hear this, but maybe you three shouldn't get involved in a rescue. You're already being hunted for the Soloheadbeg ambush and John Milling's murder in County Mayo. If the RIC spot your ugly mugs, the mission will be over before it begins."

"JJ is wanted for the same British crimes as us three," Seán Treacy reminded Finn, gesturing to himself, Breen, and Robinson. "It's my guess they'll get JJ away by rail not road, and if he is on a train and we don't get him off it before they arrive at the heavily guarded prison, they'll execute him."

Breen then added with a cheeky grin, "Besides, what sort of mates would we be, not to rescue our pal on his eighteenth birthday, eh?"

Breen had sent cyclists in all directions to try to pick up Hogan's trail, but his captors had a huge start and as the morning wore on, Danny saw the men beginning to despair. Then, Jimmy returned with news. "They've taken him to Thurles' Barracks," he told the men.

"For feck's sake. It'd be easier to get inside the jaws of hell than get in there," Breen groaned.

"They won't keep him there for long. Eventually, they'll move him to one of the big prisons … could be Mountjoy, Cork, Belfast, Dundalk?" Treacy suggested.

Breen nodded, and added, "It'll be Cork, and you can guarantee it will be by train. They usually send Munster men there. We should go now to the Maloney homestead at Lackelly. It's only a few miles from Emly railway station. It'll be a good place to pick up JJ's train. The police rarely guard it, and we've got plenty of friends in that area…"

"I don't know the Maloneys," Jimmy said.

"Well, you're about to meet them, Jimmy," Breen told him. "They'll give us shelter while we get a plan worked out."

Mounting a rescue was a dangerous, fantastical idea on paper, especially from a train. Then Danny reminded himself that the IRA were at war with the British, and every weapons' raid they carried out, every assassination of a British loyalist, every seditious word they wrote and spoke and put out publicly was dangerous. This rescue, as outlandish as it seemed, was no more, no less, than any other mission undertaken in the quest for Irish liberation. And if they succeeded, it would be a great propaganda coup.

Excitement replaced Danny's hangover, although he was still nauseous and a bit shaky on his feet. He hadn't helped himself by gulping down the lukewarm, bitter coffee Jimmy had provided earlier, but it had made him alert.

Dan Breen studied Danny for the first time with a lingering look up and down, twice over. "Finn has vouched for you. You're under Dick Mulcahy's Dublin brigade, is that right?"

"Yes, that's right. I was also in Frongoch with Michael Collins."

Treacy asked, "Well, what's up with your hands, then?"

Danny, dwarfed in size by the tall, broad-shouldered man, responded with a nonchalant shrug. "A war wound, nothing to worry about, Mr Treacy, I'm probably still the best shot in Ireland."

Finn concurred, saying, "He's not kidding, he was one of the most successful snipers we had in our Company in France. He was my sergeant in the war, and I trust him with my life."

"Good enough for me," Breen said. Then his face lit up. "I don't know about you lot, but as soon as we get to May Maloney's place, I'm having fried eggs, fried bread and bacon. I need something to soak up last night's whiskey."

Danny grinned. Breen's words fell like manna from heaven.

Chapter Thirty-One

Dan Breen had ordered that under no circumstances should any IRA member send telegrams or make telephone calls. 'We'll be giving away our plans to our enemy, so whomever we contact will have to be in person.' This instruction led Jimmy and Finn to leave the area riding bicycles that would take them to Tipperary Town, where they were to ask the local IRA battalion for reinforcements to help with the rescue.

Danny found their departure discomforting, for it left him with three hunted men who were hot-headed risk-takers. They had killed men and were on the run, yet instead of feeling apprehensive about the rescue they were putting together, they were as excited as young boys going on a grand adventure. He felt inadequate in their company and wondered why they'd brought him along instead of using him as an errand boy.

After acquiring four bicycles from helpful Republican sympathisers in the town, Breen, Robinson, Treacy, and Danny faced the long journey to the Maloney house.

"How far is it?" Danny asked. The answer shocked him.

"It'll be about fifty miles. It's thirty or thereabouts on the normal direct route, but we'll have to avoid all main roads and the neighbourhood of Tipperary town, so we'll probably do about fifty, all told," Breen answered.

Danny groaned, "Jesus, fifty…"

Treacy countered, "We've gone five nights without sleep, Danny. C'mon, hurry the feck on, and stop your complaining."

Hours later, Danny felt himself drifting as he rode, but he shook himself, pulled hard on his military fortitude, and, gritting his teeth, rode up hills and down dales and afterwards crossed the border into County Limerick through the old village of Cullen, and then onto Ballyneety where the old castle stood black against the moon and starlit sky.

On a flat piece of road, Robinson fell off his bicycle and lay prostrate on the road, sound asleep. When the other two men woke him, he mounted as though it were the most natural thing in the world, and on they rode until they arrived at Lackelly and May Maloney's house.

Danny was exhausted. His legs felt like jellified ten-ton weights as he dragged himself, shaking, into the Maloneys' kitchen where he found Finn and Jimmy, who'd arrived just fifteen minutes earlier.

Later, somewhat recovered, the men sat around the kitchen table and ate a hearty breakfast of home-made sausages, eggs and toast, washed down by a large pot of tea. After she'd cleared the table, May Maloney left on a bicycle ride of her own to Thurles to find out if JJ was still being held there. The woman was a gem, Danny thought. She was a good cook, a nice hostess, and she was not afraid of taking a wee risk or two.

Danny, his elbows on the table, his fists raised and holding up his head at the chin, listened in amazement at the speed and efficiency with which these men operated. He marvelled at the complexities of contacting the various IRA cells using dispatch riders, and how the cells had answered the call without hesitation. As it often did, his mind went back to the Easter Uprising when he'd been a courier running under barrages of weapons' fire from British and Irish defensive positions to the post office; back and forth for days, delivering messages on hastily written notes.

Now, the IRA networks were more sophisticated and expansive. It also seemed that this time around, most of the

Irish population were with the IRA, for despite the three men he'd travelled with being wanted by the British and having substantial financial rewards attached to their names, everyone they'd asked along the way had helped them.

Sitting in May Maloney and her brother's kitchen, Danny felt a pride that had been absent during his time in the army. He had fought with honour, had done his best for his men and for Britain, but this was an altogether different feeling; more like the one he'd had during the uprising three years earlier. He glanced at Jimmy and then Finn, who was leaning against the kitchen sink, chatting quietly with Breen.

"Thanks, Jimmy," Danny whispered in Jimmy's ear.

"What for?" Jimmy asked.

"For taking me with you to the dance last night. I've been in a mess for months, and now I feel as though my life is starting over. I have a purpose to my being again."

"You're not getting all weepy like a girl, are you, Danny?" responded Jimmy, eyes wide with horror.

"No, ye eejit. It's just … ah, Jimmy. This is a big day for me and … well, I want you to know I won't freeze. I won't let anyone down. I've turned a corner. Danny Carmody is back to his old self…"

******

At eleven o'clock that morning, the men lay their bicycles flat in a ditch at the side of a road and waited for the reinforcements from Tipperary to arrive. Danny noted the collective panic when, by eleven-thirty, the lads had still not appeared.

"Finn, are you certain you delivered the message to the right person?" Breen snapped, as he lost his calm exterior.

Finn retorted, "Of course, I'm bloody sure. We delivered the message in Tipperary town to a man called Johnnie Doherty, from the battalion."

"Ah, Johnnie, he's a good man. He wouldn't have let us down on purpose. No, something's happened that shouldn't have happened," Treacy stated, but didn't elaborate.

Breen looked at his pocket watch. "Christ, it's already after eleven-thirty and the train's due at noon! I'm not letting them take our JJ away without a fight."

Treacy reminded Breen, "Dan, we're going up against at least four … maybe up to eight constables armed with rifles, revolvers, and bayonets…"

"I know that, but I'll still get him or die in the trying. C'mon, we're going on that bloody train, regardless."

Danny was not a fatalist or a man to believe solely in luck, but later, he felt sure that the 'Luck o' the Irish' had been with them when they'd charged into Emly train station, then scanned every carriage on the arriving noon train only to find that Séan was not on it.

Breen and the others were crestfallen, but when they went back to their resting place, Jimmy came up with an idea that cheered them up. "What about asking the Galtee boys for help?" he suggested. "That battalion's in East Limerick Brigade. The men from Galbally and Ballylanders won't let us down."

"Right then, you and Finn go fetch them, and be quick about it," Breen answered.

At five o'clock in the afternoon, five men from Galbally arrived at Emly's railway station. Finn and Jimmy, however, were not with them. Danny, knowing they'd have swum through shark-infested waters to join the others, agonised over the reason for their absence and concluded that they'd got arrested by the RIC or British soldiers or they'd not been able to get through the roadblocks and were hiding out somewhere.

At the station, one of the Galbally men reported, "A man in our battalion got on the train at Thurles and identified JJ Hogan's carriage. He telegraphed through a coded message to a foreman he knows at the Knocklong coalmine who then told the stationmaster."

Five of the men, including Danny, were carrying revolvers; the others were unarmed. Dan Breen again surprised Danny, informing him that he would go with his small group to Knocklong station, along with Robinson and Seán Treacy. Danny had been prepared to attack the train at Emly, but being a soldier, he was accustomed to sudden, unexplained order changes.

"... the rest of you will board the train here at Emly and give us a sign which carriage JJ is in. If we fail, we'll motor to Blarney and try to pick up the escort from there. Is everyone clear?" Treacy asked the men.

Confusing as everything sounded to Danny's inexperienced ears, tactics were tactics. He surmised the reason for the change in train station was to give them more time to set up the assault and to get a signal to save time in their search for JJ Hogan. Breen told Danny the train station at Knocklong was some two miles from the nearest British garrison and was rarely guarded.

On the platform, Danny felt his loaded pistol digging into his back, just above his trousers' waistband. He shivered. It had turned cold, and it would become even colder after dark. It was also threatening to rain, and he wasn't wearing an overcoat.

Strange, he thought, how such a trivial matter could enter his mind at such a momentous time. Finn had suggested earlier that if the rescue failed, he, Jimmy, and Danny were to get back to Dublin as fast as they could by any means other than train. Danny had not imagined he'd be without his two friends, and he wondered again why Jimmy and Finn hadn't returned with the Galbally men.

At seven o'clock, the Thurles to Cork train arrived at Knocklong station in County Limerick. When the steam engine whooshed to a stop, a man stuck his head out of the door of the third carriage, pointing forward to the second carriage.

"That's the signal. Let's go get our man," Breen commanded.

Breen, Robinson, Treacy, and Danny charged onto the carriage indicated by the signal, but it was a long corridor-carriage divided into a dozen different compartments. At the corridor connection – the junction where the two carriages met – they found a couple of the men from Galbally who had boarded at Emly station.

"Hogan's in a compartment further along. He's sitting beside at least one officer facing the engine and there's another two officers occupying the seat opposite. The good news is I didn't see any guards blocking the corridor," one lad informed Treacy.

Treacy, the leader of the operation, assigned Breen to watch the railway guards' compartment at the back of the train then said, "Come on boys!" He sprang from the running board where he'd been standing and sped along the final corridor with Danny and Robinson at his heels.

"Hands up!" Treacy shouted as he burst into the compartment.

Danny, who was beside Treacy in the cramped space, spotted the constable next to the handcuffed Séan lift his pistol to the side of his prisoner's head. Danny fired with no hesitation, killing the policeman with a perfect headshot. If the man had thought to twitch his finger before dying, JJ Hogan's brain splatter would have added to the pandemonium.

In an instant, all hell broke loose. JJ Hogan launched himself across the compartment aisle and smashed his still handcuffed hands into another constable's face. The officer, with blood spurting from his nose, got up, hurled himself through the glass of the compartment's window, fell onto the platform, and then raced along it, roaring obscenities.

The tiny, overcrowded compartment erupted in individual battles. The giant, Treacy, and the RIC sergeant, also a bull of a man, were engaged in a desperate hand-to-hand battle with both men grappling for the same gun; meanwhile, Danny was struggling to take the officer's rifle from him. All four were battling for their lives, but as much as the Galbally lads wanted to help, there was not enough room in the compartment to get involved.

After a fierce struggle, Danny wrangled the rifle from the officer, and in doing so walloped it hard against the side of the man's head, knocking him out. Meanwhile, Treacy was still fighting for his life against a much bigger and stronger man, who was trying to free his right hand to grip the revolver and shoot. After the gun fired, Treacy, through sheer strength of will and desperation, eventually prevailed after getting hold of the weapon and shooting the officer at point blank range in the chest.

Danny shouted at the overly excited JJ Hogan, "Get off the train and run like hell!" But in the confusion of all that was occurring; mainly the discovery that Treacy had been shot in the neck during his tussle, the policeman Danny had knocked out managed to slip out of the compartment with his colleague's pistol concealed in his greatcoat. And before the IRA boys in the passageway could stop him, he'd scarpered off the train and reached the platform. There, in a dazed state, he opened fire, spraying the carriages with bullets, almost hitting innocent passengers in other carriage compartments. He then sent a volley of fire into the compartment where the fighting was taking place, causing glass and wood shrapnel to fly, and a bullet fragment to hit Danny's right arm.

Breen, hearing the further commotion, raced to the front carriages from the rear of the train where he'd been standing guard. Once there, he jumped onto the platform, and armed with only a revolver, tried to draw the policeman's erratic fire away from the train. When the policeman returned Dan Breen's fire, he hit the latter, first in his chest and then in his right arm. Danny, who saw the firefight from inside the compartment, saw Breen drop his pistol then pick it up with his left hand and take aim again. Possibly because he saw the gun levelled at him, the policeman turned on his heels and fled the station.

Danny's body was hot as hell. His ears rang as he staggered off the train, but they picked up the banshee sound of women screaming inside other carriages, and even more so as they fled the station. He felt disorientated, but his senses returned on the zigzagged run he made along the platform. As he rushed to the end, he noted the place looked deserted, and the few people who remained seemed rooted in fear.

Danny tried to catch his breath, worried they had left him to find his own way to Dublin. Then he spotted JJ Hogan, still wearing his handcuffs and heading to the station's main gate with two other men. Four other lads were bleeding from wounds received during the encounter, and the wounded Dan Breen was being half-carried toward the exit.

Danny came up to Treacy, who had an ugly brand of burnt, blistered skin from where he'd been shot in the neck during his fight with the officer. He followed the men carrying Treacy and panted, "Where are you going, Seán?"

"We're going to race to Shanahan's of Glenlara," one of the other men said after Seán had tried to reply with a hoarse croak. "You go with those lads over there. They'll get your wound seen to and make sure you get yourself back to Dublin. Thanks, Danny. See you again sometime."

Danny stumbled towards the exit, and as he hurried through the station's open gates, one of the Galbally boys shouted, "Get yourself in here." Danny glanced to his left, then lurched forwards in a strange, pitching gait towards a van. It hadn't bothered to stop but had slowed down considerably. When Danny reached it, a man half-helped, half-dragged him into the back, slamming the doors closed as soon as his legs were in.

In the relative darkness and silence, he started to feel the pain from the stray bullet that had hit him. The rush of adrenaline had slowed, leading towards the inevitable fatigue, and he knew of the blood oozing through the hole in the sleeve of his funeral suit jacket. The searing, white agony intensified, as if all the blood in his body had become flame, and in sympathy to their brethren blood cells seeping out of Danny's arm, rushed to that single spot, centring all the pain in the world just … right … there.

Danny didn't know the driver or the front passenger's names, and he was too tired to ask or to tell them his name or where he was from or what had happened to his deformed hand, and so on. The dance, the hangover, the fifty-mile journey that had taken most of the day and through the previous night, the waiting around, and finally the rescue and all its exertions had almost killed him. But before he conked out, he had to know, "Where are we going?"

"First, we're getting you to a doctor, then we're heading to Galbally. From there, our people will get you back to Dublin."

"Is JJ Hogan safe?" Danny uttered as he began to doze off.

"He is that. Two of my men took him across to the butcher's shop. We've got a good lad in there. He'll split open the handcuffs with his meat cleaver. Don't worry about our JJ, we'll take care of him. Well done, Danny lad. I heard you took a great shot."

"Ah, you know my name … famous at last…"

Chapter Thirty-Two

15 May 1919

Dublin, Ireland

The evening had not yet begun at Quinn O'Malley's, but as Patrick sipped his before-dinner whiskey, he felt his tired muscles relaxing and the day's worries ebbing away. Being there was a tonic that lifted his spirits and gave him a sense of well-being.

Quinn's spacious apartment was on the first floor above his woollen goods factory premises. The shop and part of the manufacturing space were on the ground floor while the stock and accounting offices were in the warehouse below ground. The apartment was homely, with welcoming warm-coloured fabrics, rugs, comfortable couches and armchairs, and it had a host who delighted in looking after his guests and having Patrick around for cosy 'dinners for two' whenever the latter could tear himself away from his studies.

Quinn had parents and a brother and sister who lived in Tipperary, his place of birth. He had once remarked to Patrick that since the Easter Uprising, his family had not visited Dublin; thus, the onus was on him to travel backwards and forwards for family reunions. 'Get-togethers are as infrequent as Christmas day,' he had added in an icy tone, and Patrick had not asked him to elaborate on his relationship with his family.

Everyone enjoyed Quinn's dinner parties. He saw to it that 'hard to come by' foodstuff and good wines rarely seen even in Mitchell's, considered Dublin's finest wine merchant, were available, and he always provided stimulating company. This evening, his guests were wool merchants who respectively supplied Quinn with carded wool and manufactured woollen products.

Patrick stood by the fireplace, as Quinn and his two guests entered the room and crossed it to join him.

"First introductions, then we'll eat," Quinn said, with a broad grin on his handsome face. "Patrick, this is my good friend and business associate, Renaldas Milavetz."

The man was short and stocky, had a mop of fair hair, a nose that was long and straight, and clear blue eyes that wore a steady, open gaze. He looked nothing like the stereotypical Jew depicted in pictures or on the streets of London's East End. Patrick stretched out his hand, saying, "Very pleased to meet you, Renaldas."

"Please, call me Aldas."

Quinn then turned his attention to the older man, a rather staid-looking fellow with a ruddy face and thick moustache whiskers, which when pulled straight would not only reach but could probably tuck behind his ears. "Patrick, this is John Kelly, a good friend of mine who has taught me all I know about the wool trade," Quinn said.

John's serious face broke into a smile. "Nonsense, Quinn, I would not have taken you on as a partner had you not known what you were doing. Good to meet you, Patrick. Quinn tells me you're a surgeon?"

"Not yet. I'm a Surgical Registrar at present," Patrick replied hurriedly. "I have another year or two to go before I can call myself Consultant Surgeon."

"He's modest," Quinn said. "He operated on men at sea during the war and saved God knows how many lives. He was on HMHS *Britannic.*"

"My God. You had a lucky escape, eh? That White Star Line is cursed if you ask me," John said.

Whilst Quinn oversaw to last-minute arrangements in the kitchen with Alister, his cook and manservant, Patrick, Aldas, and John took their places at the dining table. Patrick was curious about Aldas, who spoke with an indigenous Irish brogue, despite his foreign name. "Were you born in Ireland, Aldas?" Patrick began the table conversation.

"No, I'm a Lithuanian-born Jew. I arrived on this wonderful Emerald Isle when I was five and became a citizen at ten."

"I see. And is your family with you?"

"All dead, I'm afraid, but before they died, they taught me what I needed to know about my heritage. I don't follow the Talmud studies or Lithuanian customs, but I do speak *Litvishe Yiddish.*"

John, who had met Aldas on prior occasions, asked, "How many Jews are in Lithuania today, do you know … since the war?"

"Ah, that's a difficult question to answer, John. You see, after the 1793 Second Partition of the Polish-Lithuanian Commonwealth, Lithuanian Jews became subjects of the Russian Empire. Locally, in Lithuania, we numbered close to a quarter of a million, but that was before the war. Now…?" He shrugged.

As Aldas' words trailed off, Quinn joined the men at the table and said, "Aldas travels a great deal. He's my main wool supplier for the Eastern Hemisphere. He's been as far as Australia and New Zealand, and to the not-so-far Outer

Hebrides. We're looking into buying cotton now from America. He's just come back from the Carolinas."

"Interesting. You're going into cotton?" John asked, raising an eyebrow.

Quinn slapped John on the back, saying, "John here, operates closer to home. He's a true Irish miller."

"I am, but sadly I will never be able to compete with the mighty savage beast of the mechanised Leeds mills."

Aldas nodded his agreement. "Biggest in the world, and every year they require soaring amounts of raw materials."

"Leeds will get whatever it needs," Aldas added. "It has the great British Empire feeding it wool shipped in from Australia and New Zealand, cotton from India and the real good quality cottons from the West Indies and America, and of course, flax from us in Ireland. I understand why Quinn wants to get into the cotton business."

Aldas paused, rolled his eyes and then looked upwards. "Ah, if only I had a foothold in those Leeds Mills. What a splendid millionaire I would make."

Envy flickered across John's face, and he changed the subject, asking Patrick, "You must work long hours and see some fascinating conditions in people? I admit, modern medicine enthrals me. Do you operate on live people yet?"

"Yes. As a Registrar I'm scheduled for shorter working weeks now than as a surgical assistant, and I'm conducting most of my own surgical operations on people. Of course, Dublin's most affluent patients get full personal care from 'Sir,' or as we call him, 'God himself.' To tell you the truth, some of the most interesting and challenging cases come through the charitable trusts run by the Catholic Archdiocese of Dublin and the Sisters of Charity. This past week was a tough one, much more time demanding than usual. Two nights ago, I was on duty from eight in the morning until midnight. I'd held ward rounds and a clinic, but that afternoon we had a couple of emergency cases come up in the theatre on top of the two planned surgeries."

"Tell us about them?" Aldas requested.

"Well, that morning I made a six-inch abdominal incision and removed a man's gallbladder. He had a gallstone that resembled a lump of green-black polished stone almost the size of a bantam chicken's egg – it's the largest I've seen so far." Patrick looked at John, who seemed genuinely interested in the subject, then he glanced at Aldas who, having requested the information, now looked aghast. Patrick chuckled, "I enjoy talking about my job, but perhaps I should refrain from describing the gory details of people's insides at the dinner table. Tell me John, are you a Dubliner?"

"No, I'm County Kilkenny, born and bred, and proud of it. I'll admit it, though, business trips like these to the big city allow me to have a bit of pleasure in my dull life."

"Did the war in Europe affect your trade?"

"No, it was good for business." John's eyes narrowed in anger. "It's this Dáil and IRA carry-on that's not good for my mill. It wouldn't surprise me one bit if the British start boycotting our exports to teach us a lesson."

"Ireland will do what it has to do to get her independence, I suppose," Aldas said.

John threw Aldas a baleful look, then laid his feelings bare. "I'm surprised you would say that. You of all people must know it's the population that suffers in these situations, and not the antagonists. Sure, Germany occupied Lithuania in the war until it and Bolshevik Russia signed the Treaty of Brest-Litovsk. You must have family over there who've suffered."

"This is different," Aldas objected.

"This is nonsense, that's what it is. Look at what happened in Knocklong two days ago – two RIC officers dead while carrying out their duties, a train riddled with bullets, and women and children scared almost to death – I'd execute the lot of that IRA crowd, me."

Patrick, shocked at the ferocity of John's words, wondered whether he should intervene on Quinn's behalf and throw this topic out of the window. Discussions like these between men who were not bonded in a single belief or ideology could, and often did prove dangerous, or at the very least, unpalatable. He opened his mouth to change the subject but was beaten to the punch by Aldas, who was clearly intrigued by John's stance.

"I take it you're not in agreement with the Republican's call for total independence?" Aldas asked John.

"It's not a case of agreeing or disagreeing with the cause, it's that I don't believe violence and murder achieve anything. The Germans killed two nephews of mine in the war. The last thing we need in this island is more shooting, bombs, and deaths."

"When does any country ever *want* guns and violence on its streets?" Quinn now joined the delicate conversation. "We tried to shoot our way to glory in the Easter Uprising, and that didn't work. Now we're trying the political route, and the British won't accept our legally elected ministers in the Dáil. The underlying issue is that Ireland wants to become an independent nation. England must now choose to evacuate the country or hold it by foreign garrison in a perpetual state of war. If we won't give up and they won't leave, I see no path other than the one the Republicans are pursuing."

John shook his head in disagreement. "Have you seen the mess Dublin's in? There was nothing political about blowing up half the city in '16. A group of men cannot simply walk out of the General Post Office building holding a signed piece of paper and declaring themselves leaders of a nation when that nation belongs to another. Yes, damn right I'd have executed the lot of them, including the men who went to that prison camp in Wales."

"You'd have hanged almost two thousand men?" Patrick blurted out, his eyes blazing as he thought of Danny's time at Frongoch.

Aldas jumped into the fray. "I must disagree with you, John. Both sides made mistakes, but Britain's biggest blunder three years ago was their quick-fire executions of the Easter Rising's leaders, not to mention the British Government's efforts to extend conscription to Ireland last year."

"I agree that the British conscription demands helped to raise the membership of Sinn Féin and the Irish Volunteers." Quinn said. "If you ask me, that one misguided act changed the entire way the nationalist movement operated. We would never have got anywhere with the earlier tactic of open defiance with large groups of volunteers wielding weapons. The leaders invited arrest and with it, their executions."

Between the soup course and the roasted leg of lamb now being served by the discrete Alister, Patrick noted that Quinn was not only allowing this highly charged political discussion to continue at his table, but that he was inviting conflict between his guests by keeping the debate going. Never having seen this side of Quinn before, Patrick wondered if this were a deliberate ploy to test the political leanings of those present or if Quinn were being genuinely carried away with an excess of passion.

Whilst Alister served the roasted potatoes and well-chopped fresh spring cabbage, Quinn continued to air his views. “I think the Republican volunteers began their secret preparations for this conflict when they were in Frongoch Prison Camp. I don’t understand their tactics, but I imagine their goal is to wear the British down over time.”

Patrick, throwing caution to the wind, said heartily, “I completely agree, Quinn. To get to where they are now, they must have realised back then that small groups of dedicated volunteers striking out here and there would have more chance of success than large-scale military attacks against an empire with one of the toughest and most highly trained armies in the world. And I’ll go one step further and say that the 1916 executions of MacDonagh, Clarke and Pearse, and the rest of the fifteen leaders ending with James Connolly, despite his being grievously ill, *are* the reasons we are where we are today.” He looked at John, and added, “The Irish population didn’t like those men being shot, and they spoke out about it at the polling booths in December. It’s as simple as that.”

Quinn let Alister serve him a spoonful of peas and when the man left the table, he reminisced, “You know, it was a strange thing to see a section of the population shift their support to the Republican movements with my own eyes. I wasn’t in Dublin when the executions took place. I was home in Carrick-on Suir, in Tipperary…”

Quinn’s words trailed off, and his eyes were distant until they refocused when he continued, “On the Sunday after they shot Pearse, I attended mass in my local church. I’ll never forget Father O'Shea's voice ringing through the pews and up to the rafters. He spoke about the men who'd died, about Ireland and its dream of becoming a free nation, of how the rising was an act of desperation by men who had tried every other means of negotiation and had been let down with false promises from the British government. His words touched everyone that day. It was as if the congregation's deeply felt pathos awoke the chords of sympathy in their hearts. That was a turning point for me, too."

The mood was sombre, but Patrick again noted Quinn's unapologetic fervour when speaking. They'd never fully discussed the crisis that was becoming a war; one that scarcely merited the term 'war', but was a war, nonetheless.

A tense silence fell until John asked Aldas, "Answer me truthfully, Aldas, as a Jew, where do you stand in all this carry-on?"

Aldas laughed. "That's a dangerous question, John. Men are being shot for giving it the wrong answer. But seriously – as a Jew, I stand nowhere. As an Irishman and businessman, I have yet to decide. I work to earn money. If this 'carry-on,' as you put it, loses me my income, then I will stand for peace in whatever form it brings."

Quinn laughed. "A very ambiguous but tactful answer."

That comment ended the political discussion. As the men tucked into the tender new-season lamb and spoke about the current state of the wool trade, Patrick mulled over Quinn's political views, and found them to be in tandem with his own.

He was in love. Crazy as it sounded in his own mind, he knew his feelings to be genuine. He was scared, he admitted. For the first time in his life, he was giving his heart away. Quinn held it in the palm of his hand, and he would either crush it or give it the tender loving care it deserved. That was the risk one took when falling in love, Patrick supposed. It was, in part, a submission of power and will to the one you identified as your 'heartfelt love.'

He reached for his drink, then glanced at Quinn. It would be a long night, but at the end, John and Aldas would leave, and he and Quinn would be alone. That thought gave him much pleasure.

Chapter Thirty-Three

Patrick felt a surge of disappointment during the after-dinner brandies when Quinn whispered in his ear, "I'm behind with work. I must catch up with stocktaking and it'll take me until morning to finish it. You understand, don't you?" It had not been a serious question but an explanation, and Quinn had not given Patrick the opportunity to discuss the point.

At these occasions, he and Quinn usually planned the end of their evenings in advance. The routine rarely altered: Patrick would leave the apartment just before the other guests and then spend half an hour or so in the nearest pub. Afterwards, he'd re-enter at the rear of Quinn's building, where the forecourt and stairs leading down to the warehouse were situated. Quinn had formed the habit of dismissing the cook and his manservant just before the last guest left, presumably so they'd be tucked up in their rooms on the top floor by the time Patrick got back; however, tonight he'd said; 'Don't return, Pat.'

Patrick sat on a barstool in a pub near the docks, drowning his discontentment in whiskey. He was spending the weekend with Jenny, Kevin, and the baby, and he wouldn't see Quinn for at least a week because of his heavy teaching college schedule. Quinn knew this. They'd discussed it earlier that week. Something was wrong. He felt it deep in his abdomen and tried to drown the feeling in alcohol.

After his third whiskey in quick succession, Patrick's need to return to Quinn smashed to pieces all the reasons as to why he shouldn't go back. He glanced at the wall clock and watched its ticking second hand jump from one second to the next. *Oh, to be normal.* How different life would be were he to be attracted to women and be permitted to rejoice in his love openly, without shame. He and Quinn had agreed to the subterfuge in their relationship. It was humiliating to Patrick that he had to hide his feelings, but facts took precedence over his pride. Living an honest life was dangerous for men who loved men.

Like all homosexuals who read newspapers and books, Patrick had learnt sad lessons of highly publicised court cases, such as the one against Oscar Wilde, which had been held before the turn of the century. Wilde, the great Irish playwright, suffered a mammoth fall from grace and abject humiliation during his trial, as did all the men who'd faced the same fate.

It was hard to bear for those arrested, but for wily prosecutors, the crime of homosexuality could be the nail in the coffin for some poor wretch. Patrick recalled the trial of Padraig Pearse. It was not enough for the British to simply execute him for being one of the leaders of the 1916 uprising; no, their prosecutors had also presented dubious evidence of him being a homosexual. The truth of it mattered little when the impression had been made. The madness of Pearse's conviction was a sharp reminder that Ireland was governed by British laws mandated from the Parliament of Great Britain, such as the 1861 Offences Against the Person Act. That law saw homosexuals tried for sodomy, the conviction of which still technically carried a life sentence of penal servitude if found guilty. Patrick was only too aware of this, as well as the lesser offence of gross indecency with another man, which under the 1885 Amendment Act still carried a jail sentence of up to two years with hard labour. More, though, if he were caught, his career and social life would be over, even after serving a prison term.

Patrick downed the last of his whiskey, then slammed the glass on the bar counter. Maybe one day, society would turn a blind eye to a person's sexual preferences, but he doubted that the British or Irish populations would accept such sexual diversity in his lifetime.

He looked again at the clock; he'd been there for forty-five minutes. The pub was about to close, and they'd kick him out if he didn't go willingly. He thanked the landlord and then sauntered tipsily back to Quinn's under a black and drizzly sky.

Patrick went to Quinn's apartment door, looked up, and saw no lights on. Invited or not, he had a plan 'B;' a slew of feeble excuses to get him back in, should the guests still be there, and if Quinn were annoyed at the sight of his return: he'd forgotten his umbrella. Danny had given him a new-fangled wristwatch he'd brought back from France, and he'd left it in Quinn's indoor water closet when he'd washed his hands. Or he had forgotten to give Quinn an important message. He could lie for Ireland when the need arose.

The gates to the warehouse and forecourt were around the corner at the end of the street. He strode towards it with the spare keys in his hand but then halted at the sound of footsteps coming up behind him. He turned to look, saw nothing, and moved on. *Here I am, hesitating again, too scared to see what's around the corner but not willing to go home and call it a night,* he thought. At times like these, he admired his brother's impulsiveness and courage. Unlike Danny, he possessed none of those things. He'd needed help jumping off a bloody sinking ship!

Patrick took another quick glance behind himself, turned the corner and went in. The forecourt, which allowed trucks and motorcars to park off-road, was deserted apart from one truck. The wrought-iron gates were closed but not locked. He pushed one of them inwards, thankful that it didn't creak, and closed it behind himself. Drunk, he zigzagged on tiptoes in comical fashion across the forecourt until the hairs on the back of his neck stood to attention. He stopped but then turned his head at precisely the second a black, blunt object smashed into his skull.

******

Muffled voices, feet scuffing the floor, the metallic sounds of a rifle being loaded, and throbbing pain on the side of his head greeted Patrick as he returned to consciousness. He cracked his eyelids but otherwise remained still, keeping his head downturned. Paraffin lamps, turned low, emitted a dull, yellow glow, making it hard to see more than a few feet in front of him.

He was slumped in a chair, arms pinned behind the back of it and his wrists bound by what felt like thick cord. His front was dishevelled; dark stains streaked his white shirt … blood? His jacket and coat were ripped open, and someone had turned out his pockets. Wanting to hear what was being said, he continued to feign unconsciousness. It wasn't hard; he was groggy and had an agonising headache. Someone had walloped him across the side of his head with a hard object, and afterwards he'd been dragged along the ground, with his back and backside thumping every step on the way down to the basement – that was all he remembered.

"...are you certain he had no one with him, Jack? You went up and down the street for a look?" Aldas asked the man who'd clobbered Patrick with his rifle butt.

"He was alone, but I can't guarantee there's not more like him lying in wait somewhere." Jack shrugged and continued, "Sure, if he'd brought a squad of men with him, they'd have come in here by now."

Aldas looked across the stretch of basement at Patrick, clearly furious.

Quinn, also appearing angry at Patrick's unexpected appearance said, "Wake him up. We need to get him out of here before the British soldiers do their rounds in the morning.

"What time are Michael Collins' men coming for the merchandise?"

Quinn looked at his pocket watch. "We've got two hours."

"Fuck you, Quinn. You need to be more careful who you befriend."

"I know. I made a mistake ... he was a good customer ... harmless, I thought."

Aldas shook his head in consternation, then gave instructions to Jack, "Go back upstairs, and keep your eyes peeled. You see the slightest movement, you run back down here. Otherwise, I'll come up for you after I've put that rat down."

Aldas turned to Quinn, "We'll give him back to his British friends as a corpse in the River Liffey."

The voices were growing louder and clearer, but much of the discussion going on was still inaudible. Quinn was talking ... yes, it was Quinn. Then Aldas spoke back in a harsh tone. Panicking, his head bobbing up, down, and around like a child's doll that had been decapitated and re-capitated one time too many, Patrick struggled to speak. "Quinn. Quinn?" he finally uttered.

Two shadowy figures approached Patrick. His eyes widened as they focused on the floor instead of the men. Wooden crates full of rifles; three, no, four of them in plain sight. He looked up into Quinn's shadowy face, and asked, "What the hell's going on here?"

"You're awake, are you?" Aldas noted, while Quinn remained silent.

Patrick saw the men clearly now. He wondered which of the two had split his head open then thought, *what does it matter? They won't let me live after seeing their guns.* Ignoring Aldas, he repeated his question to Quinn. "What are you doing with rifles?"

Aldas stepped closer to the chair, rage on his flushed face. "Who do you spy for? The RIC intelligence branch? The British Army? The government? Are you a member of this new G-Force, eh?"

Patrick stared at Quinn who returned his gaze with eyes devoid of emotion. Then he saw the 38-calibre gun held casually in Aldas' hand. With a dry mouth and swollen tongue, he said, "Quinn knows the hours I work at the hospital and college. I don't have time for a second job, let alone police work. I'm a doctor." *I'm a fool, a lovesick bloody fool who's going to die for love,* he thought, stunned at Quinn's duplicity and coldness. With as much calm as he could muster, he continued, "Look, lads, granted, I wasn't meant to see whatever this is, but I'll keep my mouth shut. I was never here."

Aldas stepped closer and punched Patrick's face with an uppercut, then again demanded, "Who do you work for?"

Patrick shook his head to try to clear it. Blood poured from his nose and his open mouth.

Aldas punched Patrick twice more in quick succession and then growled, "Why did you come back here?"

Quinn's eyes continued to bore into Patrick's, which had welled with pain. Disgusted, Patrick explained, "I forgot my watch … I washed my hands in Quinn's closet." He spat blood out of his mouth and threw Quinn a filthy look, as he said, "Go look."

Aldas raised his revolver, and with a steady hand, pressed the end of the barrel against Patrick's forehead.

The bottom fell out of Patrick's stomach. Accepting he was going to die, he rushed out, "If you're going to shoot me, at least do me the courtesy of telling me what I'm dying for?"

Aldas obliged, twisting his head to nod at the crates in answer. Then he turned back and said, "You're not a hero, you're a stupid man. Know that?" Still furious, he gripped Patrick's battered chin, digging his nails into the latter's skin, and added, "And you're a feckin' traitor to your country."

Quinn's hand shot to Aldas' shoulder. "He's a traitor all right, but he's my mistake. Give me the revolver. I was stupid enough to let him into my house, and I'll be the one to shoot the bastard, not you."

Aldas lowered his gun and twirled it around in his fingers so its butt faced Quinn. The latter took it, raised it to Patrick's head, and with an icy-cold stare, said, "When you find yourself in hell, say hello to the rest of the British bastards I sent there. Close your eyes."

Shocked by the hatred spewing from Quinn's eyes, Patrick hissed, "No. I want you to see me looking at you when you shoot. I want you to say my name before you pull the trigger. Say it – Patrick Carmody – say it!"

"Close your fucking eyes!"

Heartbroken, Patrick gave Quinn one last lingering look, then squeezed his eyes shut and held his breath.

Quinn pivoted and shot Aldas through his temple. When his victim fell, he then put another bullet into his forehead.

Patrick flinched when the revolver report blasted his ears. Gasping from his long-held breath, he opened his eyes and exhaled as he watched Quinn turn his back on him and hurry across the warehouse towards the exit. Stunned, Patrick looked down at Aldas' body, seeing the blood widening like a pillow around his head, his dead eyes staring at the ceiling. In shock, yet astonished to still be alive, he muttered, "Aw, Jesus Christ, I'm not dead."

Despite his heart racing, Patrick began to shiver then his teeth to chatter as adrenaline coursed through his body. Seconds, then minutes ticked by, but his thoughts got stuck in the moment the gun had fired, making him flinch with terror, as real as if it were happening time and again. He looked down and saw to his horror that he'd wet himself. No – on closer inspection, it was blood that had dripped from his face to his crotch, not urine.

"Patrick, it's over," Quinn said several minutes later, hurrying back to the chair.

"Where did you go?" Patrick mumbled in a stupor.

"I had to deal with Aldas' man upstairs."

Still not coming to terms with Quinn's duplicity, Patrick said, "You're a weapons dealer? Are these guns for the IRA?"

"Yes." Quinn's tall frame loomed menacingly, but his expression had softened. "Patrick, you took a terrible battering.

I'm sorry," he said, going behind the chair and untying the cord binding Patrick's wrists.

"You're sorry? You're in the bloody IRA!" Patrick yelled; the announcement directed more to himself than to Quinn. "Why didn't you tell me?"

Quinn threw the discarded cord onto the floor, came to the front of the chair, leant down and placed gentle hands on Patrick's shoulders. "Truth is a complicated companion, Patrick. Nothing is ever as it seems, not even when the heart of a man is true. All you need to know is that I will clean up this mess."

"You mean my blood, or his?" Patrick snapped, and gestured to Aldas.

Quinn studied Patrick's face. "Damn it, I'm sorry," he muttered. "You need to leave now, Patrick. Colleagues of mine will arrive soon, and you cannot be here when they walk in that door. Please, for you your own safety, try to make it home."

When Quinn straightened, Patrick lurched to his feet. Despite dizziness, a damaged nose, and an eye so swollen it was virtually sightless, he smashed his fist into Quinn's unsuspecting face. "That's all you have to say to me … go home?"

Quinn stumbled backwards with the force of the punch, tripping over the dead body of Aldas as he went down on his arse. He groaned, looked up at Patrick from the ground and rubbed his chin, saying calmly, "I suppose I deserved that. I promise, I will explain…"

Chapter Thirty-Four

Patrick, distressed and in pain, set off for Danny's house under the cover of darkness, thanks to the delivery bicycle Quinn had loaned him. He hadn't wanted to take it, for it meant returning it in due course. However, he saw no other means of travel at this time of night, and he was not so out of it to believe he could make the journey on foot.

On his three-mile ride to the outskirts of Dublin, he took precautions to avoid policemen and soldiers. The bicycle had Quinn's company name on it, and they might think he'd stolen it, he'd suggested to Quinn. 'And look at me. I look like a man who's been beaten up by a crowd of disappointed football supporters!' He got on it, nonetheless.

Patrick gave himself a pep talk during his ride. At home in the city and its suburbs, he used the backstreets, lanes near the River Liffey, the outer edge of Phoenix Park, and finally the quiet streets of Dublin's suburbs, where he had the home-field advantage. He didn't know the time of night or how long he'd been unconscious in the warehouse before coming to and staring death in the face. Time eluded him during the traumatic episode that had almost killed him, but it felt like he was living through the longest night of his life.

It took a good hour to get to Danny's area. It was a mostly residential district of detached houses, some hidden by garden trees and mature hedgerows, and others surrounded by picket fences. It reminded Patrick of Victoria Street, where the family home had been. The houses here were nowhere near as grand as his father's, but Danny had purchased a good-sized property. It had come up for sale at auction following the death of its sole owner who'd had no heir. Its problem, which Patrick pointed out to Danny before he'd paid the money for it, was its grand old age. It had no inside water closet or even gas for lighting; instead, it relied on oil lamps and candles since there was no electricity or even wiring installed in any room. The kitchen, although spacious, did not have the modern cooking ranges or even outlets for indoor plumbing that were now a requisite for most homes. It was a tired-looking home and needed a complete renovation that would cost hundreds of pounds, which Danny no longer had after paying the winning auction bid.

Patrick arrived outside the house. What the hell were his younger brother and his friend Jimmy going to say when they saw him in the middle of the night with his face smashed to a pulp, his head split open, and hair matted in blood? He'd accepted Quinn's offer of a quick wash to get the blood off his face, and since his own overcoat was ripped and buttonless, he'd also borrowed a raincoat to cover his stained crotch.

The house was in darkness, as expected at this hour, but Patrick was loath to knock on the front door in case he scared his brother and instead went around the back to the kitchen.

Patrick touched the injured area on his head and flinched. The longer he waited to get it sewn up, the harder it would be to do a good job, he thought. He should have gone straight to the college of surgeons and asked a colleague to suture the wound, but he couldn't – wouldn't –answer the myriad questions they would ask about how he'd got his injuries. Whatever he now thought about the man – and Patrick truly didn't know what to think at present – Quinn had saved his life and would remain anonymous.

The kitchen door was locked, so Patrick went to the centre of Danny's back garden and gazed up at the property's upstairs windows. Danny had given him a tour of the place, and the master bedroom looking down on the back garden was the only one that had curtains, unless Danny had hung more in the last fortnight. He had pleaded with Minnie and Jenny to measure up and choose material for him and then sew curtains for the master bedroom, even though both women were heavily involved in their own decorating projects at Jenny and Kevin's new house.

Jenny also pointed out to Danny that she was still learning how to be a mother whilst relying on only a handful hours' sleep at night. Danny, with his sad eyes and little-boy-lost look won the day, however. Minnie had reminded Jenny that Danny had lost a wife who would have been happy to sew for him. Later, when he had hung the curtains to Minnie and Jenny's satisfaction, Danny had laughed with Patrick, 'If I'd known what a carry-on it would be to hang the bloody things with tassels an' all, I wouldn't have bothered. Minnie has gone wholeheartedly into the project, and now she's making me a bedspread and cushions to match. Thank God she chose green. I couldn't have lived with blue!'

Patrick finally made out the shadow of partly drawn curtains. He picked up a small stone, hoping as he let loose that he'd hit the window glass but not break it. A few minutes later – longer than he'd expected to wait – a hand drew back the thick brocade material and a face pressed against the glass. It was too dark to see who the figure was, but Patrick waved up at it regardless, then went to the kitchen door.

Jimmy Carson, dressed only in long johns, opened the door, raised the oil lamp in his hand and stared into Patrick's battered face. "In the name of Christ, Patrick, what the blazes happened to you?"

"Is Danny home?" Patrick responded, pushing past Jimmy and going into the kitchen.

"He's up in his room. He's under the weath –" Jimmy began to answer as Patrick took to the stairs. When he reached the landing, Patrick realised he hadn't made up a story to give Danny for being beaten up. On the bicycle ride, he'd gone over what had happened to him repeatedly, trying to find solace in the fact he was still alive and that Quinn had killed his weapons' dealer; the man who had made small talk over the dinner table hours earlier. *He shot the Jew to save me,* Patrick kept telling himself, yet his lover's deceit was like a knife twisting in his heart.

Patrick opened the bedroom door. Now, for the first time in their lives, *he,* the honest, reliable brother, was going to lie to Danny. This wasn't how things worked with the Carmodys; it was *Danny* who was untruthful by nature.

An oil lamp sitting on the upside-down wooden crate Danny used as a bedside table lit the room. Patrick's eyes went straight to Danny's linen-encased, strapped-up shoulder and the sling holding his arm in place. He rushed to the bed and dropped onto it, and for a few seconds each waited for the other to speak.

Even in the lamp's yellow glow, Danny's face shone pale. His mouth gaped as he took in Patrick's appearance, and twice he tried to speak but failed to get the words out.

"What happened to you?" Both men spoke the words in the same moment.

Patrick's left eye had swollen closed now. His eyelid looked like a large red bubble surrounded by bruising that was creeping downward onto his swollen cheek. His split lips were also double the size as normal and the swelling extended to his jawline on the left side of his face. "I got into a fight in a pub tonight, and I didn't want my college professors or colleagues to know about it. I couldn't think of anywhere else to go but here," he lied, a brief, ridiculous flash of pride at his own cleverness crossing his mind.

"I'm honoured." Danny reached out and took Patrick's hand in his own, examining his brother's knuckles. "I know what knuckles look like after a brawl, and you either didn't throw a single punch to defend yourself, which I find unlikely given the mess of your face, or you're lying to me. Which is it?"

Patrick, unaware that his head was bleeding again, the blood running down the side of his face, snapped, "Yes, it's a lie, but after all the lies you've told me, including the one you're going to tell me now about *your* injury, I don't give a tinker's damn about being honest with you."

Jimmy stepped into the light. "Aw, for feck's sake, you two. Stop dancing around each other like a pair of prize eejits, will you? Patrick, I'm away to get hot water and possibly a sewing kit for that head of yours. You're dripping blood, for Christ's sake. And you, Danny, you mind what you say while I'm away."

When the brothers were alone, Danny said, "I won't lie to you, Patrick. I got shot in the shoulder while trying to steal guns. It would surprise you how often that sort of thing happens. Nothing to worry about."

"Have you been to a doctor?"

"No, of course I haven't *been,* but a doctor I trust has seen to it. He removed the bullet, cleaned the wound with iodine –

with me going through the damn roof at the sting of the stuff – and then he made sure I got home. We're at war, and you know I'm involved, so … well … that's all I have to say about it."

Patrick was furious, but he also felt sick and unable to vent his anger. Heat rose from his neck into his face, and his skin was clammy. Dizziness swept over him, and as much as he tried, he couldn't keep Danny's face in focus. "Jesus, sorry about this," he mumbled, as he leant over the side of the bed, spread his legs open, and vomited on Danny's rug. Then he straightened and said, "There you go, then, that's that."

"That's my new rug ruined," Danny grumbled.

Without having to look at his head injury, Patrick knew that he, in his current state, was not capable of closing it with a needle and thread, nor was he willing to amend the lie he'd told Danny. Danny's pain-glazed eyes were full of his own lies, but his face also held genuine concern.

Patrick sighed with sorrow – regret – a mixture of both, perhaps. "You're my brother and I love you, but I can't trust you anymore. I'm afraid of telling you the truth about what happened to me tonight, and I'm afraid of learning the truth about what happened to you. It's a hell of a thing, knowing we can't be honest with each other."

"I'll always have your back, Pat, always," Danny declared, looking hurt by Patrick's words. "Tell me one thing. Just one. Did the police do this to you? British detectives? Soldiers?"

Patrick's jaw wasn't broken, but it was still painful for him to speak. "No, to the three things you asked me," he answered. Then he rose on unsteady legs. "Danny, Jimmy's right. We will get nowhere with our secrets and lies. I need to get Kevin here to stitch me. He's the only person I can trust not to interrogate me. Is it all right with you if I ask him to come see to the both of us?"

Danny nodded. "Sure, better him than anyone else around here, I suppose. I bought a bed for the room next door. Away and lie down, Patrick. I'll send Jimmy to fetch Kevin. It'll take him about twenty minutes on his bicycle, but Kevin can bring him back in his motorcar." Danny shook his head, looking genuinely shocked by Patrick's terrible facial injuries. "Ah, Patrick, if you'll only tell me who did this to you, I could get them back for it."

Patrick went to the door, and as he turned the handle, said, "Comments like that are precisely why I won't tell you a damn thing, Danny."

Chapter Thirty-Five

Kevin's fingers were gentle as they unwrapped the bandages strapping Danny's shoulder and chest; nonetheless, he was in a stinking mood. One only had to look at his furrowed brow and the tight set of his lips to know the Carmody brothers' latest antics had not amused him. Danny suspected his brother-in-law's mind was ticking away in his perfectly analytical manner, trying to make sense of Patrick being in the state he was in *and* of being in the same house as his brother. 'I'll not lift a finger to help you, Danny Carmody, unless you tell me what sort of injury I'm dealing with,' Kevin had declared upon his arrival.

'Gunshot,' Danny had reluctantly admitted. He did not add that he'd been having trouble finding a doctor to come to the house, for that would give Kevin an illusion of power, to Danny's mind, and he was a self-righteous arsehole as it was. Kevin's response was muted, as if he'd expected nothing less from his troublesome brother-in-law. 'I see,' he'd muttered before going to see to Patrick in the next room.

"How is Patrick?" Danny now asked Kevin, as the latter removed the linen pad that was sticking to tender skin around his wound.

"He has a nasty concussion and might even have a fractured skull, but unless he changes his mind and agrees to go for an x-ray, we will never know. He's being bloody minded and insisting he's staying put. Maybe you can talk sense into him?" Kevin answered.

"Sure, as if he'll listen to me. What have you done for him?"

"I've cleaned out his cranial wound and sewn it up, and I've checked his neurological signs. Thankfully, I see no evidence of brain bleeding."

Danny's eyes widened in horror, "Jesus, God, no."

"Don't worry. I've left Jimmy to watch over Patrick while he sleeps, so you and I have plenty of time to have a wee private chat."

"Yes, well, good luck with that," Danny said and clamped his mouth shut. He would not say a word about the grand rescue at Knocklong or himself being with the most famous fugitives in Ireland who had pulled off the biggest propaganda coup of the new war. The four were running rings around the police blockades being set up in many counties. For months they had avoided capture with the help of good Irish folk. He'd seen the wanted posters stuck onto lampposts and walls offering hefty rewards for information leading to the fours' arrest. He'd seen those same notices being ripped down by 'persons unknown' within hours of being posted.

To Republicans, the four lads who had ignited the war back in February were heroes being forced into hiding, but to the British army and majority of RIC officers, they were traitors and murderers who should be hanged or shot. Kevin would see them from the English point of view unless he'd had a recent change of heart, which judging by the fury on his face, was unlikely. No, he wouldn't tell Kevin a damned thing, not even about his trip to the sympathetic doctor in Tipperary with the other injured men – Breen and Treacy – who had by now disappeared with the Irish early morning mist. Danny flinched as Kevin's fingers poked around the wound's outer edges. His brother-in-law was deliberately being rough.

Danny thought, *I should tell him about my long, often-interrupted journey home with the help of many good Republican souls who relayed me off to one person after another on the way.* Kevin would hate to hear about the growing popularity of the IRA.

It had taken almost forty-eight hours to avoid police and soldiers and get back to Dublin. When Danny had finally made it home, late the previous evening and only hours before Patrick's unexpected appearance, he'd found Jimmy pacing up and down the living room floor, worrying the threads out of the carpet. He and Finn had not been able to get to May Maloney's house or to the rendezvous at Emly train station. British soldiers had set up checkpoints, and the two boys couldn't find a safe way out of Tipperary town until it was too late to be of use to the others. It had mortified poor Jimmy. 'Feck it, I missed the whole thing!' he'd wailed. Danny had joked, 'That's how it goes, Jimmy. You and Finn won't be in the history books, but me, well in years to come, your grandchildren will sing ballads about my heroic acts at Knocklong.'

Danny studied Kevin, whose fingers were still pressing down on the skin while he literally sniffed around the sutured bullet hole, checking for any putrefaction. It was impossible for Danny to determine what his brother-in-law was thinking as he worked. *It won't take him long to begin his interrogation, though,* Danny assumed. For all his romantic ways with Jenny and his tender touch with patients, *other than me,* Kevin was a hard man and wouldn't be as easily persuaded as Patrick had been to drop the questions. *No, Kevin won't leave the house until Patrick and I cough up explanations that have some semblance of truth in them.*

"You can stop staring at me, Danny," said Kevin, without looking up from his task. "I'll say my piece when I'm ready. You're not getting rid of me until you tell me what mischief you were up to."

Danny rolled his eyes. *He read my bloody mind!* "It was a shooting accident. Me and Jimmy were practicing our aim in the woods, and Jimmy accidently clipped me when he reloaded his .38 revolver."

"Sure, but you're a lying scumbag, Danny Carmody," Kevin retorted, as he heavy-handedly dabbed on Dakin's antiseptic solution of sodium hypochlorite to clean the bullet wound.

Danny winced and uttered, "Steady on, Kevin."

Kevin shot Danny a thunderous look, then began strapping his shoulder with fresh linen strips. "Right, that's it. You can take that sling off in a week, but in the meantime, keep your arm in it, and don't leave this house."

"Thank you, Kevin," Danny replied, his fingers inadvertently playing with the bed blanket as he tried his luck at getting rid of him. "You'd better be off home though now, before our Jenny has a hissy fit. I'll see you soon."

"You'll see me now, Danny. Jenny and the baby will be fine. She's got Minnie and a nurse looking after her."

"Does she know you're here?"

"No. She thinks I am out on an emergency. I don't start at the practice until next week, but I've been consulting with the doctor I'm taking over from."

Kevin rose, looking menacing as he peered through his glasses at Danny, "Don't you worry about your sister, worry about me. I'll see to your brother next door then send Jimmy downstairs to make us a cup of tea. When Patrick feels up to it, the three of us will have a talk, and I'm warning you, if you or he insults me with more lies, I swear it will be the last time the pair of you ever clap eyes on me, your sister, or your nephew.

Chapter Thirty-Six

Patrick woke to see Kevin sitting in a chair reading a book at his bedside. For a minute, he couldn't remember where he was, but when he did and the events of the previous night flooded back, the agony of betrayal and lies replaced his physical pain. *Shame I don't have amnesia.* "How long have you been sitting there?" he asked Kevin through thick lips.

Kevin put his book down. "About two hours. How do you feel?"

"How do you think I feel? I'm looking at you through one eye, and my lips feel as though they've been kissing bloody stinging nettles."

Kevin, his own eyes lacking their usual empathy, looked at Patrick's swollen eyelid and asked, "Do you feel well enough to tell me what happened?"

Patrick hesitated a long moment, then asked, "Is this in confidence, Kevin?"

"Of course."

"Well, I got caught in a weapons deal that went wrong."

"What did you say?"

"You heard me." Patrick wriggled his backside up the bed and got himself into a sitting position with his head resting against the bed's wooden headboard. "I might as well tell you the truth or you'll never let it go, so this is what happened. I went to the house of an acquaintance for dinner. When I left, I realised I'd left my wristwatch – the one Danny brought back from the war. Anyway, I went back for it and walked straight into a group of men in the alley behind my friend's home negotiating the price of guns. Before you ask, it happened too fast to see their faces. They rushed me, beat me, and I lost consciousness. When I came around, I was alone. I stole a bicycle and somehow rode it here. There's nothing more." The lie sounded solid to his own ears.

"In the name of God! Does Danny know?"

"No, and he won't. He's already threatened to kill the people who did this to me."

"And you're certain you didn't know the men?"

"I told you, I didn't get a good enough look at them."

Patrick gave Kevin a moment to digest the lies, which might or might not have been credible to his keen mind, then added, "Look, Kevin, I was in the wrong place at the wrong time. The men who did this to me left me for dead. I don't think they had any idea who I am so I'm not in danger, but Danny is. We need to go in there and get as much out of him as we can. The sooner we speak to him, the sooner you can get home to Jenny."

Without waiting for a response, Patrick swung his legs over the side of the bed, lurched to his feet, and almost fell over. "Erm … give me a hand into Danny's room, will you?"

Moments later, Kevin deposited Patrick in Danny's double bed. There, the two brothers lying side by side waited for Kevin's interrogation.

Kevin dragged an old rocking chair left by the house's previous owner to the bottom end of the bed. Patrick eyed his brother-in-law's self-assured movements while thinking that the worst part of this situation was not him lying beside his brother in his long johns, waiting for a scolding, but the expression of disgust on Kevin's face. Thankfully, Danny was the sole recipient which meant that Kevin had believed the story about the weapons deal or was willing to let it go. Guilt played on Patrick's mind. He'd never lied to his friend before – a fib or two here and there, maybe, but not an outright lie of this magnitude … although not even Kevin knew about his illicit relationship with Quinn, the lying bastard who had ripped his heart out!

Kevin sat down and looked directly at Danny. Patrick, willing to wait his turn to speak, also kept his head and eyes turned toward his brother.

"If you're not honest with me, Danny, I'm willing to walk away for good," Kevin said, his voice factual, almost emotionless with the threat. When he continued, though, he was less collected. "I know damn well you follow Michael Collins about like a bluebottle at a cow's arse. You're up to your bloody neck in his business, up to your elbows in violence, and I don't expect I'll get the whole truth out of you –"

"That's good, 'cos you won't," Danny interrupted. "You can take me to Dublin Castle, to your brother, and let him and his pals torture me like the others before me, but I won't tell you or your Charlie who shot me."

Kevin's eyes had widened at the word *torture,* and Danny considered that a point scored, albeit far from a victory.

"Do you trust me, Danny?" Kevin asked in a softer tone.

Surprised by the question, Danny muttered, "I suppose I must do … to some extent. I wouldn't have let you in my house last night if I thought you'd report me as soon as you left it." Then he sat up against his two plump pillows and glared defiantly at Kevin, his eyes full of the excess pride and passion he was known for. "I suppose I trust you, so yes, I was shot. Yes, I'm a member of the IRA, as are thousands of people in this country, and there are hundreds, even thousands more who are beginning to support us. But if you're looking for a confession, you won't get it. I will not apologise to God nor man for killing the enemies of the Irish people. Give me ten British soldiers and I'll shoot the lot of them. Give me ten of Mister Churchill's detectives and I'll shoot them, too. I will do it until this island is free of all occupying forces, and they lower the union flag at Dublin Castle. I don't know where you'll be, but I will be there when they raise the Irish tricolour for the whole bloody island to see. That's all you need to know, Kevin." Danny then looked down at Patrick. "And that's my final word on the matter to you, too."

"Our father is ashamed of you in his grave!" Patrick hissed at his brother.

Kevin, although shocked by Danny's openly hostile stance, surprised both brothers when he said, "I'm sick of this. The blurred lines governing right from wrong, patriotism from treason are disappearing in Ireland, and I'm ashamed to say I can't decide what's worse … the murdering escapades of Irish 'freedom fighters' like you, Danny, or the violent replies of the British, picking random people off the street, taking them to Dublin Castle, and torturing them to death."

Patrick placed his hand on Danny's arm and warned him with a tiny shake of his head to keep quiet.

Kevin, visibly upset, took a pack of cigarettes out of his pocket, lifted the flap, and shook one out. After he'd lit it, he continued, his voice wavering with emotion. "There was an attempt on my father's life last month. He was travelling from Cork to Dublin. Masked men ambushed his car in a country lane that wasn't even near the main road." He paused, took a long drag of his cigarette, and stared pointedly at Danny. "My father and his driver survived only because of the bravery of the protection officer travelling with them. They riddled the Rolls Royce with bullets."

"I'm sorry to hear that, Kevin. Why didn't you tell me about it?" Patrick asked, hurt.

"It's difficult knowing who to trust nowadays, Patrick, so I told no one. My father demanded that the newspapers suppress the story. My poor mother was in a terrible state, and because of the incident, my father will work from home for a while under His Majesty's protection."

Kevin glared at Danny and then he lost his calm, "He's my father, for God's sake! For all his faults, he's my dad. And now he's a prisoner in his own house, in his own bloody country!" He cleared his throat and asked Danny, "Do you know anything about that ambush?"

"No, nothing," Danny answered, shaking his head and looking Kevin directly in the eye.

The news shocked Patrick. Neither Kevin nor Jenny had spoken about the incident the last time he'd seen them. He'd not read a word about the attack in the newspapers, either, which made sense considering they had buried the story. It seemed his sister and his brother-in-law had deliberately kept the whole thing secret. Patrick wondered if Minnie knew, and what she thought of the Irish shenanigans going on. She'd have a lot to say, no doubt.

"… and I suppose you didn't hear about the prisoner rescue at Knocklong, three days ago, either?" Kevin said to Danny.

Danny's eyes flicked away involuntarily, and redness crept up his neck to his face, making Patrick gasp. "Aw, Christ almighty, tell me you weren't involved in the murder of two police officers on a train, Danny!" he spluttered.

"Course I wasn't. What would I be doing that far from Dublin when I have a full-time job here?"

Kevin snorted his scepticism, as if he too suspected Danny of being at Knocklong and of getting shot there. The newspapers had reported no shootings in Dublin in the past two days, and they *always* did, especially John Grant's *Catholic Press*. The Republicans loved to boast about their vicious victories and the martyrdom of Irish victims. "Sure, it's a sad day when Irishmen murder their own kind. The deaths of those policemen on that train at Knocklong station were tragic and unnecessary."

Patrick studied Kevin, who was clearly trying to goad Danny. Then he looked at Danny's profile: the angry set of his lips, his eyebrows drawing together in consternation, the red lies staining his cheeks.

"You're entitled to your opinion, but you weren't on that train to see what happened, were you, Kevin?" Danny snapped, right on cue.

"Sure, but you were, weren't you?"

"I already said I wasn't, but I'll tell you this for nothing. We're not *all* British, as people like you keep trying to tell us. Some of us are Irish, through and through, while others claim to be Irish but are not. Take your father, for instance. He lives a grand life, taking whatever he wants from our land, shipping his profits off to the British Empire, evicting hard-working families from their farms because they're Catholic or believe in Irish independence, and persuading the government in Westminster to come down hard on good Cork men and women while he watches Cork towns burn. Earlier, you said you didn't know the difference between a patriot and a traitor?

Well, I'm the patriot, and your da is the traitor. Maybe that's why his car was attacked on that County of Cork lane."

Kevin lurched to his feet, leaving the chair rocking hard and fast. Patrick shot daggers at Danny, but he would not say a word until after Kevin left. He had never wanted to belt his brother in the mouth as much as he did now, and he might just do it.

"Right, that's it. I've had enough," Kevin said, his voice icy as he buttoned up his coat. "You and I are finished, Danny. You will not tell me another bloody thing about what you're up to or what you think. You will not come near my house or your sister or granny while this crisis is going on. I don't care if it lasts a week, a month, or bloody years, you are banned..."

Danny let out a nervous giggle. "Don't be daft. Our Jenny will never agree to that after everything the Carmodys have been through together. And Minnie will go through you like a dose of castor oil if you try to keep us away..."

"I didn't mention Patrick, only you," Kevin replied coldly. "And don't you bring Minnie into this. She's staying in my home at my invitation, and while she's living in my house, she'll abide by my rules. If she doesn't, she can come here and live with you."

Patrick, feeling invisible in the tense battle of wills between Kevin and Danny, noted that his brother's colour had drained from his face, and his defiant expression was now one of fear.

"Jenny needs me," Danny insisted.

"Yes, well, you should have thought about her before you became a damned criminal."

Patrick tried but failed to intervene on Danny's behalf. "Maybe you shouldn't come to such an important decision..."

"The decision's made. The people who matter to me most are my wife and my son, and I will do whatever it takes to protect them. I won't allow Danny to lead the police to my door, and I will forbid Jenny from coming here. You'd do no less if you were in my shoes, Patrick."

Danny shook his head in disbelief as he uttered, "This isn't right."

"I'll tell you what's not right, Danny Carmody. You, working as a dockyard labourer," Kevin said, his voice heating as his self-control dwindled. "You, who went to the best fee-paying Catholic school, who could have got into a well-paid career using your father's good name and station. You, who won the military medal for bravery, fighting for your country. You, who threw away your future on the Sinn Féin and IRA, who have taken to violence instead of political dialogue." Kevin's voice shook as he continued, "I'm not daft enough to think these killings and the revenge murders that inevitably follow are isolated cases. No, we're at war, and I think you're embroiled in it, and more, you bloody well *enjoy* it. You're an arsehole!"

"Yes, well, the world needs arseholes, otherwise where would shite come out?" Danny's face wrinkled with rage as he asked, "Are you done?"

"Yes, I'm done, and I'll not be back, so don't send Jimmy Carson to my door again."

When Kevin walked to the door, Patrick got up and followed him, saying, "I'll walk you downstairs."

At the bottom of the stairs, they crossed paths with Jimmy, who had stayed out of the way but had probably heard the heated discussion. "Kevin was never here, Jimmy. You understand that, right?" Patrick said pointedly.

"Sure, he was never here," Jimmy nodded his agreement, made the sign of the cross to seal the promise, and bounded up the stairs.

At the front door, Kevin stared at Patrick's multi-coloured, wretched face. "I trust you with my life, Patrick, but if I find out you've lied to me about your injuries, I'll give you the same cold shoulder your brother's getting."

"I know," Patrick said in a softly spoken, accepting voice.

Kevin let out a long sigh of relief that made Patrick feel like the lying bastard he was.

"Will you come home with me?" Kevin now asked. "I'd rather you were under my roof with Minnie and me looking after you than staying here with Danny and his IRA pal. I'll go by the college and tell them you fell off your bicycle, and you won't be attending classes for a week or so ... unless you can think of another reasonable excuse."

Patrick had not vomited again. The sight in his one usable eye was fine, as confirmed by Kevin's examination, his reflexes were all right, and apart from his face and head hurting like fire, the man who'd thumped him hadn't cracked his skull open or caused bleeding on his brain. "I'll be out of action for at least ten days. Even then, they'll order me to go through a medical evaluation before being allowed to operate or touch a patient again. Are you sure you and Jenny can put up with me for that long?"

"Of course, and Minnie will love mothering you."

"I admit, I'd much prefer Minnie's cooking and bedside manner to having Jimmy Carson crow in my ear about the unfairness of life. I've had enough of the bloody IRA and the violence they foment." He winced as he tried to smile and the split in his lip reopened. "I'll go get dressed. Give me five minutes."

One year later,

June 1920

Chapter Thirty-Seven

June 1920

County Cork, Ireland

Jenny clung to the baby who wriggled to be free of his mother's arms. Dressed in his white satin christening robes, the child was slipping through her fingers as he arched his back to the side and backwards. She tried to soothe him with an Irish lullaby, but it seemed like he knew this was a special day for him and didn't want any part of it.

She let Kevin help her alight from the motorcar, then handed Robert to him, saying, "Give me a minute to fix my hat, darlin'. This little tinker tried to get it off me."

The church's entrance was awash with RIC officers. Plain-clothed detectives, requested to behave like guests but *looking* like plain-clothed detectives, were guarding all other parts of the building and its perimeter. They had cordoned off the village street and were also standing watch in windows of the houses opposite the church. *This is not my Ireland,* Jenny thought. It was a new and frightening land where people could get shot anywhere, anytime, and where the christening of an aristocratic child was a dangerous occasion instead of an event where the local population lined the street to cheer the family on.

Lord Jackson had spoken to Jenny in private about the security situation at the church. He'd been kind to her, she admitted. He had warmed to her since Robert's birth, her conversion to the Protestant faith, and her baptism into the

Church of Ireland. She liked to suppose he understood the sacrifices she had made for her husband and his family. Her old parish priest had rebuked her for turning her back on what he called 'the true religion,' saying, 'You are excommunicated in the eyes of God and the Catholic Church. You will no longer be welcomed into the kingdom of heaven,' Father Kelly had stated the words as a fact. The delicate matter had also put a terrible strain on her relationship with her brothers. She had not seen Danny, but Patrick had, and in the spirit of honesty he had relayed Danny's disgust, word for word. 'Tell Jenny she's a bloody traitor,' Danny had apparently said.

Jenny watched Lord Jackson's car arrive. A security officer opened the back passenger door, and out stepped her father-in-law dressed in a black suit and carrying a top hat. He smiled at her before walking around to the other side of the vehicle where Lady Jackson alighted.

Lord Jackson's frankness with her when they'd left the 'big house,' had stuck with her.

'I'm not taking any chances with my family's safety today. I'm sorry we had to delay Robert's christening, but you know, Jenny, dear, as a representative of the law, I will always be a target for madmen and criminals.'

Jenny understood completely. Her father-in-law had survived an ambush by armed men on the road to Dublin. What man nowadays wouldn't be afraid of a repeat performance from the IRA when that group of fanatics never seemed to give up until they eventually chalked off their target?

After the family debate suggesting that Jenny and Robert should go in Lord Jackson's motor vehicle, which had a protection officer, Jenny had got her own way by riding to the church with Minnie and Kevin in Kevin's motorcar. Patrick had driven his Ford Model T, which he'd bought new three months earlier for the princely sum of ninety-eight pounds. Patrick had also bought the idyllic country cottage he'd been longing for, and he was glowing with happiness. Jenny planned to ask him today if he had a special love interest somewhere that she didn't know about.

Standing on the pavement, Jenny murmured to Kevin, "This should be a happy family occasion, but look at the place. There's more policemen here than guests."

Minnie, unsteady on her feet and clinging to Kevin's arm, said in an equally quiet voice, "Sweetheart, those IRA fanatics almost killed Lord Jackson in his motorcar. 'E's not taking any chances with 'is own grandson's life, is 'e?"

"Even so, Minnie, it doesn't mean I have to like it," Jenny grumbled.

"Ignore the police, Jenny. We've waited long enough for this to happen, so let's get it done." Kevin, still carrying the baby, tried to soothe his wife's discomfort, but instead he angered her further.

Kevin is blind to my feelings at times, Jenny thought, clamping her mouth shut and marching into the church. She had wanted the baby christened months ago in Dublin, away from the Jackson's seat of power and while he was still an infant. She'd asked Patrick to be Robert's godfather, but the Jacksons, including Kevin, had suggested it should be a Protestant and had invited the earl and Lady Jackson to be godparents. She'd begged Kevin to allow Danny to attend, but he had not invited her brother. She supposed Danny would've said no, even if Kevin had asked, but still, she had been desperate to see him and was bitterly disappointed.

She glared at Charlie Jackson, who was talking to policemen at the doors of the church. Thank God Danny hadn't come; Charlie would have arrested him on sight. Kevin's brother was the only person in the family who hadn't tried to get to know Jenny. He adored his nephew, which she found strange, considering his aloofness toward her. Robert was half hers and bore *her* father's Christian name, not his dad's.

Now a detective, Charlie worked at Dublin Castle and thought he was the greatest asset to Ireland since Saint Patrick himself. The previous night, he told Kevin that Danny was now a wanted man with a file as thick as an encyclopaedia, and that he would arrest him and his cohorts soon. She'd wanted to slap the satisfied smirk off Charlie's handsome face, but she'd kept her own counsel and vowed to warn Danny through Patrick, who still saw their brother occasionally.

Flowers did not bedeck St George's Church for the occasion. The pews were empty, no choir was present to sing hymns, and the family members attending the christening numbered a grand total of nine – ten, including the baby.

No sooner had Minnie and the five-strong Jackson family contingent, which included the earl and countess, sat in the front pews than the minister appeared. Kevin escorted Jenny, once again holding their child, and the Earl and Lady Jackson to the water font at the side of the altar. There, he said, "Thank you for doing this at such short notice, Reverend. It's not under the best of circumstances."

"Indeed, it is not. We should have a full congregation and choir to welcome young Robert into the bosom of the church." He looked at the empty pews and added, "Ah, but we're living through terrible times."

As the ceremony required, Jenny gave the baby to her mother-in-law. As godmother, Lady Jackson was to share responsibility of the child's spiritual development and upbringing with her cousin, the earl, as godfather, should Jenny and Kevin die. She gave the baby's grandmother an encouraging smile. The poor woman looked as uncomfortable as Robert did as she tried to handle the child's multi-layered robes. Meanwhile, Robert squirmed mightily to get back to his mother.

The baby, sensing his grandmother's unease, became even more restless and began to hit Matilda, who promptly handed him over to the earl. With a roll of her eyes, Jenny shared her disapproval with Kevin, then she whispered to her mother-in-law in a voice laced with honey, "Oh, I do hope you'll be able to hold him later for the photographer." At that moment, Robert stretched out his chubby little hand and pulled a loose tendril of his granny's hair as it blew towards him in the cold draft running through the church.

"Ouch, what a naughty child," Matilda snapped.

There you have it. I was right, Jenny thought. Lady Jackson wasn't the right choice for the job, and the baby, at just over a year old, had made his feelings known.

As the minister began to open the proceedings, Jenny thought, *this is not how I imagined the christening of my first child.* This *was* a cold process, a rote formality, not a meaningful Catholic ceremony with all the beautiful words and communion and choir boys singing and the smelly incense that used to make her feel sick as a child wafting over them. She didn't feel right as a Protestant; she sensed a void inside her soul, or mind or heart – wherever the spiritual part of her dwelt. Nor did she approve of her son growing up as an 'Orangeman', a 'Proddy-dog', a 'Billy' … a British loyalist to follow his grandfather. She said a quick *Hail Mary*, then wondered if her new faith allowed that prayer. She couldn't remember the reverend's instructions on which prayers, scriptures, and psalms were in and which were now out or what she could and could no longer pray for. As her resentment swelled at having to leave behind Catholicism, she threw Kevin a filthy look; he stared back at her with a confused cock of his head. She would apologise to him later for her nasty thought.

After the quick, dispassionate service, Jenny took the baby from the earl and led the small group down the aisle and out of the church. On its steps, the group posed for the photographer who'd come with all his cumbersome contraptions. Even he was being ringed by plain-clothed policemen who were flicking their eyes in all directions while brandishing their rifles and pistols in warning to anyone who might think about starting trouble.

"I'll have the baby and his parents first, thank you very much," the photographer said, taking charge. "Then I'll have the godparents together with the child and afterwards the whole family."

Jenny had insisted upon Patrick being photographed alone with Robert, and after the man had taken three photographs of uncle and nephew together, she drew Patrick to the side as he returned her son. "Patrick, before this is over today, I must know all you have on our Danny. I miss him terribly. He's all we've got left, and I won't allow even Kevin's orders to keep me apart from him," she whispered in his ear.

Patrick, shielding Jenny from Charlie Jackson's invasive stare, said, "Hold it all in, darlin'. We'll have a chat about

Danny before I return to Dublin tomorrow, just the two of us, I promise."

******

After dinner at Kiloblane house that evening, the men retired to the library for their brandy or port and cigars whilst the ladies went to the drawing room for coffee. Minnie, for all her brazenness which Lord Jackson now respected, had become the favourite Carmody. Strange, though it had seemed to Lord Jackson and Charlie, Matilda Jackson had grown fond of Minnie and now craved her company. She found her knowledge of current affairs stimulating, the stories of her life in London during Queen Victoria's reign fascinating, and her refusal to cow to the will of men inspiring.

"I do so look forward to you coming here, Minnie," Matilda now said, taking Minnie's arm as they crossed the room to the comfortable velvet sofa. "You brighten my days and make me think of so many things I never knew existed. My husband and sons never tell me anything. They don't think I need to know what's going on in my own country, but you understand me. You're not afraid to disagree with Lord Jackson, and that's such a novelty in this house. You're marvellous, my dear."

Mary, the Countess of Cork, perched her backside awkwardly on the edge of the soft cushions beside Minnie and said with a sniff, "The men are right, in my view. Women are not meant to rule; it distorts our feminine virtues. We have more than enough with which to occupy ourselves without filling our heads with worries of things we can do nothing about."

"Well, I for one want to fill my head with information, even if that means having worries," Matilda parried, then turned to address her daughter-in-law's grandmother. "Did you know, Minnie, that Charlie and my Clifford didn't want me to have the vote? They said such a sacred and important privilege of power shouldn't be given into the careless hands of women, as we wouldn't know what to do with it! After hearing your story about the London protest march you took part in last century, I gave them what-for and felt all the better for it."

Jenny smiled. She was warming to her mother-in-law, and thanks to Minnie, she believed Matilda was also breaching the wall of class snobbery that stood between them. After the church service, Matilda had pulled Jenny aside to apologise for her awkwardness at the water-font. 'I was afraid of being shot whilst holding my grandson,' she admitted, then, after a brief hesitation, added. 'I'm not the best mother. Oh, I love my boys, but you see, like myself, my children had nurses from birth until they were five years old. I rarely held them; it … it wasn't my station. Forgive me, Jenny, I'll try to be better with our little Robert.'

Matilda was becoming kinder and more considerate, and she loved her grandson, Jenny knew, watching her mother-in-law bask in Minnie's company. She'd said recently, 'My Kevin was such a serious and sombre young man, Jenny, but you brought him out of himself. He's happier than I've ever seen him, and I'm grateful to you for that.'

"Did you vote in January's local elections, Countess?" Jenny asked, mischief on her mind.

"No, I did not. As I just said, the voice of power should rest solely with men. Why any woman would want the responsibility, I'll never know."

"Oh, yes, good idea, Mary," Matilda snapped at her cousin. "Let's allow men to make all the decisions, including those that take us to war and anarchy on our streets."

"She's right," Minnie agreed. "Look at where men's power 'as got Ireland, Mary."

The countess pursed her lips and scowled at Minnie for daring to address her by her Christian name, but Minnie was enjoying herself and continued, "I don't understand you not wanting something we fought so 'ard to get. It's madness. After all those poor women in the suffrage movement went through to give us our civil rights, and 'ere's you wanting to leave it all up to men who 'ave no conception of 'ow diplomacy works. As a woman who was on the front lines in the fight for equality, I'm disappointed in the likes of you."

It's going to be a long night, Jenny thought.

"Anyone for whist?" she asked.

Chapter Thirty-Eight

Kevin, sitting next to Patrick on the library's polished leather chesterfield sofa, had tried twice to end the unsavoury conversation that Charlie had instigated. This evening, his brother was deliberately making it more inflammatory by bringing religion and Irish nationalism into the mix. Twice, he'd spat out the derogative term 'Fenian' from his obnoxious mouth, despite Patrick's presence or because of it. Kevin was inwardly raging at his brother's lack of respect for a houseguest. Charlie, since becoming a detective at Dublin Castle, was impossible to deal with.

"... you're quite right. Quite right, Charlie," Kevin's father was agreeing with his son's statement about the country's need for more British-backed forces on the streets. "Bringing in those RIC Special Reserves from England is the best thing Dublin Castle has come up with for a long time. You'll see, these 'Black and Tans' fellows will turn this thing around."

Charlie nodded, saying, "They're already showing the IRA scum what's what, Father. Unlike the police, they're not afraid to get their hands dirty."

"It's high time someone did," the earl concurred.

Charlie nodded again to himself. "I've been saying for a while that we should inflict harsher punishments against all Republican movements, whether they call themselves politically elected or Republican Army. They're as bad as each other. Did you know the IRA burnt over three hundred abandoned RIC barracks and almost one hundred income tax offices over Easter? I say we should set the British reservists loose with their guns and armoured cars and see what they can do for us. They showed the people in that Dublin Street what they were made of."

"What happened?" the tipsy earl asked Charlie.

"The Black and Tans were patrolling one of the slum areas in the north end of the city, and people were tossing rotting vegetables out their windows at them. One reservist on the armoured car opened fire on the tenement windows, then his fellow 'Tans' joined in. They soon shut the people up and stopped that carry-on in its tracks. Yes, set them loose, I say."

Patrick, looking disturbed by Charlie's fervent desire for more violence, finally spoke out. "Set them loose, Charlie? What are they … a pack of stray dogs sent to gnaw the bones of the Irish? Christ, as if there's not enough blood being spilt on our streets…"

"Are you talking about the blood of that detective shot near the courthouse in Cork last week?" Charlie glared at Patrick.

Kevin glanced at Patrick out the corner of his eye. Their friendship had been tested in the past year; it had held in large part because both had realised that by ostracising Danny from the family, they had unwittingly protected him from arrest, execution, or much worse. The lad was up to God only knew what, but it was public knowledge in this house that no one; not Jenny, Minnie, Patrick, nor he himself knew of Danny's whereabouts or what he was involved in. Charlie, therefore, however much he wanted to make a name for himself in his new position as detective, was not wasting resources having Jenny or Patrick followed and did not bring up Danny's name in conversation. Ignorance, in this case, was bliss, Kevin and Patrick agreed.

After a terse silence, Kevin found his voice and aired his own views, which countered both his father's and brother's.

"Father, if you'd like to thank anyone for the 'Black and Tans', it should be Winston Churchill. He's the Secretary of State for War, and he came up with the idea, not Dublin Castle."

The earl, who spent much of his time sitting on the benches of the House of Lords and very little time in Ireland, slurred, "Yes, but it's all … all so ambiguous, isn't it? I had the impression they were temporary constables recruited to assist the Royal Irish Constabulary, but now it seems they're wearing a mixture of British Army khaki and black RIC uniforms, and it's being suggested in Westminster that this is the reason the fellows are being called the 'Black and Tans,' so what are they … I mean, are they army or police?"

Charlie, revelling in the conversation in which he regarded himself as being the most knowledgeable of the group, informed his second cousin, the earl, "I suppose they're a bit of both. They come under RIC command, but they don't follow our rules of engagement, not wholeheartedly. Irish nationalists would have people believe that most of the men the British recruited have criminal records and came straight from British prisons. It's a lie, of course. In fact, a criminal record would disqualify anyone from the police force."

"That might be true, Charlie, but it's also a fact that they're committing criminal activities in towns across Ireland," Kevin put his brother right this time. "Most of them are ex-soldiers and it's for economic reasons that they joined the Temporary Constables. They have no love for the Irish, and as battle-hardened mercenaries, they'll do whatever they need to do to prove their usefulness to the government, including shooting innocent people and burning towns."

"Not true," Charlie said shaking his head.

"For God's sake, Charlie, you must have heard about the recent mutiny in Listowel?"

"Yes. I admit, that was unfortunate, and disgraceful," Charlie said, strangely subdued at the mention of the town.

"Unfortunate? Disgraceful?" Kevin jumped in again. "A British paramilitary force ordered Irish police officers to shoot as many of their fellow Irishmen as possible! Would you go down to the town and shoot your neighbours and tenants and friends you grew up with on the orders of these English thugs?"

"If I thought some of them might be IRA members, then yes, I probably would."

"That's enough, you two," Lord Jackson lobbed a warning shot at his sons. "This whole thing is messy. Kevin, you seem to forget about the number of innocent people the IRA have shot and killed."

"Yes, Kevin, how many fellow Irishmen have they bombed or killed with bullets?" Charlie asked, his newly acquired smugness supported by his father's words. "Go on, then, how many innocent lives have they taken, eh?"

Kevin, still dismayed by his brother's defence of the Black and Tans' outrageous behaviour in towns and villages across the south, disobeyed his father's ineffectual order to stop bickering and spat, "You mark my words, Charlie, the excesses of the British will drive the Irish population straight into the arms of the IRA, and you'll be sitting in your office still wondering how the hell it had happened."

Charlie flicked his eyes to Patrick and Kevin, and surprised both men with a more conciliatory tone, "Look, I know I come across as being hard-hearted against the Republican supporters, but I don't want bloodshed any more than you do. I want to see an end to this political upheaval, so we can *all* live in peace on this island."

"You mean once we have achieved a total victory over the IRA, Son?" Lord Jackson queried.

"Yes, Father, of course. Peace can only come when we defeat the Republican movements. But when, not if, we do, we will still have to win their support for ongoing British rule."

"Good luck with that," Patrick said. He'd remained quiet for almost the whole evening, but he now brought up another topic. It was in keeping with the ongoing subject, but he hoped it was one they could all agree on. "What I find fascinating, is why no one here is mentioning that the RIC have neglected their duties to law and order because they're too busy trying to destroy the IRA."

"Are you saying we're not doing our jobs?" Charlie frowned.

"That's precisely what I'm saying, Charlie. You probably know the crime figures better than anyone here, so you know that land agitation is on the rise, and as a result, cattle driving and removal of fences have resulted in Anglo-Irish landowners appealing to the Dáil for help. I know this because I've just bought a cottage in Malahide where the Dáil courts have replaced the Arbitration courts. They're under the control of the Dáil's Minister for Home Affairs, now, and its judges comprise IRA members and local priests. It's no secret…"

"And you support this, Patrick?" Lord Jackson asked with accusing eyes.

"Not really, sir. I was trying to make the broader point that the longer the ordinary people rely on the IRA and Dáil for justice in their communities, the more likely they are to get behind them in future elections." Patrick looked pointedly at

Lord Jackson, and added, "You're a Justice of the Peace, sir. I'd worry about your job, if I were you."

Kevin stood. The evening was well and truly soured, and no singing or piano playing or games of bridge or whist with the ladies would save it. Patrick was like a reed that bent in the wind. He didn't like to argue or fight, but tonight, something had struck a chord in him, and he had one thing yet to say to the Jacksons.

"This has put us in a hell of a spot," Patrick said, following Kevin to his feet. "Hundreds of links in the British military chain have been severed. The Peelers have abandoned all pretence of being a police force and are openly, avowedly a military force, designed not to keep down crime but to hold this country by brute force. At long last, the Irish have had enough. Heaven help us all."

Chapter Thirty-Nine

July 1920

Dublin, Ireland

The man entered the pub and with the help of two patrons was hauled onto a sturdy pub chair, the make-do elevation serving well as a temporary dais. His excited face was red with exertion, and as he waved a piece of paper about in his trembling fingers, he shouted, "God bless you, Ireland!"

"Silence, everyone! Pat has the final tally for the rural vote!" The landlord's booming voice came from behind the bar.

Danny had arrived at the pub when the party was in full swing. He knew various places in Dublin where IRA men wanted by the police could still go to enjoy a drink and to celebrate a victory, for as long as they kept their stays short; Shanahan's Pub was one such establishment. Here, amongst the Guinness barrels, whiskey bottles, and some of the finest singing voices he had ever heard, Danny rendezvoused with saint and sinner.

"Have you seen anything of Dan Breen or Séan Treacy, or young JJ Hogan?" Danny asked Jimmy, who was standing next to him.

"They've been in a couple of times, but last I heard they were in Tipperary. Regular Houdinis, those men. On the run for well over a year, yet still finding time to enjoy themselves in a Dublin bar." Jimmy answered, as Pat, the elderly man with the news, asked someone to get him a Whiskey to clear his lungs.

Danny recognised a few men from the IRA Dublin Brigades. Sure, but Shanahan's took numerous precautions to keep its patrons safe: lookouts roamed the vicinity and acted as early warning systems; the building had trapdoors to the basement where escape exits via various tunnels had been constructed; and it also boasted numerous hidey holes on the upper floor that opened to the sweet Irish sky and access to the rooftops of Shanahan's neighbours. It was brimming with Republican supporters who shielded IRA operatives on the run, and, when not on the run, these IRA men, surrounded by admirers, loved to boast about their achievements against the British tyrants as much as the civilians loved to hear about them.

"He wouldn't have got up on that chair if it was bad news, Jimmy," Danny said, watching Pat again trying to silence the drinkers.

"How did we do then, Pat?" Jimmy, who was holding a pint of Guinness in his hand, shouted back to the man balancing on the round wooden seat after downing his whiskey.

"Great news for Ireland!" Pat yelled in his loudest voice. "We won. Westminster and all its trickery failed to hinder Sinn Féin's popularity. We have taken control of twenty-nine of the thirty-three councils on the Irish ballot!"

Danny cheered, then his euphoric voice melted into the universal chorus of, "*Give me the Irish Republican Army. Give me the green, white, and gold every time.*"

"We did it," Danny said, nudging an elated Jimmy Carson when the song was done. "Despite Westminster's act to bring in proportional representation with a single vote and all the other machinations and deceit they used to undermine Sinn Féin's support, we swept the whole bloody country. Can you believe that, Jimmy?"

The man on the chair shouted again, "We faced this election with our political wing being suppressed by the British Government. But despite Westminster's obstructions, its imprisonment of our political leaders, and our press being stifled, we thrashed them…!"

Jimmy, eyes glistening with emotion, raised his empty pint glass and told Danny, "The Irish have spoken! They have answered, if possible, more emphatically than two years ago. This is it, Danny. The English bastards can't keep us down for much longer…"

Jimmy kept whatever else he was going to say to himself as the man on the chair continued with his forceful rhetoric. "…and this is our answer to the brutal and dastardly regime to which we have been subjected. We have intensified our desire to rule our own land, and we have done it at the ballot box!"

Jimmy shouted, "Good on ye. You tell them, Pat!" Then he said to Danny, "Fancy a whiskey?"

Danny looked at his wristwatch and shook his head. "I can't. I'm meeting Patrick. I'll see you later."

After his fib to Jimmy, Danny left the pub and headed to his secret meeting. Since taking on his new position in the 'squad,' he answered directly to Michael Collins, who along with his other titles was now the IRA's Director of Intelligence. At first, Danny had been reluctant to get involved with the 'squad'; Collins' nickname for his assassins' unit. As one of the first to join, Danny often looked back to the day in which the 'big fellow' had put the proposal to him and others present at the secret meeting. Collins had begun with a rousing speech about how he, the Dáil, and the IRA leadership had tried to reach independence using softer and more political means. 'We have tried low-level acts of violence, such as our attacks on RIC barracks, to demoralise the officers and make them abandon their rural outposts, the public's boycotting of the RIC, our intimidation and threatening policies against its officers to get them to resign, and the killing of known British spies and informants. And in my opinion, none of it is working well enough or quick enough to impact the British government's decisions on Ireland's future.'

Now, ecstatic about the election wins and enjoying the tram ride across town, Danny searched his heart for guilt over the assassinations he'd personally performed, thus far. He was not an evil man or a murderer. He *despised* the British for making him the killer he'd become and for forcing him to live like a hunted animal. He loved his family and his country. He wanted peace. Christ, how he yearned for a quiet night walking in the park without wondering if he were being followed. How he'd love to visit Jenny and the baby, and to talk with Patrick over a pint in a pub. Yet, in searching his heart, he found no regret or guilt for the killing he'd done; he felt instead a quiet, sombre pride at the success of his deeds.

Danny recalled the fateful meeting almost a year earlier, when he had shrunk at the idea of killing one man, much less having a fulltime job as an assassin. Every man present had told Michael he was crossing the line of decency, yet despite the universal reluctance, Michael eventually won over not all, but most, of the men. His speech had begun: 'We all know the RIC is not a police force in the true sense of the word. It has become a semi-military and political force, armed and drilled and concentrated in those little forts of theirs that are the block houses of Imperial rule in Ireland.'

At that point, Danny had agreed with the big fellow's perception of the Peelers. They had become increasingly violent towards the Republicans after Churchill had sent in his handpicked detectives and intelligence officers, who'd formed the new G-division. However, Danny also accepted now that it was only *after* the squad had shot Patrick Smith, a G-man, that Dublin Castle began to suppress the Dáil and Republican movement in earnest. Sure, both sides made mistakes. There was no neat orderliness to war, whether fought in muddy, bloody trenches or in backrooms with curtains on the windows. It was all bloody and filthy.

'What I want is a full-time unit devoted to eliminating British intelligence assets in Ireland,' Michael had got straight to the point. 'Dick McKee has chosen you because you're young and ambitious and most of you don't have wives or children to worry about, but that doesn't mean you have to accept. I'm asking you to do terrible things that you might not be able to bear, and I'm not going to force any one of you to say yes if your conscience won't allow it. It is a rotten thing to kill a fellow Irishman under any circumstances, but they're coming for us. They're putting everything they have into eliminating us, of killing our dreams of a free Ireland. The way I see it, and I do, clearly and precisely, it's either them or us now.'

Danny remembered the men in that room.

He'd seen the torture in the eyes of the ones who refused outright; their desire to serve pitted against their revulsion at putting bullets into fellow Irishmen. The targets of assassination worked against the Nationalist cause, but they also had families and lives within Irish communities up and down the country, and many were good men despite the political differences between them. Danny saw and felt the pain of the refusers most acutely. The majority of men in the room were more like Danny himself, he recalled; they were unhappy about it but agreed anyway, feeling the greater good demanded their sacrifice. A few of the men saw no problem in doing whatever was asked of them and fewer still seemed almost eager to be handed their weapons and their kill orders. Danny had studied their faces, committing them to hard memory. He knew that day whom he would want spotting for him and whom he wanted nowhere near him.

In Danny's mind, killing a British asset who would do whatever it took to bring down Sinn Féin, IRA leadership, or Irishmen in the street suspected of sedition was not only necessary, but it was his sacred duty. To date, he had killed two G-men, shooting them at close range, on different days and in different locations in Dublin. It was a grubby, high-risk job that came with a death sentence if captured, but Danny was at the tip of the spear, doing more damage to the enemy, both physically and in terms of tearing down their morale, than any other IRA section.

Danny entered Mary Street and found the house he was looking for. As always, he looked surreptitiously in all directions before going inside. For months, Michael Collins had been evading arrest using his own cunning talents and help from loyal Dubliners. He'd been successful, in part, by moving between safe houses in the city, rarely sleeping in the same place twice, and going after spies and police informants before they could get to him. His survival owed no thanks to Éamon de Valera, who had taken himself off to America to raise funds for the Nationalist cause. He'd left Michael in the firing line as 'leader', and with those lofty six letters, to take the entire fall for Republican crimes should the British find him. Danny surmised that 'Dev,' as Valera was known, wouldn't be happy about the big fellow's assassination squad, but to hell with him; he'd jumped ship and had no right to dictate policy.

Michael and a man Danny had never seen before were already in the sparsely furnished bedroom of an old tenement flat. After greeting the men, Danny joked, "Jesus, Mick, sure you're going down in the world with your living quarters."

"If I go down any further, Danny, I'll be sleeping in a gutter," Michael said good-humouredly. Then he introduced the stranger. "This is Quinn O'Malley. Quinn, this is Danny Carmody, the lad I've been telling you about."

Danny eyed the man, who stared back at him with equal curiosity and with a strange, knowing smile on his face. "And to what do I owe the pleasure of this little get together?" Danny asked as his eyes scanned the papers, maps and photographs strewn across a table. Meetings with Michael in person were rare occurrences nowadays, and they almost always led to orders that included assassinating someone. It didn't take Michael long to prove Danny correct in his assumption today.

"I want you to do a job with Quinn. He supplies us with guns and information and is a pillar of the community. Isn't that right, Quinn?"

"I'm a gem of a man, Mick, that I am."

Collins continued, "He's meeting a man tomorrow night, who wants to meet me." Michael paused to place a photograph of the person in question in front of Danny. "This is a clipping from John Grant's newspaper. Meet Mathew Brady. He's a councilman, a purported IRA supporter…" Michael let his words trail off, then said, “Quinn, you’d better tell Danny what you’re thinking.”

Quinn nodded. “Last week, Brady came to me with six rifles, ten .45 calibre revolvers, and some boxes of bullets. After I paid him, he started talking about his desire to meet Mick. He asked me three times to set up a meeting, said he had important information that he could only give to Mick in person.”

“Quinn has a good nose for sniffing out traitors, Danny. I went to his warehouse last year and found him standing over the bodies of two dead Jews who had delivered guns to him. Tell him about that one, Quinn.”

“The Jew came to me, offering guns – top of the line – he said. He told me he’d be back the next night with them, so I said all right but took it upon myself to watch his offices at the docks the next day. There was something off with him, like a strange smell I couldn’t figure out. Anyway, I saw him having a meeting there with one of the G-men who’s on Mick’s list, and after a while the pair of them came out of the Jew’s office and shook hands. Well, I didn’t need to see any more to come to a decision. That night, I waited until he came back with the weapons. He didn’t come alone, though, so I had to dispose of his sidekick outside before me and the Jew, name of Aldas, by the way, had a nice wee chat with him at the end of my fist and tied to a chair. Seems the lying scum was double dealing with the British at Dublin Castle, so I killed him. Mick and his men got rid of the bodies in the Liffey.”

“He doesn’t mess around, our Quinn,” Collins told Danny. “So if he thinks there’s something off with this Mathew Brady, I believe him. Carry on, Quinn.”

"I do think there's something off with Brady," Quinn continued. "Three nights ago, I sent Finn – you know Finn, Danny?"

"Yes. He's a good friend of mine," Danny answered.

"Well, I asked Finn to follow Brady, which he did, and he reported back to me that after Brady had left my place, he went to the house of a known RIC intelligence officer, where he spent the night. They left that house together the next morning and got into an unmarked RIC car."

"Finn spent all night in the street waiting, did he?" Danny asked.

Quinn's eyes twinkled. "No, he got a bedroom for the night, opposite the house Brady went into and watched from the window. In the morning, he shadowed Brady right to the castle. Thank God the British have not been able to despoil Irishmen of the spirit of kindness and hospitality. I've never been turned away from a home and a cup of tea when I've needed shelter. Dublin is with us, and that stirs my heart."

Not all Dublin, Danny thought. He remembered not long ago, being tossed out on his ear from a house he was trying to hide in. He eyed Mick, who seemed comfortable in Quinn's company. Their apparent friendship was enough for Danny to decide not to contradict Quinn, or to ask questions about the two Jews he'd shot, where he'd shot them, and how he managed to put them down by himself. If Michael trusted him, that was good enough. And Finn, whom he hadn't seen for months, also seemed to trust the man by the sound of it. "I take it you think this Brady fellow is a spy trying to draw Mick out of hiding?" he asked.

"He wouldn't be the first. Every British loyalist in Dublin is trying to get our Mick into the open," Quinn answered, then he continued, "I knew for certain Brady was a spy when he came back the next day, offering me more guns but implying that he'd only give them to me if I took him to speak to Michael in person. I set up a meeting for tomorrow night at a place close to the river – the old tannery building – you know it?"

Alarm bells went off in Danny's head at the mention of the tannery. That place was cursed, as far as he was concerned. He hated the thought of going anywhere near it. He stared at Michael whose eyes were still on Quinn and said, "Mick, tell me you're not going to meet him."

"No, I'm sending you in my place, with Quinn and Finn to back you up. I want you to kill Mr Brady. Can you bear it, Danny?" Michael asked.

Can you bear it? Danny had rented his house out to a good Catholic family who had nothing to do with politics. They paid the rent on time every month but were constantly harried by visits from the police and detectives, looking for Jimmy. Someone had given his name up to the G-men under torture, and Jimmy was now a suspect in the murder of an Irishman called Joseph Docherty, a police informant. As it happened, Jimmy had nothing to do with *that* assassination.

Danny accepted the hardships of living out of a small bag that carried only essentials and of flitting from place to place to rest his head at night. No place was safe in Dublin anymore, at least not for the likes of known IRA soldiers and sympathisers. The hardships of the Irish War, added to those of the Great War, had become too much to bear for some Dubliners. Misguided traitors became British informants in exchange for a fat stack of pounds sterling and police protection, but they never seemed to learn that in doing so, they sold their freedom cheaply. Should they not be able give viable information to the

Black and Tans when they came calling next time, their blood money could just as well be coffin nails.

Danny gave Michael a cheeky grin and finally answered, "Which part is hard to bear … my life being upended? Me not being able to go home to my own house, and having to sleep in places far worse than this, or not being able to speak to my family for months on end? You know what I said to you when you asked me to join the squad, Michael. I said I'd let God judge my deeds and conscience, and that's what I'm doing. Yes, I know the cost, as do we all, and I can bear it for as long as it takes to end this war in victory."

"Good lad."

Michael smiled at Quinn, who seemed amused at Danny's passionate declaration. "Quinn, I met Danny during the uprising when he was just a lad of seventeen and vowing to fight to the bitter end while the British army were trying to smoke us out of the GPO building. We spent time together at Frongoch Prison Camp, where he fell in love with a wonderful girl called Anna – God rest her soul. Ah, Anna, she was a real beauty. Every man in the camp was jealous when she fell for young Carmody, here."

Michael pressed both his hands down on Danny's shoulders, squeezed reassuringly, and nodded. "I knew you were a feckin' true believer the first time I…"

Michael turned sharply to the door as it swung open to admit Aidan, one of Michael's lookouts. The man, panting for breath, rushed out, "Police and Black and Tans are about Henry Street and Mary Street. They're conducting door to door searches in the whole sector; you need to get out now, Mick…"

"Shite, not again," Michael sighed. "Right, Aidan, thank you. You know the drill." As Michael packed his briefcase with the sheets of papers and photos that were on the table, he lifted humour-filled eyes and apologised to Danny and Quinn. "Sorry, you two, we're going to have to cut this meeting short. Come with me, and don't stop for a cup of tea along the way."

On Henry Street, Danny followed Mick and Quinn as they entered a house and took to the stairs inside. The three men bolted along the stair landing until they came to a bookcase. There, Michael pushed a book which depressed a spring and the "bookcase" swung inwards into a darkened room with no windows and only a hole to let in air. Ushering Danny and Quinn inside, he said, "Sorry, boys, this is where we'll be spending the night. Batt O'Conner, a Kerry man, built this years ago. It won't be comfortable, but it should be safe enough." With that said, and with no other recourse available to them, Michael closed the entrance and turned a contraption with levers on it to lock the door.

A few minutes later, they huddled silently with their backs against the wall, listening to the rough and tumble cockney voices of the Black and Tans in the hallway outside.

It was going to be a long night.

Chapter Forty

The next morning

"All clear, Mick."

After spending the night inside the cramped cubbyhole, Danny, Mick, and Quinn let out collective sighs of relief. 'All clear,' coming from Aiden on the landing was music to Danny's ears and knotted muscles.

In the hallway, Danny stretched his back and neck. "Jesus, I never thought I'd be able to walk upright again," he groaned. "Mick, you snore and fart for Ireland. And you were rambling on in your sleep, Quinn."

"And you, Carmody, were jumping about all over the place. I thought I would have to hold you down again." Mick playfully slapped Danny's back.

Embarrassed, Danny told Quinn, "That'll be my cursed dreams of the war in France. My brother's a doctor. He says they'll go away, eventually." Not being able to speak all night for fear of being heard by police officers or reservists who might still be in the hallway had been hard on Danny, for his curiosity about Quinn had grown during the hours of darkness.

Often in Republican areas, the police and men from G-Division came, went, and came back repeatedly during their searches for suspects and arms. They recurrently knocked on the same doors, shouted in gruff voices to scare babies and small children, thumped heavy boots in corridors and hallways … all to punish tenants because the English knew them to be Sinn Féin sympathisers who supported the IRA and the Dáil's lawful government.

The G-men were relentless, like sniffer dogs. They even attended Sinn Féin gatherings where they took notes of the speeches despite being known by appearance to almost everyone in Dublin who had a stake in the war. The blighters who were staying the course were not afraid … or if they were, they didn't let fear disrupt their duties.

As in the RIC and Metropolitan Police, some G-Division officers *had* resigned. Danny surmised that, unable or unwilling to operate under threat of death from the IRA, they'd either thrown in the towel or they had realised which side they belonged on and were now spying for Mick Collins. These were the bravest, and often most committed of men.

Mick went into the kitchen of a small apartment downstairs, where a woman was frying eggs. He kissed the woman's cheek and grinned. "How about a spot of breakfast, Mrs Walsh?"

"Ah, that sounds grand," Danny said, and got a violent shake of the head from Mick for his cheek.

"Not you, Danny. Go with Quinn. You've got a job to do," Mick said.

Later, Quinn and Danny ate a big breakfast at Quinn's apartment, and afterwards Danny slept for a while in a proper bedroom while Quinn went about his business downstairs. Then in mid-afternoon, Finn arrived.

"What do you think about this Quinn? Do you trust him with your life?" Danny asked Finn over a cup of tea upstairs in the apartment.

"He's a good man, and he's got Mick's ear. That's good enough for me."

"But have you worked with him before this?"

Finn bit into a soda scone, and with his mouth full, mumbled, "I've come across him many times. He's in procurement and acquisitions. To be honest, I don't know how he runs a business *and* does what he does for us. The cheeky bugger has men from Dublin Castle here for dinner parties and gets useable information out of them before dessert arrives. Cool as a sheet of ice on the Liffey." Finn chuckled then repeated, "The cheek of the devil. Did you know he supplies the Metropolitan Police with uniform accessories – socks, woollen overcoats, scarves, blankets – that sort of stuff? Now, if you're asking me if I think he's a British spy, then the answer's an emphatic, no. He's as loyal to the big fellow and de Valera as they come. Put it this way, I trust Quinn as much as I trust you, and that's saying something." Finn cocked his head to the side and mused, "He must like you to bring you here."

As Finn dozed in an armchair, Quinn offered Danny a hot bath. "No offence, Danny, but you stink like my dear departed mother's old garden closet. Forty people shared it."

Danny studied Quinn's manservant, Allister, as he emptied the last bucket of hot water into the half-full bath. Quinn had remarked earlier that day, 'Allister is one of us and you can trust him. He'll lay a clean shirt and long johns out on the bed for you.' Danny wanted to ask the dour-faced man why he was working as a manservant, but he added that question to the list of the others rambling in his head.

"Ah … lovely." Danny sucked in his breath as the heat of the steaming water caressed his skin. For a while, he lay there thinking about numerous things. Relaxing in the candlelit room without windows and feeling the heat of the water loosen his knotted muscles set free repressed thoughts and memories in the back of his mind. They were always there, chirping away, waiting to jump out in an unguarded moment: Anna, his parents, the friends he'd lost in the war, and the man he had shot on the Knocklong train … all ghosts from his past. His mission tonight, Jenny, the baby he hadn't seen for almost a year, Patrick, and Minnie living her final years just up the road from him were his present, and those contemplations – all of them – hurt and made his heart feel as heavy as a sack of rocks.

After the bath which left the water a dirty-grey colour, he went into Quinn's bedroom to borrow the shirt. He'd been wearing his for more than a week and Quinn was right; it smelt rotten, although he still thought the man had exaggerated the extent of his body odour.

When dressed, Danny looked in Quinn's wardrobe. *Well, well, here's a man who likes nice clothes,* he thought fingering the row of hanging garments. On a shelf, he spotted a wooden box. He reminded himself that both Mick Collins and Finn trusted Quinn, but he thought, *it won't do any harm to peek inside it. Sure, every man in Ireland is at least a bit paranoid about being duped by a spy or a traitor. Who knows what might be in a box hidden in a wardrobe?*

He looked at the bedroom door, then went to it and quietly locked it. Returning to the box, he set it on top of the bed and removed the lid. It was full of photographs – childhood memories, family and friends, he presumed – nothing seditious – not that he could see.

He studied the people and backdrops in the pictures: Quinn with older people, perhaps his parents, children playing in the sand, a boy dressed in his first Holy Communion outfit, Quinn with a group of men drinking pints, Patrick in his naval uniform … Danny's breath caught. Finally, he pushed it out and forced himself to inhale again. Patrick, his brother, *his* Patrick's sombre face staring back at him.

As Danny dressed, he wondered what action to take. The sensible thing to do would be to call Quinn up to the bedroom, question him, and beat the shite out of him or kill him, whichever course seemed best. He could see no reason for the man having Patrick in his sights other than that he was working for the British as a spy and suspected Patrick of something nefarious. But why *Patrick*, for Christ's sake? He was a civilian; a political atheist, a nobody. Could they be using Patrick to get to him and through him, possibly, Mick Collins? No, Quinn was already well in with Mick. So how did Patrick fit in?

Puzzled, Danny replaced the box carefully in the wardrobe but tucked Patrick's photograph into the inside pocket of his jacket. He was trembling, but he accepted that the mission must go ahead, and that, for now, he needed to focus on his job and put Patrick's safety to the back of his mind. Then, and only then, he would take Quinn O'Malley aside, interrogate him, and if needed, put a bullet in the bastard's brain.

******

After darkness had fallen, Finn, Danny, and Quinn set off on their bicycles. The three men were carrying loaded .45 calibre revolvers, but before joining Quinn and Danny that afternoon, Finn had also hidden two rifles in foliage at the place where they were to meet with Mathew Brady.

The men dismounted, hid their bicycles within the wood's thick undergrowth and then walked the final hundred yards to a bridge crossing the Tolka, the biggest tributary that fed into the River Liffey. It stood about one hundred and fifty yards from the old tannery and at parts ran from about thigh to waist deep. One couldn't find a more secluded spot in Dublin.

Finn retrieved the rifles and gave one to Danny. A minute later the men heard three soft whistles. Quinn raised his fist, army style, and hooted his response, sounding like a common tawny owl.

With confident swaggers and armed with rifles slung over their shoulders, John Grant and the five men with him approached the bridge. Danny and John faced off, for once unable to ignore the other's presence in the confined space. Quinn, knowing the history between the two men from Patrick, allowed the confrontation to take place – he'd never been able to look at Grant in the same way since learning about his betrayal of a severely wounded woman.

They expected Brady to arrive in a half hour, which gave the men plenty of time to get into their respective positions. Quinn was interested to see how the youngest Carmody would perform against the powerful and more experienced John Grant.

Patrick's brother impressed Quinn. The lad was a hardened criminal and murderer as far as the British were concerned, but from Mick Collins' point of view and the perspective of thousands of IRA volunteers or supporters of the Republic, he was a brave and dedicated soldier who had suffered terribly for one so young. John Grant, on the other hand, was an aggressive dog who felt he deserved the biggest, meatiest bones and a pat on the head because of his illustrious surname.

"How's that broken nose on your face, John? Sure an' you'll remember it was the Carmodys' parting gift to you in London," said Danny, striking the first verbal blow.

"How is your poor, deformed sister?" John answered, drawing gasps of disapproval from the men standing beside him.

"She's blissfully happy," Danny smiled, making eye contact with each of the men in turn. "She and her husband have a son. He was born in their beautiful five-bedroom house in central Dublin. Sure, the best thing she ever did was to get shot of a turd like you, John Grant, and get herself a real man."

After giving Danny a look of disgust, John told an amused Quinn, "I've got our perimeter marked out where you instructed. If the DMP or Black and Tans come that way, we'll know about it. We're all set … that's if Danny here doesn't freeze or have one of his famous fits before he fires his kill shot."

"Danny never misses a shot," Finn said casually to John.

As Quinn began to unravel the strings of the mission, the old saying; *he who sets the trap becomes trapped,* came to his mind. "Look lads, Brady will show up and we'll deal with him, but I'd be lying to you all if I suggested he's coming alone."

"We already gathered that, Quinn. You wouldn't have asked for the six of us if you thought Brady intended to take Mick by himself." John grinned at Finn, the tallest of them, and the man chosen to play the part of Michael Collins. "We've got your back, Finn. Like I said, anyone comes into those woods behind us, and we'll give them a fireworks' display they won't forget in a hurry."

"They'll forget everything, ye eejit, 'cos they'll be dead." A man with John laughed at his own smart mouth.

"Don't you worry yourself, Quinn, we're expecting a fight. I hope this Brady brings a dozen of those detectives with him.

That'd be a good show for Mick Collins," another man from John's unit said.

Danny, looking around the immediate area, mused, "At least they can't get any motor vehicles into this place, which means they'll have to fight their way out, same as us."

Quinn nodded his agreement, then he looked at the bridge's waist-high stone wall to his left. "Danny, that's your spot up there. We'll position Brady in your line of sight with his back to you."

"And we'll make sure we're far enough away that you don't hit us by mistake," Finn joked.

"Who'll take care of his backup man?" Danny asked.

"Finn and I will deal with him. Brady won't want to break through those trees with a legion. If he's smart, he'll tell any men he has with him to wait in the wood until the meeting is over."

"True enough," Danny said. "He'll confirm he's talking to Mick Collins before he makes his move."

"And when did you become an expert in this sort of thing, Danny?" John Grant sniggered.

"Around the same time that I smashed your face in and left you whimperin' for your da on a London pavement."

"There's only one path through the woods, and we'll have it covered." John dragged his eyes off Danny and spoke directly to Quinn. "Are you certain he doesn't know what Mick looks like?"

"Do I look daft to you?"

"No."

"Good, 'cos if I wasn't certain, we wouldn't be here, would we?" Quinn answered.

Chapter Forty-One

At eleven o'clock, two dark figures emerged from the treeline and onto the narrow dirt track that ran behind the riverbank and led to the tannery. Quinn couldn't make out their faces, but as they drew closer, he recognised Brady's confident swagger and his peaked cap and raincoat billowing outwards like a cape as he faced the wind. When the figures neared, Quinn spotted the long army canvas bag slung over Brady's shoulder. He also saw that the man trailing behind held a smaller carpet bag. Even in the dark, he recognised the second man; he'd come with Brady to the woollen factory two days earlier.

This is looking good, Quinn thought. He saw only two men and was not hearing a single warning shot from John in the woods, which meant Brady had probably not brought the authorities with him, or they were yet to arrive. He found the thought of John's men ambushing detectives and police exhilarating, but he also worried that John would start a war in the woods before Finn and he could interrogate Brady about who else was spying on the IRA and what the British were planning at the castle.

Quinn greeted Brady with a handshake and said, "Glad you could make it, Mathew." Then he shook the other man's hand, "Good to see you too, Séamus. Right, let's get this done before it pelts down."

Brady set his bag on the ground, then gestured to Séamus to do the same. When both bags were open, they revealed an assortment of weapons. Brady informed Quinn, "We've brought you police carbines, five Lee-Enfield rifles, three shotguns, two Webley revolvers, and some ammunition…"

"Don't forget the two grenades, Mathew," Séamus said.

"Ah, yes, and two grenades, right enough…"

"Where did you get them from?" Finn interrupted, his gruff voice matching his rod-straight stance. For the guise of Mick Collins, he'd decked himself in a baggy raincoat and fedora hat pulled down at the front. He strategically stood in Quinn's shadow, making it difficult for Brady and his man to see his facial features but able to note his towering figure. Something everyone agreed upon about Collins was that he was a big fellow, hence his nickname.

"I got them from the lads at IRA Dublin Brigade 4th Battalion," Brady answered Finn's question. "They're procuring weapons from the Quartermaster at Wellington Barracks and smuggling them out by the canal at the rear of the complex." Still staring at Finn, he continued, "It's good of you to meet with me, Mr Collins."

"It's an honour," Séamus echoed Brady.

Brady began a polite conversation in which he uttered his devotion to the IRA and his admiration for Mick Collins. In the meantime, Danny's head peeked over the top of the bridge's stone wall. Finn and Quinn faced it while Brady and Séamus stood with their backs to it. A strategically placed hurricane lamp was also on the ground near to Brady to help guide Danny's aim.

So far, so good, Quinn thought again. Now he needed to draw Brady out and get solid information from him before any assassination took place. He was fighting this war with grim sobriety, and there was nothing more sobering than murdering a fellow Irishman. He'd informed the men earlier that despite Finn's firm evidence, he wouldn't kill Brady unless he was certain of his treachery. But if Brady *was* a spy, Quinn was most interested in who he took his orders from at Dublin Castle.

Before Brady's arrival, Quinn had told Danny, 'Do not shoot until you see me removing my cap. It's not an inventive signal, but you won't misinterpret it in the dark as a natural gesture.'

As the conversation between Finn and Brady continued, Quinn played out the assassination in his mind, step by step, seeing it through to its conclusion. ... *we'll then have the other man to kill before he gets to his concealed weapon – they are carrying, that's a given – so after Danny's kill shot, we'll have only seconds to react against Séamus.* "Well, are you going to stand there kissing Michael's arse all night?" Quinn finally grumbled to Brady. "You said you needed to meet him 'cos you had something to tell him, so get on with it, man."

"Wait a minute, Quinn, let Mathew tell me about his boat," Finn said harshly. "Did you know he had a boat?"

"No, I didn't."

"Well, he does, and I'm interested in it – go on, Mathew – tell me what sort of fish you catch."

Keeping in mind that Finn was supposedly Michael Collins, and his superior, Quinn was reluctant to cut off the friendly conversation. Inwardly, however, he was annoyed with Finn for prolonging the meeting with useless chatter, when they both knew damn well that every minute they stood there, the danger of being caught breaking curfew grew. Eventually, his anger outweighed his need to play the role. "Bejesus, to hell with the boat and the fishing. Go on Mathew, hurry the feck up. It's going to rain any minute now and I don't like getting wet."

Brady looked nervously at Finn and began, "I have information for you, Mr Collins. You need to know that you…"

At the sound of gunfire from within the wooded area, Finn, impossibly fast and way ahead of the others, drew his Colt and pulled the trigger twice on Brady who was still fumbling to get his gun out of his pocket.

When Brady fell dead to the ground, his pal, Séamus, almost immediately joined him with a bullet to the back of his head, courtesy of Danny's rifle. Danny then ran off the bridge to join Finn and Quinn, who hadn't fired his weapon or even removed his cap.

The firefight, in and around the treeline, seemed in bloody earnest. Gunshots, rifle fire and grenades causing explosions and balls of flames vibrated the ground Quinn and the others stood on even though they were at least a hundred yards from the trees.

"Jesus Christ, that's John and his boys trapped in there!" Quinn panicked.

"What the hell's happening?" Danny panted.

When a rifle shot narrowly missed Quinn and ricocheted off the bridge's wall, his questions were replaced by the urgent desire to scarper. Black-clad figures rushed out of the mist-shrouded woods like dark crusaders closing in. Quinn looked longingly at the guns in the bags, dived to the ground and rummaged through the big one until his hands gripped one of the grenades. "Run!" he shouted, even as Danny and Finn were already wading through the mid-calf high river to get to the other side. To buy time, Quinn removed the pin and lobbed the grenade at the oncoming men, and when the explosion came it also brought a smokescreen that allowed him to rise and wade into the Tolka.

Quinn lost sight of Finn and Danny to the darkness almost as soon as he cleared the chilly water, but as he ran through a field of tall grasses, ferns and wild weedy shrubs behind the tannery building, he mentally mapped out different routes into the city. Seconds were like minutes, minutes like hours as he ran, head and body crouched low amongst the shrub cover, and him not looking back despite hearing a sporadic shot echoing in the distance behind him.

When he neared the first dilapidated city tenement buildings, he detected nothing but the sound of his own breath being released through his gaping mouth in sharp, pained gasps. He was finished; his arms were flailing awkwardly, his chest was on fire, and it was becoming painful to swallow. To compound those egregious symptoms, he was hit with dreaded stitches in his sides; cramps so painful, they sucked the breath out of him. "Feck it…" he wheezed. "I'm done in."

Doubled over, he entered the first building he came to. The old warehouse, a longstanding customs post from a bygone age, had a maze of rooms off a main storage space. Empty wooden packing crates were piled high, probably unmoved since the old place had shut down and given way to more modern dockyard buildings.

An hour passed, with Quinn in his hiding spot behind a tower of crates. He was gaining confidence that the police had probably given up their search. He was fast on his feet and had great stamina, despite crashing at the end. The chances of the police catching him on foot had been slim from the outset, but it didn't mean they might not now be scouring the city on bicycles or trucks. He did some easy stretches to keep his muscles loose. *Where were Danny and Finn? Had John and his men been captured or, God forbid, killed?*

Deciding to wait it out until dawn at least, Quinn settled down and tried to make sense of what had happened. The trap laid by Brady and the police, who'd probably been led by detectives from G-Division, completely baffled him. They had planned the ambush with precision and seemed to have had prior knowledge of where the IRA lads would be positioned in the woods. It was a certainty that men *were* dead or captured. Both sides had probably suffered multiple casualties in the intense gun battle.

He rubbed his eyes and stared unseeingly in the darkness. If they planned the police ambush, why had they not lain in wait by the bridge, to capture the biggest prize, which had been Mick Collins? The other puzzling aspect was that Brady had started giving information a second before Finn pulled the trigger. *'You need to know you have a…'* … a what? What did Michael Collins have? Also, at the first snap of gunfire, Brady had looked genuinely unprepared and as shocked as everyone else. He hadn't looked like a man who was planning an escape or waiting for help, nor had he dictated the length of the meeting. Finn, the hot-headed idiot, had been too quick off the mark with his shots, and now there were more questions than answers.

As morning light crept into the warehouse through the broken wood panels at the entrance, Quinn stood up and stretched. In the cold light of day, he wondered if he could claim any victory at all from the previous night. Another two British spies in Dublin were dead, but that small win didn't make up for him not getting his bloody weapons, and possibly losing eight good men. *Mick will go through me like a steam train when he hears about this.*

Cautious, Quinn looked outside but saw nothing untoward happening. He sucked in his breath then released it slowly, to calm his fluttering heartbeat, then he stepped into the thoroughfare and blended in with rush hour foot traffic.

The roads throughout the dockyard and beyond were busy with men going to work on foot and bicycle. Periodically, they skipped aside to let the odd horse and cart trundle by, and quickly scattered again as modern motor trucks rumbled along like kings of the road, brushing aside everything in their paths.

Again, his mind played with a plan. He couldn't go home for fear of being named by a captured IRA man. Chances were, they'd be torturing the lads at the castle. Quinn's inner voice was screaming, *lie low!* It would be at least a day or two – maybe longer – until he found out who had survived in the woods, and whether Danny and Finn had got away safely. It might be a week or more before he could risk a meeting with Mick.

Until now, Quinn had not been a suspect in any Republican crime, as far as he knew, but after the previous night's disastrous operation, he expected to be hunted down along with the rest of the IRA fugitives on G-force's extensive lists. It appeared the 'good life' might be over for him.

Quinn cheered and stepped up his pace when he decided where he was going. At a junction, he got on a tram that went to the train station. From there, he took a train to Malahide, or as the Irish called it: Mullach Íde – or sand hills of Íde – in Fingal, County Dublin. It was about thirteen miles north-east of the capital city, and it was also the village where Patrick now lived.

It had taken months for Patrick to forgive Quinn for the debacle at his business' warehouse. Patrick had sustained serious injuries, inflicted by Aldas and his man, and being a gentle soul, he'd also been traumatised by the dirty war he'd tried to ignore for so long. Aldas was a good man, and Quinn often regretted shooting him and the other Jew, even though he acknowledged that he'd kill any man who endangered Patrick's life. He smiled as he recalled the many days and nights when he'd stood in St Stephen's Green with his eyes glued on the College of Surgeons' entrance. It had not been easy winning the love of his life back. Outside the building, and on four separate occasions Patrick had seen him and snapped, 'Get lost,' but on Quinn's fifth try, he'd agreed to one drink and to talk. During that evening, which had eventually led to a late supper, they had finally reconciled.

Quinn sauntered through the village, enjoying its relative tranquillity and fresh air. Malahide lay between Swords, Kinsealy and Portmarnock. Much of the County Dublin area comprised a series of villages. This one was situated where the Broadmeadow River estuary came to the sea, and on the opposite side of the estuary was where Donabate stood. To the east of the village, the Gaybrook Stream passed through the Yellow Walls area to reach the estuary in a marshland. It was breathtaking scenery, and its beauty reminded Quinn of why he was fighting for a free Ireland.

Before buying the cottage, Patrick had invited Quinn to explore the county with him. Riding bicycles instead of motorcars, both had decided that it was an idyllic place to make Patrick's home; not too far from Dublin, yet far enough away to feel free of the city and its grimy atmosphere. Today, it would be Quinn's haven.

As he stood outside Patrick's detached cottage at the edge of the village, clutching the spare key in his hand, Quinn swallowed hard with dread; the living room windows were open, which confirmed Patrick was home. He'd finished his end-of-year final surgical exams and had passed all of them with distinction. He had three weeks' holiday now before going on surgical rotations at the hospital and had mentioned a week earlier that he might visit his sister for a few days. Apparently, he'd changed his mind about going to Jenny's. Quinn had nowhere else to go – nowhere was safe – but the thought of endangering Patrick was intolerable.

"Damn it," Quinn muttered as he put the key in the lock; he'd hoped for a rest before coming clean about his criminal exploits. "It's only me," he called out as he opened the front door and entered the hallway.

"I'll be down in a minute," Patrick replied from the upstairs' landing.

"Well, this is it," Quinn muttered as he filled the kettle with water. He was about to inform Patrick that he'd met Danny, who was now in police custody, dead, or fit and well but in hiding.

To lie to Patrick meant breaking their bond of trust, and he would *not* do that a second time.

Chapter Forty-Two

End of June 1920

Malahide, County Dublin

Patrick allowed himself to relax completely and enjoy his hot soak in the bathtub. His muscles no longer felt tense, and his mind was relatively unburdened by an accumulation of facts and figures, procedures, Latin names for every organ in the human body, where to cut with the surgical blade, how deep and how long. He had passed every exam as he'd hoped and was now being rewarded with three weeks' holiday during which he planned to hike around the countryside, eat, sleep, and spend time with Quinn and his family. He was in heaven.

Although proud of his performance during this last term, he admitted it had been a harder course than he'd imagined a year earlier, when he'd strolled into the Royal College of Surgeons in Dublin thinking he knew more than anyone else in this his final residency year. He'd been over-confident and cocky, for in the written exams, he'd floundered like an upturned beetle more than once until he finally realised the study texts weren't *suggested* reading. Ah, but his success had been worth every sleepless night, the pressure, the anxiety, and all the sacrifices made, for when the college board formally confirmed his exam results, he could add FRCSI after his name: Patrick Carmody, Fellow of the Royal College of Surgeons in Ireland. Oh, how he wished his parents were alive to share his wonderful news.

Fully dressed, he stood in front of the bedroom mirror and flattened his wet hair back from his forehead with an ivory comb…

"It's only me!" Quinn's familiar voice called up the stairs.

Downstairs in the kitchen, the kettle steamed and whistled on the stove, and next to it, Quinn stood with his head bowed as he shovelled a spoon into the tea caddy.

Patrick crossed the kitchen, removed the kettle from the heat, wrapped his arms around Quinn's waist, kissed his neck, and asked, "Why are you here this morning?"

Quinn's dirt-smudged face looked tired even as he responded with a bright smile. "What sort of greeting is that to give a man who's travelled far and wide to get to you?"

"Jesus, would you look at yourself," Patrick took a step backwards to study Quinn, then said, "You look as though you've been down a coalmine, and haven't been to bed all night What mischief have you been up to?"

Quinn slumped into a kitchen chair, put his elbows on the modest kitchen table, and ran his fingers through his hair. "I've been in service to Ireland. I'm ready for my bed. Can I stay here for a few days?"

Patrick sat in the other chair, crossed his arms, and contemplated his response. Whenever Quinn was doing 'whatever' in service to Ireland, it usually meant he was raiding a British facility for weapons or involved in a gunfight with the police or Black and Tans. Ever since they'd got back together, Patrick had steeled himself for bad news: Quinn's body being found pitted with bullet holes in some town; or his name appearing in the newspaper, saying he'd been arrested and imprisoned or executed; or his business being closed by order of the authorities, and Quinn missing, like others who were never seen on Dublin's streets again.

Patrick knew the dangers to Quinn and the cost to himself for being involved with active IRA operatives, but he had put his fears aside and finally embraced the Republican cause. Gone were the days when Irish men and women sat on the fence, thinking they could ignore the troubles. Violence was spreading, both in its intensity and frequency. Both sides were committing atrocities, but he supported the Irish right to freedom, despite their murderous ways, over the British Black and Tans or G-division. The Black and Tans were indiscriminately harsh with innocent bystanders, and the G-division officers were even worse; they took pleasure in assassinating non-combative Sinn Féin members and their supporters. The brutalities perpetrated by those forces and soldiers as they patrolled the streets to uphold curfews were unforgivable.

He stared across the narrow table at Quinn, and despite his love for the man, said with a stern tone, "Yes, you can stay, but I want you to tell me what you've been up to. The truth and nothing but the truth." Patrick then regarded Quinn's dust-matted hair and changed his mind. "Christ, would you look at the state of you? On second thought, you'd better get yourself upstairs and into a bath before you tell me anything. The water's still warm, and I'm not filling another tub for you. Oh, and so you know, Kevin's bringing Jenny and the baby and Minnie for a visit this afternoon, so you'll need to make yourself scarce or make up a plausible reason for being here – do you have one?"

Quinn cocked his head, looking pensive.

"I thought not."

Whilst Quinn obeyed and got into the bathtub, Patrick left the house on his bicycle and headed to Mr Sullivan's nearby farm for breakfast goods. Living in the village had its advantages. One was his friendship with the local farmer and his wife, Alice. David Sullivan had limped into the village pub one night. Patrick, standing alone at the bar counter had struck up a conversation with the man, and after a couple of pints had asked to see his sore leg. Mr Sullivan had sustained a long gash to his shin; a painful spot on the bone and notoriously difficult to heal. The cut had become infected, was turning septic and had the faint but discernible smell of putrefaction.

Patrick had taken the man to the back room of the pub to treat it and had then taken him home. The next day, understanding the urgency of treating the infection as quickly as possible, he'd gone to the man's farm loaded with a variety of antiseptic medicines, such as Dakin's solution of sodium hypochlorite and his old standby from the ship, iodine, to initially clean the wound and surrounding skin. In Dr Alexander Fleming's research papers from the war years, it was suggested that iodine use was also a better preventative of gas gangrene than carbolic acid, so he'd taken plenty along.

As a doctor, the war had taught Patrick so much more than the average medical student would ever learn at the college; for instance, sodium hypochlorite was an effective germicide but stung the skin. He found that adding boric acid neutralised the solution, making it effective but non-irritating. Along with what he'd absorbed from Doctor Fleming's papers, he'd also learnt about a technique used by a Doctor Carrel, who during the war had invented an Indian rubber tube with several holes along its length. Patrick had used such on the farmer's shin by placing it along the wound and covering it with towelling, thus, the antiseptic solution continuously poured down it. Also, the towelling absorbed the fluid and kept it in contact with the surface of the wound bandages.

As thanks for saving her husband's leg, Mrs Sullivan baked for Patrick whenever he was home while Mr Sullivan provided fresh eggs, milk, cheese and freshly churned butter directly from his dairy herd. All were in short supply in the shops; some food stuffs were still being rationed, and although Patrick insisted on paying for whatever they gave him, he appreciated the gesture and the Sullivans' friendship, which they had also extended to Quinn, whom Patrick had explained was his lodger, from time to time.

After visiting the farm, Patrick returned to the cottage, geared up with freshly baked soda bread, cinnamon-spiced fruited bread pudding, four eggs and a large pat of butter. It had started to rain, and a strong wind was chilling him to the bone – hard to imagine it was almost July – it felt more like an early April's wintery day, he thought, parking his bicycle at the back door.

He unbuckled his saddlebag and removed the food wrapped in brown paper and tied with string. At the back door, he thumped the toes of his boots against the step to dislodge mud, then halted abruptly at a scuffling noise coming from behind him.

"It's me … it's me, Patrick," Danny said, with his hands in the air.

Shaken, Patrick pivoted to stare at his brother, whom he'd not seen for over a month. He was relieved to see Danny looking well, albeit as grubby as Quinn had been when he'd arrived. Thinking about Quinn, he said, "Danny, I told you not to come here unless it was an emergency. Who are you hiding from this time?"

"Ah, but it would take a while to answer that question. You should have asked, who's not looking for me?" Danny said good-humouredly as he took a step forward. "I need a place to stay for a couple of days. Can you put me up?"

Patrick opened the door, choking back the word *no.* His worst nightmare had become a reality; Danny and Quinn were in the same house and he was not prepared for the encounter. "Come in. I'm making breakfast," he muttered, as he went into the kitchen.

The brothers faced off; Danny looking guilty as sin with his hands in his pocket and his eyes looking everywhere other than at his brother, and Patrick looking just as furtive as he flicked his eyes to the door leading to the hallway.

Patrick cleared his throat then began, "Danny, I have…"

"Shh … someone's in the house!" Danny's eyes widened at the unmistakable sound of footsteps on the creaking floorboards in a room upstairs.

"Well, you see…"

"Hush … stay here, Patrick!" Danny hissed again and made for the door.

"Wait a minute! I have a guest … stop!" Patrick called out as he followed his brother to the hallway, but Danny was already bounding up the stairs, apparently deaf to Patrick and shouting, "Come out, ye bastard!"

Then, things got worse.

Chapter Forty-Three

On the top landing, Danny met a fully dressed Quinn coming out of the bedroom with his revolver in hand. Both men were shocked. Quinn was more surprised than threatened, whereas Danny, after seeing Patrick's photograph in Quinn's house, was shaking with suspicion and rage

Quinn lowered his weapon. He turned to the bedroom and tossed it gently onto Patrick's bed and then said, "Danny…"

Danny pounced on Quinn with all the rage a protective brother could muster, and with his own momentum behind him, fell on top of Quinn in the doorway.

"Stop it!" Patrick yelled from behind the men as they became entangled on the floor.

Danny, trying to straddle Quinn, panted, "You think you're going to put the heat on my brother? I'll kill you, ye git."

Quinn gasped, as Danny pressed his full weight on his opponent's chest.

Danny swung his arm back and threw a punch, catching Quinn square in the face. "Tell me why you're spyin' on him, ye sack of shite!" Incensed, his fist flew a second time, but Patrick entered the fray, grabbing Danny's wrist with one arm and getting his brother into a sloppy headlock with the other.

"Get off him – get off my guest, Danny, or I'll put you down myself," Patrick roared, as he pulled Danny backwards by his neck.

Surprised by his brother's fierce intervention, Danny relaxed enough to allow Patrick to pull him until he was sitting on the floor and clear of Quinn.

"Stay, Danny," Patrick warned, both arms now wrapped around his brother's throat.

"Get … off me," Danny choked in return, shrugging half-heartedly. He tried to process what was happening. In his mind, Quinn was a danger to his brother, but his ears were hearing a completely different story. Danny started to get the sick feeling that, once again, he might have leapt before looking.

"Quinn, are you all right?" Patrick asked.

Quinn got to his feet, wiped his bloodied lip and then approached Danny, who was still in Patrick's grip. "I'll take that .45 calibre Colt from your waistband," Quinn said, retrieving the weapon even as Danny stiffened. He went to the bedroom and set the gun on the bed beside the other one. "You can let him go now, Patrick," he said, returning to the landing.

Patrick's arms slackened, but before he completely let go of his brother, he said, "This is over, Danny, you hear?"

Danny remained on his backside, mystified as he looked up at the two men. Patrick was trying to examine Quinn's eyelid, which was beginning to swell. Quinn gently pushed Patrick's hand away and began tucking his shirt tails back into his trousers. The cotton was torn, buttons had popped, and one of his trouser braces had snapped in the tussle.

"Have you gone entirely off your head?" Patrick demanded, looking down at Danny.

Danny stared balefully at Quinn as he got to his feet, and then said, "Patrick, I don't know what the feck's going on here, but I do know this bugger is spying on you. He had a picture of you in his house. His house, Patrick!" Danny went into his jacket pocket and whipped out the photograph, now somewhat crumpled. "Look at it." Then he demanded answers from Quinn, "Explain to my brother why you have his photograph.

What was your plan? Were you sent here to kill him? Are you a spy? Out with it!"

"Oh, don't be so bloody dramatic. He's not a spy," Patrick said, eyeing the photograph he'd given Quinn months earlier. "We're friends, Danny, just friends." Patrick, also looking puzzled, asked both men, "And how do you two know each other?"

With the photograph still in his mind, Danny flicked his eyes from his brother back to Quinn. "I'll ask you one more time –"

"No," Patrick snapped. "You will not. For once, Danny Carmody, you will sit down and feckin' listen, or I'll have you out of my house as sure as Kevin banished you from his."

The words stunned Danny into silence. It lasted all the way through the trip downstairs and the making and pouring of tea, which Danny said he didn't want then changed his mind.

The three men sat at the kitchen table, Danny tucking into a soda scone and washing it down with the tea.

Whilst Patrick was refilling the teapot with boiling water, Quinn gingerly touched his reddened eye and said to Danny, "Your brother and I are friends. Sometimes we have dinner together in Dublin. To be honest with you, I didn't know where else to go last night, so I came here. You evidently had the same idea."

He's lying, Danny thought. "Do you keep photographs of all your friends in a box in your wardrobe?"

"Not as – wait. I gave you my hospitality, and you went into my wardrobe? You had no right!"

"Ah, but sure I did it, anyway."

Patrick said, "I met Quinn on a packet boat crossing the Irish Sea eighteen months ago. We got talking and enjoyed each other's company. I promised to keep in touch with him, so when I returned to Dublin, I went to his shop … he's in woollen goods. Anyway, I bought Minnie a scarf …"

Danny didn't miss the quiver in Patrick's voice, his stuttering and insecurity. Oh, yes, his brother was lying, but why? "Patrick, what are you not telling me?"

"Well…"

"Please, allow me, Patrick," Quinn jumped in before the other could answer. "Patrick has not been entirely honest with you, Danny. I've been indoctrinating him into the IRA. I can't get a gun into his hand for love nor money, but I saw his potential as an emergency doctor for our wounded. I put a proposal to him, which he has not yet answered, but I think he's coming around to the validity of our cause."

Danny's eyes widened as he stared at his brother who was nodding his affirmation.

"It's true, Danny," Patrick confirmed. "When I came back to Dublin, I had no friends. Unlike you, I never lived in Ireland much before the war. And I lost Kevin as soon as he married Jenny. You've seen how hard it is to prise them apart."

"That's true enough," Danny admitted.

"Anyway, I met Quinn, and while I don't like the killings that are going on and will have nothing to do with them, I do believe that saving the life of a Republican or easing his pain agrees with my Hippocratic oath to medicine. In that vein, whenever Quinn needs a doctor or a place to lie low, I oblige him, as I do you."

"And you say you're willing to help us whenever we come for you?"

"If I'm in Dublin and I'm called upon to treat a wounded man, I will attend him." Patrick then gave Quinn a sharp telling-off. "Why did you not tell me you knew my brother?"

"We met for the first time yesterday," Quinn answered, raising his hands apologetically.

"That's right," Danny said, but the photograph still bothered him. "Look, all this is very nice. You two are friends, and Patrick, I'm thrilled you're finally coming around to the cause, but it still doesn't explain why Quinn has a picture of you?"

Quinn shook his head as if the answer were obvious. "C'mon, Danny, you know as well as anyone we must be careful at the hospitals. When I send one of my couriers to fetch a physician, I sometimes need to show them a picture of the doctor in question. Would you rather I told them to go to the College of Surgeons and ask for your brother by name? 'Pardon me, pal, I'm looking for Dr Patrick Carmody. I have an IRA man, wounded and on the run, that he's agreed to treat. Fetch him, please, there's a good rebel.' Patrick would have a big, red target on his back before my courier got the words out."

Danny nodded. Photographs and newspaper clippings were almost always used to identify Republicans and British targets alike, so why wouldn't Quinn use Patrick's image to aid a messenger in a more subtle approach? "Hmm, right then. That's sorted. Sorry, Patrick, I'm still trying to take this in. I'm happy you've joined us. Sure, we'll be able to see more of each other now, and we might even get rid of some of the secrets between us."

Then he cleared his throat and stuttered to Quinn, "I apologise … you know, for jumping the gun. I hope that eye of yours doesn't give you too much trouble."

Patrick snapped, "See, that's your problem, Danny. You jump in with both feet before ever knowing what you're getting yourself into and then try to say 'sorry' like a little lost boy afterwards. Now, can we finish breakfast before our sister and the family show up? Look at the time, will you? I haven't even peeled the potatoes for lunch!"

Quinn, with a peculiar glint of amusement in his eye, said, "I'm going to leave you two to your family business. You'll have a lot to talk about before your sister arrives."

"Where will you go?" Patrick asked.

"I'll go to Mr Sullivan's farm for the day."

Danny, having calmed down but still feeling guilty for his violent outburst, said, "Quinn, before you go, do you think we could talk about what happened last night? I've been thinking about it all night, and I'm certain we were set up. Not by Brady, but by one of our own men."

"I think you're right. I'll be back tonight. We'll talk about it then."

Chapter Forty-Four

A rush of love warmed Patrick as he looked around the dinner table where his family congregated. Jenny gave little Robert a crust of bread to bite into, then settled him on her lap. She and the child sat next to Danny, who was curiously emotional as he too gazed at the faces at the table. It had been grand seeing his young brother and sister weeping in an embrace, and for now getting along fine; their sibling banter once again flourishing between them.

Patrick looked at Kevin, who was behaving himself, but who had made a scene upon his arrival, 'What's Danny doing here?' he'd demanded, as if it were his own bloody house he'd walked into.

'He's here at my invitation. This is my house and all Carmodys *and* Jacksons are welcome,' Patrick had retorted, putting his foot down and ending the contentious moment.

Minnie, who had also shown up with a surprise guest, namely Uncle George, was in fine fettle and wearing her Sunday best for the occasion. And it *was* a wonderful occasion, for it had been a year since the whole family had broken bread together or even tolerated being in the same room.

Patrick had often wondered if the fight for independence was worth the cost to his somewhat broken family, but recently, he'd answered his own question with a confident *yes*. It was worth it if only to see the back of the Black and Tans, who'd lately been threatening his small village with their overpowering presence. Almost every day before dawn, they swept in on the backs of their armoured trucks bearing rifles, verbally abusing people in their homes with shouts of 'Paddy bastards!' and firing their guns in the air to disturb the still-sleeping population in the most terrifying way. Patrick wanted them gone from all Irish towns and villages. Finally, he had come off his perch on the fence, and in doing so had bonded with his brother.

"How long are you planning to stay in Ireland, Uncle George?" Danny asked, half a sausage hanging off the end of his fork.

"Four days, Danny. Long enough to make sure Minnie gets the proceeds from her house in London sorted out, and for me to get to know my great-nephew," he answered, before saying to Jenny and Kevin, "Young Robert does you both proud. He's a handsome-looking lad."

"Thank you, Uncle George," Jenny answered.

"I asked my George to stay longer. Gawd knows when I'll see 'im again," Minnie smiled at her son.

"Sure, he'll be back soon, Minnie. Won't you, Uncle George?" Jenny asked.

"No, I won't, sweetheart," George answered rather harshly. "To be honest, I haven't felt safe in Dublin since the minute I got off that packet boat. What the hell are you lot doing to this country? There are men walking around with guns in their pockets and shooting His Majesty's servants of law and order in the streets, bombs exploding and soldiers patrolling the roads, day and night. It's like the bloody Wild West! I hope you're not involved in any of this carry-on, Danny?"

"Yes, I am involved, and I'm proud of it," Danny responded, sticking his chest out like an aggressive turkey.

"Proud of murdering policemen, are you? Proud of blowing up their barracks and threatening the lives of men who have sworn to protect the population? I'm disappointed in you,

Daniel. You and that bunch of thugs you support should be ashamed of yourselves."

Patrick groaned inwardly. The truce was broken, and it had only taken Danny's innocent question of 'how long are you staying' to do it. He shared a worried glance with Kevin. Both men had agreed after their initial altercation that today would be Jenny's day. She was overjoyed at being in the company of both her brothers and her closest family. Patrick noted Jenny's face reddening, as she tried desperately to keep her mouth shut. Danny, however, unbound by good manners or common sense, would soon dig himself into a hole filled with conflict and nasty exchanges he'd not be able to take back.

"Uncle George, don't pretend to know what's going on in this Republic of ours," Danny responded, unfettered, as Patrick had predicted.

Kevin then attempted to nip the growing hostility in the bud, failing miserably when he said, "We prefer not to speak of politics with each other, George. Danny sees things differently to the rest of us, so we decided a long time ago not to bring up the subject of our Irish troubles when we're together."

"That's the trouble with you, Irish. You use your fists instead of your brains. Did it ever occur to you that if you *did* talk to each other, you might avoid the killings?" Uncle George suggested, although it was more of a statement of his opinion than a question.

Minnie, who'd been unusually quiet, surprised everyone when she snapped at her son, "George, as Patrick said, there is a good reason we don't talk of these things when we're all together, and I'm sure there's a good reason the Dáil and IRA 'ave stopped talking to the British. Now, eat your dinner, there's a good boy."

"You've changed your tune since being here, Mum," said George, looking embarrassed by his mother's patronising order. "You've always said, a problem not dealt with becomes a crisis. It seems to me, no one is dealing with this conflict sensibly. That's exactly what I read in *The Irish Times* newspaper I bought while on the boat coming over."

Danny snickered and said, "*The Irish Times* is a British organ, as is *Freeman's Journal.* They're both beneath the contempt of any decent Irishman. Uncle George, you're falling for their lies. You talk about how terrible the IRA are; how we are cruel murderers going about the streets killing people, but did it ever occur to you that the British are experts in not recording their own hostile actions, perpetrated against the Irish civilian population."

"Oh, is that right? And what actions might they be?" Uncle George asked, his voice dripping with scepticism.

Patrick, unable or maybe unwilling to stop the conversation because of seeing a young man bleeding to death in the street a few days earlier, answered for Danny, "Well, for a start, the British-backed newspapers haven't reported that the Dáil Éireann, the democratically elected representative government of Ireland, has been denounced by the British as an illegal assembly. Parliament even declared its building schemes and plans for developing industry to be illegal."

"Thank you, Patrick," Danny said, beaming at his brother before he continued. "You see, Uncle George, you're missing the whole picture because the British don't want the likes of you to see it. Did you know they've listed the Irish Volunteers, and the Gaelic League that wish to promote Irish language and culture as criminal organisations? I bet they don't mention the raids on homes of peace-loving citizens, or that it is now a criminal offence for Irishmen to be outdoors between the hours of midnight and 5am. In Limerick, they permit no one to leave their house after 7pm, and that's not the worst of it. It's become customary for the British to clear the streets using volley after volley of gunfire. Do you know how many Irishmen and women, not to mention sweet babies and children are being killed with indiscriminate bullets made in England? Do you know about our politicians being gunned down by British murder squads? Take Tom Mc Curtain, the Lord Mayor of Cork. The king's thugs murdered him in front of his wife, for Christ's sake. Did you read about all those crimes in your bloody, prejudiced propaganda newspapers?"

Patrick had allowed Danny to continue, as what he said was true. Kevin had not interrupted either, and even Minnie had looked stunned at the mention of women and children being gunned down for breaking curfews. "Danny's not lying, Uncle George," Patrick added. "I've seen it with my own eyes."

George's lips were tight and fidgety as he fought for a suitable response. Eventually, after a rather uncomfortable silence, he asked Danny, "Why don't Irish newspapers loyal to your proxy government, or whatever you call it, mention all this carnage you're talking about?"

"They do, but our newspapers don't manage to reach the wider audience across the Irish Sea. According to the British press, England has proclaimed the whole of Ireland an illegal assembly, which we will not tolerate."

Minnie laid down her fork. She had hardly touched her food and looked upset. "Maybe if the British were to openly state that the Dáil was a legal organisation but that it also 'ad no chance of ever ruling Ireland, the killings might stop. As Lord Jackson recently said: it would be better if the Irish 'ad no hope of victory rather than fighting for an impossible dream at a great cost to life."

Kevin cleared his throat. "My father is biased, Minnie. I wouldn't pay him any heed in the independence question. He's been against it from the start and nothing will change his political views, not even you who wraps him around your little finger."

Minnie blushed with pleasure. "But it makes sense, Son. I mean 'ow can your little bands of men roaming the countryside possibly defeat the might of the British Army? David Lloyd George 'as just sent more troops 'ere. At the last count, there were over thirty thousand British soldiers in Ireland. A British defeat seems unthinkable."

Danny, showing great restraint, leant in towards his granny, who was sitting opposite him at the rectangular table, and said, "Oh, really, Minnie? Even though British authority has collapsed in most of the south and west, which has forced its government to introduce the emergency powers we were just talking about? We've almost obliterated the RIC Barracks in rural areas, and every day we're winning public favour. Ask Kevin what happened in Fermoy, County Cork, a while ago. No, on second thought, don't bother, you won't get an honest answer from him."

"Enough, Danny," Kevin hissed.

"Enough from you! I'm talking to my granny – I'll tell you the truth, Minnie – you see, there was an incident there in which the IRA killed a British soldier, and the judge gave the suspected Republicans a not-guilty verdict. Do you know what the British army did? It sent in *two hundred* soldiers who looted and burnt the town's main businesses and caused untold suffering to the population." Danny glared at Kevin. "You don't tell Minnie about those sordid details, do you?"

Robert, as if sensing the soured atmosphere, began to cry. Jenny rose with the child in her arms and went to his pram. When she'd settled him in it, she covered him with a blanket, and began to rock him to sleep.

With all talk stalled at the table, Patrick excused himself and went to the kitchen to boil water for coffee. Alice Sullivan's fish pie topped with mashed potatoes and accompanied by vegetables had gone down a treat, but the discourse at the table had been harder to swallow. *Let them carry on without me,* he thought, saddened that he was no longer surprised when conversations turned ugly in his family.

Danny followed Patrick into the kitchen, armed with the empty dinner plates. He set them down near to the sink, then placed a hand on Patrick's shoulder and said, "I'm sorry."

"Will you get the dessert plates out of the cupboard for me?" Patrick responded without looking up from his task. Jenny had brought a sponge cake, which she had ordered from her local bakery rather than making herself.

"I'm sorry about that, Patrick," Danny repeated, as he put the fresh plates down next to the cake stand. "I tried to behave today for your sake, but I'm tired and irritable, and when Uncle George sniggered like the Englishman he is, I lost my temper. I heard you and Kevin arguing about me when he and Jenny arrived. I know this hasn't been easy…"

"What hasn't?" Patrick interrupted.

"You know, breaking Kevin's ban on me being anywhere near Jenny."

Patrick gazed into Danny's worried eyes and had the urge to hug him. It was easy to forget all that his brother had been through. He'd suffered far too much pain and sorrow, both physically and mentally for a man so very young. Patrick often wondered if Danny might have been a different sort of man had Anna lived to help steer his course. "Danny, this is my house. You'll always be welcome here, and no man, not even Kevin Jackson, will say otherwise."

Patrick lit the stove then turned to lean against the small preparation counter next to it, and there, the two brothers began one of the most candid conversations they'd ever had together. "Whenever I see Quinn, he tells me things are going well for the IRA, like you did in there. But with your hand on your heart, Danny, do you think the Republicans can win?"

Danny hesitated, as though the question took him aback. He looked shiftily at the kitchen door and eventually responded, not with his answer but with personal observations that were just as telling. "When this war kicked off with the Soloheadbeg ambush, where the IRA shot and killed the two policemen, the Dáil government weren't happy. They wanted a purely political path to victory. Even now, our war policy is not popular. Our GHQ seem to have lukewarm feelings about it, our political wing opposes it, and more than one of their number has denounced us for our violent acts. But truth is, they have left the IRA to carry on this war, using its own initiative and finding its own resources. We receive neither the approval nor disapproval of the Dáil government, but while they don't want to be associated with our actions, and up until now they've denied having any part in this conflict with the British, they want us to win for them. People call me and men like me murderous criminals and selfish bastards because the British retaliate with much more force than we've *ever* used, but we are the ones doing what *needs* to be done. I hate the killing. I see the faces of the Irishmen I've killed in my dreams. I hate myself. I hate all of it, Patrick."

Patrick believed his brother's sincerity and asked, "Do you think you have the majority of the public behind you?"

Again, Danny seemed to measure his words, but when he next spoke it was with tears in his eyes. "What the public forget is that their vote in the general and subsequent elections *led* to the establishment of the Republic. So many of them think we can win our freedom with no effort on their part. At one time, I resented their apathy, but then as slowly but surely as the sun rises, people began to stand by us and take their share of the burden and risks involved." Danny placed a hand on Patrick's shoulder and added, "I count you as being one of those people."

"But can you *win*?" Patrick repeated his first question.

Danny, with all honesty on his face, sighed, "We're not doing well in Ulster. We're outgunned and outmanned, yet we've taken countless RIC barracks, from Cork to Kilkenny and everywhere between by using crude, often hand-made, weapons. Yes, we'll win. We'll be victorious, Patrick, but victory won't come easy. We'll win this war by using force and guerrilla tactics against the occupation army and its mercenaries. It's the only way, because Britain is clearly not honouring the will of the people of Ireland. I'm certain of that."

Chapter Forty-Five

After the late lunch ended, Jenny suggested that Danny accompany her on a walk through the village with the baby. She had wanted to tell him about the disturbing news she'd learned that morning from the moment she saw him at Patrick's house, but she'd not been able to get him on his own all day.

As they set off on what was a cool, windy day despite being summer, Jenny eased into the conversation with her estranged brother. "It's a beautiful village and right by the water. I can't believe we never visited here as kids."

"We probably missed it because we always went to Minnie and Uncle George's in London for our holidays. I've been seeing a lot of the countryside these past months. It's stunning compared to dreary London and the awfulness of the Somme." He gave her a wry smile. "France was like another world … one chewed, eaten, and spat up like black vomit by some monster from another planet up there."

"Are you getting over it, love?"

"No, Jenny, it'll haunt me until my dying day. Some days are better than others, but … no, I never will."

Choked by her brother's silent pain, Jenny thought; *poor Danny, lost and alone, and neglected by his family. It's not right.* "I sometimes wish we had bought a place further out of Dublin," she said, trying to cheer him up.

Danny gazed down the length of the main street bordered by pretty cottages and a few shops, and behind them, Malahide Castle and gardens. He looked proud as he pushed Robert, who was sitting alert in his pram, looking about at all the sights and happily babbling a nonsensical conversation. "Hmm, I can see why Patrick likes it here, although I don't think he gets much free time to spend in his house. He works hard, our Patrick. Dad would have been proud of him."

Jenny wondered if their father would have been proud of Danny. She was conflicted. She hated that he was a criminal in the eyes of the law, but she understood – and privately sympathised with – the cause he was fighting for. "Are you still angry at me for becoming a Protestant? You can be honest."

Danny considered the question before replying. "I'm hurt, Jenny. You betrayed your family and the church we worship in, but what hurts the most is that you despoiled your father's memory. Being Catholic is not just a religion in Ireland, it's a statement of our identity."

"I know, but the way I see it, my son is a Jackson, and I'm no longer a Carmody, and … unlike you, my religion doesn't define me."

Danny stopped pushing the pram and looked her in the eye. "Maybe not so much now, but it will be religion that divides us. It'll divide this whole island."

"No…"

"Yes, it will, Jenny. We lack the support of people in the north because they're predominately Protestant and loyal to the crown. It's a pattern that's been emerging for a while now. Take the Jacksons. I believe if they were Catholic, they'd support the Republic, because they'd have suffered as only Catholics have and still do under British rule. The Westminster Government have always favoured Protestants. They give them the best jobs, the best housing. Over there in England, they won't even consider having a Catholic monarch or a Catholic marrying into the royal family. By all the saints, but I wish you hadn't done it, and that's me being honest."

Jenny had asked, and she accepted Danny's answer with good grace. She hadn't gone to the bother of getting him alone to speak about religion, though. "Danny, I got news this morning which might interest you. I couldn't tell you at lunch because I knew it would start an argument, plus it's a secret."

Danny laughed, "We kicked off an argument, regardless."

"True, we seem to find fighting easy in our family," Jenny replied, with a weak smile. She took a deep breath to prepare herself. She was about to disobey Kevin and possibly lose his trust by betraying his confidence, but she had never agreed to ostracise Danny. Sometimes, she resented her husband for mandating the rift in her family while still expecting her to grow closer to his own. She loved her brother, had missed him terribly and now wanted to make amends for pushing him away. "Charlie Jackson came to our house this morning. He lives at Dublin Castle now, and as it's near to us, he sometimes pops in to see Kevin before his shift begins. He was full of his own importance, as usual when he arrived –"

Danny halted abruptly and snapped, "He shouldn't go to your house. Kevin banned me from seeing you because he thinks I'm a danger to you and this little fellow here, but I'm telling you, Jenny, Charlie Jackson's job is *far* more dangerous to you than I'll ever be. You know what he does now, don't you?"

"He's in the police."

"Yes, and no. He's moved over to G-division. He's known to the IRA. We have a dossier on him, and when we get back to Patrick's, I'm telling Kevin to keep his brother away from you and the baby."

"Danny don't, he'll know I told you. Say you won't – say it."

Danny gazed into Jenny's torn, pleading eyes and relented. "Okay, okay, I won't do it." Rage still coursed through him, though, at the thought of Charlie Jackson near Jenny, Robert, and Minnie. "No one will ever lay a finger on you. I'll make sure of it, darlin'. Tell me, what did Charlie want on a Sunday morning?"

"I'm not sure he wanted anything. But he … well, I don't know if he meant to or not, but he let something slip and it upset me. It shouldn't have, but it did."

"Oh?"

Jenny looked furtively around her. Being Sunday morning, the post office was closed, as were the grocer's shop and the butchers. She stared at her brother's expectant face, and as a penance for deserting her faith and him when he was a lost soul, not in his right mind with grief, and needing his family who'd abandoned him, she repeated the disturbing conversation between Charlie and Kevin. "When Charlie arrived, he said he'd been up all the previous night because of an operation against the IRA. He'd got a tip from a man inside the Republican camp and had followed it up. You should have seen the grin on his face when he told us the police had killed three and captured three armed Republicans and bags of weapons near the old tannery."

A flicker of pain sparked in Danny's eyes. Jenny placed her hand on the pram's handle and urged brother to walk on before continuing with, "Charlie said they'd killed traitors … that's what he calls anyone in the IRA."

"Oh, is that right? I'm surprised he said that in front of you, knowing you're my sister and I'm a Republican. Does he ever talk about me?"

"No. Kevin made a big thing about banning you from our lives, but he did it to keep you safe –"

Danny's boisterous laugh cut Jenny off. "Yes, right, Kevin cut me off from you and my nephew and Minnie to protect *me* while he lets his brother come and go at your house with a big red target on his back and more blood on his hands than I've ever carried in mine. That's rich."

"It's true in one way, though. Charlie no longer asks about you because he knows we've not seen you for almost a year. He believes what Kevin tells him. He looks up to him." Jenny placed her hand on Danny's arm. "This isn't easy for any of us. Minnie misses you as much as I do. She's terrified she'll die of old age before she gets the chance to see you as often as she'd like."

"Sure, it's a bloody shame, but what can I do?" Danny then softened his tone and went back to Charlie Jackson. "What else was Charlie saying this morning?"

"Kevin sent me into the kitchen to make tea, so I might have missed some of their conversation, but I heard Charlie from the hallway saying he had John Grant in custody. He joked to Kevin that John was not such a big, cocky fellow anymore … that he wouldn't be writing anything else in his newspapers … and he thought it funny that John had wet himself during interrogation…"

"Jesus, John Grant," Danny muttered. "Did Charlie mention anyone else's name? Think, Jenny."

"No. I suppose he only mentioned John because he knew of my past betrothal to him." Jenny recalled Charlie looking angry when she'd returned with the tea tray. "Charlie also said he couldn't understand why suspects wouldn't talk under torture while knowing they might not get out of the castle alive. I have no love for John Grant, Danny, but the thought of the British authorities brutalising him makes my blood boil. His poor mother will be beside herself, and his father will have a heart attack. You know how close father and son are."

Jenny studied Danny's white, frightened face, looking everywhere but at her. She had no reason to suspect her brother of anything, since she hadn't seen him for a year, but she knew his guilty look, which led her to believe he already knew about this news, or at least part of it. "Apparently, the IRA killed two policemen during the operation. Do you know anything about that, Danny?"

"No, not a thing. Shall we get back, darlin'? It's getting nippy for the baby."

******

On their return to the cottage, Danny found Uncle George helping Minnie on with her coat. "You're off, Minnie? We've hardly had time for a blether," he said.

"I know, Son, but whose fault is that? I'm still waiting for an invitation to your house. Maybe I could bring Uncle George with me while he's here?"

No! "That would be lovely, Minnie, but I'm working long hours at the docks. I'm hardly ever home. And you know jobs are scarce."

Danny wrapped his arms around Minnie's bony frame, hating that he was lying to his granny, whom he adored. He no longer worked at the docks. His IRA business with the squad and other related jobs were his full-time occupation now, for which he was paid wages. "I'll pick you up one day and take you for lunch, how's that?" Danny suggested, pulling away gently.

Kevin appeared just then, adding with a threatening tone, "I can't see that happening anytime soon, can you, Danny?"

"We'll see, won't we?" Danny responded, throwing him a filthy look.

After the visitors had left, Danny went into Patrick's cosy living room where the fire was blazing. When Patrick joined him, he was pacing the room, going over what Jenny had told him on their walk. John Grant, for all his faults, was dedicated to the cause. He'd rather die a painful death than give up his fellow Republicans, but he was not the only person from the previous night being tortured.

"What's up with you? I thought you'd be happy after spending time with our family," Patrick said, as he dug the poker into the red-hot coals.

"The police captured John Grant and two other men. They were with Quinn and me last night. If you know where Quinn went when he left here, you need to tell me."

Patrick's face drained of colour. "He's probably still in the village. He went to visit a friend of ours. Why? What have you two got yourselves into?"

"The same as John Grant, and he's in custody being tortured."

Patrick replaced the poker on its hook on the fireside tools companion then came to stand before Danny. "Will John tell the police you were with him?"

"I don't know."

"Did the police officers see your face? Will they be looking for you and Quinn?"

Patrick's questions were coming thick and fast, and Danny had no answers to give him, except one he would not like. "John's not a traitor, but who knows what he and the other two lads will say under torture. Quinn was in charge last night. He gave the orders, so if those men break, they'll give him up first."

"What do you want me to do?" Patrick asked, looking shaken.

"Go get Quinn, right now. He needs to know, and we need to talk and make our plans. Neither of us can go back to Dublin, at least until we know more, and I don't want you involved in this."

"How much trouble is John Grant in?" Patrick asked, as he pulled his coat on.

"I don't know … but it's possible we might never see him alive again."

Chapter Forty-Six

July 1920

Dublin, Ireland

Danny, dressed in a hastily bought black suit, white shirt, and black tie, marched in the long funeral procession that snaked its way through Sackville Street and eventually passed the General Post Office. The British had forbidden processions that looked like organised marches, so the population strode in single file on opposite pavements, flanking the funeral carriage carrying the coffin and the horses pulling it.

Earlier, he'd gone to the church service where an outpouring of grief was on full display for John Grant, the deceased man. Although Danny's good memories of John were tainted and he had no great love for him, his old friend had died a hero under torture in Dublin Castle, as had the other two men who'd been captured with him.

For two weeks, Danny and Quinn had hidden in various houses in villages and towns surrounding Dublin, not knowing if they'd been named in the tannery ambush or if the three captured IRA men were alive or dead. What he and Quinn were agreed upon, however, was that they had been betrayed on the night they met with Mathew Brady.

Only when three dead IRA men were found where they'd fallen near the tannery, John Grant's bloodied, battered corpse was thrown off the back of a police van in central Dublin, and the other two IRA men were discovered face down in the River

Liffey did a picture of bravery emerge. None of the captured men had given up the names of their comrades who had been at the bridge that night; that wasn't a fact one could put one's signature to, but a belief stemming from the lack of police presence at Quinn's business premises and Danny and Finn's most recently known foxholes. Also, their family members had not been harassed and apparently no 'wanted' notices with monetary rewards had been posted with the three men's faces on them.

Still, it was a risk being out in the open this morning, what with the police and Black and Tans patrolling the streets, watching the thousands of mourners openly march in support of the IRA man in the hearse. On the other hand, a man could easily get lost in such a big crowd of supporters, many of them carrying revolvers on their persons. Danny was not surprised by the turnout. John had been an important figure in the fight for Irish freedom; from the Easter Uprising to Frongoch Prison Camp and beyond, he'd been a loyal soldier … if not a loyal fiancé or friend.

As the street narrowed, the crowd's slow amble replaced the earlier brisk pace. Danny walked alongside Jimmy Carson, who was limping. Before returning to Dublin for his friend's funeral, Jimmy had been working with one of the Cork battalions. Danny accepted that John and Jimmy had shared a close friendship, which had not waned over the years despite John's animosity towards the Carmodys. Jimmy was an honest fellow and his true character was now on display as tears rolled down his cheeks.

"What happened to your leg, Jimmy?" Danny asked above the noise of Irish pipes lamenting John's passing.

"I fell off my bicycle and went into a ditch full of loose branches. Don't ever get stabbed by a stick, Danny; it's not pleasant." Jimmy stared at Danny's profile and continued, "I heard you were with John that night. Where have you been hiding these past weeks?"

"Here and there."

"I was with Mick last night. We've got to leave this lot as soon as they reach the graveyard. The big fellow wants to see you."

Relief swept through Danny. "Good. I want to see him too. I take it you know where he is?"

"I do."

Glasnevin Cemetery was packed, and many of the mourners couldn't get anywhere near its gates. Danny had seen enough, done his bit, remembered the good times with John when they'd got each other through their incarceration in Wales. He now chose to recall those fond memories, not what happened on the night of the Zeppelin attack in London and its aftermath. "We should go, Jimmy. We've paid our respects," he said, placing a comforting hand on the other man's shoulder.

An hour later, and after constantly checking they were not being followed, Danny and Jimmy found Mick Collins in the attic of the old abattoir near the dockyard. Michael tended to hide in staunch Republican areas, where he'd have back up and means of escape should the authorities raid. He still managed to sleep in certain loyal Republican-owned hotels on occasion, where he was treated like the Irish leader he was. He was revered by many, and against stiff odds had eluded the British net strangling the capital.

Mick, who was in deep conversation with Quinn and Finn, the latter of whom Danny had not seen since the night of the tannery attack, grinned as he saw the new arrivals.

"Good, you're here, Danny – Jimmy. You're just in time to hear what I have to say about John, Tommy, and Harry."

"God bless their souls," Danny added, removing his flat cap.

"God help them find peace," Mick echoed before saying, "If I had a bottle of whiskey on me, I'd drink to their bravery right now. Our man inside the castle has confirmed that the G-men got nothing out of our lads before they killed them. Not a word except for some cheek and a rendition of the Irish anthem."

"Is your man one hundred percent certain?" Danny asked.

"As certain as he can be. He finally got into the archives room, to see if there were any files with your names on them. He didn't find Quinn's name anywhere, nor Finn's, but you and Jimmy have a lovely, shiny folder each, going back to 1916."

"Sure, we already knew that," Danny acknowledged, shrugging.

"Ah, but the good news is, they've not been updated with recent accusations of crimes or warrants, so, boys, it looks like you're in the clear for that tannery business."

For a while, Mick spoke about his need for revenge and his plans for a massive strike against G-division officers, but then he stopped the meeting unexpectedly to issue orders to Finn and Jimmy. "I want you two to take this envelope to John Grant's father. Slip it to him at his house, and be discrete, lads."

"Shall we say who it's from?" Finn asked, taking the envelope.

"He'll be expecting something from me. When you've given it to him, stay with the mourners, have a cup of tea or something, but don't leave until you get Mr Grant's reply."

As soon as the two men had left, Mick's tone changed to one of anger. "We have a British spy in our midst."

Danny, not surprised to hear Mick say this, didn't hesitate to voice his own concerns. "I think I speak for Quinn when I say we both agree with you. We've been wracking our brains as to who it might be and have come up empty." Danny wondered if Mick and Quinn had discussed the matter before his arrival.

Danny trusted Quinn, but ever since they'd left Malahide together weeks earlier, he'd been mulling over the man's association with Patrick. Good coincidences were grand when they could be explained away, but after spending two weeks on the run with Quinn, Danny was still trying to wrap his head around the unlikely friendship between his brother and the IRA man.

"Quinn, what did you make of Brady when you met with him that night?" Mick asked.

"I thought him honest. I didn't see anything untoward in his demeanour. In fact, I'd swear on the Holy Bible he was just as surprised as I was when the gunfire kicked off in the wood."

"And what about you, Danny?"

"I agree," Danny answered.

Mick then shocked Danny and Quinn by stating, "It gives me no pleasure to say his name, but I know who the traitor is, and I'm sending you two to deal with him."

Chapter Forty-Seven

Quinn and Danny left the abattoir and headed to Mr Grant's sprawling mansion in the back of a food delivery truck that had been waiting for them downstairs in the old building's deliveries bay. Danny's teeth were chattering, and his nerves tingled as if electricity from a bared cable were coursing through his body. In the back of the truck, he double-checked the bullets in his Colt. He'd placed six bullets in the chamber but would need only one to do the job … to end a life.

"Will you be all right, Danny?" Quinn asked.

"No. I don't think I'll ever be all right." Devastated and angry beyond belief, he tried for the second time to hand over responsibility to Quinn. "What's Michael playing at? Is this a test to see if I have the stomach for it … for me to prove to him that my loyalty knows no bounds? Jesus Christ, have I not done enough for the man? I can't do it!" Then, inconsolable, he punched the inside panel of the van with his left hand until his knuckles bled and he panted with pain. "This isn't right. Mick can be a feckin' arsehole sometimes." He scowled at Quinn. "And why are you here if you're not going to pull the trigger?"

"Mick ordered me to come in case you needed backup. You signed up for this, didn't you?"

"I signed up to kill the enemy, yes."

"Then do your job. We don't let traitors live. That's the rule."

Motorcars were parked in a line outside the front entrance to the Grant's family home. The delivery truck drove past them and made its way around to the rear of the house, finally stopping near the tradesman's entrance by the outside basement stairs. "We're here," the driver called over his shoulder.

"We follow the plan to the letter, Danny. No deviations, no changing your mind or making a scene or giving him an apology," Quinn warned. "He gets a spy's death, same as all the others. Are we clear?"

"We're clear," Danny answered, choking on the words.

After traipsing through the basement kitchen where servants were preparing food on silver platters to take to the mourners, Danny and Quinn went up the backstairs to the main hallway. Danny knew the house well; he'd been in it plenty of times in the old days when he and John were youthful friends planning grand adventures. In their young minds, both were heroes, and neither ever got injured nor tarnished by the world's cruelties. Fantasy was so much better than reality; Danny had learnt that the hard way since those bygone, innocent days.

People were milling about the hallway and adjoining reception room with cups of tea in one hand and a cake or sandwich nestling in a napkin in the other. Danny spotted Finn and Jimmy chatting in the doorway between the hall and living room, then he saw Mr Grant, who waved him over.

"Please accept my condolences, Mr Grant," Danny said, shaking the grief-stricken man's hand.

"Ah, 'tis yourself, young Danny Carmody. Good, I'm glad they sent you."

Danny bowed his head. "Mr Grant, I wanted to tell you how sorry I am. I feel rotten that John and I parted on bad terms. He and I go way back to the days when we played in your back garden, and I'm upset we were both too hot-headed to make up." Losing his only son had devastated the man, and platitudes and sincere condolences weren't going to make him feel better, Danny knew, anticipating some form of forgiveness.

"It's all right, my boy. You were both at fault," Grant responded gracefully to Danny's admission. "You shouldn't have punched John in a London street and then left him destitute, but he was wrong to humiliate your sister and leave her at the altar. My son wasn't a saint when he was alive, and I'll not make him one now he's dead, but…" Grant let his words trail off as he leant in to whisper in Danny's ear, "He was my only child, Danny, and I'll have my retribution today through you. It *must* be you."

Quinn approached as Grant drew away from Danny, and asked, "Are you ready, sir?"

"Yes. I want this done now so I can get back to my guests and honour my John. I suppose my heart will still be broken, Quinn, but it'll be more peaceful."

Danny followed Mr Grant to the vast garden at the back of the house whilst Quinn went to fetch Jimmy and Finn, who were also to attend the private meeting.

After passing trees and flower beds, the two men arrived at the bottom of the lawn, situated a good distance from the house. Mr Grant led Danny into what he called his summer house. It was in fact a one-storey building with a cellar, and the place where John and Danny had played together as kids. As a boy, Danny had joked that it was bigger and better furnished than the downstairs of Minnie's London house, which comprised a living room and kitchen. Today, though, this previously magical garden house was a shell of a place, cold and smelling musty from neglect. He wondered if John had ever come in here to reminisce about their boyhood larks.

Mr Grant left the door open and walked along the narrow hallway to a door at the end. He went into his pocket and took out a key, opened the door with it and said in a dispassionate tone, "I chose here because it's soundproof downstairs. I wouldn't want to scare my guests away, would I?"

Minutes later, Quinn appeared at the top of the basement stairs and called down with a cheerful voice, "Anyone home?"

"We're here. Lock the front door before you come down!" Mr Grant shouted back.

Danny observed the room's layout. A sturdy chair sat in the centre of the room on top of a large ground sheet, like the waterproof ones Danny used in the trenches. An overturned apple crate served as a small table. Mr Grant lit two oil lamps and set them on top of it. He was staging the place for an execution, and under the lamps' yellow hue, his scowling face wore the somewhat macabre expression of one who was looking forward to witnessing death.

Grant turned from Danny to watch Quinn, Finn, and Jimmy plod down the wooden steps. He studied the newcomers in silence until he eventually said, "I'm glad you three could join us. Let us begin."

Danny gasped at the speed in which Quinn and Jimmy restrained an unsuspecting Finn, who began struggling against the two men as they pushed him into the chair and then pinned his arms behind the back of it.

"What the fuck are you doing? Get off me. In the name of Christ, what's happening here?" Finn panted with shock as he tried to free his wrists of the rope tying them together.

"Sit still and shut up!" Quinn snapped, as he clipped Finn's ear.

As his eyes welled up, Danny, the silent onlooker still, searched Finn's face, and despite Quinn's earlier warning uttered in a lame voice, "I'm sorry, Finn."

"What are you sorry for?" Mr Grant demanded to know.

Quinn rolled his eyes at Danny, but Mr Grant was not as lenient, "Well, what are you sorry for?"

"Nothing," Danny replied.

"Whatever you think this is … it's not! You've got it wrong. Danny, tell them I'm not a spy…" Finn pleaded.

Danny, who knew Finn better than any man in the room, realised to his horror that the soldier he had fought with in France was pleading for his life and using the word 'spy' before anyone had accused him of being one. The fear in his eyes was not borne of confusion or shock, but of guilt. "You're working for the British," Danny blurted out, as the truth slapped him on the face. "You told them about the weapons' deal at the bridge. I didn't believe it, not even when Mick showed me the evidence against you. My God, you gave away John's position! Finn, what have you done, ye daft bugger?"

Finn's eyes flicked from Danny to Grant and then to Quinn and Jimmy, whose expressions spat hatred. Instead of cowering, as he had at first, he vehemently shook his head, then shouted his innocence, "No … no, you've got it wrong! It's bloody ridiculous. I've risked my life for Ireland, same as you. I'm loyal. I'm as faithful to the cause as any man here!"

Michael had gathered the evidence against Finn in the two weeks since the tannery business, and on paper, it looked indisputable. Danny, forgetting the official order of things, snapped, "I read the report…"

"That's enough, Carmody. I'll do the talking now," Mr Grant growled with impatience. "I have the evidence right here." His reddened face was sleek with sweat, and when he pulled a sheet of paper from the envelope Finn and Jimmy had delivered from Michael less than an hour earlier, he waved it in Finn's face. "Your wife and two children moved to a nice little cottage in County Tipperary recently, courtesy of the British authorities. Isn't that right, Finn?"

"Yes … yes, she moved three weeks ago, but it was to get away from the police." Finn's voice stuttered. "She had to leave Dublin. The men from G-force were calling at her door every day looking for me and threatening her. Ask Danny and Jimmy – they'll tell you I haven't lived at home for months. Aww, c'mon now, Mr Grant, I did what any man would do to keep his family safe."

Grant shared his scepticism with Quinn and Danny with a disdainful snort. "Did you hear that, lads? He did what any man would do."

Finn squirmed in his chair as Grant stepped towards him. "Mr Grant. If you would just listen – please, I swear on –"

"Shut it! You don't get to swear on anything or anyone – begging for your miserable life because you think you did what any man would do is an insult – a bloody insult! Do you know how many families the British have destroyed because good men *refused* to spy for them?" Grant leant in and spat in Finn's face, then continued, "You fell into the classic trap of treachery because you're weak and selfish. You traded the lives of my son and the five good men with him for British protection, that's what you did."

"I didn't…"

"You came to my house last night and saw my John lying battered and bruised in his coffin," Grant said, talking over Finn. "You told me how sorry you were that you couldn't save him or the men who were with him. You blamed yourself for not running into the woods to help him! You drank my whiskey and ate my food. You kissed my wife's hand and swore to her you'd get revenge for her boy. Is that not the truth of it?"

"Yes," Finn muttered.

"Right, so why don't you say sorry to me again but this time for killing my lad, for making a deal with the police, for falsely accusing Mathew Brady of being a traitor, and then killing him before he could deny it. Why don't you be honest with me before you die?"

"I didn't…"

Danny's chest constricted as if a giant hand were crushing it and trapping the air inside. His breath came out of him in tiny gasps as he finally admitted to himself that he'd suspected Finn since the night of the slaughter in the woods but had been unwilling to accept the truth of his betrayal. Still conflicted and unwilling to look at Finn, who was now crying like a baby, he closed his eyes, and listened to Grant detailing the formal charges.

"The IRA man undercover at Dublin Castle, saw you come out of G-Division's offices and shake the hand of one of His Majesty's detectives. At no time did he see Mathew Brady in the halls of that place. After John and the others were captured, Michael's spy inside also heard that same G-man bragging about your deal with him. He said you delivered the men in the woods, but he still wanted to go after you, all the same, for not telling him there were men at the bridge, one of whom had lobbed the grenade that killed two police officers giving chase…"

As Mr Grant continued to read aloud the evidence, Danny recalled Finn's behaviour at the bridge, and the subsequent conversation with Quinn about it when they'd been on the run together. Both agreed that Finn had tried to stall Brady's interrogation, and the subsequently planned assassination, by holding Brady in a trivial conversation about fishing and boats. It was clear now that he'd been playing for time, hoping the police would show up before Brady got the chance to defend himself against Quinn's accusations. Maybe Brady knew about Finn's betrayal? Was that why, at the sound of gunfire in the woods, Finn immediately silenced the man? Maybe the police were supposed to arrive earlier. 'I have information for you, Mr Collins. You need to know that you…' *That you ... what? Have a rat under your roof?*

Yę stupid bastard, Finn. Look at what you've done to yourself. Danny's eyes welled. He squeezed them shut, inadvertently sniffled, then opened them to see Mr Grant's tearful, red face continuing to read the charges. This was painful, Danny thought, but he finally condoned Mick's decision to sentence Finn to death; to not do so would make him a traitor to the men who'd died.

When Grant finished reading the IRA's official charges, Danny finally gazed at Finn, who was now looking petrified. His forehead was sleek with sweat, and his weepy eyes fixed on Grant were begging for mercy. "I disagree with your evidence," was all he could manage.

Grant asked, "Why won't you confess? Show me some remorse, a piece of your bleeding soul, blackened already with shame? Show me something and I will make sure you get a quick death and proper burial."

"Go fuck yourself!" Finn retorted, surprising everyone.

No, he won't confess, Danny thought. Finn was a proud man who knew what was going to happen to him, regardless of the thousand apologies he might want to give Mr Grant. Had G-division purposely targeted Finn's wife to gain his cooperation? Probably. The British were copying IRA policy, which was to threaten the families of government officials, metropolitan police officers, detectives, and RIC officers in other parts of the country. Many of them had capitulated to the Republicans' pressure and had either joined the IRA or had resigned from the police forces and disappeared with their families. Finn, unfortunately, had fallen to fear, and right into British hands. Danny wondered what he'd do if the enemy threatened Patrick or Jenny, and it shocked him when he couldn't answer the question.

Finn's wide, flooded eyes stared up at the ceiling. Pensive, he bit his upper lip then lowered his head and shook it; as if he now couldn't fully comprehend his situation. But as the men's breathing grew louder with their exasperation, he sighed with defeat and turned his attention to Danny. "I won't try to defend myself … but you, Danny … will you tell them how I saved your life in the war, and how the trenches change a man's thinking about the importance of family? You once said you would do anything to save them from danger. Remember what you said about Anna? That she had become even more precious to you despite suspecting you would probably not live to see her again … remember, Danny?"

"I do, Finn," Danny answered and got a filthy look from Mr Grant; however, the grief-stricken father allowed Finn to continue to make his case.

"These men, here, will never understand how desperate we were to cling to our loved ones as men fell all around us," Finn now said, as though Jimmy, Finn, and Grant couldn't hear. "Danny, I could have told the police about you and Quinn being at the bridge, but I didn't. I saved you because I love you like a brother. You're more than that to me. Please, Danny, for the sake of our friendship, ask them to show mercy. I'm begging you!"

Danny stared at Finn, unable to hold his stony expression. His top lip quivered, and his eyes filled with regret. Grant, Jimmy, and Quinn knew nothing of the bond forged between soldiers on the front line. Men who'd survived war together, like Finn and himself, later shared an unspoken but lifelong pact in which each felt responsible for the other's well-being. He wanted to plead for Finn's life, but if he did, the three men standing next to him wouldn't understand why, for they had not shared that living hell together.

"I see," Finn said, when it was clear Danny wouldn't ask for mercy on his behalf. "Well, I suppose that's it then. I know what happens next. I've stood where you three are. You remember the man from Limerick, Jimmy? Remember, we went down there to do to him what one of you three are about to do to me now? We had no doubts, no regrets, and no guilty conscience. He was a traitor, and we didn't give a damn why he'd betrayed us. I get it. Sure, but I'd be the first of you to put a bullet in me. All I ask is that you don't retaliate against my wife. She's a good woman."

Mr Grant let out an angry sigh. "Right, Danny, I'll not get an apology from this piece of shite, so go ahead; finish this."

Finn sucked in his breath. Danny pulled his Colt from his pocket and aimed it at his friend's head. For a few seconds it wavered in his shaking hand until he pulled back the hammer to the cocked position. His finger was wrapping then unwrapping around the trigger. He tried to steady his arm, and in turn, his hand, but it now trembled so much he was apt to hit the bloody wall behind Finn's chair. *Christ, I can't do it. I won't...* he thought.

"It's all right, Danny. I forgive you," Finn croaked.

Upon hearing Finn's voice, Danny lowered his gun. Defeated by sentiment and for the love he bore the man, he took his own life in his hands and told Grant, "I can't shoot Finn. I can't take the life of a man who saved mine more than once. I'm sorry, make of it what ye will."

Quinn stepped forward and took the gun held limply in Danny's hand, raised it, and double tapped Finn between the eyes.

The two cracks of gunfire reverberated around the confined space. Danny winced at the shooting pain assaulting his ears. He shook his head to clear the bells, then wrenched the gun from Quinn and slipped it, warm barrel first, into his pocket.

Danny stared at Finn, who now bore two bullet holes almost merging as one just above the bridge of his nose. His neck stretched backwards, his Adam's apple protruding while gore continued to drip over the top of the chair. His eyes, staring sightlessly at the ceiling, still wore a wild, terrified expression; as if he'd expected death, but not at that precise second. *I'll miss ye, Finn,* Danny thought.

Grant stood over the body and spat again in its face before taking a sheet of paper from his jacket pocket and pinning it to Finn's jacket with a sewing needle. It read: *Beware of spies – sentenced to death by order of the IRA.* After staring for a moment longer, he turned around and aimed his anger at Danny. "I'm disappointed in you, Danny. I'll be reporting your conduct here today to Mick Collins."

"Do what ye see fit, Mr Grant. I'm not going to make a single excuse for not doing my duty," Danny said with a measured tone that could brook no argument

Grant stared balefully at Danny, which in the latter's mind added more bricks to the wall of bitterness already standing between the Grants and the Carmodys.

"What now?" Quinn asked, evidently gauging the sour atmosphere.

In response, Grant gestured to the body. "Wrap this piece of shite up and get it off my property. And lads, make sure you leave him in a public place. I want an audience present in the street when the police get to him. Jimmy, come with me – I have a reply for Mick."

Danny sank to his knees, covered his face with his hands and wept.

Quinn got down on one knee and placed his hand on Danny's shoulder, saying, "This is the worst of it now, but it'll be over soon. Don't worry about Mr Grant. I'll sort it out with Mick."

"I don't need you to fight my battles," Danny spat.

"I know that, but I'm going to, anyway."

Danny straightened, only now realising the enormity of Quinn's timely actions. "Thank you, Quinn."

As he began rolling Finn in the bloodied sheet, Danny turned his thoughts to Jimmy. He hadn't offered to shoot Quinn. He didn't even offer a kind word when it was over. He wasn't half the friend Finn had been, and that was the sad truth of it.

Chapter Forty-Eight

Five months later
20th November 1920

Dublin, Ireland

Late on a Saturday afternoon, Danny trooped into a burnt-out warehouse in north Dublin, along with twenty other men. Twelve were in the assassination unit – the squad – and the others, he presumed, would be part of the backup team. His spirits were still at an all-time low, but for the first time in months, he felt an upsurge. After being banished from Dublin, he was back in the city at Mick's request.

"Over here, Carmody!" Danny pivoted at the familiar voice and grinned. "Jimmy, you're all right, I see. How's life been treating you?"

"Shite. Same as it's treating everyone else in this war, I imagine. Are you over your wee spat with Mick, then?"

"I must be if I'm back in Dublin." As expected, Mick had punished Danny for not carrying out the explicit order to execute Finn, and he had sent him to Cork where he'd participated in armed raids and retaliatory strikes against British loyalists; low-level stuff. Danny hadn't thought it possible to break the same heart twice in one go, but he'd smashed his into pieces on the day of John Grant's funeral. He'd let the great Michael Collins down and had lost his friend, and to this day, he didn't know which aspect of that execution caused him the most pain.

"I'm getting married," Jimmy informed Danny. "She's the love of my life..."

"You mean she's the only woman who'll have ye," the man standing next to Jimmy said.

"Oy, ye gobshite, away with ye," Jimmy laughed, just as Mick entered and called the meeting to order.

Danny headed to an empty oil drum and sat on it. Jimmy followed him while others found more comfortable places where they could see Mick. Revolvers and ammunition lay strewn on a table in front of the men. Each member of the squad carried, without exception, two guns, usually an automatic and a Webley Mk VI revolver, mass produced during the war and easier to conceal on one's person. He was grateful that Mick hadn't confiscated his. Even after all the arms' raids they'd carried out in the past year, guns remained scarce, and they were expensive to purchase from the black marketeers profiting from the conflict.

The squad in Dublin no longer used .38s. Danny and the other men in the unit had found out early on that they were not up to the job. The assassins wanted clean kills, but the .38 had often caused their victims to linger for weeks before death by infection took them. Danny, still troubled by the killings he'd been a part of as shooter or backup, told himself every day that blood *had* to be shed in order to get the peace treaty they desired. A free Ireland, a Republic, liberated from the monarchy and the British occupational forces was the goal, and the Irish in support of such a nation had long since decided they would pay whatever it cost to achieve that end.

"Something big is about to happen. I can feel it in my bones, Jimmy," Danny whispered while watching Mick put sheets of paper and files in order on the table next to the weapons and ammunition.

"And I know what it is," Jimmy whispered back, then looked front as Michael Collins came to face the men.

"Right, lads, listen to me, now. This is the biggest gathering I've held for a while, so remember this day; it might win or lose us the war." Mick gazed affectionately at the men, and for a second his and Danny's eyes met. Danny had asked to have a word with the big fellow before he left, but he was shocked at the leader's changed appearance after less than half a year. He noted the burden of power hunching Mick's shoulders, lost hours of sleep sitting in the heavy bags and dark circles under his eyes, the faint shadow of stubble on his normally clean-shaven face. The war was taking its toll on everyone.

"I bloody have it," Mick said, waving a handwritten sheet of paper in the air. "In my hand, I hold a list of G-division officers and those nasty fellows in what we call the 'Cairo Gang.'"

The men booed, then one of them asked, "Hey, Mick, why do we call the bastards that?"

Danny jumped as Jimmy answered in a loud, authoritarian voice, "It's their nickname, Tommy. We've seen them a lot in the Cairo Cafe on Grafton Street."

"No … sure, it's because they're scared of being shot and wrapped in bandages like Egyptian mummies," another man laughed at his own feeble joke.

Mick raised his hand, good-humouredly. "That's enough, you two. Some of them were in British Military Intelligence in Egypt and Palestine during the 14-18 war, which is now being called the Great War by the press, apparently. How bloody stupid is that, given millions of men died? Can I get on now?"

His expression grew serious. “Whatever they’re called, they’ve come here to mimic our methods of assassination. That lot and undercover RIC ‘squads’ are murdering members of Sinn Féin unconnected with our military struggle. They’ve assassinated the Mayors of both Cork and Limerick, and don’t think they’re not compiling lists like the one I have in my hand, with your names on it.”

Danny’s emotions grew. Goosebumps rose on his arms, heat spread from his throat to his face, and as he continued to listen to Michael’s enigmatic voice, his desire to kill increased.

After the mutterings had died down, Mick continued. “They’re not in Dublin to fight a fair war against us. They’re here to kill lawfully elected civilians. It’s them or us, lads, but – and I can’t stress this enough – any man here who doesn’t want to get involved in this counterstrike, tell me now. There will be no going back for any of you later.”

As he became more excited, Mick slammed his fist on the desk with the paper still clutched in his hand. His usually animated, half-serious expression was absent. Today, his sombre eyes held a deadly promise as he swept them over the men. “C’mon now, men, you’ve all been through a hell of a time of it. I won’t think badly of anyone who pulls out.”

“Are you certain you want to do this, Mick? They’ll rain terror down on our heads,” a man standing close to Danny warned their leader.

“I don’t think any man here wants to kill, Johnnie,” Michael replied, “but our one intention must be the destruction of the undesirables who continue to make the lives of ordinary, decent citizens miserable. I have proof enough to assure myself of the atrocities which this gang of spies and informers have committed, and I feel in my bones that their destruction will make the very air sweeter. My conscience is clear. There is no crime in detecting the spy and the informer who have destroyed countless lives and dispatching them without trial in wartime. We're paying them back in their own coin, boys. That's all this is. It's up to you each to decide if your soul can carry the extra weight."

Mick stopped speaking as two men left the room, looking ashamed but evidently not able to go through with the multitude of killings Michael was planning. Danny didn't hate them or even think them cowards. They just weren't committed enough to shoot someone in cold blood. Every man there had a conscience of varying magnitudes, and a moral compass that lost its direction from time to time. If he were to ask each person individually if they would lay down their guns to stop the death and destruction going on and return to the previous conditions and accords of 1918, not one of them would say yes, not even the two men who'd left the room. Remaining under the yoke of the British Empire was and never would be a viable option for any true Irishman.

"Right. Good – let's get on." Mick went back to the weapons and ammunitions' table, to brief the squad members and backup teams on their targets, which included twenty British agents at eight different locations in Dublin. When he finished, he said, "God willing, we'll rub out every name on this list tomorrow. We'll begin at daybreak. No one goes home tonight. Find a safe bed and stay away from any of our usual haunts and hotels and don't go near Shanahan's Pub. If we're caught, we're dead men. That's it, thank you. Stay safe, do the job, and then run like blazes."

Danny took a handful of bullets and then approached Mick, who'd agreed to a private meeting with him. The two men stood in the crowded warehouse floor, just out of earshot of men who were now beginning to file out. Only Jimmy remained after arranging to partner with Danny as his backup man the following day.

"What have you got to say then, Danny?" Mick asked, towering above the latter.

Danny swallowed painfully, but he was determined to speak his mind. "I've had a long time to think about this, Mick, and though I'll apologise to you now as I did on the day, I maintain you were wrong to order me to execute Finn, given that you knew what he and I had gone through together in the big war."

"Is that right?"

"Yes, that's right. You could have asked Quinn or Jimmy to shoot Finn, but you forced me into a corner and gave Mr Grant another reason to stick a knife in my back. Finn was wrong to do what he did, there's no denying it, but he didn't deserve the humiliation of a coward's death at the hand of his best friend. You could have handled it differently…"

"Should we have shot him with a bouquet of flowers?"

"Don't be flippant, Mick. It doesn't look good on you. Men who came back from the Continent are not the same men who went to it. Finn suffered with the same curses I live with every day. Whenever men like us see a rolling mist in a valley, we automatically go for our gas masks. Every time we leave our families, we fear we'll never see them again. To understand Finn, you must put yourself in his boots…"

"Carry on."

Danny continued, "Finn was never going to get over the shock of that war. I know this because neither will I. Every time I take a stroll along a street, I have flashbacks of men getting their heads blown off as they walked through the trenches. I suffer dreams that are sometimes more real than my waking hours. Then there's the insomnia and anger I feel at the drop of a hat. Sometimes, I'm so filled with terror, I can't bloody move. Finn felt the same way. He was afflicted, but he tried his best to serve in the Republican Army whilst fighting his demons."

"You're wrong. He didn't do his best. If he had, he'd have told me the British were making deals with him, and *we* would have protected his family."

Danny was stumped. Mick, his hero, stood before him with a blank, bored expression on his face, as if he couldn't give a shite about the sufferings of men who'd been to war. This was his final insult to Finn McClure, and it sickened him enough to state to his boss, "You don't give a damn, Mick."

"I do, Danny, but I can't let informers and traitors off the hook just because nightmares and tremors affect their judgement. If I let traitors live, they'll eventually get our people killed … like Jimmy over there, like yourself, like *John Grant.* You went into the army, Danny, and you came out of it alive, so as much as it pains me to say it, I need you to learn to live with your ghosts or get out of this fight. I'll not tell you again."

Disappointed that nothing had been resolved, Danny still surged ahead with the reason for this meeting. He expected a 'no' to his request, but at least he could say he'd asked. "Would you consider giving a sum of money to Finn's family, for the years he gave you? They must be on the brink of starvation by now."

Mick raised a somewhat scornful eyebrow. "You want me to give money to traitors, is that the crack? Sure, why don't I gift a few pounds to the men of G-Division while I'm at it? No. I'll not be giving Finn McClure's family anything, not even a complimentary word about him."

"Right, Mick, I understand. I'll mention it no more."

"Good to hear."

Fuming, Danny went to fetch Jimmy, who was still examining the second-hand revolver he'd acquired.

"Where do you want to sleep tonight?" Jimmy asked.

"I don't care!" Danny snapped back, then quickly apologised, "Sorry, Jimmy, anywhere near the assassination site will do."

"Ah, would you look at the colour of Ireland's beloved sky up there," Jimmy said when they got outside the building.

Danny craned his neck to search for the beauty Jimmy apparently saw. It was dusk. The weather had been horrendous all day, with thunder clouds smashing into each other and frequent downpours that had soaked his very bones as he'd peddled the final miles back to Dublin. He saw a brighter sky now, despite the sun's waning rays. A reddish-pink ribbon streaked across a grey backdrop, as if someone had painted it on to add a jot of colour to the dreariness. "As much as I like a nice sky, Jimmy, I'd prefer to find something with a roof tonight, if that's all right with you?" And with that, the men got on their bicycles and headed to a Republican area in the city to seek shelter for the night.

Chapter Forty-Nine

19th November 1920

Kiloblane House
The Jackson Estate
County Cork

"Wake up – darling, open your eyes!"

Jenny reluctantly roused herself from a deep, peaceful sleep, as rough hands shook her by the shoulders. Coming to, she heard a muffled voice along with a child's cries and a crackling sound like that of a blazing garden bonfire. She moaned with annoyance at the assault on her ears, and then coughed as her nostrils and mouth filled with a smell and taste akin to that of dying embers in a hearth. Her eyes snapped open. Fully awake, she saw Kevin's face – behind him a thick fog – and her father-in-law's shadowy figure carrying her child to the door wrapped in a blanket.

"My God, Kevin, what –?" she cried out, slipping her legs over the side of the bed.

"Hurry, you two!" Lord Jackson called as he disappeared with Robert.

"The house is on fire," Kevin said, covering Jenny with a blanket.

"I gathered. Where's Minnie?" Jenny snapped back.

"One of the footmen went to fetch her. She'll be on her way downstairs by now."

Kevin guided Jenny along the length of the hallway until they got to the main staircase, made almost invisible by the thick fog of smoke creeping up them like a rolling mist. Smoke began to choke her and sting her eyes, and for the first time she saw the bright orange hue and shadows of flames dancing on the walls, which made the cracking sound of wood from the rooms downstairs even more terrifying.

The fierce heat searing her face startled her when she got halfway down. Kevin, with an unusually harsh tone, shouted, "Hold on to me. Don't touch the bannister!"

As they cleared the bottom stair, Kevin halted abruptly to let three male servants carrying buckets of water and sand cross their paths on their way to the drawing room. Jenny's immediate thought was that they wouldn't even be able put a dent in the fire if it had taken hold.

From the centre of the reception hall, Jenny's eyes darted to the rooms adjoining it. Both the drawing room and library were on fire, and the family room, to which she didn't have a good line of sight, was also ablaze, judging by the reddish glow and noisy racket.

Jenny covered her mouth with her hand and stared through stinging eyes at the entrance to the exquisitely decorated drawing room. The flames reached for the ceiling, devouring everything they touched. They seemed to have taken hold of the curtains first. The dreadful sight of rich brocades aflame and semi-disintegrating before they fell to the floor with a whoosh was not as horrific, however, as the more violent echoes of crystal glasses shattering, wood snapping like kindling, and china ornaments exploding. It was enough to crush the spirits of the bravest of the men beginning to fight the blaze in that room.

"We were attacked," Kevin told her grimly. "Someone must have gone around the outside of the house and thrown fire torches through the windows to set the individual rooms alight." For a moment longer, he stood rooted as he assessed the damage, but then he got over his initial shock. "Let's get you out of here," he shouted, pulling her towards the main doors just as his father rushed back inside.

"Are the women safe?" Kevin asked his father in the doorway.

"Robert is with Matilda and Minnie on the lawn. Go, Jenny. We men have work to do," Lord Jackson commanded, then he kissed her cheek before hurrying past her.

Kevin kissed Jenny hard on the lips, and said, "I'll join you soon. I love you, darling. Go, Jenny. Now!"

"No, Kevin, don't do this, it's too much! Get everyone outside and wait for the fire trucks," she shouted, gripping his arm.

Kevin kissed her again, but when he drew away, his voice was hard and unyielding. "Do as I say; I can't be worrying about you. Go now!"

Halfway down the semi-circular lawn that met the curved gravel driveway, Matilda Jackson stood with Robert in her arms whilst Minnie had her frail arm hooked over the housekeeper's arm. Behind them, three housemaids huddled together, wide-eyed, their usual neatly pinned-back hair flying about their faces in the breeze. The bright orange flames licking up the side of the house's façade gave the women ghoulish, spectre-like appearances, as their white nightclothes billowed around them in the strong wind. It was a freezing cold night, and ethereal, misty breath left the women's mouths as they panted with shock.

"Oh, my gawd, Jenny, what took you so long, love?" Minnie asked, looking stoic and serene next to a trembling, weeping Matilda Jackson.

Before responding to anyone, Jenny took her child from her mother-in-law and began kissing his face until he pulled away and sobbed, "No, Mama!" When she swooped in for another kiss, he smacked her face with his tiny hand. Despite Robert's protestations, Jenny pulled his cot blanket more tightly around his body and head, swaddling him and pulling him closer to her breast.

"It's all going!" Matilda cried, her voice desperate with fear for the men still inside. "Every room is on fire. They want to destroy our home. Why? What did we ever do to them? Oh God, my life is over!"

Jenny rocked Robert in her arms. The child was becoming heavy, uncooperative, and distressed at being outside in the cold during the night. She looked down the driveway but saw no help arriving: not a fire truck, nor trucks of any kind, nor any local men running towards the house from the nearby farms or local village homes to assist them with fighting the fire. *Who had started the blaze?* It seemed likely that the multiple rooms afire were, as Kevin had suspected, individually set by one or more men, but only now that she had a view of the house from outside, could she see the smashed windows. They could have broken and exploded outward because of the heat … but she went back to Kevin's first impressions; they might have been smashed deliberately by arsonists. Maybe the noise of breaking glass had alerted the Jacksons, but she'd not heard a thing asleep in Kevin's arms.

She moved closer to Matilda to offer comfort, but then her mother-in-law unleashed a tirade against the IRA, leaving

Jenny in no doubt that Lady Jackson thought she knew exactly who was responsible. To make matters worse, Minnie threw her threepence into the ring, saying, "Matilda, dear, maybe some angry people started the fire as a reprisal against the British for indiscriminately burning houses in Cork's towns and villages. Did you not once think this might happen?"

"No, I did not, Minnie! What have we to do with all that nonsense? This is about the Republicans' hatred for the aristocracy. My husband said only last week that the IRA want to see us lose our financial capital from the Irish economy, but you tell me, if we're not living here, who will pay the servants or people that work the estate? What will they do if they have no jobs to go to? It makes no sense to me, and it shouldn't to anyone with half a brain, not even to the Republicans."

"But you're not the first 'big 'ouse' to go, are you?" Minnie insisted on pushing her point home.

"No, nor will we be the last!" Matilda began in a shrill voice, inadvertently confirming that this had not been the complete surprise to Lady Jackson that she had claimed. "This is the work of the republican gangs roaming around Cork killing and burning police barracks. They won't be happy until they kill us all."

Jenny uttered, "You don't have any proof –"

"I don't need proof, Jenny. Criminals are trying to destroy our country houses, so we don't billet British forces in them, as the earl has done in his estate. Mark my words, heads will roll for this disgrace. Heads will roll!"

Jenny handed Robert to one of the maids, with strict instructions to hold him tightly: his full-time nurse had not joined them for this weekend break in the country. With still no outside help in sight, she began to wonder if the people from the village were deliberately ignoring the fire that was now licking up to the roof of the house, or worse, if they were the arsonists. At the very least, the smoke should now be visible to the tenants and the alarm sounded, despite the late hour.

"Maybe it's because you're Protestants?" Minnie began again, angering Matilda further.

That may be true, Jenny thought, but *she* had no intention of airing her views. The 'big houses' belonged to the Anglo-Irish aristocracy of Protestant ancestry, and as a class, most of them were opposed to the notion of Irish independence. Additionally, they held key, lucrative positions in the British administration of Ireland.

"Rubbish," snapped Matilda, between chattering teeth.

"Well, what do I know?" Minnie at last capitulated and pulled her blanket tighter across her chest. "I'm British, and far be it from me to speak against our armed forces here."

"Quite right," Matilda snipped.

Minnie, not liking that patronising tone, added, "But I did read in one of those Republican-supporter newspapers that your Kevin buys that the British Army are taking to burning and defacing the homes of nationalists engaged in actions against our administration in Ireland. Seems to me, nobody's without blood on their hands. I'm not making it up; it's a fact, Matilda."

"But why our family?" Matilda retorted, looking genuinely puzzled. "We have no influence over British Military Police in the area, and what if we are Protestants? It doesn't mean we *must* be Anglo-Irish loyalists…"

"Oh, for goodness' sake, is this really the time for you two to be debating politics? Our men are in there!" Jenny snapped, having heard enough from both women.

"Look – thank God – listen!" Jenny exclaimed as the women's shrill voices stilled at last. A bell ringing on each of two fire trucks grew louder, and finally the vehicles came into view as they raced across the lawn, past the women, and headed to the house. Behind them came the local grocer's truck filled with men and lads in the back, and following that, a military vehicle carrying RIC officers and British soldiers.

Jenny, desperately worried about Kevin and the other men inside the house, ran up the lawn towards the truck full of locals from the town, and when it stopped and the men were jumping off the back of it, she shouted to the driver, "Can you take the women and one child into the village for sanctuary, please. They'll freeze to death out here."

The man, at first gazing with admiration at Jenny's breasts through her frugal attire, said, "I will do, Lady. By the looks of this fire, we'll need more men, anyway."

Jenny climbed into the cab, then it headed back down the driveway. When it stopped to pick up the women and toddler, she got out to help Minnie, Matilda, and Robert to get into the truck's cabin while the three housemaids and housekeeper climbed up onto the backboard. Standing beside the passenger window, Jenny instructed the driver, "Please take them somewhere warm. My granny's quite frail."

"I'm as fit as a bleedin' filly, thank you very much," Minnie countered sharply.

"Hurry dear, get in," Matilda told Jenny.

"I'm staying. I might be able to help here. Please look after Robert until I join you."

Jenny raced back to the house over their objections. Flames engulfed the ground floor and as she stared fixedly at the front doors, she was both angry and fearful that Kevin had not yet appeared. Experienced men had arrived, and they were going inside or working the hoses of the fire truck, but she knew Kevin too well to believe he'd walk out of his home without fighting to save it until someone forced or carried him out!

Twice, she thought about going inside to drag him out by the hair. Twice a memory of her own hair being on fire when the Zeppelin struck made her step backwards until she was once again standing helplessly on the lawn a fair distance from the house, her entire body shaking and not from the cold. This was the first time she had recalled the seconds before unconsciousness on that night in London, and the shock and horror of what she was experiencing in her mind's eye struck her so hard her legs buckled and she dropped to her knees.

Two men appeared at the still-intact front doors, half-carrying Lord Jackson between them. Once outside, they dragged him with his toes scraping the ground until they reached the grass, where they laid him on his side.

Seconds later, Kevin staggered out, coughing and spluttering, but thankfully, on his own two feet. Behind him came the three footmen; one of whom was being carried by two newly arrived men. And then came all the men who'd gone in.

It was over; the fire was out of control, and it seemed no one wanted to risk their lives trying to save their detestable Protestant landlord's property. How terrible that she should even think that.

Upon seeing Kevin, Jenny cast aside Ireland's hatred of Anglo-aristocrats and her nightmarish images of being burnt and rushed to his side. He squatted on the grass with his head almost between his knees, but she was so incensed by his foolhardy attempts to save the burning house that she lashed out. "What the bloody hell were you playing at? Look at you, black with soot and smoke, not to mention the stuff you're coughing up. You should have known better than to put me through this worry, Kevin Jackson! I could kill you myself!"

Without responding, Kevin allowed Jenny to help him sit on the wet grass, where he continued to cough his lungs up. She turned and regarded the three brave footmen who had fought the flames without being ordered to do so. Finally, Jenny paid attention to Kevin's father who was being looked after by the men who had carried him outside. "How is he?" she asked, heading toward him.

"Father, are you all right?" Kevin finally stopped coughing and crawled behind Jenny to Lord Jackson. "Father?" he asked again.

The three grim-faced men rose and moved aside. Kevin, now kneeling by his father's head, rolled Lord Jackson onto his back, felt for a pulse, and muttered urgently to Jenny, "Oh dear God, he's not breathing! Jenny, my father..."

Chapter Fifty

21 November 1920

Dublin, Ireland

It had been a long, cold night with much tossing and turning and very little sleep. Jimmy's uncle, Jerome O'Leary, had been kind enough to offer Jimmy and Danny a bed for the night, which had resulted in one of them lying underneath the kitchen table and the other on the floor next to the stove, wrapped in their own overcoats, with no pillows or cushions. 'Still, we had a safe bed, and what more can we ask for nowadays?' Danny tried to cheer up a grumpy Jimmy in the morning.

At eight o'clock, when daybreak had transformed the pitch-black sky to a wintry dark-grey and fiery red, Danny, Jimmy, and a man called Conner rode their bicycles to the corner of Sackville Street. There, they dismounted and propped them outside an office building. It was Sunday, and the street was mostly deserted. Danny, smoking one Woodbine after another to calm his torn nerves, took a long drag, exhaled, and said, "Well, this is it, lads."

"Are we waiting here for you, right enough, Danny?" Jimmy asked.

Danny looked down the length of the vast street and shook his head in response to Jimmy's question. This was Dublin's main thoroughfare. He knew it well but observing the details of its layout was particularly important today. "Hmm, I'm not sure if we should maybe go further up the street, given that it's Sunday and there's no one about," he mused.

"Well, make up your mind, it's bloody freezing," Conner, the sixteen-year-old boy tasked with looking after the bicycles, said.

Danny playfully cuffed Conner about the ear, and with an amused twinkle in his eyes, said, "Rule number one, Conner: have respect for your elders and betters." The previous night whilst lying on the floor, Danny had studied the map of Sackville Street by the light of a candle. He now reminded Jimmy and Conner of its vastness, "This street is fifty-four yards across at its southern end and fifty yards across at its most northern point, and it's five hundred and forty-seven yards long. Sure, I'd have to bloody fly back here to you from the Gresham Hotel if I want to get away without being spotted by people going to Mass at St Agnes'. We need to get closer."

Another five-minute discussion ensued before Jimmy and Conner agreed to move the appropriate number of yards up the street and park on the far side of the Catholic Church. From that spot, Danny only had a short distance to walk to the Gresham Hotel, where he was to meet the other IRA members involved in the operation.

Danny gave Jimmy and Conner a wry smile. "Right, this is it, lads. I'm off, and if you're not standing here with my bicycle at the ready when I get back, I will haunt the pair of you to your graves."

"When have I ever disappointed you, Danny Carmody?" Jimmy said, slapping the other on the back.

Alone with his thoughts, Danny imagined what the other squad members were doing right now. Most of the assassinations were to occur within a small middle-class area of south inner-city Dublin. Mick had planned only two hits on

Sackville Street; both at the Gresham Hotel and involving a twelve-man team.

Every stride he took towards his destination, Danny pictured not the shooting itself but the aftermath in which he and the other men scattered to their pre-planned hiding places. Prison and death awaited him if he failed to evade the authorities. This was now a war where no one showed mercy, such was the virulent hatred each side felt for the other. "God help me," he choked aloud when the hotel came into view.

Danny surveyed the wide street with a few trees running down the centre of the road. He had seen no tram buses, but a few horse-driven carts were passing by in both directions, most loaded with scrap and old furniture. Being Sunday morning, the area was calm and devoid of the weekday morning rush, but there were still stragglers rushing to St Agnes' for nine o'clock Mass. He'd come back this way at least ten minutes after the top of the hour to best avoid foot traffic.

At five minutes to nine, Danny entered the Gresham Hotel. Once inside, he assembled in the vestibule with two other members of his team; one of them being his old friend Donal O'Donnell and the other an acquaintance called Tom. He liked Tom. He had an impetuous nature and a very fine character, but from what Danny had seen on prior missions, he was a rotten shot. Also present were three other groups of three men.

As planned the previous day, four men were tasked with controlling members of the hotel staff and residents, covering the exits and preventing communication with the outside during the operation. Once they were in place and had checked the hotel's register, Danny, Donal, and Tom, the third man, set off.

In the hotel lobby, Danny passed two of the assassination team members holding up a few staff members and some guests. Another IRA man was disconnecting the telephones by ripping out the wires. Danny stood before the hotel staff, and not conversant with the layout of the hotel, ordered a porter to guide him to room 14.

In an upstairs corridor, the group halted when they saw a man opening a bedroom door to step out. He was of foreign appearance and carried himself with an air of superiority. Danny was on his way to kill a British agent called McCormack, but he had a hunch that *this* man might be the other agent Mick had targeted. On the spur of the moment, he approached the guest, thinking that if he ignored the situation and the man were a British agent, he might barricade himself in his room and call for help, thus mucking up the mission completely.

"What's your name?" Danny asked, covering the man with his gun.

The man promptly replied, "Alan Wilde, British Intelligence Officer, just back from Spain. What's going on out here?"

Behind the men, footsteps pounded the hall carpet. Danny spun around and welcomed the arriving group that had been detailed to deal with Wilde. "Here's your man, Mr Wilde," he told Mick Kilkelly, the unit's leader. Mick raised his revolver and fired three shots into Wilde's body and one in the head.

"A head's up would've been nice. I didn't have time to plug my earholes," Danny slated Mick for being inconsiderate.

"How did you know it was him?" asked Mick, ignoring Danny's remark.

"He told me. He probably mistook us for a British raiding party; otherwise, why would the stupid bugger just give us that information?"

As Danny, Donal, and Tom moved away from the dead man, Danny saw through a window a lorry of British soldiers patrolling at an idle pace along Sackville Street. Regardless, he continued to his target, hoping the patrol wouldn't hear gunfire and come into the hotel.

McCormack's bedroom door was closed but unlocked. Danny, whose legs had been trembling at the knees since the killing of Wilde, adjusted his grip on his revolver, his forefinger resting on the frame close to the trigger, and used his free hand to turn the door handle. As he entered, with Donal right behind him and Tom remaining to guard the door, he expelled a long shaky breath.

Inside, Danny moved to the bed where McCormack was partially sitting up. McCormack fired his gun with incredible speed and stony calm, the bullet passing between Danny and Donal to bury itself in the door jamb. Although shocked, Danny fired almost at the same second, and unnerved by McCormack's speed, put five bullets into the man in quick succession.

When Danny and Donal emerged from the room a minute later, they saw no one milling around but Tom. *It took less than a minute to do the job,* Danny thought, as he walked head bowed along the corridor, but it had seemed much longer.

It stunned Danny that outside in the street, the usual Sunday morning calm prevailed, allowing him to amble towards Jimmy and the bicycles without drawing undue attention.

"I thought we'd be running for our lives down this street," Donal said, mirroring Danny thoughts.

As Danny passed St Agnes' church, the choir boys' dulcet tones singing a hymn, reached his still-ringing ears. He looked at the crucifix engraved in one of the wooden doors and silently begged Jesus to pray for him.

Donal and Tom went their separate ways after about twenty yards, leaving Danny's mind to run riot with images of the bedroom and hotel he'd just left; its walls and carpets bespattered with blood and gore, the colour of the carpet on the stairs and in the hallway, the fearful hotel staff being held at gunpoint, the squad members' excitement, and the face of the man he riddled with bullets. But while those images were sharp in his mind's eye, he never thought to look down at his clothes, covered in a dead man's blood, until he reached Jimmy and Conner.

"Give me your coat," he snapped at Jimmy, as he removed his own.

Jimmy, eyes wide at the sight of Danny's bloodied jacket and the specks of blood on his face, unbuttoned his overcoat and handed it to Danny, along with a grubby handkerchief for his face. "I take it you shot someone, then?" It was a statement, not a question.

Danny, putting Jimmy's coat on, replied, "I did the job." Then he got on his bicycle and asked Jimmy, "Where are you going?"

"Back to the O'Leary's where we spent last night. Me and some of the lads are going to the football match this afternoon." Jimmy mounted and asked, "Where are you going?"

"Patrick's house. I'll see you when I see you." And without further ado, Danny began his thirteen-mile journey to Malahide.

Chapter Fifty-One

The next morning, Danny woke up on Patrick's couch feeling euphoric. He had helped rid the world of two British intelligence officers at the Gresham Hotel, and he knew that in doing so he'd saved Republican lives. Today, he would read the newspapers' accounts of the operation. They'd print the number of other agents the IRA had rubbed out – they always publicised British deaths – and with those numbers, Mick would measure the IRA's success.

Undaunted by the journey, Danny had left Jimmy to set off alone to Malahide. The choice had been simple; stay somewhere in Dublin, which would be overrun by British soldiers and Black and Tans within hours of hearing about the British deaths or leave the city and wait it out until the authorities sated their thirst for revenge.

He got up, stretched, and then folded the blanket he'd taken from Patrick's bed the previous night. In the kitchen, he filled a kettle to boil water and through the window above the sink, saw Patrick parking his bicycle in the back garden. *Shite, he's home. So much for a quiet day,* he thought.

The previous day, Danny had got in using Patrick's spare key. 'I'm not sure I want you coming and going as you please,' Patrick had quibbled when handing over the spare set. But Danny had a knack of wrapping his big brother around his little finger and getting his own way, and eventually with gentle persuasion, he'd gained both front and back door keys and an open invitation.

Patrick strode to the back door, pale-faced, his eyes red-raw and narrowed in anger, and with an uncommon stubble on his chin and jawline that gave him the hardened look of a pub brawler. Under one arm, he held a stack of newspapers. In the other hand, he carried a brown paper bag, and the smell of freshly baked bread wafted into the kitchen as soon as he turned the doorknob and entered. Danny noted that although his brother said nothing as he carelessly tossed the newspapers onto the kitchen table, he was unsurprised to see Danny.

"Morning, Patrick," Danny initiated in a sweet, innocent voice.

"I thought you'd be here. Every time the city suffers atrocities, you turn up," Patrick uttered, affixing no 'good morning' or 'how are you, Danny?' to ease the sting.

Danny measured his words before responding, but as Patrick emptied the bag filled with Irish baked goods, he decided not to pop off a smart retort, but instead keep the peace for as long as he could manage.

"Well?" Patrick demanded, laying the newspapers on the table with the front pages and headlines visible. "What have you got to say about this?"

Danny looked at the headlines printed on the assorted newspapers. A lump of bile climbed his gullet, and as he turned from the table, his legs gave way. Forced to sit in the chair closest to the newspapers, he read the words again, his entire body shaking with shock. "Oh, Jesus Christ Almighty, no, no," he moaned, covering his face with his hands.

"Yes, Danny, damn you, yes!" Patrick shouted. "This is what your Republican Army caused yesterday!"

Incensed, Patrick gripped the back of Danny's neck, twisted it, and then pushed it downwards until his nose was touching the newspapers and he could smell the ink from them.

"Leave off," Danny muttered, shrugging Patrick off him.

Undeterred, Patrick growled, "Read what's written, and then tell me this war is good for the Irish people – read the bloody headlines – every word!"

"No!" Danny, who was still trying to wrap his head around what was at the top of the front pages, reacted to Patrick's grip by lashing out with his elbow, which jabbed his brother's ribcage. Mortified, he gasped, "I'm sorry … sorry, Patrick."

Patrick coughed, then pressed his hand against his ribs and sat in the chair next to Danny's, pushing the first newspaper towards his brother.

Danny swallowed painfully as he searched his brother's still-enraged face. "Back off, Patrick. I'll read them if that's what you want."

Patrick, winning the first battle of wills, sat back. With a catch in his voice, he said, "When you do, know that I was at that football match yesterday with my colleagues from the hospital. I watched it happen. The whole thing, Danny. I saw every broken and crushed bone and skull, every dead man, woman, and child, and those trampled or riddled with bullets screaming in pain while they died."

Patrick went to the stove to boil water for tea, cursing the Metropolitan Police on his way there. Danny spread the newspapers out on the table, and before reading the stories, scanned the different headlines. *The Evening Herald* led with: *Deadly Hail. Thousands of football spectators under fire. At least twelve killed, seventy injured. Indescribable scenes of panic at Croke Park.* Another stated: *A day of carnage in Dublin.* And another: *Three IRA men, Peadar Clancy, Dick McKee and Conor Clune, killed after they were captured and then attempted to escape Dublin Castle.*

Danny's head shot up as he pictured the men in his mind's eye: Peadar Clancy and Dick McKee were Commandant and Vice-Commandant respectively of the Dublin brigade … dear God, but their loss would be a blow to the IRA. Murdered during their attempted escape? No, probably shot or hanged in their cells, Danny concluded. And the final newspaper, along with the same awful headline of carnage, had also included the IRA's operation on its front page: *Between ten and twelve British officers massacred along with civilians. Death toll expected to rise.*

At first, Danny experienced a heady rush of victory. Michael Collins was a ruthless, unforgiving warrior who had organised a brilliant raid on the enemy the previous morning. Together, the loss of the 'Cairo Gang,' which would devastate British Intelligence in Ireland, and then what appeared to be the carnage at the Sunday football match at Croke Park, would decimate the cause of British rule in Ireland. It would also increase support for the Republican government under Éamon de Valera. For a few seconds, he continued to bask in the IRA's success, but then he jolted himself out of this state of mind to focus on the murders of the innocent Irish people at the football match.

He went first to *Ireland's Freeman's Journal* and began reading, not all, but selected excerpts from the story:

…the spectators were startled by a volley of shots fired from inside the turnstile entrances. Armed and uniformed men were seen entering the field at the Canal End gate, and immediately after firing broke out, scenes of the wildest confusion took place. The spectators made a rush for the far

side of Croke Park and shots were fired, some reports say, 'over their heads,' and others reported, 'into the crowd.'

The police kept shooting for about ninety seconds: their commander, Major Mills, has admitted that some of his men were "excited and somewhat out of hand." Some of the police fired into the fleeing crowd from the pitch, while others, outside the Park, opened fire from the Canal Bridge at spectators who'd climbed over the Canal End Wall trying to escape. At the other end of the Park, the soldiers on Clonliffe Road were startled first by the sound of the fusillade, then by the sight of panicked people fleeing the grounds. As the spectators streamed out, an armoured car on St James Avenue fired its machine guns over the heads of the crowd, trying to halt them.

It hadn't taken the British bastards long to get their revenge, Danny thought, giving Patrick a furtive glance. His brother, not made of stern stuff, was probably still reeling from his experience. "Are you all right, Patrick?" he dared to ask.

"No, I'm not all right, not after what I saw there, nor saw later in the hospital in the operating theatre. Every surgeon in Dublin was out trying to save lives," Patrick blazed back.

"Is the *Freeman's Journal* story accurate?"

Patrick let out a shaky sigh, as the water came to the boil. Ignoring Danny's question, he poured it into the teapot then swirled it around, filled two cups with the tea and a little milk. Without a word, he left the kitchen for the living room with his own cup in his hand whilst Danny took a sip of his before following his brother with the newspapers under his arm. *It's time to face the music,* Danny thought, and as usual, he'd take Patrick's sermon like a good little brother.

Both men sat in comfortable armchairs facing the fire, which had not yet been lit. The room was cold, and the ugly grey sky with black clouds outside made it dim and unwelcoming. Patrick, still waiting for the Malahide area council to install electricity wires into some of the cottages, leant over to the small round table next to him and lit an oil lamp. Then in an excruciating silence of the brothers' own making, he sipped his tea until he finished it.

"I was standing at the highest point in the stadium and could look down and see the entrance," Patrick eventually began. "It was about half past three when I spotted nine … maybe ten military lorries and three armoured cars pulling up outside the Park. People packed the stadium; there had to have been about five thousand spectators in there. Anyway, at least a hundred RIC men spilled out of the lorries. Hmm … at least, they were wearing the dark green uniforms of the RIC. And I don't care what those newspapers are reporting, I saw them firing their weapons, unprovoked, the moment they got off their vehicles."

Patrick paused and squeezed his eyes shut, as though he were trying to recall the tiniest of details. "A few of the ticket sellers started running away from the Peelers and into the ground, up the Canal End. That's when the police opened fire and chased them into Croke Park. I couldn't believe what I was seeing. The bastards were blazing away at the crowd *and* the players. Hundreds of rounds, Danny, spraying in every direction."

"Mary, Mother of Jesus. All those poor people, with their kids?"

Patrick nodded. "People were throwing away their overcoats and dropping shopping bags to run faster … and some were getting trampled on by others as they tried to get away. I don't know how many were crushed to death in the stampede, but to add to the pandemonium, one of the armoured cars fired round after round from its machine gun. The newspapers say the Peelers fired over our heads, but I saw bullets hitting the crowd as we fled."

"Thank God you got out," Danny said, shaking his head in disbelief.

"We did, but a few of us doctors went back in after the shooting stopped, to give first aid to the wounded. There were at least fifty men, women, and children lying around the field … shot or crushed or both. After the ambulances arrived, we loaded up the wounded and headed off to the hospital to scrub for surgery. We worked on the wounded for hours, one after another. It was like re-living scenes from my time in the war…"

Danny's mind shot to Jimmy Carson, who'd said he was going to the match. "Patrick, did you see Jimmy?"

"No."

"Thank God," Danny sighed.

"It doesn't mean he wasn't there."

"Sure, but of course." Danny wondered if Patrick had come straight from the hospital or if he'd stayed the night somewhere. He had a lot more questions, but most were regarding the IRA's situation in the city, and the strength of British security on the streets. Patrick would not take kindly to those questions. "Did you leave the hospital last night or did you stay there until you left the city for home?" he asked.

"After I'd handed over the last of my patients, I left the hospital. It was just before curfew began, but I didn't want to stay in the city centre because of the noise of police and Black and Tans' lorries and trucks. I knew Kevin and Jenny were away in County Cork, so I went to Quinn O'Malley's flat. Danny, those British troops had blood in their eyes. I swear they wanted to kill as many of us as they could get their hands on. All night long, we heard sporadic gunfire, heavy motors and sharp commands echoing along the streets near the port. People were shouting, 'Go home ye bastards, go home!' I don't know if the voices belonged to the police, the Black and Tans, or Irish civilians daring to break the curfew."

Danny asked, "When did it all calm down?"

"About four this morning."

When the wave of guilt smothered Danny, it rendered him shocked and speechless. The event at Croke Park was without a doubt a retaliatory strike by the British and their Irish whores in the RIC. Nothing he could say would bring comfort or justify his own murderous actions in his brother's eyes, but perhaps telling the truth would appease some of Patrick's anger? "Now that you've told me what happened, I expect you'll be wanting to know where I was yesterday. Will you let me make you another cup of tea first?"

In the kitchen, Danny felt his stomach sour with self-disgust. He couldn't picture what had happened at the football match, for he'd not been present, but he imagined the police going in, guns blazing, their only intention to punish the Irish for their brazenness in killing what he'd just read were at least fourteen British agents, and unfortunately, a few civilians probably shot by mistake. He'd let his guilt surface later for the deaths of those civilians, and for his compatriots at the football match, but for now, he'd try to defend himself to Patrick without losing his temper.

"What did Quinn say about it all?" Danny opened the conversation when he returned to the living room with a fresh brew.

"He'd been home all day and knew nothing about any of it. He didn't know about the IRA raids that morning, either. As far as he and I were aware, the police and Black and Tans had mounted an unprovoked attack on the people of Dublin. It was only when I read the newspapers this morning that I found out about the British forces in the city being shot up yesterday."

Patrick, as though he'd just run out of tolerance, slammed the cup down on the table, and pointed his finger at Danny, blasting, "You killed one of those intelligence officers yesterday morning, didn't you?"

"Yes." Danny replied, "but as far as I know, nobody's looking for me."

"Oh, you don't think anyone is looking for you. Sure, and that makes it all right then."

"Patrick…"

"And did it not occur to you that there would be grave consequences for Dublin after you and your boys ran around the place like bloody bandits?"

"Yes, we expected reprisals, but never this." Danny swallowed a sob and repeated, "Never this. I'm devastated, truly, but I'm also not my own boss, Patrick. There's an order of things in the IRA, and I must follow instructions, same as when I was in the army. Yes, I shot and killed a man, but to be honest, those British officers were about to do to us what we did to them. They had a hit list as long as their arms, but unlike us, they were killing non-combatants as well – non-violent Sinn Féin leaders. They're assassinating us, Patrick!"

Patrick remained unimpressed, and Danny accepted that his brother was too shocked to see the military reasons for the IRA's killing spree. He knew his brother, and in his mind, cold-blooded murder was ugly. Period. Unexpectedly, even to himself, Danny became angry. He and Patrick had tackled this subject repeatedly without Patrick ever stating whether he supported one side or the other. He was a still a true fence-sitter, as were Kevin and Jenny, who'd never to this day given their oath of allegiance to the Irish Republican cause *or* to the British government.

"I won't defend myself to you," he snapped, airing his angry thoughts. "Yes, I killed a man yesterday, and I watched another bastard being shot in front of me after he stupidly introduced himself as a British intelligence officer. He was standing so close to me, his blood spattered my face, and you know what, Patrick? I felt nothing but satisfaction as he slid down the wall outside his hotel bedroom. I'm sick of this … always having to excuse myself to you and Kevin Jackson, always begging your forgiveness when *I'm* the one fighting for the future of this island. You know, it's the disapproval of cowards and fence-huggers like you that's the highest praise for the brave soldiers, like those in the IRA. When have you ever done a brave thing in your life?"

"You know nothing about me," Patrick snorted. "And is that what you tell yourself? That you're a brave man, with a righteous gun put into your hand by God himself?"

"Bloody right, it's what I tell myself. In the future, you and people like you will be thanking God for me and men like me, who risked death and torture and imprisonment so you could get yourself a passport that the bloody King of England hadn't issued!"

Both men jumped at the sudden banging on Patrick's front door. "Who the hell is this now?" Patrick snapped.

Chapter Fifty-Two

Patrick opened the door and found Jenny standing underneath his arched porch. “Jenny?” he uttered.

“Can I come in?”

“Good morning to you, too. Of course. Danny’s here,” Patrick answered.

“Good. This concerns both of you.”

Jenny swept past Patrick in the hallway, vowing not to take out her anger on him. Her older brother wasn’t guilty of a thing. Danny, on the other hand, would get a piece of her mind.

In the living room, she faced her younger brother, who was lounging in an armchair looking like a man who slept well at night with an innocent conscience. She wanted to slap his smug face and pull him out of the chair and tell him to stand in the corner in shame. She wanted to cuff his ear and use language reserved for dockyard workers. He probably hadn’t started the fire, but he was an IRA man and therefore guilty by association. “What are you doing here?” she asked Danny in a cold voice.

“Why shouldn’t I be here?” Danny retorted.

“Are you all right, darlin’?” Patrick asked, concerned.

Jenny’s white face bore her pain. She wasn’t wearing her usual lip rouge, and she hadn’t brushed out her tight curls. She looked awful, and felt sick, tired, and over-emotional. She sighed as she collapsed into the chair facing Danny’s at the fireplace. “It’s freezing in here.”

Patrick sat on the arm of Danny’s chair and asked again, “Tell us what’s wrong, then I’ll light the fire and make us some breakfast.”

"Lord Jackson is dead," Jenny croaked.

Danny gasped. Patrick asked, "How did he die?"

"Kiloblane House … that beautiful old home went up in flames on Saturday night. We were asleep when it caught fire. My son was in his cot. In his cot sleeping!"

"My God," Patrick muttered.

"I'm sorry, Jenny," Danny muttered.

"The police say it was arson, but we knew that already, because the IRA in the area claimed responsibility yesterday morning." She glared again at Danny.

"What are you looking at me for? I've not been anywhere near County Cork," Danny said.

"That's your story and you'll stick to it, I suppose," Jenny grunted, more sad than angry. Her brother's relationship with Kevin was a pile of ashes. Memories of comradeship during the war in Europe no longer lingered in the men's minds, nor did their coming together in a common goal on the night the zeppelin injured her. Her brother owed Kevin his life, but nothing would rekindle the peace and friendship between them, not even her urgings that they get along for the sake of her child.

Patrick, visibly shocked and upset by the news, asked Jenny, "How did he die, sweetheart?"

Jenny burst into tears. She'd held them back for Matilda and Minnie's sakes, but an accumulation of physical tiredness and grief had opened the floodgates. She hadn't cried like this since her mother's untimely death. She wiped her eyes with her handkerchief but was still gasping for breath when she began to explain what had happened, "We all got out safely, but then Kevin and his father went back in to try to douse the flames. They knew it was an impossible effort. Every room on the ground floor was on fire by the time your nephew and I got to the front doors." She gulped, then continued, "After the fire trucks finally arrived, two men helping Lord Jackson and Kevin came out. They were as black as soot and … and then Kevin's father fell to the ground and minutes later he must have stopped breathing … or maybe he was already dead when they brought him out … I don't know, it was all so awful."

"Oh, my poor Jenny," Danny's defensive posture had turned to sympathy, as he leant in to hold his sister's hand.

"Kevin thinks his father might have had a massive heart attack caused by breathing the sooty smoke," Jenny started again as Danny squeezed her fingers. "Kevin did everything he could. He tried for ten minutes to revive the poor man, but nothing worked."

Jenny had recently come to realise that she'd grown fond of her father-in-law. It had taken hard work and persuasion on her part, but she was certain he had also softened towards her, and he had adored his grandson. "Strange – despite our shaky beginning, he and I had become friends – no, it was more than that." She touched her cheek and continued, "He was almost like a father to me. He kissed me before he ran back inside the house." Then she scowled at Danny, drew her hand away, and spat, "Why are you and your friends filled with such hatred…?"

"Why are the British still occupying our country?" Danny parried and broke the truce.

Patrick raised his hand, palm facing Danny to shut him up, and said, "Please accept my heartfelt condolences, Jenny. Where is Kevin now?"

"With his family at the Earl of Cork's estate. Lord Jackson's body is going to the estate's chapel for a five-day wake. Kevin is inviting his father's associates from the House of Lords to his funeral service, but he doesn't think they'll come because of the security situation in Ireland."

"Is there anything we can do?" Patrick asked.

Jenny sniffed, and looking directly at Patrick, answered, "Yes. Kevin will be pleased to see you. Minnie and I are returning to Cork tomorrow. I'll leave Robert at home with his nurse. I don't want him to see any of this. He loved his Papa. It's not right, Patrick! It's not fair."

Danny surprised Jenny by getting off his chair to kneel in front of hers, then he took her hand again, saying, "I would like to support you at the funeral, if you'll allow it?"

Jenny swallowed painfully, as she recalled Kevin's warning to her as he was getting into his motorcar to return to Cork. 'Do not bring Danny back with you. I don't want to see his face.' She'd have liked him with her, but even as she looked into his genuinely concerned eyes, she respected Kevin's wishes. "I'm sorry, Danny. You're not welcome in Cork."

"You can't blame Kevin for not wanting to see you," Patrick suggested.

"Bloody great when my own family don't want me, eh?" Danny said, getting back in his chair. "That's it, then. I'm to be ostracised, even though I'm fighting the people who are massacring *our* people. Even after they burn towns and make people homeless, even though I'm trying to give my nephew a brighter future, Kevin Jackson still thinks I'm a criminal – feckin' marvellous."

"I'll make breakfast, then I'll pack a few things," Patrick said, brushing off Danny's tirade.

"Will you get time off work?" Jenny asked.

"Yes, as compassionate leave; not a problem under the circumstances."

When Patrick left the room, Jenny watched Danny light the fire, already laid and set in the hearth. To avoid further conversation, she closed her eyes. She hadn't wanted to have words with Danny today. She'd got used to never knowing where he was or what he was up to. She'd read the newspapers earlier that morning, and probably like everyone else in Ireland, regardless of which side they were on, was appalled by the stories of gratuitous death and murder on what should have been a lazy Sunday in Dublin.

She hadn't wanted to stay in Cork, and she didn't want to go back, she admitted. As carnage was reigning in the capital, the RIC and Black and Tans were causing havoc in Cork by burning houses and businesses, and by stopping and arresting anyone who dared to walk along the street for the most trivial of reasons or for no reason at all. Smoke had billowed into the sky all day from the fire, and she had demanded that Kevin return her and their child to the safety of Dublin's suburbs. Safe? Nowhere was safe nowadays.

"Did the Peelers arrest anyone for arson?" Danny asked, interrupting Jenny's thoughts.

"I heard they'd detained three men suspected of setting the fires," she responded, her eyes still closed.

"I very much doubt the men the police have arrested are those who've done the deed."

Jenny shivered as the fire's heat caressed her cold skin. "Did you know the Jackson's manor house was over two hundred years old?"

"No."

"Well, it was, and it has always belonged to the Jackson family. They're as Irish – No … they're more Irish than we are. But you're right about the men that were arrested yesterday. Even Charlie once admitted the mistakes the British forces are making. He said the Peelers and Black and Tans often detain men they know are innocent. It's all about making the public believe that Westminster has the upper hand against the IRA."

Danny sneered, "And how many times is Charlie Jackson going to torture innocent people before he admits he's a bigger murderer than any member of the IRA? Bloody hypocrite."

Jenny wondered where Charlie was now. Not even Lady Jackson knew of her youngest son's whereabouts. "Can I ask you something, Danny?"

Danny sat again, but then he began poking the coals around the fireplace with the iron poker. "Ask me anything you want, but I can't promise you an honest answer."

"Minnie warned me not to question you if I saw you, but I want to know … did you kill any of those British agents yesterday morning?"

"No. I had nothing to do with anything that went on in Dublin. Why are you asking?"

"Why do you think? Charlie Jackson is a detective, and he's based in Dublin, that much we do know. I imagine Lady Jackson will be beside herself with worry for him. Kevin couldn't even reach his brother to inform him of their father's death. Charlie's disappeared apparently, and Kevin's thinking he might have been killed by the murderers yesterday morning."

Danny looked uncomfortable. Jenny always knew when he was lying or keeping something from her, as had Anna. He pulled at his collar as if it were choking him.

"Oh, Danny, tell me your people didn't –"

"As far as I know, Charlie Jackson is alive, but for how much longer, I can't say. I'm sorry, Jenny, but I'm a small cog in a large wheel, and I don't have all the answers."

Jenny and Kevin had discussed Charlie's safety. She had a feeling his days were numbered, as the tit-for-tat killings were becoming regular occurrences. "How long are you staying here?" she asked.

"I'll leave tomorrow, probably." Danny leant in. "I really am sorry for Kevin and his family. My condolences are sincere, but it would be best if you didn't tell Kevin you saw me here. I've come to agree with him that it would also be better if you and I stayed away from each other. It'll hurt me but keeping you and your son safe matters more than you and me having a blether together."

This time Jenny took Danny's hand. "Do you ever wonder where you'd be if Anna hadn't left us? Do you ever think maybe you'd have turned out…?"

"Respectable?" Danny jumped in to finish what his sister was going to say. "Good? Law-abiding? I used to think that, but not anymore. No, this was always my destiny." Danny's eyes smarted and his lips trembled as he fought to keep his voice steady. "I miss her every single day. Sometimes, I pretend I'm in the trenches in France, longing to see her and to hold her in my arms, and in those daydreams, hellish as the trenches are, I feel her love. But dreams don't last, Jenny. Reality is always waiting in the wings to drown us in despair. Ah, darlin', let's face it. She brought out the best in me; she was the one who believed in the man who could put his gun away forever."

"You can still do that," Jenny sniffed, as her eyes welled.

Danny shrugged, then rubbed his own eyes as if trying to erase what he saw in them. "No. I'm not that person anymore. Some days I hardly recognise myself. Sometimes I'm disgusted by what I do, but the thing is, I hate the British more than anything. If they had only given in to our demands for independence four years ago, we would now have a peaceful Ireland, as it is meant to be. No, Jenny, I'm too far gone now to turn back. We all must finish this, and you must let me."

Danny stood and placed his hand on Jenny's head, like a priest blessing a member of his congregation. "I can't promise I'll behave, but after it's all over, I'll see if I can find myself again and live as Anna would have wanted. I can promise you that."

After Danny left the room, Jenny sat on, basking in the heat. The future of Ireland was in the hands of people like Danny; like those who had burnt the Jackson's ancient manor house to the ground. She wondered if her brother and others like him would *ever* find peace? Or were their souls too mired in hatred to be rehabilitated? She loved Danny, but she didn't like what he had become, and that was the truth of it.

Chapter Fifty-Three

Six months later
5 June 1921

Dublin, Ireland

Jimmy and Danny left Shanahan's pub around eleven o'clock that night to catch the last tram before midnight, when Dublin's curfew began. On the crowded car, alongside the anonymous faces of working-class men, they blended in by singing the chorus to an old Irish folk song; *Goodbye, Sweetheart, Goodbye.* Jimmy was enjoying himself; Danny, however, was uneasy and planning to escape, even as he sang the haunting lyrics. He recognised a man who'd got on the tram at the same stop as Jimmy and himself. He was a member of the British raiding party that had barged into a house he'd been staying at in the north of Dublin some weeks earlier. Danny had got away by the skin of his teeth that night and had been close enough to one detective to see his face. It was the same man who now occupied the back seat of the car. *There's no way he doesn't know me,* Danny thought, feeling his mouth go dry.

Danny was at a disadvantage. If he turned his head to look, the man might make a move. If he didn't look, the man might shoot him in the back of the head, anyway. His only saving grace was the slight reflection in the window glass at the front of the tram. In it, he could see the top of the man's fedora hat, so he kept his eyes focused on that spot.

"Why aren't ye singing, ye miserable bugger?" Jimmy asked, nudging Danny's ribs.

Danny, who'd decided not to alarm Jimmy, caved in and joined in the sing-along whilst keeping a tight grip on his Mauser revolver concealed in his jacket pocket, just in case the man were to make an aggressive move or get off the car at their same stop. He'd riddle the bastard like a watering can.

At the next stop, the man got off without a backwards glance. Danny let out a long sigh of relief. He was always being told he had a forgettable face, that he wasn't handsome and tall like Patrick, or as smart and ambitious as either of his siblings. Well, having a forgettable face was coming in handy nowadays.

Two stops later, Danny and Jimmy alighted from the tram and made their way on foot towards the bridge that crossed over the River Dodder. Danny looked behind himself, saw no one following, then picked up his stride as they approached the bridge. This would be a long walk, but he'd find a good supper and a warm bed at the end of it.

"I've always liked this river better than the Tolka," Danny remarked, as they walked along its embankment.

"One river's the same as another to me," Jimmy shrugged, a couldn't-care-less gesture.

"Did you know the Dodder's about sixteen miles long? When I was growing up in the Rathfarnham area, I frequently cycled the whole length of it. I used to pass Firhouse and Templeogue, and that nice wee place with all the streets ablaze with flowers in summer and the shop that sold ice cream cones. What was it called…?"

"Rathgar?"

"That's the one."

"It's still there."

"Right." In the darkness, Danny tripped over a root vine on the ground. On the other side of the bridge, the Dodder's bank was lush with moss-like bryophytes, and thanks to the teachings of his late schoolmaster, Mr O'Connell, Danny remembered that name and the names of many other plants to this day. Once a term, the late Mr O'Connell walked his pupils down to the riverbank on nature rambles, across the bridge, and through the wooded area, to explain what grew, ran, jumped, flew, and lived at or near the Dodder, the longest tributary feeding into the River Liffey.

Danny smiled at the memory of those informative years. He'd never be that mischievous but innocent lad again. Never would he look upon Dublin's beauty without seeing the ugliness of British occupation and violence, nor associate this river with anything other than a place to hide from the law. Shame … for his childhood around here had been glorious.

He chuckled, and wrapped up in the images of the past, recited aloud his old teacher's nature lesson. "Watch your feet, now. There are three divisions of non-vascular land plants here, lads. You've got your liverworts, hornworts and mosses amongst which foxes, badgers and otters make their home. And you will not throw stones at these God-made creatures." He tittered again and remarked, "Ah, those were the days, Jimmy."

"What are you going on about?" Jimmy panted behind him.

"Nothing. Forget it. I was remembering my school years."

Jimmy was tired and irritable, Danny thought. Like most of them involved in this war, he'd had enough of striking the enemy then running away to hide. They were all sick of holing up in this place or that, of missing their families, of being able to walk along the road without worrying about being shot by some man looking like every other man in civilian clothes but carrying a Crown-approved weapon. Jimmy's sense of humour seemed to have left him at the same time his girlfriend dumped him. He hadn't been the same man since she'd shattered his dreams of getting married.

Eventually, the two men came to a weir just above the bridge at Ballsbridge. Near there, the river became tidal, roughly where they crossed another bridge at Lansdowne Road. Danny loved this area. It conjured up other wondrous memories of summers at the Botanical Gardens. They belonged to Trinity College, which had leased land from the Earl of Pembroke. The place brought Danny's father to mind, for he'd wanted his youngest son to attend Trinity College. Little did his da know that his seventeen-going-on-eighteen-year-old son would graduate towards his adulthood in a prison camp and the muddy, rat-infested trenches of war instead of in a study hall.

At Mr O'Brien's detached house, Jimmy said, "I've been fidgety all day. I can't stop thinking we're being followed."

Danny was also becoming paranoid. He often thought he was seeing British intelligence men he'd already killed. He saw no point in telling Jimmy that he too was anxious; the detective on the tram had got off before them – end of story. "Relax, Jimmy. You can hear a twig snap in these woods. Believe me, if someone was following us, we'd have heard them by now."

Mr O'Brien's street was deserted, but before going to the garden gate, Danny and Jimmy looked around the pitch-black area.

"I can't see a bleedin' thing, can you?" Jimmy whispered.

Danny answered softly, "They'll be sleeping by now, so be quiet." Then he took the latchkey from his pocket. Besides Patrick, a few good friends had given him keys to their houses. Mr and Mrs O'Brien were a lovely old couple who had never turned him away, regardless of what time it was or the danger to themselves.

"Hurry up, will ye? I'm dying for a hot cup of tea," Jimmy hissed, while Danny fumbled in the darkness to find the keyhole on the door.

It was well past one in the morning when they arrived, but upon hearing them, Mrs O'Brien got up and insisted on making the pair cheese and pickle sandwiches and freshly brewed tea. She then went back to her husband in bed after offering Danny and Jimmy the spare bedroom which had a made-up double bed. The men didn't take long to finish their supper and climb the stairs as noiselessly as possible to the room that Mrs O'Brien had shown them.

The bedroom overlooked a lean-to conservatory, the end part of which adjoined the wall of the house just under the bedroom's windowsill. Danny looked through the window at the garden, bordered by a waist-high stone wall. The first time he'd been there, Mr O'Brien had called Danny's attention to it. 'You probably won't need it, but just in case you ever do, you can get away over that wall into next-door's garden,' he'd assured Danny.

Sharing the solitary bed, but fully dressed apart from their boots, the two men tossed and turned, each unable to sleep. Jimmy was lying on the inside, next to the wall, and Danny's side was next to a chair on which sat his newly acquired Mauser C96 pistol. Jimmy let out an angry sigh. "Jesus, I can't sleep now. I've got this strange feeling I can't get rid of; like my luck's running out."

Danny joked, "Well, if there's a raid here tonight, at least we'll die together as the good Lord would want."

Danny, struck by his own premonitions of doom, admitted to himself that he'd been lucky. British murder squads made up of Irish, Scottish, Welsh and English officers had got close to him on numerous occasions, and once, he'd had to shoot himself out of a predicament on a Dublin street. Thanks to Charlie Jackson's gaffes or deliberately dropped information when bragging to his brother and Jenny, Danny knew that the hefty-sized file in Dublin Castle with his name on it travelled from desk to desk, allowing each 'G-man' ample opportunity to get to know Danny Carmody. Since the previous year, Charlie had worked in an office. He wasn't in any of the murder squads, nor did he go on raids. 'He's playing it safe by having a desk job, where he sits on his backside filing reports all day long and sends others out to face the danger,' Jenny had told Patrick and Danny during one of their clandestine meetings without Kevin.

"When you've had as many near misses as I've had, you start to think the odds are against you. Know what I mean, Danny?" Jimmy now whispered in the dark.

"It's your destiny to live, Jimmy," Danny muttered with a yawn.

"I don't believe in that destiny shite. I'd like to be the author of my life, not have some unseen hand writing it for me."

During the next silence, both men dozed off. Danny, slipping into a wonderfully relaxed state, sensed rather than heard something and sat bolt upright. "Jimmy, wake up!" he hissed.

Jimmy instinctively went for the Parabellum pistol he'd hidden beneath his pillow, then sat up, straining to see or hear.

Danny picked up his Mauser and slid his legs over the side of the bed. Now, hearing the distinctive tramp of marching men, followed by murmuring voices at the rear of the house near the conservatory, he whispered with remarkable calmness, "This isn't looking good, pal."

Both men rushed to their boots, and whilst Danny was lacing his up, he heard a hand groping the knob of the locked bedroom door.

Downstairs, Mrs O'Brien screamed, and her husband yelled, "Get out of my bloody house!"

In the bedroom, Jimmy pressed Danny's arm and said, "Goodbye, Danny. I'll see you in the next life, I suppose..."

Loud cracks heralded the first two bullets to go through the bedroom door from the landing. Instantly, Danny fired his Mauser twice in reply; his two bullets also going through the closed door between himself and the enemy forces beyond it. Blinded by darkness save the flash of the gunfire, he retreated to Jimmy who was now crouching underneath the windowsill. Outside in the hallway, a cockney accent shouted, "Where's Carmody? Find him!"

Bullets began firing from both directions, making it clear the men on the other side of the door believed they'd found Danny. Someone began to kick in the door, forcing Danny to blast away at it until he heard men's bodies falling to the floor.

Danny spun around to see Jimmy climbing out the window. "On you go. I'll join you when I fight my way through." Danny shrieked in surprise then looked down at his bloody hand, giggling hysterically when he saw his thumb hanging on by a fleshy thread. *Oh, Jesus, we're both going to die tonight!* He laughed again, louder this time, and changed shooting hands as a momentary pause in firing silenced the hallway outside the bedroom. "That's right!" Danny called out maniacally. "I'm a demented, half-mad fecker – come get me, ye gobshites!"

Another bullet flew into the room, hitting the wardrobe and suggesting that more men had climbed the stairs to replace the ones who had fallen to Danny's initial salvo. From the back garden, the massive crash of glass followed by the sharp report of rifles evoked images of Jimmy falling through the conservatory's roof and being immediately fired upon by the loyalist forces at the rear of the house.

Danny kept blasting away in reply to bullets coming at him. He'd reloaded when the first gun battle ended with the men in the hall retreating, dead, or wounded, but others had come to replace them, and his ammunition was running dry.

In the next hail of bullets, a projectile struck just below his shoulder blade, then seconds later another round punched a hole in the fleshy portion of his thigh. Enraged with the heat of battle and the thought of Jimmy's probable death in the garden below, Danny rushed to the bedroom door, opened it, and nearly tripped over two dead bodies as he blasted away into the hallway, facing the battery, electric torchlights pinpointing him as a target. "English bastards!" he screamed, firing continuously until the reinforcements broke ranks and ran back down the stairs.

Danny turned around and ran to the window. There, despite the agony in his leg and shoulder, his adrenaline-fuelled body urged him to swing over the sill, step on a steel conservatory rafter, and then jump to the ground.

Dazed by the fall, the pain excruciating, he crawled in the pitch blackness to the front of the conservatory. Two dead policemen, their rifles beside them, lay on the ground. He picked both rifles up, slung one over his shoulder, and readied the other to fire.

Jimmy got away, Danny thought, as he began to move forwards, to the best of his ability. A bullet whizzed past him, and he returned fire. Finally, he reached the waist-high garden wall where he found another dead body. Bolstered by the thought of Jimmy having come this way, Danny forced his body up the wall to its ledge and rolled over it to the other side, landing with a thud on the stony ground. Bullets followed his path and hit the bricks on the side of the wall he'd just escaped over, but Danny got up and stumbled onward; sheer stubbornness and strength of will kept him going.

Grenades exploded close to Danny, rendering him deaf and off-balance. Drenched in blood, dizzy with the ringing in his ears and enduring screaming pain receptors from every part of his body, he determined his death wouldn't come cheaply. He'd been through worse, and in the direst circumstances of his past, he had survived by surging on, regardless of the hellfire and brimstone coming after him. This time, however, he was seriously wounded and was already feeling his strength and mobility failing him.

As he stumbled to the next garden wall, which was the same height as the first, he went over it by collapsing against the wall and dragging himself upward, pulling one leg to the top for momentum, then falling head-first to the ground on the other side of it.

The gunfire was relentless behind him, but he continued to stumble on in an almost dreamlike state through the subsequent garden plots, now separated by low strands of fencing, until he eventually came out of the final garden onto the thoroughfare.

There, an armoured car with a man in its open turret confronted him.

Danny, with his good night vision, fired, hitting the surprised man. He hobbled over to the side of the road, thinking the others in the armoured car were holding their fire, but they opened on him with a machine gun before he got twenty paces. He staggered on, as bullets sprayed walls and fences, and showers of splinters from the road flew up at him. No matter how much he wanted to ignore the searing pain, it was now impossible to make his leg react normally, so when he reached the next bridge over the Dodder, he slithered across it on his belly, and then headed for the relative shelter of the suburban woodland where he'd played as a child.

Chapter Fifty-Four

Danny pressed his hand hard against his thigh and kept it there as he stumbled through bushes and undergrowth bordering the river. Knowing he hadn't broken a bone in his leg gave him hope, but the thigh, his shoulder, and the stump where his thumb had bled copiously made him feel dizzy. It was a strange thing to look at his hand and not see a thumb in its rightful place, but in his dazed state, he felt the pull of laughter rather than tears. He didn't even know where or when the bugger had dropped off!

He peeked through the bushes, saw the river, and once again recalled the late Mr O'Connell and his botany lessons. He remembered the teacher saying that Achilles had used the plant yarrow to stem haemorrhaging. *I'm bleeding out, so what do I have to lose?*

In a thicket, he pulled a handful of the yarrow leaves and flowers, and then added some mossy bryophytes for good measure. He slumped to the ground and groaned in agony as he leant towards his sock and retrieved his knife tucked inside it. Without attempting to pull his trousers down or stripping off his shirt and jacket to get to his one-piece long john's, he went straight to the blade and began cutting slits into his trousers and cotton john's until the thigh wound was visible.

Danny picked up a stick and shoved it between his chattering teeth, where it instantly began to rattle. Then he packed the three ingredients deep into the wound. The circumference of the bullet hole after being stuffed was larger than before, but the wound felt cooler, as if the leaves had absorbed the heat, somehow. He kept going, despite the pain and the hurry he was in to find shelter, and with one agonising push, crammed the yarrow and moss into the bullet hole in his shoulder.

Afterwards, he struggled to his feet, getting into all sorts of awkward positions before he was upright. The area appeared deserted still, and apart from the odd sounds of night creatures, was deathly quiet. He eyed the other side of the river, with its steep embankment leading up to the backs of houses and gardens. It would be madness to head back to Dublin using the main road, he thought, for he'd either come across an armoured car or bump into another patrol. Apart from that, despite his first aid attempts, he'd not make it in his condition.

He was familiar with this part of Dublin, and near to his current position were other rows of houses, one of which hosted Michael Collins. The reason Danny and Jimmy had chosen Mr O'Brien's house was because it was near to Mick's latest headquarters. They had planned to meet with him just before daybreak, when British patrols returned to their barracks as the night's curfew ended.

Going to see Mick was now out of the question. He, Danny Carmody, would *not* be in the history books as the man responsible for getting Michael Collins shot by inadvertently guiding the enemy to his door. His aims now were to put distance between himself and his pursuers and to find help from strangers sympathetic to the cause.

Knowing he'd be exposed if he crossed any of the Dodder's bridges, Danny forced himself into the shallow water and waded to the other side. There, unable to walk any further, he crawled in agony up the steep embankment. He didn't know who lived in the homes he saw, but he accepted that his survival depended on him finding shelter under a roof.

Danny chose one of the closest back doors, knocked on it, then waited for the hand of fate to decide his future. What a sight he made, half-clad, dishevelled, wet, and bloodstained. He hadn't prayed for a while, but he did now, for he had as much chance of confronting a policeman, British loyalist or Black and Tan billeted here as he did a friendly face.

After a time, the door opened to reveal a middle-aged man who looked over Danny's bloodied body. The latter swayed on his feet and muttered like a drunk man, "Can you help me?"

"No," came the sharp rebuke. "I don't approve of gunmen. I'm calling for the police."

A woman with her head full of rollers covered with netting pushed the man aside, snapping, "You will do no such thing, Colm Byrne. If you try to send this lad away, I'll go straight to Michael Collins and tell him what you did." Then she pulled a pliant Danny inside, where he dropped unconscious, folding like a rag doll at the woman's feet.

Sometime later, Danny half woke from a dreamlike state and saw the woman's kindness in results. He had no recollection of getting inside the house, nor did he remember lying on this bed or having his wounds cleaned and bound. Even now, as he tried to keep his eyes open, he felt he was in an otherworldly place, filled mostly with a black void that kept trying to pull him into its abyss.

"…you'll be all right, Danny," a familiar voice, coming from very far away, told him.

Mick? Was that Mick Collins' voice? Danny, making a monumental effort to wake up properly, dragged himself out of the darkness and forced his eyes open.

"That's it, stay with me," Mick was saying, perched on the edge of Danny's bed.

Danny cracked half a smile. "Sure, but it's good to see you. Did you find Jimmy? I lost him, along with my thumb." Then he drifted back into that black place once more.

******

Before dawn, Michael Collins sent a man to Quinn, informing him of Danny's condition and the address of where to find him. An hour later, Quinn and Tom, the man who'd been Danny's partner in the Gresham Hotel assassinations, carried Danny between them to the car and began their journey to the Mater hospital in Dublin, where one of Mick's scouts had already arranged for Danny's admittance.

Danny came around again almost as soon as the motorcar moved off. Quinn worried about the amount of blood Danny had lost, and even as he drove through dangerous streets where Black and Tans raided, his thoughts went to Patrick and whether he should send for him to say goodbye to his brother.

"I left five pounds and my wristwatch in Mr O'Brien's bedroom," Danny moaned from the back seat.

Before leaving the house, Quinn and Mick had removed Danny's clothes, which were bloody and cut to shreds. He now wore a fresh shirt, buttoned-up jacket, and trousers, but fresh blood was already seeping through to stain the garments.

"Sure, you'll never see the money or your watch again, Danny. Some policeman will enjoy a good night out with his windfall," Tom informed Danny.

"Tom, if you can't be tactful, keep your bloody mouth shut," Quinn grumbled.

"Do you want me to lie to a dyin' man?" Tom retorted, as Danny drifted off again.

After driving along Botanic Road and then through Phibsboro' without problems, Quinn came upon a Metropolitan Police Officer standing on the corner at the turnoff for the hospital. He swore under his breath as he slowed then stopped the car. With trepidation, he rolled down his window. "Good morning, Constable. What can I do for you?" he asked, keeping his voice pleasant.

The policeman looked at the men in the back of the car then flicked knowing eyes once again to Quinn. "You need to move over to the kerb. A convoy of Auxiliaries are coming this way."

The officer didn't say, but Quinn believed the man had guessed who the car's occupants were. Having not been arrested, he replied with a friendly nod and a "Right you are, sir."

Soon after, the convoy carrying a detachment of Black and Tans passed the vehicle and the policeman, who chanced to be standing at the rear door, his bulk blocking the window. When it had disappeared at the end of the long road, the policeman returned to Quinn's window and said, "If I were you, I'd get off these streets, and get that man seen to. God bless you, and God bless the Republic of Ireland."

"Down with the British," Quinn replied, with another grateful nod.

Five minutes later, Quinn saw Michael's scout at the side of the road leading to the hospital's entrance and brought the motorcar to a stop. "How is it looking, Declan?" he asked the man.

"No good, Quinn. I saw two inspectors accompanied by some military and Auxiliaries going in there to raid. Our man is inside. He says they're looking for wounded fugitives. If I were you, I wouldn't go near it until we give you the all clear." Declan then peeked his head in the car window and said to Danny, "According to our man in the hospital, you killed four or five detectives last night. They were on Michael's list for special treatment. You did a grand job, Danny."

"Jimmy got a couple … is he in there?" Danny slurred.

"No, not that I know of."

"We'll wait at our usual place, Declan. Send someone to me when the hospital is clear," Quinn told the man.

"Don't you worry, Quinn, I know where you'll be. I'll get word to you the minute the bastards leave."

With no intention of taking Danny into a place filled with the enemy, Quinn turned the car around and drove towards the city. He crossed from Dorset Street into Mountjoy Square, and from there into an old stable on Great Charles Street. It was one of his dumping grounds for weapons stolen by the Dublin Brigades. It was considered a safe site, but Quinn suspected that nowhere in Dublin would be safe from British raids this morning.

By eight o'clock that morning, Declan reported in that the inspectors, Black and Tan unit, and Auxiliaries had moved on from the hospital. Quinn, desperate to get Danny under the skilled hands of a surgeon, moved without delay back to the Mater hospital whilst Danny drifted in and out of consciousness the entire way, unaware of the danger on the streets of Dublin that morning.

At the hospital's back entrance, two orderlies laid Danny on a gurney and cut his new clothes off him as they rolled him inside. Soon after, they took him to the more discrete private nursing home, where a surgeon appeared and did an initial examination of the wound sites.

"Will he make it?" Quinn asked.

The surgeon, a man the IRA relied upon frequently, answered. "I'll let you know after I remove this plant matter, which seems to have stemmed the bleeding. I'll operate immediately. If he's got family, Quinn, I suggest you get them here."

Quinn went to the nearest manned desk and asked the young man sitting behind it to place a call to Patrick at the College of Surgeons. Patrick had mentioned a couple of days earlier that he was planning to stay at his hospital digs all week because of his heavy work schedule. *All the better,* Quinn thought.

After the call went through to the College with the message for Patrick Carmody to go to the Mater Hospital straight away, Quinn found a seat and waited. Half an hour later, Patrick hurried to his side.

"Tell me it's not Danny?" Patrick rushed out.

Quinn nodded. "It is. He's with the surgeon now."

Patrick slumped into the chair, and promptly declared, "That it. I've had enough. I don't know yet how I'm going to do it, but my brother will not lift another gun. He's finished. You hear me, Quinn? I'll lock him up and throw away the bloody key if I have to." Only then did he ask about Danny's condition. "Aw, Jesus, how badly hurt is he?"

"I don't know. As I said, he's under the surgeon's knife. They shot him in three places…"

"Christ."

Quinn dared to squeeze Patrick's hand, saying, "He's tough, Patrick. He'll make it. Danny's far too cocky to die."

Chapter Fifty-Five

13 June 1921

Dublin, Ireland

"I admit I was disrespectful and cruel to you and Jenny when we first met," Charlie Jackson confessed to Minnie. "Please believe me when I say I'm deeply ashamed of the way I belittled you."

"Yes, well, we appreciate you saying that, Son, and now you 'ave, 'opefully, we can move forward with a better understanding," Minnie responded.

As Minnie gave Charlie her forgiveness, Jenny bit her tongue, wondering what her brother-in-law was up to. He'd arrived at her house twenty minutes after Kevin had left for work at the medical practice. This was an unusual occurrence, for Charlie seemed to time his visits so Kevin was always at home. As for his apology? No, that was a ruse still to unfold.

Jenny despised Charlie's unchecked, bombastic disposition, his need to goad her with his open hostility towards Republicans, and his unbending loyalty to the British authorities, even when their heavy-handed reprisals resulted in the deaths of innocent people. She wanted to like him, but he was the major cause of friction between herself and Kevin, who often defended his brother even whilst admitting Charlie's gleeful, violent tendencies disturbed him. This morning, however, Kevin's brother was contrite, and using Minnie like a priest in a confessional box, about to give him his penance.

Charlie seemed in no hurry to speak again, Jenny noted, as she regarded him from her comfy armchair. There he was on the couch, wallowing in pleasure as he bit into his soda scone, then washing it down with a generous slug of tea, and while he was at it, giving Minnie sickly sweet smiles. She wanted him out of her house!

"Was there a particular reason you came to see us this morning, Charlie, apart from to apologise for your past behaviour?" Jenny asked, fed up with waiting for him to finish stuffing his cakehole.

After clearing his throat with a cough, Charlie wiped his mouth, and then placed his teacup on the saucer. "Yes, I have an ulterior motive for coming to see you while Kevin's away. I'd like to ask you if you will take my mother in for a few weeks. She's unhappy in Cork … not sleeping … worried about further attacks from the IRA, as you can imagine. I know how much she enjoys your company, Minnie, and she's devoted to you, Jenny, and my nephew. Would you be willing to have her as a houseguest?"

Jenny, certain this request was not the sole reason for his visit, said, "It goes without saying that your mother will always be welcome here. She can stay for as long as she likes…"

"And is the worry about Matilda really why you're 'ere today, Charlie?" Minnie's question mirrored Jenny's thoughts. "I ask because you could have spoken to Kevin about your mother in a telephone call."

Charlie began, "Well, there is…"

"I knew it. I knew you wanted something else. Come on then, out with it!" demanded Jenny, casting aside all decorum.

Charlie, also ditching the short-lived pleasantries, sank into the cushion at his back and for the first time since his arrival, looked like his usual superior self. "All right. Let's dispense with the niceties, shall we? I need you to tell Danny to hand himself over to the police. It's for his own good, Jenny, you must agree."

Jenny fought for an appropriate response that didn't include telling him to bugger off, but Minnie had no qualms about putting Charlie in his place. "Oh, Charlie, Charlie. You've 'ad a wasted journey 'ere. We've not seen our Danny for over a year. Your Kevin banned 'im. No, *banished* 'im from the family."

Charlie sniggered, "That's what he said, but I know how close you Carmodys are. C'mon, Minnie – Jenny – be honest with me. You've both seen him. You know where he is."

"Are you calling my granny a liar?" Jenny hissed at him.

"No, I wouldn't do that. I'm … look, the thing is, if you don't help us, we'll send men to periodically raid this house. It'll be a terrible disruption for you and the child. Is that what you want, Jenny? We'll also have to watch Patrick's cottage in Malahide more closely. I'm not in charge, and I don't know how long I can protect you, especially now."

"Why now?" Minnie spat.

Charlie spread his arms for dramatic effect, and replied, "Danny has a substantial reward on his head. He's a murderer who killed five policemen with help from his pal. It'll be bad for all of you if you don't cooperate. You don't want me to name you as IRA collaborators, do you? Please, for my brother's sake, *and* for young Robert's, either tell me where Danny's hiding or take me to him. It's the only way out of this mess for you two."

"Get out. Get out of my house now." Jenny, rising with shaky legs, stood her ground and let her contempt for him surface with gay abandon. "How dare you come in here and threaten my family. Your brother's child is asleep upstairs in his cot, for God's sake. Would you have the police drag him out of it?"

"Never!"

Jenny went to the couch where Charlie sat. She towered over him, hands on her hips, furious, and unrepentant, "I will *not* ask Danny to hand himself over to the British authorities. I've heard what you do to prisoners, Charlie Jackson. Everyone knows you torture and hang people in your custody without even giving them their day in court. Listen to you, talking about the *murdering IRA* every time you come here, when you should take a good look at yourself in the mirror. I'd sooner see Danny on the other side of the world than give him to the likes of you!"

Minnie tried to stand but couldn't quite raise her backside off the armchair, so she ended up perched on the edge of the soft cushion, gripping the chair's arms. "You've got a bloody cheek asking us to betray our Danny. You wait till I tell your mother what you're up to –"

"What's going on here?" Kevin stood in the doorway, his arms crossed tight across his chest, fists clenched, and his eyes spitting fire at his brother. "What are you saying to my wife, Charlie?"

Charlie, still cowering under Jenny and Minnie's combined verbal attacks, sank deeper into the couch and refused to answer.

"I'll tell you wot 'e's sayin', Kevin," Minnie piped up. "E's threatening your wife and son, and Patrick into the bargain. 'E wants Danny, and if 'e doesn't get 'im, your brother 'ere will raid your 'ouse with 'is thugs in tow. 'E also says 'e'll report me an' Jenny as IRA collaborators! And on top of that, 'e wants your mother to live 'ere."

Jenny crossed the room and helped Minnie out of the chair she was still trying to leave. She glanced at her husband, and fearful of the thunderous glare he directed at his brother, left Charlie to his fate. "I can't listen to this man any longer," she told Kevin, as she hooked Minnie's arm in her own. "We're going upstairs. You can join us after you've let him out the door."

Charlie, who'd been intimidated for a few moments, found his mettle again and turned his ire once more on Jenny. "I have an obligation to my job, you two, and Kevin understands that more than he lets on … more than you want to admit. Do *not* defy me…"

"Away with you, Charlie Jackson," Minnie flung over her shoulder as she and Jenny reached the door. "The only job you're good at is causing conflict and thrashing people who can't hit back, but guess wot? You've got a lot to learn about 'ow to scare the women in my family. You 'ear me, you poor, misguided boy?"

******

For months, Kevin had felt like a reed bending in the wind; this way for Jenny and that way for his brother, who, to be fair, was suffering the terrible loss of the father he'd idolised. But this time, Charlie had crossed a line, and Kevin, no matter how much he loved his sibling, could not let it stand. He had overheard enough while he'd been at the parlour door to agree with Minnie's account of the matter.

"You've gone too far, Charlie," Kevin said, standing near the chair Minnie had vacated. "I don't want you to come back here."

Charlie's eyes widened in surprise. "Are you serious? You're sticking up for *them,* instead of taking the side of your own brother?"

"You're damn right I am. Jenny is my wife. She's not a pawn in your crusade against Danny Carmody. I told you months ago not to bring the war into this house."

"It is my duty…"

"Your duty is to your family first, country second."

"In that, I can't and won't agree." Charlie, whose hubris had diminished upon Kevin's unexpected arrival, stared at the carpet, with his shoulders hunched and heaving with rare emotion. "Ah, Kevin, I can't believe you're saying this to me. What a pickle we've got ourselves into. I'm worn down with this carry-on … with myself. I do terrible things every day, yet I know I'm doing right by my country. It's a difficult situation I'm in. Do you not see that?"

Kevin, torn between his love for Jenny and his brother, wondered if the man Charlie had once been would ever return, or had he never truly known his brother's nature? "I don't recognise you anymore, Charlie," he said airing his thoughts. "I suppose you grew up when I was away fighting in the war."

"I don't recognise parts of myself, either," Charlie admitted. "Minnie and Jenny were right. I've tortured and even killed men in my custody. I feel like shite afterwards, I do, but I'm driven by the need to end this conflict."

"We all are, but we mustn't lose ourselves in the process."

At that, Charlie's self-righteous arrogance returned. "You're a fool. Father knew it, and even mother said you'd lost your way. Let me tell you about Danny Carmody, who's the real villain of this story. He's killed so many men, he's now one of the most wanted fugitives in Ireland. He's a coward who murders then hides in the houses of traitors and criminals. He has no conscience, no remorse, and no love for his sister or for you. I swear to God, if I could go back in time, I'd have arrested him the day he set foot in Kiloblane House. If I had known for a second that you, my brother, would take his side over a mine, I'd have cut you off a long time ago. Tell me, make me understand why you protect a man like that, when I'm the one on the right side of the law?"

"I'm not protecting him. No one in this house knows where he is."

"That's what you say…"

"That's the truth!" Kevin snapped, looking up at the ceiling. Robert was crying. Jenny and Minnie were probably seething up there as they waited for Charlie to leave. Kevin knew that, but for chance, he would never have known the true extent of Charlie's machinations, even if Minnie and Jenny had told him. He had come home to get a patient file he'd left on his desk after having treated a man who lived close by. He'd thought to surprise Jenny with an unexpected visit and a quick cup of tea. Now, he didn't fancy staying for a cuppa and the earful from Jenny and Minnie he'd be sure to get with it. "I'd better get back to the practice. C'mon, I'll show you out." Kevin walked to the door. "Move, Charlie. I can't have you here."

Charlie reluctantly stood, but before he took a step towards his brother, he asked, "Did you mean what you said about me not coming back here?"

"Yes, I meant every word. Jenny's expecting again, and I don't want you upsetting her. And don't tell mother about the pregnancy, either, you hear? That is our privilege."

"I won't … well, congratulations, I suppose."

Charlie looked genuinely upset at the front door and offered his hand to Kevin in a bid to make peace. "Will you shake my hand, brother?"

"I'll shake your hand when you learn to respect my wife."

Kevin went back inside, shutting the door behind him and leaving Charlie to walk alone to his motorcar, parked on the street at the end of their substantial driveway. Worried about Jenny, he took to the stairs and headed to the nursery. There, Jenny, Minnie, and the baby's nurse watched little Robert banging two painted wooden blocks together.

Jenny's pleasant expression immediately reverted to her earlier scowl. "Is he gone?"

"Yes. I'm sorry about that, dar –"

The explosion rattled and cracked the windows and seemed to shake the entire upstairs' floor. A whoosh followed, shooting billowing flames and debris skywards from the end of their drive.

Kevin's stomach did somersaults, and he shouted, "Stay here!" as he ran from the room and down the stairs two at a time. In his mind's eye, he was already seeing his brother's death in graphic detail.

Outside, he rushed towards the burning motorcar with the government's registration plates. He'd almost reached Charlie's blazing vehicle when a neighbour pounced on him and pinned him to the ground, preventing him from jumping into the inferno "No! My brother's in there, Colm. For the love of God, I have to help him!" Under Colm's weight, Kevin stared up at the vehicle and gasped, "Charlie!"

A wall of fire engulfing the car's underside and shooting upwards to fill its interior was obscuring, but not completely hiding the leather seats, the steering wheel, and Charlie Jackson sitting behind it, head upright, as if he were looking out of the window. Kevin wept, "Charlie, not you as well."

Jenny rushed down the drive to Kevin and got on her knees beside him. He was no longer struggling, but instead allowed Colm, his neighbour, to hold him down using his full body weight. More people appeared on the street to encircle the burning car at a safe distance.

"I telephoned the operator to get the fire brigade here!" a man shouted as he arrived, and at that, Colm got off Kevin.

Kevin sat on the ground. His entire body shook with grief and the shock of glimpsing his brother's burning body through the car's windows. He found no comfort in knowing that Charlie had probably died almost instantly, and that no one could have saved him. All he could think about were the harsh words he'd spoken and his refusal to shake his brother's hand. "Jenny, my Charlie's in there … my wee brother. Mother of God, not again … not again."

Chapter Fifty-Six

13 June 1921

Dublin, Ireland

Danny woke up in Quinn's spare bedroom to see the familiar, smiling face of his nurse, Grace. "Any news of Jimmy Carson?" He slurred, due to the after-effects of his nightly medication.

"Still no news, I'm afraid, Danny," she told him in her soft, lilting voice.

"How many days have I been here?"

"One more than yesterday. Tomorrow will make a week." She smiled patiently at him, cognisant of the mind-clouding effect of the medications.

In his drowsy state, Danny stretched his leg, forgetting the severity of the thigh wound. He groaned as pain shot from the bullet-hole site to his toes. *This makes six days. Six days, and Jimmy's whereabouts are still unknown,* he thought, six days he'd lain in this bed at the mercy of his brother and Quinn, who had spirited him away from the hospital soon after the surgeon had removed the bullets from his body. Six days, and he could not yet stand on his own two feet or raise his arm above his head.

He watched Grace as she filled the enamel basin with warm water for his washdown. She was a lovely girl, with a warm smile and a patient manner. She was an attentive listener; someone who laughed at his somewhat dry sense of humour when others rolled their eyes instead. She also told him stories of her own life in the hours he was awake. She'd been born and raised in Dublin, so she was accustomed to the pace of a big city, and she was cheekily good at chess, beating Danny in almost every game they played. She was also a competent nurse who took no nonsense from him, even though he was now eager to get out of his bed and becoming irritable because he couldn't.

"How are you feeling this morning?" she asked.

"Better," he lied.

"Good. Your brother is here. Why don't we give you your wash before I call him? I think he wants to redress your bandages today."

Why don't we give you your wash, she'd said, when she would be the one doing the washing. He smiled at her as she unbuttoned his pyjama jacket and thought, *is she falling for me?* Strange though it seemed to him, he was open to the idea of affection, maybe even intimacy for the first time since Anna's death. Not love – the concept still chilled him to the bone. To open his heart completely to someone who might eventually smash it to pieces, either deliberately or through some quirk of fate that went against him, was a terrifying thought; a pain he could never face again. He wasn't certain what frightened him the most: the overpowering strength of love coursing through his veins or the agonies brought about after losing the person who had consumed his heart. He liked Grace, was fond of her, even, but he would never allow himself to love her as he had his Anna.

Danny kept his eyes closed during the washdown for fear of blushing and looking like an eejit, despite the towel covering his John Thomas; Grace then covered his nakedness with his underpants, a sheet, and a blanket. "You must wait for your breakfast until after Patrick has seen to you," she said, wringing out the washcloth.

"Very good, I'll look forward to eating it with you."

She gave him a sweet smile and left, leaving the door open. Moments later, Patrick appeared with a teacup and saucer in one hand and his Gladstone bag in the other.

"And what torturous things are you going to inflict upon me today?" Danny asked his brother, tacking on a good-natured smile.

Patrick wore a serious expression. He looked tired; not surprising, for he came to treat Danny before and after his official working hours every day. Danny had learnt that Kevin had refused Patrick's request that he help with Danny's care. Apparently, he'd said, 'I don't want to know anything about it.' Kevin was being true to his word. They'd never recover their relationship, albeit it had always been tenuous. Not even after the war was over and Ireland was at peace under an Irish government, would Kevin say, "Thank you for freeing Ireland. Thank you for the sacrifices you made. Sorry about the friends you lost to British torture and bullets."

After setting his bag on a chair, Patrick said, "Drink your tea then we'll get started."

Danny wriggled his backside up the bed on his own and got into a sitting position. "See what I can do? I'm making progress." He took the saucer and cup, noting Patrick's sombre expression and his unwillingness to share as much as a glance. "Is everything all right?" he asked.

"Yes. How are you feeling?"

"A bit better, as you can see. Groggy with the medicines I'm taking. They've given me a dry mouth and swollen tongue. Let me guess, you're angry with me about something?"

"Ah, Danny, but I have no more anger left in me." Patrick took the cup off Danny once he'd wet his lips and set it on the bedside table. Then he pulled the covers off the bed.

Danny tilted his chin downwards and peered down the length of his body. A bandage was wrapped around his underarms and across his upper chest and looped over his shoulder. His right arm nestled in a sling, and his hand was dressed with his four fingers visible and the thumb area padded out and protected with linen pads and cotton wool under the bandage. He glanced down at his bottom half and noted that the bandage covering his entire right thigh looked clean. The leg, elevated on a pillow, was still the most painful of his wounds. The surgeon had been worried about infection, primarily, but it looked like Danny had made it past that hump. Secondarily, he was concerned about damage to the muscles or even nerves. He had warned Quinn and Patrick that it could take weeks to heal, and, even then, it was possible Danny could have significant pain and limited mobility for the rest of his life. "Sure, I've really done it to myself this time," he muttered.

Patrick set to work in silence at first, unwrapping Danny's shoulder bandages and disinfecting the wound, sutures, and the surrounding area with a solution of sodium hypochlorite and boric acid. "It looks clean. The surgeon who handed you over to me mentioned you used yarrow and moss to pack the wounds. The efficacy the plants had in stemming your bleeding amazed him. Did your knowledge come from that old botany teacher you used to idolise? Was it one of his remedies?"

"Yes. Good old Mr O'Connell. Funny, I was telling Jimmy about him on the way to Mr O'Brien's house."

"Hmm … there's some research needed there," Patrick mused, as he carefully inspected the wounds. "Can you lift your arm?" he asked in a flat expressionless tone.

"No, not yet. What's the matter with you today, Patrick?" Danny asked again.

Patrick sighed, "I have to tell you something…" Whatever he was about to say remained unsaid when Quinn walked in.

"Have you told him?" Quinn asked.

"I was just about to."

Danny eyed Quinn, then shifted his gaze back to his brother, who had finished with the shoulder dressing. For days, he had drifted in and out of consciousness, at times forgetting who had been to see him and who had said what to him. This morning, he was fully awake, and for the first time, interested in what was happening outside his four walls. "I need to know what's going on, so get on with it. Leave nothing out."

Quinn responded with a nod while Patrick abandoned all further medical issues for the moment.

"We have a clearer picture of what went on the night they shot you," Quinn began. "Our spy at the castle told Mick Collins that they grabbed Jimmy near the house you'd both been hiding in. He'd taken a bullet in the arm and stomach and his head was bleeding. The police took him straight to Dublin Castle, where according to Mick's man, they didn't bother to treat his injuries. They interrogated him the next day, beat him until his face was purple, and then they hanged him in a cell…"

"No, no, not like that, not Jimmy," Danny, enraged, grief-stricken, and overcome with guilt for surviving and finding time to flirt with a pretty woman whilst having his non-lethal injuries treated by his own brother, wanted to scream in fury.

He wanted to get out of the bed, ready or not, and go kill every man inside Dublin Castle!

"The word in the street is that Jimmy committed suicide while in custody, but it's a lie, like so many others the bastards at the castle tell the people of Ireland. I'm sorry, Danny, I know how much Jimmy meant to you."

Patrick added, "We knew you'd want the truth of it."

Danny, whose eyes had filled with tears of foreboding as soon as Quinn had mentioned Jimmy's name, tried desperately to separate his rage from his sorrow. He'd not expected to hear Jimmy had survived, not if he were being honest with himself, but he hadn't thought for a minute that he might have been tortured then murdered at the hands of the enemy. Not his best friend.

Through his tears, Danny noted Patrick's sympathy, and the rare absence of disapproval in his eyes. His brother's understanding brought him comfort in this, his darkest moment since the war in Ireland began. "I've lost my two best friends. Aw, poor Jimmy! He was a brave, loyal soldier. He was the perfect pal, the man who shared my hopes and adventures, who never lost his vision of a free Ireland, even when we were in prison or on the run. It breaks my heart to think he won't be here to see our victory." Tears then ran down his cheeks unashamedly, and he swiped them away as an image of Finn pleading for mercy in his final moments replaced Jimmy's ruddy, cheeky grin. "Both of them gone, and here's me still here. It's my fault Jimmy's dead – my fault."

"Don't be daft. It's war that kills men," Patrick said.

Danny sniffed, "Not this time. I recognised a G-Division man on the tramcar. He got off a stop before Jimmy and me, so I thought we were safe, but … but what if he reported that he'd seen us and…" Danny stopped talking to stare at Patrick and then Quinn. Both men had dropped their gaze the moment he had said, *G-Division.* "What? Tell me."

"The DMP and Black and Tans *were* mobilised after a G-man reported you to the headquarters in the area. The call for men also went out to the castle." Quinn said reluctantly. "They had fifty of them scouring the length of the Dodder for you and Jimmy; there was no way you could escape them … so they thought. They took tracker dogs onto the river's embankments, suspecting you were headed to a safe house in that area. They lost your scent, but the O'Brien couple are known IRA sympathisers, and their address fell within the force's search perimeter. That's why they raided his house…"

The news devastated Danny, his ashen face and red-rimmed eyes displaying his grief. He shook his bowed head repeatedly until he raised it to ask, "How are Mr and Mrs O'Brien?"

"They shot Mr O'Brien dead in the first exchange of fire, and his wife was severely injured and is in hospital."

"No!" Danny cried out again, uncaring that his brother and Quinn were witnessing the weakness of his grief. He wanted to be alone to mourn, but he suspected that Patrick and Quinn had more bad news for him. He didn't know if he could bear it.

"Danny, there's a sizeable reward out for your capture. Your face is on every lamppost and shop window. Dubliners are ripping them off, but the next day the police are putting them back up. If you remain in Dublin, your days are numbered," Patrick stated. "Nowhere is safe now … not this apartment, or a dilapidated building, or the river's embankment. Nowhere."

Quinn continued, "It's bad, Danny. The British have touts and spotters everywhere. They're offering liberal rewards for information whilst trying to restore their intelligence service and match it to the IRA's. Armed Black and Tans on the backs of trucks mounted with machine guns fill Dublin's streets. They're jumping off vehicles randomly to stop, question, and search people and boarding tram cars to frisk passengers trying to get to or get back from their workplaces. Hospitals and nursing homes, convents and churches are being raided every few hours, and they've started to surround entire blocks of houses, keeping tight cordons around those areas for hours while they systematically search every house from cellar to attic."

Quinn paused, then shot Patrick a sideways glance before continuing, "Time is running out for me too. Sooner or later the British will come to my premises looking for evidence against me…"

"But you have business arrangements with them up at the castle," Danny interrupted. "Why would they come after you?"

"I have it on good authority that they're already beginning to suspect me of having ties to the Dáil and Sinn Féin."

"Do you know this for a fact?" Patrick asked Quinn with a worried frown.

"Yes, but you needn't know how or where I heard about it. The less you hear of this conversation the better, Patrick."

"Am I getting my marching orders, then?" Patrick retorted.

"No … I didn't mean you had to leave."

Danny, seeing the strain on his brother's face, suspected he was about to suggest a move to his cottage in Malahide. It was clear from what Quinn had said that it was no longer safe to use this apartment as a safe house. "Patrick, before you try to sort the rest of me, will you give me five minutes alone with Quinn?"

When Patrick left, muttering to himself, Danny said what had been on his mind since being informed of Jimmy Carson's death. "Quinn, listen to me, Jimmy must be avenged. Someone has to answer for his murder."

Quinn sat on the edge of Danny's bed, then leant in and said in a soft voice, "It's being dealt with as we sit here. The target is Charlie Jackson. Our spy said he gave the order to hang Jimmy."

A strange mixture of satisfaction and dread fell upon Danny. He hated Jackson and wouldn't be sorry when he was in the ground, but some part of him felt bad for Kevin. A man could not forget the debt of gratitude he owed to another for saving his life, and he owed so very much to his brother-in-law. He was man enough to admit that. "Charlie Jackson, is it? Good, but I hope the squad were told not to assassinate him while he's anywhere near my sister and her husband."

"I'm sorry, Danny. I don't know the details of the assassination, only that Jackson is the target."

"Does Patrick know?"

"He does not, and you'll not be telling him today, tomorrow, or any other day."

Quinn got up. He looked at the pile of bandages on the bedside table, then he stared at Danny's bandaged thumb-less hand. "I'll send Patrick back up to you. As soon as he has you sorted, we're moving you to Malahide…" Quinn paused, as if he were measuring his words.

"And?"

"I spoke to Mick," Quinn responded, with a catch in his throat. "The good news is the British have made a conciliatory gesture by calling off their policy of house burnings as reprisals. Also, it seems the King has made his unhappiness at the behaviour of the Black and Tans known to his government."

"That's something, I suppose. And the bad news?"

"Mick doesn't think we can continue indefinitely. The British have declared martial law in the province of Munster. They've deployed regular British Army troops in greater number and they're mounting 'sweeps' across the countryside. They're executing dozens in response to our assassinations of individuals."

Quinn's eyes drifted to the window, and for a moment he stared through it, lost in his own thoughts until he eventually continued, "We've got about another month left in us. We don't have the resources to hold on any longer than that."

"We must be able to give a reply, throw something back at them?"

"We're doing what we can. We stepped up our own executions of informers. We've extended our attacks on off-duty British personnel, and we've begun a campaign of burning loyalists' properties. The British are executing prisoners in their custody, so we're doing the same to our captured British soldiers and police. But we're short of ammunition and weapons, and we lost eighty men when we conducted that damned raid on the Customs House in Dublin. Mick told de Valera it was a bad idea."

Quinn seemed to know everything that was going on, Danny thought, feeling resentful that he was not privy to the facts and figures he'd just heard about. "Why haven't I been told about all this?" he asked.

"Why? Isn't it obvious? The situation is fluid, Danny. I've been out on the streets, closely involved and up to date, while you've been in here, lying on your backside sleeping most of the day. It's as simple as that."

Chapter Fifty-Seven

15 June 1921

County Cork, Ireland

Patrick felt out of place, though he was precisely where he was supposed to be. He stepped from foot to foot near to Charlie's coffin and from his location in the room gauged the mood at the wake. The men in the spacious drawing room, including Charlie Jackson's RIC colleagues from Cork and Dublin Castle, were not what one would call 'mourners.' Instead, they were a group of furious, scheming men planning retribution – no, *revenge* – for the death of their fellow officer.

The women were in an altogether different frame of mind, Patrick noted. They sat in two rows of four on hard chairs facing the casket, wallowing in their grief behind black veils, which were unnecessary given that they were at home and not in church, nor were they Catholics. On their laps, they balanced china plates laden with cake and a sandwich or two, and when they nibbled from their plates of goodies, they had trouble lifting their face netting to get the food into their mouths. *Veils: the quintessential mourning garb outdated in any religion,* Patrick thought.

Jenny, whose tummy was just beginning to round with the baby inside her, sat between her distraught mother-in-law and Minnie, while the countess was on the other side of Matilda. None of the women present appeared to give a damn about the men's vengeful machinations, which Patrick thought strange, for Danny's name had been mentioned twice since his arrival.

No, the women had their gazes fixed on the closed coffin, as if they were expecting Charlie's charred remains to open it from the inside and tell them it was all a silly joke.

Patrick noted that everyone in the room sat or stood in a group, apart from himself taking up a solitary position near the deceased. Again, strange, that he should be the one attending the dead man, for he couldn't abide Charlie in life and felt only grief for Kevin and Lady Jackson at his death.

Kevin had warned Patrick upon his arrival that although he was most welcome, he was to avoid telling the mourners his name. He had also spoken to the family earlier that day, advising all of them, including the earl and countess, not to say the name Carmody aloud. Danny Carmody, it seemed, was infamous even in Cork, and sharing his surname might cause friction, Kevin had said bluntly.

As the subject of Patrick's thoughts approached him, Patrick cast aside his worries for Danny and gave in to his sympathetic side. Kevin was still a very good friend and deserved his 'heartfelt' condolences for the death of his younger brother. Oh, how he wished Quinn were at his side to offset the feeling of being the only unwanted guest at the party.

"Here, drink this," Kevin said, handing Patrick a whiskey. "It might dull your ears to the talk of revenge going on in the corners of the room. I asked my mother not to invite any politically motivated person, especially anyone from the police force, but she insisted that Charlie would have wanted his pals here, and she told me that if the IRA turned up, she'd shoot them herself. Would you look at us, Patrick, policemen and detectives coming out of our ears."

"That's your mother for you. I think Minnie's been a bad influence on her," Patrick said dryly.

"No. Minnie's been a good influence. I think for the first time in her adult life, my mother is discovering herself as a woman who has her own mind and was not just the wife of a powerful man – God rest my father's soul."

"May he rest in peace."

The men then grew serious as they shifted their attention to the coffin. Matilda, as she had done twice before, approached it now, to place her hand on the lid and weep. "Why?" she'd been asking that question for days. "Why my son? What did my Charlie do to deserve this?" As she cried, Patrick wondered if she knew a tenth of the evil Charlie had done in the name of duty or had even an inkling why he might have deserved what he got.

"I have something to tell you, Patrick. You won't like it, but I'll ask you not to try to talk me out of it."

"Go on," said Patrick, staring at Kevin's frowning face.

"I've had enough … we've had enough. This war, or whatever they're calling it, has worn us down. We're moving back to London until it's all over."

"Good."

"I thought you'd be upset?"

"I am. I'll be sorry to see you go, but after losing your father and now poor Charlie, I don't blame you for wanting to take your family far away from this madness. The truth is, for as long as Danny is a target, you and Jenny will be in danger from the police, the Black and Tans, and even Charlie's detective pals sitting over there eating your mother's cake. I've heard enough in this room to know this lot want revenge on the IRA, and we both know they'll use just about anyone or any means to get it."

"That's true. Jesus, I can't believe the IRA's audacity to place an incendiary device under Charlie's car right outside my house. When the detectives came, they questioned my neighbours from the top of the street to the bottom, and not one of them claimed to have seen a damn thing. I don't believe that. The street's crawling with IRA supporters."

"They might not have lied, Kevin. The driveways are long, some are curved or hidden by trees and walls, and the IRA, like the British murder squads, are now experienced assassins. It might have taken only a few minutes to place the device." Patrick leant in and murmured in Kevin's ear, "You think these people don't know who I am, but I guarantee some of these men from Dublin have already recognised me as being Danny's brother, and you can bet your life they know Jenny is Danny's sister and Minnie is his grandmother. I'm afraid we're all targets, bound by blood and a common thread."

"Danny being the thread," Kevin spat.

Refusing to get into a debate about his brother's shortcomings, Patrick asked, "When will you get the boat?"

"On Saturday morning."

"Four days?"

"Yes, and my mother is coming with us." Kevin tittered, then continued, "Don't worry, I'll rent a house big enough for Jenny and me to find quiet times alone. Both Minnie and my mother can be wearing."

Kevin excused himself and went to his mother who was still weeping, her cheek pressed against the coffin lid. He put his arm around her shoulder, and led her back to her chair, speaking a few soothing words to her.

Patrick wanted to tell Kevin about Quinn; not about their loving relationship but as an example of how lives were being ruined. Quinn's suspicions had been proved true. He was no longer safe from the British authorities who were offering money for information leading to his whereabouts. Like Danny, he had spent the last week at Mr Sullivan's farm.

The Sullivans were kindness itself. They asked for nothing in return, but Patrick knew how much they appreciated the money they were receiving for the men's board and food. Quinn was also being a good help around the farm, and through work, he tried not to think too much about what he'd lost. Running from Dublin had taken its toll on his business premises, which now boasted of smashed-in windows, and a break-in that had resulted in the theft of his entire shop stock. 'At least they didn't burn the place to the ground,' Quinn had said, as he tried to look on the bright side.

When Kevin returned to Patrick's side, the latter asked, "Do you have a job to go to?"

"Yes. The administrator at Charing Cross Hospital wants me back. I accepted primarily because of this damn war we're in, but to be honest, Patrick, I miss practicing medicine, especially the variety of urgent care patients within a busy hospital. The monotony of a general practitioner's life is making me feel old before my time."

"Too many haemorrhoids and abscesses to deal with, eh?" Patrick chuckled at Kevin, who rolled his eyes in response. "It's hard to believe that five years have passed since you and I stood in front of my father's coffin, with him looking grand in his suit. Five years of strife and war, Kevin – five years, and still with no end in sight to the bloodshed…"

"Right you two, that's enough of hiding in the corner," Jenny said, joining the men. "Kevin, you have guests looking like they're ready to leave."

"I'm leaving soon, too," Patrick said.

When Kevin left them, Jenny curled her arm around Patrick's and said, "I take it he's told you of our plans?"

"He has, and though I'm sad, I'm not shocked at the news."

"Come with us, Patrick. Get a job with Kevin. Charing Cross is desperate for doctors, especially good surgeons," Jenny blurted out, looking excited. "There's nothing holding us here apart from our homes, and God willing, they'll still be standing when we return, and one day we will come back."

"I can't leave Ireland. Danny needs one of us…"

"Danny chose to participate in this insanity," Jenny interrupted. "He chose it, Patrick, and look what he's doing to us all. Do you even know where he is?"

"No," Patrick lied to his sister.

"Then admit it, we won't be a family again until this is all over. C'mon, pack your suitcases and cross that Irish Sea with us."

Jenny was being brave, holding back her tears. Patrick wondered; *were it not for Quinn, would I agree to leave?* Yes, he'd probably be leaving for Malahide right this minute to pack up, as she suggested. "Darlin', I'll visit you often. It won't be like the war years when we didn't know when or if we'd see each other again. You don't think I'd let you give birth without me being there for you, do you…?"

"You'd better be," Jenny rushed out.

"He'd better what, Jenny?" Minnie asked, sneaking up on her grandchildren.

"I was saying, I'll be over to London often, to visit you."

A shadow of grief crossed Minnie's eyes and when she spoke it was with a sorrowful, broken voice that tore at Patrick's heart. "Oh, would you look at me? I'm nearing the end of my days, Son, and I'm spending them at the funerals of those who should 'ave long outlived me. Can I 'ave a word with you before you go?"

An hour later, Patrick said his goodbyes to Minnie. She had given him much to think about, and now, he was eager to return to Malahide.

Kevin was showing the last of his guests out. The policemen and detectives had already slipped away, as had the minister who had christened Robert. Only the ladies remained, and they were still clucking around Matilda. It was almost eight o'clock, however, and in Ireland, it impolite to leave a wake after that witching hour.

"Kevin, do you have a moment?" Patrick asked.

The two men went into the library, and there, Patrick put Minnie's idea to Kevin. When he'd finished his proposal, he said, "I can't do it without you. Will you help me?"

Kevin chewed over the idea as he stared at the carpet. He was taking his time to give an answer, making Patrick's heart thump in nervous anticipation. His friend's mind was probably filled with misgivings – pros and cons – each being weighed up against the other until he thought his head would explode. "Kevin, please, I need you."

Kevin raised his head and nodded, looking unhappy. "All right, I'll do it, but I swear to Jesus, Mary, and Joseph, this will be the last time I ever get involved with Carmody shenanigans."

Patrick sighed with relief, "Thank you. To be honest, I've been mulling this over for weeks, but tonight Minnie gave me the push I needed. The timing is right. I'll set it up for Friday and see you at eight o'clock on Thursday night at my house. Is that good for you?"

"It's fine."

Patrick stepped closer to Kevin, who was standing in front of the fireplace, and he now continued candidly, "We don't deserve you, Kevin, I know that. Time and again you've proved yourself a good friend, despite losing your father and brother. I have a cheek to even ask you to do anything else for Danny..."

"You have the cheek of the Irish in you, all right," Kevin retorted, then he let out a long sigh, "Ah, but I've learnt the Carmody way."

"And what's that?"

"That you'll stop at nothing to help each other. That brings me comfort. I know should anything happen to me, you and Danny will step in to protect and care for my Jenny and my little boy." Kevin then smiled. "And though you're a troublesome lot, you're *my* troublesome lot."

Patrick would miss his friend's counsel and his constant faithfulness. As they shook hands to seal their pact, he said, "Tell me I'm doing the right thing?"

"I believe you are, Patrick, but what I think isn't important. Do you think you're doing the right thing?"

"I don't know."

Chapter Fifty-Eight

Thursday, 16 June 1921

Malahide, County Dublin

Patrick arrived at Mr Sullivan's farm just before nine o'clock in the evening to find Danny and Quinn sitting in front of the house chatting in the reddish glow of the dying sun. As he got out of his Ford, he watched Danny make his way across the yard towards him with the aid of a pair of crutches. His leg was healing well; he put his full weight on it about every other step. "How are you?" Patrick asked him.

"Not too bad, still sore. My thigh muscle is pulling, and the leg pains me when I walk. I mostly use these crutches for show, now, so there's that, eh?"

"It'll feel better after tonight. I'm here to take the sutures out of your wounds."

Danny's mood brightened as the two men began walking towards Quinn. "Oh, that's a welcome surprise. I didn't think you'd be back from Cork until the weekend."

"I left straight after the funeral. I've got a busy few days on surgical rotation coming up. I still haven't chosen my speciality."

"Does that mean you'll stay in Dublin? What about me?"

"Yes, I'll be staying in Dublin. Contrary to what you might think, Danny, my job is not all about patching up IRA fugitives every five minutes, nor is it about babysitting my little brother."

"Patrick, it's good to see you. How are you?" Quinn asked, joining the brothers.

"He's in a stinking mood, Quinn. I'd leave him be if I were you," Danny grunted.

Patrick smiled. Being happy to see Quinn was an understatement. He'd never felt as lonely as he had during the last few days. "I'm happy to see you took my advice and stayed here, Quinn. The Peelers are up in arms about Charlie Jackson's murder, and I have a feeling Dublin will see more violence this week. You two are in the best place."

"I suppose Jackson had plenty of protection on his way into the ground?" Quinn muttered.

"Half of Dublin Castle were there, vowing to kill as many of your lot as possible. Danny, your name is at the top of their list. Did you know you're worth a thousand pounds?"

"Is that all?" Danny tittered. "I'll be worth a lot more when I get back in the fight. I might have lost a thumb, but I'm betting I'll be able to hold a revolver soon enough, and if I can't, I'll learn to shoot better with my left hand. Wait and see, I'll be the sniper I once was before the month is out."

"We'll see about that," Patrick grunted, then he seemed to cheer up. "Right, let's get your stitches out before there's any more talk of fighting and shooting, shall we? Go inside and get stripped off. I need a few words with Quinn before I start on you." As Danny made his way inside, Patrick called after him, "Ask Mrs Sullivan to boil some water for me, and if she wouldn't mind, could she make me a cup of tea? It was a long drive."

"Patrick, I know that look on your face, and it's not good. What's up?" Quinn asked, when the two men had been alone for a few minutes.

"If I ask you to do exactly as I say without question or objection, will you?"

"I'll do anything for you, but can you be more specific?"

Patrick looked up at the first floor and saw the flickering orange glow of a lit candle. Danny was already in the bedroom he shared with Quinn. When he'd turned his back to the window, Patrick studied Quinn's inquisitive eyes, noting his raised left eyebrow. He wouldn't be at all pleased with the plan he and Kevin had concocted. "I don't want you to have any surprises, so this is what's happening to Danny tonight..."

******

At eleven o'clock, Quinn greeted Kevin, Jenny, and Minnie, who were getting out of Kevin's car. Kevin's grim face matched Jenny's, as she asked timidly, "Are you Quinn?"

"Yes, and you must be Jenny. Patrick and Danny speak of you often. It's nice to finally meet you."

"Yes, well, I wish it were under better circumstances. This is our granny, Minnie."

Quinn's eyes twinkled as he looked over Minnie's slight form, and then he grinned. "You know your Patrick adores you, don't you, Minnie?"

"Well, I've been around for a long time," Minnie giggled with pleasure, like a flattered love-struck girl, as Quinn bent over her hand to kiss it.

"This is my husband, Kevin," Jenny said.

As the two men shook hands, Jenny had a good look at Quinn under the light of the storm lamp he carried. At last, she was meeting the elusive man whom Patrick had talked about on several occasions. Patrick was probably oblivious to the glimmer of love that sat in his eyes whenever he spoke of his friend; however, Jenny had not missed the pink romantic glow on his face nor the slight tremor in his voice. He was in love with the man who stood before her now, and although the very idea both shocked and frightened her, of all the disturbing questions she could have about this revelation, the one thing she wanted most to know is if Quinn returned Patrick's affections.

When Patrick crossed the yard, Jenny studied him in a new light. Oh, for so long she had watched her brother suffer alone and in silence. She'd suspected for years – since before he'd become a man – that he was not interested in girls. He'd never blushed in a woman's company, had never spoken to anyone in the family – as far as she knew – about liking a woman. Not in the way boys liked them, at least. Sure, but he had always been more comfortable in the company of men, although it was more than that … it was something within him she'd not been able to put her finger on until right this moment, as he looked ardently at Quinn. Jenny shifted her gaze to Kevin, and thought, *he doesn't know. After all their years together at university, he doesn't know what Patrick is.*

"Right, shall we make this a memorable night?" Patrick said, taking Minnie's arm.

As Mr and Mrs Sullivan and Minnie busied themselves in the kitchen making sandwiches for the guests, the Carmodys, along with Kevin and Quinn, congregated in Danny's bedroom. Jenny had insisted on accompanying Kevin, although she expected it would be a difficult night, which would leave her shrouded in sadness and regret.

"Will you look at all of you, even Kevin, standing around my bedside like I'm about to die on you," Danny said with his feet up on the bed. "Christ, all we need is a priest to say a few last words over me."

Jenny said, "Oh, stop it. I didn't get to see you on your birthday last month, so when we visited Patrick earlier tonight and he told us you were here, we thought we'd give you a nice surprise."

"It's certainly that, darlin'," Danny grinned at his sister.

"Kevin and I hadn't heard you were hurt. I would have come sooner had I known. Oh, Danny, what has our family come to when I don't even know if you're alive or dead or sick or well? When will you learn you only have one body to play with?"

"There's nothing to learn, Jenny, darlin'. A man either gets a bullet with his name on it or he doesn't." Patrick had not re-bandaged Danny's hand after removing the sutures. Danny stretched it out to Jenny and joked, "Ah, well, this hand's been ugly since a bullet went through it in Belgium. I thought I'd finish it off by getting rid of its thumb. I think it's in the Dodder, by the way. It's a strange sight to see, is it not, Jenny? I might even go for the fingers next – you've met Quinn, I see."

Kevin, who'd not said much since their arrival, answered with his eyes on Quinn, "Yes, we have. Tell me, Quinn, are you IRA as well?"

Quinn flicked questioning eyes to Patrick.

"You can trust Kevin with your secrets," Jenny answered on behalf of her husband. "Were that not the case, our Danny here would've been captured more than a year ago."

Again, Quinn looked to Patrick for instruction, and this time he nodded. "Kevin's my brother-in-law, but he's also my dear friend. Speak freely, Quinn."

Jenny had been present earlier when Patrick had warned Kevin that Quinn was at the farm. At first, Kevin had refused to meet him and had snapped at Patrick, 'Have you forgotten my brother was just blown up by the likes of him?' To which Patrick had responded, 'He's a good man. He hasn't assassinated anyone.'

"Well, are you IRA?" Kevin repeated his question to Quinn despite Jenny giving him a dig in the ribs to shut up.

"Yes, but I'm also a businessman," Quinn finally answered. "I've been staying here with Danny because there are people in the occupation forces who'd like to see me locked up or dead. They've already destroyed my life's work."

"I see. And why do they want you dead?"

"That's enough, Kevin," Minnie said in her strictest tone. "We're not here to talk politics."

"It's all right, Minnie, I'll answer Kevin's question," said Quinn, maintaining his good humour. "It seems my long-term, and up to now, amiable relationship with the DMP is over. I've made no bones about wanting freedom for this country, Kevin, and they've now made it clear they no longer want to do business with me. In fact, I have closed my premises indefinitely, for the sake of my employees – you know how the British occupiers like to burn profitable enterprises to the ground with its workers still in them?"

"I know your lot killed my father when you burnt my family home to the ground," Kevin interrupted.

"Please darlin', not tonight," Jenny took his hand.

Quinn, trying to make light of Kevin's interrogation and thinly veiled accusations, addressed Minnie, and continued, "Apparently, I now have a sizeable file in my name, for crimes committed against the occupation authorities. You see, Minnie, the British might see them as crimes, but I see myself as a true Irishman, declaring love for my country and hatred for the Imperialists who subjugate my people." Then he shifted his gaze to Kevin and asked, "As an Irishman, where do you stand?"

Jenny sighed with relief when there came a crisp knock on the door and Mrs Sullivan stepped inside. "I know it's late, but I've set the table downstairs with a bite to eat for all of you. I'm thrilled to finally meet the rest of the family. Come down while the tea is still hot – oh, and I've made Gur cake and a vanilla sponge."

Jenny enjoyed the comparatively jovial atmosphere at the table. Danny and Kevin were being polite to one another, even though Kevin was not happy to be in the company of men who supported the rebels who had taken his father, brother, and childhood home from him. He would not forgive, never. Earlier that day, he'd told Jenny, 'I'm doing this tonight for you and Patrick, but after it's done, I'd rather not see or know what's going on with your family. I'm hurting Jenny. I'm hurting, and I'll hurt no more because of them.'

Mr Sullivan, who'd already downed two tumblers of good Irish whiskey, asked those at the table, "Did you read in the newspaper about King George's address the other day, to the Parliament of Northern Ireland?"

Kevin answered, "I did, and I think he made sense. I doubt anyone will listen to him, though."

"I think he's as blind and as stupid as the rest of the British politicians in Westminster," Danny said.

"I read it top to bottom," Minnie declared.

"What did it say?" Jenny asked her.

Mr Sullivan got up and fetched the newspaper. "I have it right here." Then he disappointed Minnie by reading a snippet of the piece aloud, normally her honour.

"I urge all Irishmen to pause, to stretch out the hand of forbearance and conciliation, to forgive and to forget, and to join in making for the land which they love a new era of peace, contentment, and good will."

"Contentment and goodwill? While they still bloody occupy us and shit on us after every meal? Forgive and forget? He won't find that anywhere in Ireland, the silly … the self-righteous … Mrs Sullivan, what did you put in that tea? It's … strange. I don't know…" Danny slurred his words, letting them trail off as he looked fearfully at the faces around the table.

Jenny searched Danny's face as his eyes drooped, his mouth grew slack, and his head wavered before it slumped downwards, his chin hitting his chest. Struck by the enormity of what they were doing to her brother, she promptly burst out crying for her part in the subterfuge. "Oh, my poor, wee Danny, I'm sorry! You're a foolish boy at times, but I'm going to miss you terribly."

"Don't cry, Jenny," said Minnie, with tears in her own eyes. "This is for the best. We must go through with it for 'is sake."

Patrick checked Danny's breathing and with a broken voice, said, "Right, let's get him into the car."

"I feel horrible for doing this to my own brother … this is wrong," Jenny continued to sob, as Quinn, Patrick and Kevin lifted a soundly sleeping Danny between them.

"You know he'd never have agreed to it, Jenny," Patrick said, as he and the others carried Danny out of the kitchen and into the yard.

"Can he breathe all right in there?" Jenny asked Patrick when Danny was lying curled up on the floor of the car's boot.

Kevin placed his arm around Jenny's shoulder, "Of course, he can, darlin'. He'll sleep just fine until Patrick and I get him to the ship."

Minnie said, "Long enough for that ship to sail, I 'ope. Knowing 'im, 'e'll jump right off the thing."

"It'll be all right. When he's in his cabin, I'll give him more morphine that will keep him under until well after the ship is at sea. There's no turning back now. It's either this or certain death for him." Patrick's voice broke as he added, "We must be brave."

"Kevin, must you go, too? Wot 'appens if a police or Black and Tan patrol stop you?" Minnie asked, as she held onto Quinn's arm.

"It must be me, Minnie. Quinn's a fugitive. He might be recognised," Kevin, still a reluctant partner, got into the driver's seat and snapped at Patrick, "C'mon, we need to go. No more talking."

"Quinn and the Sullivans will keep you company until we get back. Pray for us," Patrick said to the weeping women as he got into the motorcar.

Chapter Fifty-Nine

Friday 17 June

Danny stirred as the bed rocked gently beneath him and his ears caught the chugging sound of a heavy diesel engine. They had drugged him. He'd long since recognised the strange taste and dryness in his mouth, along with the wonderful feeling of having no pain anywhere in his body. Only morphine gave him that relaxed, delightful feeling that everything was right with the world. Still … something wasn't right … not as it should be.

Even without opening his eyes, he knew he wasn't in his bed, and Quinn wasn't in the one next to him. He wasn't at the farm; no birds chirped, no cock crowed, no chickens clucked, and no luscious smell of breakfast being cooked wafted up the stairs. If only he could escape the pull of sleep.

He slept on until he woke up anew to the sound of a woman's voice. He cracked his eyes open and saw her blurry outline. "What?"

"Danny, I said, good morning. I've got tea for you."

More alert now, he stared into Grace's lovely, untroubled face. "Grace?" he muttered, as he looked around the cabin. "Where am I? What are you doing here? Where is here?"

She answered, unable to contain the excitement in her voice. "We're on a passenger ship bound for New York, in America, Danny! We've been at sea for over four hours. Look, I slept in the chair over there … oh, but don't worry about my innocence, your brother got me my own cabin next door. We'll get there in six days, maybe seven."

"In the name of God, what have they done to me?" Danny cautiously sat up, and then slid his legs over the side of the single bed. He slouched at the edge of the mattress, his head dangling between his knees while his dazed mind tried to digest what Grace had told him. Jesus Christ and all the saints above, he was on a feckin' ship going across the Atlantic Ocean? Eventually, he raised his eyes, spotted the cup of tea on the night table and lifted it in shaky fingers to his lips.

"I'll kill the feckin' lot of them," he hissed, then slugged down the contents of the cup. As the tea lubricated his dry throat, he focused on his surroundings until his eyes finally settled on Grace. "Did my brother force you to get on this ship with me?"

"Don't be daft. Nobody forces me to do anything." Her golden hair was loose. She tucked some strands behind her ears and continued, "Your brother was kind to me, and his proposal thrilled me – so generous! Me going to America, Danny! Who'd have thought it? Oh, I nearly forgot…" She took an envelope out of her dress pocket and smoothed its creases. "This is for you. It's from Patrick. It should explain everything, including the bit about me looking after you until you get your bandages off."

Grace opened the envelope and then unfolded the letter. She handed it to him then went to sit in the chair she'd slept in, to drink her own cup of tea.

Danny was furious – more – shattered at being duped by his family, and Quinn … and the Sullivans. Christ, they'd all been in on it! "I'll get on the very next ship home, Grace. I swear I will."

"Just read it, Danny, all of it," Grace said, looking pleased with herself.

She had a bit of rouge on her lips, he noticed, and a smudge of kohl around her eyes. She looked quite beautiful in what was clearly a new and fashionable gown.

Danny's uninjured hand was trembling as he gripped the letter in his fingers, "Damn you, Patrick," he mumbled as he began to read.

Dear Danny,

I imagine you are angry, hurt, and sorely disappointed in me, but before you take your bad temper out on Grace, whom I have charged to look after you, please hear what I have to say.

It was made clear at Charlie Jackson's funeral that you are a high value target for all sections of the British Authority Forces. This fact, and my own suspicion that the Peelers and Black and Tans were about to use us, your family, as hostages in order to flush you out, made my decision to spirit you off to America an easier one. And just so you know, this was Minnie's idea to begin with.

Perhaps you don't think about the repercussions of your actions, Danny, or maybe you do. Either way, they are grave, and affect not only your life but that of your old grandmother, Jenny's, her child's, and her husband's, as well as my own. By now, Kevin will have been to the British administration at Dublin Castle, to inform them that you are no longer hiding in any part of Ireland or Great Britain. Only he could do this because of his somewhat reasonable relationship with the DMP and Auxiliaries, who went all the way to Cork to attend his brother's funeral. You owe Kevin a debt of gratitude, again, for without his intervention on numerous occasions, you would have come to great harm, and probably death. I know this in my heart.

Do not even think about returning to Ireland, Danny, until this land is at peace, either with itself or with Britain in some form or another. I repeat, do not think to return until all former combatants on both sides have been given amnesty; if you do return, and harm befalls any member of your family, it will be a stain on your soul.

I am sorry that I drugged your tea at supper. I am sorry that I stuck you in the back of a car and whisked you off without your permission. I am sorry that I injected you with morphine after Kevin and I got you into your cabin on the ship – by the way, we had help, thanks to Grace. After speaking to Michael Collins, she arranged with some IRA boys to escort us through the dockyard, into the port, and onto the ship.

I know you too well, Danny. You, with your spirit and overabundance of passion, would've gone back to the fighting the minute you felt well enough, and you'd have been dead within the week – so, yes – I am sorry for the deceit and trickery, but not for sending you away. I did this for you, to keep you alive, but I did it mostly for myself. I cannot lose you. I cannot.

You will be in America for quite some time, Danny. Grace has an envelope containing pounds and dollars. The generous amounts should allow the pair of you to have a comfortable life for as long as you are there. You should also know that Michael Collins was happy to agree to the plan; he said your body had taken enough bullets. He instructs you to find two of your colleagues in New York. There, you will continue fundraising for the Irish cause. Enclosed are their names and the address of the hotel where they are staying. You might even enjoy yourself. It is high time you put away your gun and had fun in life.

I love you, Danny. You are my own fine brother, and you are in our thoughts and prayers.

Until we meet again

Patrick.

"Until we meet again. I'll kill him!" Danny threw the letter and watched it zigzag its way to the floor. "And Mick Collins was in on this?"

"He was, and his instructions were clear."

"I'll kill him too."

Grace came to the bed and sat on the edge. Her sombre eyes met his, and with instinct, or perhaps pity, she held his hand. "My father died before I ever knew him. My mother and little brother died of the Spanish flu … God rest their souls. I was an orphan at eighteen, without a brother or sister or anyone else to give a damn about me. Be grateful that you have a family who loves you, Danny. Be happy we are going to work on behalf of the Republic. This is not a punishment; it's an honour, a reward for all you've done for Michael and for Ireland."

Danny's scowl softened, but almost instantly the flash of anger returned to his eyes. "Are you daft, woman? I was drugged and smuggled onto a ship that's taking me away from my beloved land in the middle of the night, and all without my permission."

"And is that the bramble you caught your pants on? Sure, Danny, it doesn't matter how we got here, it's what we do now that's important." She cocked her head to the side in thought before continuing, "What we do in America will be just as significant as shooting up our own country, don't you think?"

"I think you and I are seeing a completely different story here." Tutting and muttering, he limped to the porthole and looked out at the ocean. In all fairness, Patrick must have paid a pretty penny for this cabin, he thought. It had a window with a sea view – a sea feckin' view for days on end until they reached a strange shore that would look nothing like the beauty of the rolling hills and lush green valleys of the home he had left – no, been forced from. "They shouldn't have done this. It's not right, Grace. My brother and sister have taken my choices away from me."

"No, I don't believe they have," Grace shook her head. "They have *given* you choices, choices you wouldn't have had in Ireland, and they saved *themselves* into the bargain, don't be forgettin' that. You don't know the latest casualty figures, but I do. One thousand people have died in Ireland this year alone, and we're still in June. The violence is becoming more intense, and it's not just in Dublin, but also in south Munster and Belfast. They have killed five hundred people in County Cork, three hundred in Dublin. How long do you think they would have lasted – or you, with your wild excess of passion, and your need to fight? Sure, it's as if there's nothing else in you but the need to kill and your grief for your dead wife, but for the rest –"

"I'll not have you speak of her like that!" Danny snapped.

Her wet eyes stared back at him, and he was immediately contrite. "I'm sorry, Grace, I shouldn't have shouted at you." He stretched out his hand and took hers, then he kissed her fingers. "This is an adventure, you say?"

She nodded. "A grand adventure for us both, Danny," she said, her voice subdued but still hopeful.

This might not be too bad, he thought, back to staring at the ocean waves. He was exiled for now, no denying it, but what man wouldn't want to jaunt away with a woman like Grace by his side and a ready-made job to help the Republic? And, sure, he'd go home soon enough, when the war was over. Michael might even reward him with a seat in the new Irish Parliament – Danny Carmody, MP for Dublin – why not? He'd earned a voice in government.

At her sweet, lilting tone, he turned and asked, "Sorry, what's that, Grace?"

"I said I'll need to change your hand bandages before we go out. I think we should take a wee turn about the deck and get some breakfast up there while we're at it."

Danny felt the urge to kiss her, to smile, to look forward to this new undertaking. With that, his rage began to dwindle. "Right then, darlin' you'd better smarten me up. A wee turn around the deck it is."

Epilogue

January 1922

Dublin, Ireland

Quinn was furious, feeling betrayed by the man he'd idolised for years. For months, he and every other Irishman had waited for the British and Irish to sign a treaty that would give Ireland its freedom; instead, Mick Collins had brought back from London a treaty that declared only half a win and part of the country lost.

On the first floor of the Dáil building, Quinn faced Mick from the other side of the desk. His eyes blazed with indignation, his throat burned with bitterness and deep regret. He went into his jacket pocket, pulled out a cigarette and lit it. He took a deep drag and then slowly exhaled a cloud of smoke before saying what was on his mind. "There are thousands of people gathered outside, Mick. Do you even give a damn that you're going to disappoint them or throw them into another war?"

"There'll be no more wars if we handle this right," Mick responded, with a scowl on his face to match Quinn's.

Quinn snorted aloud, a bitter reproach for his leader. "Lie to me, but at least be honest with yourself. All this truce has done is to allow the IRA to regroup, recruit, and train openly. Most of us think this is just a temporary end to hostilities, but go ahead, say what you think sounds good instead of what is true."

"And what in your mighty opinion is true?"

"That by the end of today the Dáil, Sinn Féin, and IRA will be splintered beyond repair. I can see by your face you're predicting the same."

When Mick didn't respond, Quinn snapped, "Mick, for God's sake, you must know our members won't agree to this farce!"

Mick, still struggling with his reply, lowered his head and focused on his well-prepared speech. Quinn knew what was on the pages; he had read every word, which confirmed Mick's capitulation and disloyalty to the men who had fought and died for him. There he sat, devoid of any decent defence and with no plausible reason for letting down his countrymen and women, and every single child and their future in Ireland.

Quinn was desperate to get out of there and find Patrick, who was in the crowded street outside waiting for news, but before he walked out on his leader, he wanted to end the meeting with some measure of sincerity between them. "I was a happy man in July when the truce took effect," he said, breaking Mick's concentration. "I thought to myself back then … Mick and de Valera will put up a good fight for us in Westminster. It won't happen overnight. It'll be a difficult negotiation, but they'll bring us home our freedom."

Mick finally raised his eyes and responded in a stern, unyielding tone. "If you're going to sit there whinging about my negotiation skills, I suggest you go get yourself a stone and join every other bugger in the street waiting to pelt me."

"I'll be glad to leave, but am I not permitted to say what I think before I go?"

Mick thumped the desk with his fist. "Sweet Jesus, Mary and Joseph, I'll never hear the end from you, will I? Go on then, say it and be done."

"What you did wasn't good enough," Quinn began, undaunted by Mick's growing anger. "We had the British on the ropes, Mick. In July, they thought our guerrilla campaign would continue indefinitely. You made a point of saying the spiralling costs in British casualties and capital and the severe criticism they were getting at home and abroad would give us an advantage, yet it seems to me now that all our efforts have been for naught. Is it for *this* treaty that Jimmy Carson, Finn, Séan Treacy, Aiden, Colm, John Grant and all the other good men under your command died? Is *this* our homage for the men the British executed at Dublin Castle without charges being laid against them? Look at you, sitting there like a victor with your grand speech ready for parliament while knowing you're selling our people short. You'll go out there to tell the world that the fight for freedom has been won even though the new Free State government will be obliged under oath to pledge its allegiance to a foreign king. How many of us do you think you'll fool with those fancy words of reconciliation?"

Mick stood up and went to the window. There, he looked down on the street before turning back to Quinn. "Do you think you could have done better?"

"I think I would have stayed in London until we got the North with us," Quinn retorted.

Mick sighed, "You were a good commander, Quinn, but you've never understood the complexities of politics. I agreed to the six counties in the north being excluded from the free Ireland agreement because I'm confident they too will eventually join a united Ireland. I'll make sure of it, even if I have to induce them into it at the point of a gun."

Mick came back to the desk and repeated, "And I think it will have to be at the end of a gun."

Quinn put aside his anger to plead this point, "Postpone your announcement. Try again to get Ulster with us on this treaty. We can bear bending the knee to the king for a wee while longer, but we need our brothers and sisters in the north now. We might not get another chance."

Mick shook his head. "We don't have the advantage. The British crippled our organisation in Belfast when they arrested three hundred and fifty IRA men and formed the Ulster Special Constabulary filled with bloodthirsty unionists. We lost even more ground when our men killed those two Protestant police officers in Belfast last year." He paused then uttered reluctantly, "I'll admit to you, I didn't expect them to attack Catholic areas in reply, but they did, and do you know how many people died, Quinn?"

"No."

"A hundred, maybe more – hundreds of Catholic homes burnt out – another seven thousand Catholics expelled from their jobs in the Belfast shipyards. How can I get the north when the Protestant and loyalist majority population up there don't want to join us?"

"You could have fought harder."

"I fought like the bloody devil, but I got all I would get from the British. When de Valera went to London to meet with the Prime Minister, Lloyd George made it clear he wanted Ireland to remain within the British Empire as a dominion state, much like Canada. He told Dev at the time that he and his government wouldn't accept the name, 'Republic of Ireland.' He thought it had a whiff of Russia about it, and you know as well as I they've tried for years to blacken our name by tying us to the communists."

Mick banged the desk again with his fist, bouncing objects and dislodging his neat pile of papers. By now, his anger outweighed Quinn's, as his mind appeared to be squabbling with his heart. "Why do you think Dev sent me to London to negotiate for him?"

"He said you were the obvious choice…"

"Rubbish." Mick glared at Quinn across the desk. "When he ordered me to go, I could see his scurrilous brain working to cover his own arse. I kept thinking on that boat going over to England … if I make compromises, the fundamentalists on our side will see me as a traitor, not de Valera … if I go back home without an agreement for complete freedom for Ireland, I'll be signing my own death warrant – Dev would see this country burn if he could be King of the ashes. He's a coward, and I hope to God he goes down in history as one for making me his damned scapegoat."

Those who were near to the top of the Republican movement knew that de Valera was afraid of Mick's popularity, Quinn admitted. People wanted to follow Michael Collins. He drew supporters the minute he opened his mouth at public gatherings. De Valera didn't have that magic touch with the people. He was not a great orator, nor as diplomatic or as humorous or heart-warming as the man sitting before him. "Sending you to London was a piece of Machiavellian genius on de Valera's part," Quinn responded, finally agreeing with Mick on something. "Sure, you could have made a friend of the Kaiser had you met him, but I'm sorry to say you've lost me today."

Mick's eyes bored into Quinn as he asked, "Will you not stand with me?"

"In good conscience, I cannot. I didn't give my oath of allegiance to half a country, I gave it to all of Ireland … north, south, east and west. And not only are we now a divided nation, but you agreed to the Dáil swearing allegiance to the British crown. You've also agreed to us calling ourselves a 'Free State' instead of a 'Republic.' I can't tolerate it nor bear it."

Mick, visibly upset by Quinn's announcement, said hurriedly, "Don't you worry about that, the Free State moniker will disappear once we begin running our own affairs." He stood, stretched out his long arm, and opened his palm to shake Quinn's hand. "I know you're disappointed, but I'm asking you not to abandon me, not after everything we've done together."

Quinn was sad but resolute as he stood. Even with the greatest will in the world, he couldn't bring himself to support the Anglo-Irish Treaty that Mick, Arthur Griffith, Robert Barton, George Gavan Duffy, and Eamonn Duggan had negotiated over the past five months. Those men were already written into history. They'd tried their best, but they hadn't gone to London as conquering heroes, dictating terms to a vanquished Britain. Had that been the case, they would have signed the peace treaty in Dublin, not London, and the horde outside would be celebrating on Irish whiskey and barrels of Guinness, not standing in the cold waiting to hear the bad news for themselves.

If one analysed the treaty with an objective mind, one could see some positive outcomes, Quinn thought. Amongst its terms and conditions, it disestablished the desired Irish Republic of 1919 but created the Irish Free State, an entity encompassing twenty-six of Ireland's thirty-two counties. Yes, it would mean much more independence than the Home Rule Act of 1912 would have granted, but it did not attain complete freedom from the British yoke. For this reason and many others, he had no intention of being present during Mick's announcement in the Irish parliament session, which was to begin downstairs in fifteen minutes. He was disillusioned, finished with all of it.

"Don't call on me. Goodbye, Mick," Quinn said, finally shaking Mick's hand.

******

Patrick stood as close to the main doors of the Irish Parliament building as possible, but people desperate to get the best view of the treaty negotiators as they entered repeatedly pulled and shoved him. It had been an hour since Quinn had left him to meet with Michael Collins, and during that time, speculation and impatience had grown in the street, as had anger from many who suspected that the end of one war would herald the beginning of another.

At last, Patrick spotted Quinn standing on the steps of the building behind a row of DMP officers. He searched the crowd to his left and right, then smiled wanly when he saw Patrick's wave.

"Is that it, then?" Patrick asked, after the two men had pushed through the centre of the incoming crowd in Dawson Street.

"That's it, and now I need a whiskey or three," Quinn answered, as he walked into the first pub they came to.

Patrick sat at a recently vacated table while Quinn went to the bar to order two pints of Guinness and double whiskey chasers. Like every other crowded corner, street, hotel and restaurant in the area, the pub was crammed with folk desperate to hear the outcome of the Dáil's debate, which was about to begin. Quinn had said nothing about his meeting with Michael Collins, but his pale, glowering face said more than words ever could. Patrick was not confident; on the contrary, he was afraid of what was to come.

Before Quinn told Patrick about his meeting with Collins, he downed his first whiskey, then took three slugs of Guinness from his pint tankard. He wiped his lips afterwards, then said, "I'm out. I want no more of this."

"But it's over … isn't it?" Patrick queried.

Quinn sneered, "No. It's about to begin." Then he relayed to Patrick his conversation with Mick, word for word.

The first thoughts that came to Patrick's mind were about the increase in violence; more guns on the streets, more burnings, more deaths. "Quinn, you say you're out, but how will you stay out?" he asked. "I know your commitment to this cause. Do you really think you'll be able to remain neutral? And what about the men you've fought with? What if they turn on you?"

Instead of looking at Patrick, Quinn stared at his pint glass, and answered, "For the first time in years, I don't know how I'll manage anything. I'm bankrupt, Patrick."

Patrick stared, wide-eyed. "Why didn't you tell me? When did this happen?"

Quinn took another swallow, then shrugged. "I didn't want to worry you. I've been hanging on by the skin of my teeth for years. During the war in Europe, my earnings went down and manufacturing costs went up. I was still solvent when peace came … only just, but still in the game. I might even have weathered the storm and eventually turned a profit, but … well, my biggest mistake was closing the business last year when the

British Army cancelled my contract with them and threatened my life and those of my employees. Afterwards, I carried on paying my workers. Every Friday they got their pay packets even when I was on the run, even when I wasn't making a penny. I suppose I just ran out of money."

"You have nothing?" Patrick asked.

"I have a small amount tucked away, but since I reopened the business after the truce came into effect last July, I've been in debt. And before you ask, the bank won't give me a loan. They don't think I'm reliable."

Patrick was torn between genuine sympathy for Quinn and relief. Quinn was well known in Dublin, and it was a good bet that if he were no longer on Michael Collins' side, he'd be regarded as an enemy, no matter how hard he tried to remain neutral in the conflict to come. And it *was* coming.

"You won't want to hear this, but better your business going under than you taking an assassin's bullet."

Patrick recalled those terrifying days when Quinn was in permanent hiding from British murder squads, and policemen and detectives were persistently harassing him at his business. "What will you do?"

Quinn's shoulders heaved with a sigh. "I spent my youth building up that business, despite having no help or encouragement from my family. I remember my father saying I could never compete with the Jews. 'They succeed every time because they're cunning and sly, and much smarter than the rest of us.' Quinn sniggered, "I never got a congratulatory pat on the back from my da when I tasted success, and I'm bloody sure I won't give him the opportunity now to tell me he told me so."

In a lull in the conversation, Patrick glanced around the bar area. As he looked at the strangers' faces; some angry, others animated or filled with aggression, he realised that he was as alone without his family as Quinn was with his parents only a county away. "I miss my family being here, Quinn."

"I know. It can't be easy with Jenny and Kevin, their son and new baby daughter, becoming settled in London with the grannies."

"I'd hoped they might return, now that the Irish and British have signed the peace treaty, but I don't think they'll come back after hearing all this talk of division between the south and the north, a free state and a Republic. Jesus have mercy, but how long will it be before all Irishmen reconcile their differences?"

"I don't know. I can't see an end in sight."

Patrick studied Quinn's downtrodden face: his eyebrows drawn together in consternation, the sharp line of his jaw, his lips set in a tight line. He felt the mad desire to hug and kiss him; both impossibilities in a public house or anywhere in public, so instead, he changed the subject from Jenny to Danny, to give them both some cheer. "I got a letter from my brother, yesterday."

Quinn's eyes lit up. "Oh, and how is Danny doing over there?"

"He seems happy. He and Grace are still together and living in Philadelphia. He doesn't say, but I think he's taken by her … might even be love…"

"Sure, and that'd be grand if it were true."

"Danny's working for an Anglo-Irish society. He didn't go into detail, so that could mean just about anything, and Grace is nursing in a hospital. She says the Americans are crying out for qualified doctors and surgeons in most major cities … and their salaries are twice those of here."

"Did he say when he was coming back?" Quinn asked, but he still looked distracted.

"No, that's the surprising part; he doesn't want to return. He seems to like the life there. He's not keen on their prohibition laws but says he can always sniff out a drink in illicit bars. He says there's unimaginable opportunities for men like him. You know, I think the fight for Ireland has finally gone out of him."

At last Quinn smiled. "I doubt that, but it's good news."

"Why don't we go?"

"What?"

"Let's pack up and join him and Grace in America." Patrick looked shiftily around the bar. "I can practise my skills as a surgeon in a fine American hospital, with that huge salary I mentioned, and you can see for yourself what opportunities there are. We might even find a modicum of acceptance there. I've heard about organisations in some cities that work to advance our civil rights. They say there are even bars where men like us mingle together, where we can kiss and have fun, and meet interesting people. That's a step in the right direction. It might open up a new world for us too."

Patrick was breathless with excitement. "Think about it, Quinn … a new start in a new land full of people who don't hate each other; don't answer to another powerful country, don't spit in the face of a person who belongs to a different faith. No more IRA, nor Loyalists. No more funeral processions in the streets every day of the week or worrying that one of us will be murdered by an assassin's bullet."

"You're serious about this?"

"I am."

Quinn stared at his empty whiskey tumbler, with a pensive frown creasing his forehead. "There's a civil war coming, Patrick, where Irishmen will kill Irishmen and Britain will sit back and watch all of us burn. If I stay, I will fight, not for a Free State within the British fold but for a bona fide united Republic, and I will most likely die. But how can I desert the cause I've lost so much to?" He gazed at Patrick, his eyes tearing up with a fistful of emotions. "How can I walk away now?"

Patrick gulped down the last dregs of his Guinness. Overwhelmed with love and the possibility of a future with Quinn, he had not contemplated being turned down. *What now?* He thought back to the darkness before they'd met, but as quickly at those gloomy recollections came: the Easter Uprising, the war against Germany, and the family tragedies that now scarred the Carmodys and Jacksons, they gave way to light and hope and infinite promises. "Why choose to die when we have each other to live for? Life is full of moments, Quinn, and I've spent some of my best and worst with you. You've done your bit for Ireland; now it's time to take a chance on us across an ocean. What do you say?"

Patrick studied Quinn's face, almost hearing his inner debate as he stared at the men at the bar counter. Discussions were morphing into arguments. Soon, fists would fly, and insults would be as blue as the smoky air. "Quinn, is this what you want?"

"No." Quinn gazed at Patrick's hopeful face and dared to squeeze his hand. "I'll take a chance on you, Patrick Carmody. Sure, but I see good odds for the two of us marching along a new path together."

Follow the Author

Jana hopes you enjoyed *Oath of Allegiance*. Find out more about her books:

Website: http://janapetken.com/
Facebook: https://www.facebook.com/AuthorJanaPetken/
Twitter: https://twitter.com/AuthoJana
Pinterest: https://es.pinterest.com/janpetken/
Youtube: https://www.youtube.com/watch?v=gmrLECGgP8I
Goodreads: https://www.youtube.com/watch?v=gmrLECGgP8I
Email: petkenj@gmail.com